AMERICAN

Fuji

Sara Backer

A Marian Wood Book

published by

G. P. Putnam's Sons

a member of Penguin Putnam Inc.

New York

AMERICAN

Fuji

A Novel

A Marian Wood Book
published by
G. P. Putnam's Sons
Publishers Since 1838
a member of
Penguin Putnam Inc.
375 Hudson Street
New York, NY 10014

Library of Congress Cataloging-in-Publication Data

Backer, Sara, date.
American Fuji : a novel / Sara Backer.
p.   cm.
"A Marian Wood book."
ISBN 0-399-14691-1
1. Americans—Japan—Fiction.   2. Women sales personnel—Fiction.
3. Funeral consultants—Fiction.   4. Japan—Fiction.   5. Culture
conflict—Fiction.   I. Title.
PS3552.A259 A44   2001   00-056146
813'.6—dc21

Printed in the United States of America

1   3   5   7   9   10   8   6   4   2

This book is printed on acid-free paper. ∞

BOOK DESIGN BY JUDITH STAGNITTO ABBATE

TO MY FAMILY OF THE HEART

Fuji

One

Toilets and cars. That's what Mr. Eguchi had trained Gabriela Stanton to notice whenever she made house calls. She was to report the year, make, and model of the cars, and—her boss's pet obsession—whether the toilet seat was padded, heated, musical, or equipped with a panel of buttons that produced douche sprays of various strengths and temperatures. *Toilets tell truth about people,* Mr. Eguchi insisted. He might be right, but Gaby wouldn't want anyone to analyze her by her toilet. Or her car: an old stick-shift Honda with broken air-conditioning.

She drove slowly, straining to see through a blurry cascade of water the frantic windshield wipers couldn't slap down fast enough. When the traffic light turned green, the white sedan ahead of her abruptly halted, and she barely braked in time to avoid tapping its rear bumper. She rolled down her window to see what the problem was. The storm had completely flooded the intersection, turning it into a shallow lake. No one dared to be the first to cross it.

Rain blew on her hair and Gaby closed her window. She could take advantage of the traffic jam to determine if she had passed the temple Mr. Aoshima had mentioned in his directions to his house. While rain pounded the roof, she carefully opened her well-worn map of Shizuoka City, trying to keep the fold lines from breaking apart in her hands. After living in Japan almost five years, she was used to nameless streets and addresses coded with nonsequential numbers only the post office could decipher. The trick was to steer by landmarks. She counted the intersections she had gone through. A small temple was hard to spot in the middle of a storm. She'd assume it was in this block and hope for the best.

A delivery truck boldly crossed the street, leaning on its horn all the way through, spraying up rooster tails of water. Other cars began to move, and Gaby took her turn, keeping a steady speed through the sunken intersection. After she turned left, the road got narrower and houses grew larger and farther apart. This was one of the wealthiest neighborhoods in the city. She wasn't surprised; since she'd started to work for Gone With The Wind ten months ago, all of her clients had been rich. At the end of the road, she checked the two *kanji* characters on the gatepost: "blue" and "island." She had reached the Aoshima residence.

The Aoshimas owned a double lot, and their extended front yard was an impressive rock garden. Rocks that large cost the equivalent of $8,000 each. The pine trees were well pruned, with stakes and wires to contort their branches against gravity. A three-car garage was nearly as large as the house behind it, an old-fashioned farmhouse with a wraparound porch and a steep roof made of curved ceramic tiles.

Gaby parked in the ample driveway. She twisted the rearview mirror, licked her finger, and tried to flatten the few wayward white hairs that sprang out of her dark brown French twist. The fine lines in her forehead and around her eyes hadn't been there when she'd arrived in Japan. At thirty-six, she felt too old to be starting over in a job that had nothing to do with her education and experience. Last year at this time, she had been an English professor at Shizuyama University. It still rankled—getting fired, out of the blue, for no reason. But in Japan, she had learned to expect the unexpected. Gaby took a deep breath and grabbed her briefcase. She had to stop longing for the job she used to have and get to work on the one she did.

She opened her car door and her umbrella before getting out. While the wind whipped her pink linen skirt against her legs, she tiptoed between puddles in the gravel drive. Under the eaves of the front porch, she leaned her umbrella against the wall and rang the doorbell.

A short, suspicious woman opened the door. Gaby handed her a Gone With The Wind business card, and they bowed for a few minutes.

"Namae-wa Gaby Stanton. Yoroshiku onegaiitashimasu."

"Hajime-mashite. Aoshima desu."

Mrs. Aoshima wore a faded blue housedress with an apron. Her gray hair had a touch of purple, and two of the teeth among the crooked tangle in her mouth were gold. She didn't look like a rich man's wife. Although she had used polite verb forms, her eyes burned with hostility as she stared first at the top of Gaby's head, then at her breasts, and then down to her legs.

The constant gawking still made Gaby uncomfortable. Her dark brown eyes and hair and fair skin hadn't helped her blend in as she had hoped. Her five-foot-seven-inch height and her figure always stood out. Wherever she went, whatever she wore, men and women alike scrutinized her breasts and legs.

Last month, a client had begged her to model his department store's new line of shoes for a television ad. *"You have the legs Japanese girls dream of!"* Gaby tactfully made him aware that he didn't make shoes big enough to match her American size eight. Five minutes later, he wanted her to model brassieres. *"You wouldn't have to show your face. We'll put a Japanese head on you."* Gaby, alarmed at the idea of her body appearing on TV in part or whole, claimed her boss wouldn't allow it, though, in fact, Mr. Eguchi probably wouldn't mind and might even get a kick out if it.

Gaby stepped out of her damp shoes and into a pair of slippers lined up at the border of cement and tatami. She had learned to wear loose pumps that came off quickly inside the door, and industrial-strength nylons that resisted runs in case the floor was old and splintering. Not every house had guest slippers. She followed Mrs. Aoshima to the room where her husband waited.

Mrs. Aoshima, believing herself out of earshot, whispered in Japanese, *"That foreign woman is here, you stupid fool."* Then she turned to Gaby and gestured for her to enter the room as she spoke in her formal voice. *"You are most welcome to our poor, shabby home. Please sit. I will bring some tea."*

Gaby heard the television snap off, and Mr. Aoshima stood up and said in English, "Come in, come in." He shook her hand and didn't do a bad job of it. He must have been a businessman who dealt with Westerners. Unlike his wife, he had dark skin, a curious, small-featured face, and a thick brush of white hair. He continued in English. "How do you do? How are you? I'm fine thank you, and you?"

"Nice to meet you," Gaby answered.

"Your English is very good!" Mr. Aoshima laughed at his joke.

Gaby smiled. "So is yours."

"Oh, no, no. I don't speak English now that I'm retired." But he looked pleased. "Guess how old I am."

In America, she would guess sixty; that meant around seventy in Japan. "Fifty-five?"

"No!" he crowed, delighted. "Guess again."

"Sixty?"

"Older, older!"

"Oh, you can't be," Gaby protested.

"Seventy-seven!"

His wife came back with a tray of teacups, a pitcher of iced tea, and cookies. Pepperidge Farm Milano—a good sign, indicating a willingness to break with tradition. Mrs. Aoshima knelt on the floor, arranging the cups on the low table. She served her husband first, then Gaby. She took nothing for herself, a bad sign. She sat on her knees, looking sullen.

"We're going to speak in English," Mr. Aoshima said. "My wife majored in English in college." His wife responded by slapping his arm and muttering something in Japanese Gaby couldn't catch.

Gaby switched to Japanese. *"I noticed your large garage. Do you collect cars?"*

"English, English! Where are you from?"

"America."

"I knew that by your accent. Which city?" His English actually was very good.

"Portland. You probably haven't heard of it."

"In Washington, right? South of Shiatteru?"

"Yes, south of Seattle, just across the Oregon state line. How do you know about Portland?"

"I did a lot of business on the West Coast. I like America. I like American freedom. Americans are so creative."

"You're too kind," Gaby said.

"That's why I called Gone With The Wind. A big American book, eh? Scarlett O'Hara, right?" He pronounced O'Hara like the Japanese name, OH-hah-lah. "So, tell us about your services." He glanced at his wife. "In Japanese."

Mr. Aoshima was efficient in his own flamboyant way. Gaby often had to endure an hour of small talk before introducing the business of her visit. He fit the Gone With The Wind client profile perfectly, but his wife might cancel the order behind his back. Gaby opened her briefcase and placed a brochure on the table as she began her pitch.

"Our basic departure party is fully catered at our own Gone With The Wind ballroom and accommodates an unlimited number of family members, up to one hundred guests, and ten chanting monks. The honored person enters with a laser light show, circulates through the room on a conveyor belt, and leaves for his ultimate destination in a stunning display of dry ice to his favorite Japanese song, or if you prefer, an American song—"

"Which one?" Mr. Aoshima cut in.

"'Yesterday,' 'My Way,' *or* 'Whistle While You Work.'" Gaby coughed until she had stifled her urge to laugh. Japan: where reality was absurd. This was why she had gradually stopped writing letters to friends in America; it hurt too much that they simply would not believe her firsthand perceptions, so unlike their preconceived ideas about modern Japan. Her own sister resolutely claimed nothing could happen in Japan that didn't happen in New York City. Even her mother, who had recently moved to Brazil with her new husband, continued to think all expatriate experience was like the Peace Corps. The job Gaby held now sounded like science fiction, yet here she was, in Japan, at work. She went on: *"But more popular and memorable are our theme departures. We have three theme parks fully equipped not only for your ceremony, but for future anniversaries of your special trip."*

Gaby took a videotape out of her leather briefcase and gestured toward their television system. The screen was almost one meter across, which was a good sign. Mr. Eguchi always said, *Big screen means big dream. "If you please?"*

Mr. Aoshima looked surprised, but turned on the set and inserted the video. Gaby spoke as the video deftly shifted between rotating computer graphics and close-up film, constantly moving to make the theme parks appear much larger than they were. *"First, our Field for Dreams. The honored person is carried around the bases as he makes his way safely home, accompanied by the song of his high school baseball team. Family members may play baseball at this theme park to observe anniversaries of this home run."*

She waited for the GWTW logo to appear and spin itself into a ball before starting her next speech. *"Next, our exclusive golf shrine Whole in One, distinguished by its moss and rock gardens maintained by Zen monks. The honored person rides among the guests in a golf cart, receiving flags at each hole. As a bonus, family members may play golf at the shrine on the one-year anniversary party. Notice the fine rake work done every morning on the sand traps."*

After the logo appeared, revolved, and fractured into fireworks, she moved to her conclusion. *"Our most impressive package is our Star Flight Memory. Family members join the honored person on an indoor roller coaster ride, similar to Space Mountain."* Gaby could safely assume the Aoshimas had been to Tokyo Disneyland.

"The theme songs are 'Twinkle, Twinkle Little Star' *or* 'Fly Me to the Moon.' *For the finale, the first car, carrying the honored person, breaks away and rises through the roof in a display of shooting stars while the guest cars slow and form a circle to wave goodbye."* Gaby reached over to turn off the TV before the video stopped. A sudden switch from tape to television could lose the sale. A few seconds of a samurai drama or a beer commercial could lure the client back to tradition and waste all her work. *"And, all veterans of this package will receive a trip to the moon."*

"*Really?*" Mr. Aoshima exclaimed.

"*Liar!*" Mrs. Aoshima said at the same time.

Gaby nodded solemnly. *"By the year 2020, gardens on the moon will be a reality. Of course, prices will be much higher in the future, but everyone who purchased a Star Flight special before then will be launched on the first available spaceship."*

"You can't own the moon," Mr. Aoshima muttered in English, but his eyes showed a hint of appreciation of the idea.

Gaby switched to English to match him. "That's a technicality we're working on," she agreed, packing away the video and producing a gift-wrapped box. "A present from Gone With The Wind for letting me talk to you today. Please."

Mrs. Aoshima didn't touch the box, but glared at her husband.

Gaby knew whose party it would be by who took the box. When Mr. Aoshima absently untied the silk ribbon, she felt a bit sad; she was getting to like him. "Of course, you don't want to make a decision today. But if you were going to order one of our parties, which one would you like?"

"To the moon," Mr. Aoshima mumbled. He took the fan out of the box and absently started fanning himself.

His wife snatched it out of his hand with a sharp cry. "No! It bad idea! It your Korean heart say such thing. We are Japanese. We Japanese die Japanese way!" Mrs. Aoshima ran from the room, pulling her apron skirt up to hide her face as she cried.

Gaby pretended not to notice and concentrated on a long sip of cold barley tea.

Mr. Aoshima looked hurt, then turned to Gaby with a face prepared for photographs—straight, serious, revealing no emotion. "There you have it. My family tomb won't accept my Korean heart. Do you allow Korean hearts at Gone With The Wind?"

Gaby didn't know how to answer. Mr. Eguchi had not prepared her for this. "I think it is not disallowed." In matters of caution or delicacy, Japanese preferred to use the double negative. "Hearts, you see, are muscle, and muscle burns away, all turns to essence." She thought of a hedge in case his wife wouldn't want his remains in an integrated tomb. "As for entire bodies, now, I'm not sure—"

"No body," he said. "I'm Japanese except for my heart."

"Well, I believe that's all right."

He smiled and slapped his knee. "Because my heart will burn! Burned out, all gone, bye-bye, right? Yes! Send me up in flames! Fry me to the moon!"

"Um . . ."

He scooted on the floor to a cabinet and pulled out a bottle of rice wine. "Now, we drink *sake*. I tell you about my heart."

Gaby thought about the half-million-yen commission for a "moon package." "Oh, yes, please."

He poured two small cups and knocked his back in one gulp after the *kampai* cheer, obliging Gaby to do the same. He poured again. "I was a marathon runner, always in good shape. But my beat got off. My heart was too big, maybe. It couldn't pump hard enough. Breathing became a chore. I had white pills, yellow pills, pink pills. Nothing worked. Going upstairs was like climbing Fuji-*san*. In the hospital, they told me I should prepare to die. Only a transplant could save my life. And as you know, we Japanese don't donate organs when we die. My doctor is progressive and he put me on a special list for a transplant at another clinic. But there are so many people in the world, and so few hearts! I was dying with my name at the bottom of the list. And then, a very lucky event happened. A Korean laborer got in a bad traffic accident. His death was very nice; he hit his head on the road, so his middle was in good condition. His blood type matched mine, so when he died they cut his heart out of his chest—snip, snip—and put it in mine! And here I am, still alive today. A miracle."

Gaby felt queasy. "That is amazing."

Mr. Aoshima filled the cups again. His face was flushed. "That's when I began to believe in God. God killed this man for me—for me!"

"Indeed," Gaby said. "That's quite a story, isn't it?"

"And when I die"—Mr. Aoshima tipped his head back to drain another shot—"I want my heart to fry to the moon!"

"Gone With The Wind can do that for you," Gaby said. She worried about his drinking—was alcohol allowed for transplant patients? "Eguchi-*san* will call to make arrangements tomorrow. But perhaps your wife needs time to get used to the idea?"

Mr. Aoshima waved his hand and settled it on Gaby's knee. "She'll complain, but she will do whatever I say. I am the man of the house. Are you married?"

Every time. She never managed to avoid that question. "I was," she said, "but no longer." The words were true, but she was acting stoic-in-the-aftermath-of-tragedy when, in fact, she wished she'd divorced the jerk earlier.

Mr. Aoshima looked sympathetic. "He is dead, isn't he?"

Gaby pulled out her handkerchief and pretended to stifle tears. "I'm sorry . . . I can't talk about his . . . departure."

"Here, drink this." Mr. Aoshima pushed more *sake* at her. "So, that is how you got into this business. Naturally, you didn't work before he died. Suddenly, bills to pay. You don't know what to do. You stay with your husband's body as long as you can. The funeral man whispers that it's time to leave. You look at him with your big brown eyes and ask if he has a job for you. You poor thing. You are very brave."

Gaby put the handkerchief down and sniffed. "Thank you for your kindness. I'm sorry for my rude outburst. Could I . . . could I please use your toilet?"

"Please, go ahead. Down that hall."

Driving back in the rain, Gaby telephoned Mr. Eguchi with news of her success. *"The toilet is a Toto Home Sound Princess, with a button that produces a fake flushing sound to disguise your own noises, and above the tank there's a wedding cake–like thing with ballerinas that rotate to the tune of 'Swan Lake' when the water drains. We've got a big dreamer here."*

"Wonderful!" Mr. Eguchi exclaimed. *"I'll call him tomorrow to finalize the details. Does he know you're not married?"*

"He thinks I'm a widow. Invented a romantic story about me."

"Good, good! We'll take this one to the moon, Gebi-san. Good job."

She turned the telephone off. Half a million yen, she reminded herself, as the wipers dejectedly batted the rain left and right. The moon, invisible behind storm clouds, was growing full.

Two

箸 Alexander Thorn lowered himself onto a floor cushion at the long, black lacquered table in the banquet room of the restaurant. Instantly, he was assaulted with the question he'd heard at least twenty times since his arrival two days before:

"What are your impressions of Japan?"

This time, the question came from directly across the table, from a young Japanese man with a crew cut and a blotchy red face brought on by rapid beer drinking.

Alex shifted his legs on the tatami floor, unable to sit in the half-lotus position Japanese men casually assumed as they took their places. The problem with that question, Alex realized, rubbing his cramped calf muscle, was that his impressions weren't good and it was difficult for him to lie. Tokyo was crowded, expensive, and so hot and sticky that he sweat through a fresh shirt in less than an hour. His back ached from sleeping on his hotel futon, a mere blanket compared to the fat American futon he used in his apartment in Seattle. It killed his knees to balance over a squat toilet. The food was bland, repetitive, and always the perfect tepidity for salmonella. The best he could say was that the women had beautiful hair, and that was too sexist to mention.

Alex needed his son Cody to coach him how to answer. But if Cody hadn't died here a year ago, Alex wouldn't be making this painful trip. He reminded himself that everyone here thought he'd come to Japan only to promote his self-help book, *Why Love Fails,* which, for reasons Alex couldn't fathom, had just been released in a Japanese translation. They didn't know that the book promotion, which brought about receptions like this one, was just something Alex was getting through—something to please his agent and help pay his way. These first three days in Tokyo had nothing to do with the death of his son, but he tried to be polite and conceal his impatience.

"Japan is beautiful," Alex ventured, crossing his legs Indian style.

The young man's face formed a dull mask. There were pimples next to his sparse sideburns. "Do you go to Kyoto next?"

Obviously, "beautiful" had been a bad answer. In Japan, everything he said turned out to be wrong. "No, I'm going to Shizuoka City."

The young man's mouth twitched into a slight frown. "Shizuoka is not so interesting. You had better go to Kyoto and see the temples."

Alex had no idea what to say to that polite threat. "I have business in Shizuoka," he explained. Shizuoka was where Cody had died. Almost a year ago. A long, wretched, worthless year.

The young man and the other guests began to eat. With his legs crossed, Alex's knees were too high to fit under the table. He stretched forward to pick up a plate and balanced it in his left hand while he reached for chopsticks with his right.

The man changed the subject. "I was very exciting to hear

your book, *Why Love Fails.* I want to marriage, but Japanese girls are so selfish today. I am twenty-eight years old. My mother wants grandchildren."

Twenty-eight! The young man looked like a college student, eighteen or nineteen. Alex nodded encouragingly and tried to pick up a snail shell. The long lacquer chopsticks slipped out of position, and the shell rolled off his plate. When he tried to snag a piece of salad, the chopsticks slid on the oily dressing and flipped a scrap of lettuce onto his tie. One of the few women in the room, sitting to his right, put her hand over her mouth and giggled. Alex folded the lettuce and snail inside his napkin. He had never had trouble using chopsticks in Japanese restaurants back home. These polished sticks didn't grab the food the way rough wood ones did.

The red-faced man continued, ignoring Alex's mishap. "I hope your book teaches women to do their duty."

"Well, that's not my point—" Alex began.

He was cut off by an older man who reached across the table to fill the remaining inch of Alex's almost-full beer glass. "Is your wife dutiful?" He had roly-poly cheeks and stank of aftershave.

"I don't have a wife," Alex said.

The room went silent.

As Japanese murmurs circled around the dinner guests, Alex realized he had made yet another mistake.

"But your book . . ." the boldest one murmured.

Ah, that was it. How dare an unmarried man write about marriage. His personal life was more important than his license to practice psychotherapy. "As I said earlier, *Why Love Fails* shows how feelings and intuition aren't a good basis for a lifelong partnership. Since I'm divorced, I can offer myself as a bad example."

Now there was total silence. Alex decided trying to explain his joke would only make things worse. Instead, he worked on dislodging an oyster from its shell. His chopsticks skidded out of control again, and the oyster popped off suddenly and landed in his lap just below his fly.

Fortunately, the others were distracted by the arrival of

the feature course, which involved setting up boards, knives, and dishes. Alex dabbed at the stain with a wet finger towel while the chef grunted instructions to his staff. The conversation ceased when a waiter brought in a frosted glass bowl of water.

Everyone watched the chef lift a large fish out of the bowl. The fish had been sedated by partial freezing, but curled its body from side to side, attempting a slow-motion escape. First, the chef attached the fish to a cutting board with a skewer right below the eye, and another in the midpoint of the tail. Then, with a thin, sharp knife like a scalpel, he carefully cut diagonal slices in the fish's side. Alex could see the fish gasping through its gills and felt sick. The fish suddenly took on disturbing symbolism. The fish became Cody, on an operating table in a Japanese hospital. It was his son on the cutting board, struggling to live while his own flesh was carved away.

Dizzy, Alex concentrated on breathing, four counts in, four counts out, while the roly-poly man beside him explained that this method, the finest way to prepare *sashimi,* was called *ikezukuri,* which translated to "cutting down alive." The trick was to keep the fish alive as long as possible while removing the meat down to the bone, first from one side, then the other. The guests applauded as the chef removed the first slice and placed it on a small dish for Alex, the guest of honor.

He had to eat this.

He understood the need to accept cultural differences. He was a guest required to participate in the customs of his host. Yet knowing this didn't change the fish back into a fish again. To be polite in Japan, he would have to force himself to be a cannibal.

Dark eyes and beer-flushed faces watched him, watched his chopstick hand. Alex gripped the *sashimi* between his sticks. It seemed to be flopping on its own, but maybe that was his hand shaking. As he raised the bite to his teeth, bile flooded his mouth. He took a breath, shut his eyes, and placed the fish between his lips. Immediately, he vomited. He tried to bend his head low to his plate, but was peripherally aware of splattering someone's glasses and someone's Armani suit jacket.

Next thing he knew, he was the vortex of a whirlwind of long, drawn-out ascending "aahs" of questioning concern. A damp white towel appeared under his nose and he quickly wiped his mouth. When he raised his head, he faced a young woman with prominent eyeteeth and black glasses that magnified her brown eyes. "Are you okay, *sensei*?"

Alex wiped his mouth and started apologizing. "I'm sorry. I didn't want to ruin your party. I think I'm sick. Flu or something. Sorry." He hoped they would believe he had the flu and allow him to escape to his hotel.

There was great group muttering in Japanese, eventually shaping into a consensus to allow Alex to leave. The woman with the black glasses offered to walk him to his hotel. Yes, it was working; his coat was fetched by a waiter. He heard some comparison to an American president who had thrown up during a key trip to Japan. His exit from the room was slow, hampered by handshakes and bows. But when he passed the chef, the chef glowered and cut a quick gesture in the air with his knife.

Outside the air-conditioned restaurant, immediately shocked by the heat, Alex slowed down. His female guide walked quickly, and he tried to keep sight of her bowed legs and pigeon-toed gait as he followed her through a neon maze of flashing *kanji* characters. She stopped on a bridge and waited for him to catch up.

"I'm sorry," she said. "I thought you were pretending. Are you sick really?"

"Maybe," Alex answered. He felt guilty about his pretense, but it didn't seem to bother her. "Maybe more homesick than anything else." Struck by her concern, he felt guilty about his unkind assessment of her legs. "What's your name?"

"Jiyuko. My parents made up my name. It means 'freedom child.'"

"Are you free?"

She shrugged. "No."

Alex smiled sadly. "Neither am I."

Jiyuko put her hands on the stone rail and turned to face

the river, which reflected neon in pink and orange ripples. "But America is the land of the free. Americans can have whatever they want."

"I can't have what I want." Cody, alive. Alex didn't want to talk about Cody, but he couldn't think of anything else to say. The silence grew awkward.

Jiyuko waited, then said, "I am sorry about your divorce."

Alex almost laughed—that she thought he had feigned illness to escape questions about his ex-wife. "I'm not. My marriage was a mistake from the beginning." Alex waved his hand. "Anyway, that's all ancient history."

Jiyuko tilted her face toward him, and her hair slanted down to her waist. Her eyes seemed large behind her glasses. "You didn't love your wife?"

Alex felt obliged to be fair. "Well, I thought I did at the time. Jane gazed at me when I talked, made me feel important. We were only twenty-two."

"Why did you marry her?"

"Well, I was moving across the country to go to graduate school, and it was either marry her or leave her. I didn't want to be alone. I was very insecure."

"Was she beautiful?"

Alex could easily picture Jane's college face. "She was blond, a little chubby. She wore overalls. She didn't intimidate me with jewelry or hair spray."

"So you like blond girls?"

"I didn't like her for her hair color. I liked her because she was nice to me."

Jiyuko took off her glasses and studiously polished them on the hem of her skirt. She glanced at Alex. "Do you think Japanese girls are nice?"

Alex caught himself watching the rise of her skirt over her thick thighs. Was Jiyuko making a pass at him? She couldn't be. At his youthful best, he'd been a skinny guy with thick hair, a long nose, and a lot of energy. Now his hair was gray, his stomach flabby, and his energy gone. Looks aside, why would she flirt with a forty-five-year-old American man? Especially one who had recently thrown up. He still tasted fishy bile in his mouth. "Sure. Maybe too nice."

"I'm not," Jiyuko said.

"What makes you say that?"

"My boyfriend says I'm a bad girl."

Ah, the boyfriend. She wasn't flirting; she wanted counseling. This, Alex could handle. "Why would he make such a cruel comment?"

"He wants me to be like everyone else. We Japanese have a saying: The nail that stands out will be struck down."

"Well, then, leave him and find a man who appreciates you for who you are." Alex felt comfortable now, having switched to his professional role of psychotherapist.

"In Japan?" Jiyuko asked.

"Wherever."

"But I'm twenty-five. I'm Christmas cake. It's too late."

"I don't understand. Christmas cake?"

Jiyuko's explanation sounded like a memorized speech. "Everyone wants fancy decorated cake for the night of December twenty-fourth. But on Christmas, the twenty-fifth, the cake is stale, and no one wants it. It is the same with girls. If a girl is not married by the age of twenty-five, she is too old, and 'Jingle Bells' are 'Single Bells' for her."

"That's total nonsense!"

"Not in Japan," Jiyuko said darkly.

Alex changed his approach. "What's your boyfriend like?"

Jiyuko shrugged. "A typical Japanese boy. He works at a small desk in a big room. He wears soft suits. He smokes. He likes to drink beer and play mah-jongg. He lives at home. His hobby is watching television."

"An exciting guy, huh?"

Jiyuko looked puzzled.

"Sorry. I was being sarcastic."

A group of businessmen, arm in arm, drunk, stumbled

down the sidewalk, bumping into Jiyuko first, then Alex. One of them fixed bloodshot eyes on Alex and said loudly, "Hallo! This is a pen! Are you a pen?" The others laughed, pulling him away. He heard the word *gaijin* repeated as they looked back at him, one at a time.

Jiyuko said, "My boyfriend is like them."

Alex had a sudden urge to rescue her from the horrors of Japanese conformity and the martyrdom of wifehood. They could fall in love. He could be patient and tender. So she was twenty years younger; in her culture, that wasn't a barrier. He could whisk her back to Seattle, put her through graduate school if she wanted, give her room to grow. "What kind of man do you like?"

Her eyes got misty. "Keanu Reeves."

On the other hand, twenty years was a big gap. Alex felt sweat running down his chest. "Is it much farther to my hotel?"

Jiyuko looked coy, which didn't suit her. "Why are you in such a hurry?"

Alex sighed. "I'm tired, and I need to get somewhere cool."

"I thought—" Jiyuko broke off and shrugged. "Okay, your hotel."

He followed her off the bridge, past brightly lit sporting equipment stores, an entire block of them, followed by a block of stores selling nothing but measuring instruments. This interested Alex, the idea of grouping rulers, scales, scoops, thermometers, barometers, and clocks together in one shop, but Jiyuko hurried on.

The next turn brought them into a street full of red lanterns, the emblem of old-fashioned, informal bars. Here were more drunks in gray suits, many of them getting escorted to taxis by women in kimonos. A short bald man reached inside a kimono fold and was scolded with a practiced smile and a light slap. An older woman with hints of purple in her upswept bun pinned a note on the lapel of a staggering drunk, fastened his seat belt, and shut the taxi door. Alex had a sense she was a bar hostess, if not a prostitute, but her motherly aspect gave him the creeps.

Right after the bars, incongruently, all the buildings were bookstores. Not only were they open late at night, but they were packed with customers standing in front of the shelves, reading what looked like telephone directories.

Jiyuko noticed his interest. "Those are *manga*. We Japanese love comic books."

"Even adults?"

"Oh, yes. There are action comics, literature comics, men's comics with naked women. All kinds. Do you like sex comics?"

"I've never read any." They were walking uphill, only a slight slant, but his heart sounded too loud; he was out of shape.

Jiyuko nodded. "I prefer novels to comics. I want to be a novelist." She said it as if it were a reasonable career choice. "Do you know Eimi Yamada?"

Alex wondered if this was someone he'd met at the party. "I don't remember. Is he a friend of yours?"

Jiyuko laughed, covering her mouth with her hand.

Alex stopped to catch his breath. "What's so funny?" He wiped his forehead with his hand; sweat flew off his fingertips, spattering the pavement. Jiyuko had no perspiration on her face.

"Eimi Yamada is a famous lady author."

"Oh."

"She writes about sex. With foreigners." Jiyuko took off her glasses and polished them on the hem of her skirt again. Alex wondered if she copied this gesture from some movie. She glanced up. "Are you looking at my legs?"

"I didn't intend to." Alex looked away into the street. He had never been in this part of the city before. It occurred to him that Jiyuko might not know which hotel he was staying at or was deliberately getting him lost. He had a flash fear of walking all night in the heat in Tokyo.

Jiyuko persisted. "You are not looking at my legs?"

Alex deliberately looked only at her face. She was ever so

slightly cross-eyed. Her cheeks had the thickness of youth; her chin, a few pimples. She could pass for fifteen. "Jiyuko, please, take me back to my hotel. I'm exhausted."

Jiyuko sighed. "I hoped you would help me."

"I don't understand."

"There is a story I want to write, about a Japanese girl and an older American man. Like you."

His instinct told him this had to be a sexual invitation, but it conflicted with his image of Japanese women as demure, shy, even prudish. He forced himself to assume she wanted him to read her stories or give her the name of his publisher. "How could I help you?"

"I would like to see an American penis."

Alex cringed. "Jiyuko, I'm . . . flattered by your interest, but that would be inappropriate. I'm afraid I can't help you." He hastened to change the subject. "Jiyuko, where are we?"

Jiyuko pointed up to a neon *kanji* sign. "Your hotel."

It couldn't be. It was. The neighborhood seemed to have changed its buildings at night. "Well, thank you for escorting me back. I'm sorry about . . . your story." After a pause, he added, "Good night." Alex would have shaken her hand, but hesitated to make any physical contact at this point. He bowed from his shoulders, feeling awkward and foolish, and walked into the relief of the air-conditioned hotel lobby. As the door closed behind him, he thought he heard her giggle.

The hotel clerk handed him his room key before he could say his room number. They all knew which room the *gaijin* had. Alex took the elevator to the ninth floor, walked the length of the narrow hall, and unlocked his door.

The maid had spread out the futon that used up most of the floor space. She had also straightened up his suitcase and turned off the fan. The room looked and smelled like a shoe box. Alex turned the fan on and took off his clothes. He put on the thin cotton robe provided by the hotel to walk across the hall to the bathroom. This time he remembered to wear his room slippers, which had to be kicked off inside the bathroom and exchanged for the special toilet slippers to use on the tile. These communal slippers were grubby plastic, and Alex hated to cram his toes into the moist tips, but the floor was usually covered with hair and urine and that was worse. In a nation that scrubbed sidewalks by hand and washed before taking a bath, the filthy toilet rooms surprised Alex. He considered taking a bath, but the water was scalding and at night would be packed with Japanese men who might also be curious about American penises. How had Cody dealt with communal tubs? He couldn't picture his son here, bathing with strangers. Had Cody also been solicited to display, and perhaps demonstrate, an American penis? If only he had talked to his son more often . . . enough! It wouldn't help to wallow in regret.

He went back to his room and lay on the futon as still as he could to feel the moving air from the slow fan. Memories were bad for him. He needed to move forward. Tomorrow, he would go to Shizuoka. For tonight, he would concentrate on nothing but the timed breeze from the fan grazing over his body.

Three

Gaby had planned to go back to her apartment, open one of the splits of champagne in her refrigerator, and put Beethoven on the CD player, turning up the volume on her cordless headphones so the orchestra seemed to come from inside her brain. But she stayed home too much. She felt obliged to force herself out, to try to meet new people or at least maintain her ability to speak English at normal speed. At the deciding stoplight, she headed downtown to Nature Squib, the *gaijin* bar. Maybe she'd find someone to celebrate her sale with her.

As soon as she'd ducked under the curtain at the door, she regretted her choice. Lester Hollingsworth was drinking beer at a table directly in front of her and with him was Michael McKenzie, the young Australian heartthrob who'd taken over her job at Shizuyama University. Before she could turn around, Lester called out to her.

"Gay Bee *san!* Am I hallucinating? Is the Queen of Hermits making a public appearance?" The accent was British; the tone, sarcastic. Lester claimed "The English Face" was either beefy or doughy. His was doughy, with a bulbous nose. He had angelic blond curls, but his round blue eyes made Gaby think of frogs rather than cherubs. He patted an empty chair beside him. "Sit down, Gabe. McKenzie just lost a bet. Care to have a go at it?" He held up a five-thousand-yen banknote, purple, with a picture of Mount Fuji in the center.

Gaby sat in the chair, trapped. "What's the bet this time?"

"Decoding Japanese English into English," Lester said. "In less than a minute."

"He gave me five minutes," Michael warned her, "and I still couldn't figure it out." He turned over a clean tumbler from the tray with a quart of Kirin on it and poured her a beer.

"Thanks," Gaby said, taking the glass. She had to admit Michael had charm. There was something masculine and sexy in the way his jacket creased around his elbow, and in the definition of his wrist bone. He was friendly in a boyish way that matched his freckles, and he sat close enough to Gaby to make her aware she hadn't had sex in over four years. Michael was only twenty-six; Gaby imagined all of her former female students—now his students—must have a crush on him.

"Ready?" Lester checked his watch. "Here it is: *Taaminaru beruteigo kiirudo zhionazaan suifuto.*"

Gaby said, "Is it true?"

"Is what true?"

"Terminal vertigo killed Jonathan Swift."

Lester sputtered beer. "No fair! You cheated."

"How could I?" Gaby became irritated with Lester. He had no right to make fun of the Japanese for pronouncing English with Japanese syllables; at least they were trying to learn another language. She leaned forward on her elbows. "You can keep your five thousand if you can translate that same sentence into actual Japanese."

Lester wiped his chin with a napkin. "Never mind. I wasn't serious about the bet."

"You took *my* money," Michael chimed in. "Go on, translate."

Lester shook his head. "It's impossible. There isn't a Japanese word for 'vertigo.'"

"Yes, there is," Gaby said. *"Memai."* She was, she realized, getting back at Lester for his snide comment on her arrival. Suddenly, she felt sorry for him. "Keep the money. I never actually agreed to the bet, after all."

Lester went silent while Michael regarded her with new respect. "Your Japanese is pretty good."

"It has to be, for my job. Today, I met a man who—"

"Could you help me read my mail?" Michael dug around in his book bag. "I get all this stuff at the university and I have no idea what it means." He pulled out a sheaf of photocopies.

Gaby glanced at the familiar notices and didn't reach for them. "Can't someone else help you?"

Lester dropped his know-it-all façade. "Michael . . ." he said softly, signaling no with his hand.

Michael looked from Gaby to Lester and back. "What? What is it?"

Lester murmured, "Don't add insult to injury."

Michael turned to Gaby. "I don't get it. Don't you want to help me?"

Gaby chose her words carefully. "It's hard for me because I wish I still had the job you have now."

"Then why did you quit?"

Lester's eyebrows raised. He answered Gaby's questioning glance with a shrug.

"I didn't. I was fired," Gaby said evenly. "The official reason was that my written Japanese wasn't good enough."

Michael snorted. "Then why the hell did they hire *me*?"

Gaby liked him for saying that. "Because it wasn't the real reason. Everyone knew that."

"What was the real reason?" Michael asked blithely.

"I honestly have no idea," Gaby replied. "What were you told about my . . . departure?"

"Professor Marubatsu said you had to concentrate on getting a husband before it was too late."

Gaby was glad Michael didn't try to soften the quote. He didn't seem to be in collusion with the faculty member she disliked most. "Figures that Marubatsu would say that. Did the dean say anything?"

"He said he regretted losing you and he hoped I could fill your shoes."

"So he had regrets, did he?" Gaby looked across the table at Lester.

Lester gulped some beer. "Put it out of your mind, Gabe. The dean was saying pleasant words in order to save face. What the Japanese say is not what they mean."

"No, Les! It has nothing to do with 'the Japanese.' I'm talking about two real people. The dean is a fair man. Marubatsu, on the other hand, has been nothing but a devious, self-serving—" Her voice began to rise.

Michael stood up. "We need more beer. Lester, it's your turn to buy." He swiped the purple banknote lying on the table and walked to the counter for faster service.

Lester slid into Michael's chair and held Gaby's hand. "Lower the volume, love. It's not Michael's fault he got your university job."

"I'm not blaming him." Gaby sighed. "I'm sorry. I thought I was over this. Guess I'm not."

"Listen." Lester leaned close, his blond curls tipping to touch her hair. "Whether or not the dean likes it, you're still canned. Even if you can prove Marubatsu acted unjustly, you'll never get your job back because Marubatsu is a tenured professor and a Buddhist priest and there's too much face to lose. The best thing to do is forget it."

"I know. I wish I knew what really happened, that's all."

Lester shook his head. "You Yanks place such importance on having everything out in the open. It's not a good way to get along."

"You Brits place such importance on getting along you fossilize out of fear of embarrassment."

"Which is why we Brits do better in Japan," Lester concluded.

Michael returned with a new quart bottle of Kirin and the requisite dish of crackers that came with every beer purchase. He took the chair Lester had vacated, pushing it closer to Gaby as he scooted it in. "What shall we toast, Lester?"

Gaby thought about bringing up her sale, but Lester was already saying, "To Nature Squib!"

"Nature Squib!" Michael echoed, clinking glasses.

Lester went on. "To the place where we pretend we're not in Japan. A sanctuary from our role as *gaijin.*"

"Here comes a Lester speech," Michael announced. "Make it a good one."

Lester drank beer and pontificated. "Our Japanese hosts spend a great deal of energy defining what is Japanese. The role of *gaijin* is to demonstrate what is not Japanese, and therefore not desirable. It is our duty, as outsiders, to regard the Japanese as superior. That is all they want from us. To respect them for having more education, making more money, and holding social values forged thousands of years ago. *Kampai!*"

Michael clapped. "Well done, well said. More beer?" His elbow brushed up against Gaby's and rested there.

Gaby checked her watch as an excuse to move her arm. Why had she come to this smoky bar full of expatriates? She could have been drinking champagne with Beethoven right now.

Lester grabbed her other hand and held it down. His fingers were cold and damp from the beer glass. "Don't even think about leaving. You just got here."

"I made a sale today," Gaby ventured. "Mr. Aoshima had quite a story."

"I'm learning counters in my Japanese class," Michael said, ignoring her comment. "How did you get through it, Les? Eight for days of the week is *yoka,* eight for cylindrical objects is *happon,* eight for pairs of things worn on feet is *hassoku,* eight for living beings—except birds—is *happikki.* I'll never manage it."

"Well, in English, we have flocks of geese and bevies of quail and what-not."

"But eight is eight. The number itself doesn't change."

Gaby sipped beer quietly. Lester could always drum up an audience for his shallow generalizations about "the Japanese" but the life story of one Japanese man wasn't worth listening to. While Lester and Michael argued about how to count birds, she glanced around at the memorabilia on the walls. The decor was American nostalgia, from Elvis Presley album covers to Golden Gate Bridge T-shirts. The menu included pizza made with bread, hamburgers that were meat loaf, something close to a cold taco but with rice and soy flavoring, and, the special treat, imported Budweiser. Lester had it wrong. Nature Squib wasn't a place where foreigners pretended not to be in Japan; it was a place Japan pretended to be foreign—and couldn't. The T-shirts were printed "San Furancisco" and Elvis had Japanese eyelids. Gaby would have felt more comfortable in the cramped six-stool bar in her neighborhood, where businessmen in gray suits drank in silence, watching *sumo* wrestling on TV.

"Do you mind?" Lester was saying.

"Sorry. What?" Gaby asked.

"She doesn't notice," Lester intoned in a mock-wounded voice. "I called a Japanese Babe Alert. I thought I'd engage in some international goodwill. If you can stand being left alone with McKenzie for a while."

Gaby looked over to a table with four young Japanese women dressed alike in beige sweaters and tight short skirts.

Each had long hair pulled back in a huge plastic barrette decorated with hearts or ducks. Their faces displayed garish experiments with eye shadow. In the States, you'd guess they were fourteen, but they had to be over twenty in order to get into a bar. The waiter handed each a pink concoction spiked with umbrellas and cherries. "They're so young," Gaby said.

"Oh, I'm in luck!" Lester rubbed his hands together. "One of them is my student. Emiko. Well, that settles it. I'd be rude not to say hello." He picked up his beer and headed toward them.

Michael popped a few squid crackers into his mouth, crunching loudly, and glanced at Gaby. His eyes were green and speckled. Unlike Lester, he wore his hair short, parted on the left, corporate style. "Could I talk to you about something personal?" Michael's arm was resting next to hers again. "And promise you won't laugh?"

"If it's about the university—"

"No, it's about me. Rao-*san* and me."

"Who is Rao?"

"Don't laugh." Michael's face was solemn. Gaby nodded assent. "He's a character in my Japanese textbook. The main guy."

"What's the problem?"

Michael checked to make sure no one was listening. "I'm turning into Rao-*san*."

Gaby drew back. "What do you mean?"

"Well, in chapter three, Rao-*san* buys a leather bag. That same week, my backpack broke and I had to buy a new bag." Michael patted the book bag at his side. "So far, coincidence, okay? But the next week, I had to make appointments with students, and in chapter four, Rao-*san* learns to tell time. What he said, I said. I'm not kidding."

"Michael, shopping and telling time are basic foreign language lessons for a reason; people have to do it."

Michael held up a finger. "But! In chapter five, Rao-*san* meets a cute Japanese girl in the train station, and so did I!"

"Japanese girls are unavoidable. So are train stations. We're in Japan." Gaby glanced at the table with the four girls. Lester was doing impressions of Mick Jagger and didn't seem likely to return soon.

Michael fortified himself with a swig of beer. "It's got me afraid to look ahead in the book for fear of what will happen to Rao-*san* and me."

The episodes seemed familiar to Gaby. "I know that textbook. Rao gets lost, mails a package, learns how to ski—"

"Stop! I'm going to Kyoto this weekend." Michael rummaged in his new bag and pulled out the book. "Look at chapter twelve." He handed the book to Gaby.

Gaby thumbed through until she found the right page. "Rao-*san* visits Kyoto."

Michael slammed his fist on the table. "I knew it! I knew it! Don't tell me what happens. Does anything bad happen?"

Gaby skimmed the dialogue. "He had a good trip . . . it was a little cold." She closed the book. "Kyoto won't be cold in late June."

"I'll pack a sweater, anyway," Michael said. "Did you say he goes skiing?"

"Yes. I believe a cute Japanese girl invites him to go with her."

"He doesn't break a leg and learn hospital vocabulary?"

"Nothing bad ever happens to him," Gaby said firmly, handing the book to Michael. "I'm sure you'll come through just fine." She felt a little envious of Michael's ability to turn into Rao-*san*. There were no foreign women in the dialogues.

Michael put his arm around Gaby. His hand was warm on her shoulder. "You won't tell Lester about this, will you?"

"Of course not," Gaby said.

Lester came back, frowning briefly at Michael's arm as he reclaimed his chair. "Have either of you heard of a writer called Alexander Thorn? The girls were asking me if he's famous."

"Never heard of him," said Michael.

"Rings a bell, but beats me why," said Gaby. "What does he write?"

"It sounds like he's in the self-help racket—which, of

course, would make him American." Lester turned to Gaby for a reaction but she gave none. "He's giving a talk tomorrow night. Emiko asked me to go. It's required for her American Culture class."

"What's the topic?" Michael asked.

"Marriage," Lester said. "His book is called *Why Love Fails.* Optimistic chap, isn't he? Spouse hunting for the bitter and the burned. You should go, Gabe."

"No, thank you."

"So what does this Emiko want with you?" Michael teased.

"She wants to pass her test, I think. The lecture is in English, so the students are nervous." Lester poured the last of the Kirin, already warm. "She thinks you're handsome, McKenzie. Says you look like Michael J. Fox."

"That twerp?"

"He comes across better in subtitles."

"Which one is Emiko?"

"Long hair, beige sweater, dark brown eyes."

Michael squinted. "They all have brown eyes, long hair and beige sweaters."

"The brown plaid miniskirt."

"You're kidding! The gorgeous one."

Gaby turned to see what Michael considered beautiful, but didn't notice any woman looking better than the others.

"How's her English?" Michael was asking.

"Okay. She's in my advanced class. But I thought you were seeing Kirstie."

"Kirstie's just a friend. I didn't come to Japan to date white women." Michael straightened his collar and brushed off his jacket. "My turn for some international goodwill." He winked and pivoted on his heels. He wore quality leather dress shoes. A sure sign of a newcomer. They would grow mold unless he dried them carefully each day and stored them with desiccant packets.

"More beer?" Lester asked. "Your treat, of course."

Gaby shook her head. "I'm going home."

"Without buying a round?"

"It's past eleven. I'm tired. I worked hard to make a sale tonight."

"Don't talk about *that*. I want to tell you about a new native speaker position."

"I already have a full-time job."

Lester drew a breath and exhaled a speech. "Gaby, there are some jobs we expatriates simply shouldn't take. Yours is one of them. You must quit before the men with missing fingers appear at your flat."

"Don't be melodramatic. Gone With The Wind is completely legitimate."

"But you have a Ph.D. You should be teaching. This native speaker position isn't as lucrative as fantasy funerals, of course, but it's decent work. I hear the pay is 300,000 yen a month."

The word "decent" irritated her. "My job is decent. And I made half a million yen tonight." More than Lester made in a month.

Lester whistled low and long. "What a whore you are."

"No more than you," Gaby stated testily. "I sell parties, you sell conversations."

"Parties. Good God, what a euphemism. They've brainwashed you."

"Lester, please, let's drop the subject, all right?" Gaby knew Lester's talent for cumulative nastiness. At times, he was uncannily like her ex-husband, Ron. You could never win an argument with Lester; he only got more and more personal, finding your weak spots and then aiming for them.

Lester watched her closely. "Don't you miss teaching? The smell of the chalk dust, the snores of the students?"

Gaby looked away. Michael had become the center of attention at the table with the four young women. They could have been in her university classes. Japanese women acted silly around foreign men, but even flirting in a bar was reaching out to the world. She had enjoyed the energy of her female students and their search for a new identity as Japanese women. These days, her life was a parade of dying rich men. "Yes, I miss teaching."

"So what's keeping you? Pride? After university prestige, you can't bear to slum it in the Berlitz league with me?"

Whatever she said now would come out wrong. In a way, Lester had it right. Gaby had a doctorate and college teaching experience. She was a qualified, legitimate English professor. She didn't want to work for a language school and be bossed around by the typical twenty-three-year-old *gaijin* upstart who believed in conversation classes without grammar because he had poor grammar himself. Was this pride? Gaby preferred to call it justified indignation. Either way, it was a point she couldn't argue with Lester. "I'm not entry-level anymore," Gaby told him. "I have to support myself, you know. I have to save money for the future." She wouldn't mention her need to live in a country with national health care. She kept her poor health a secret.

"That's morbid nonsense," Lester said. "You have to have confidence that money will find you, confidence in the *next* job. Stay loose, swing from limb to limb in the jungle of the workplace."

"Fall off the limb when they decide they want a *man* for the job."

"Then forget Japan. It's a man's world here, I'll grant you that. Go home. America has all that marvelous feminism. Be a professor there."

"There are no university positions in the States. Every job opening has at least four hundred applicants. I'm not exaggerating. That's why I moved here in the first place."

Lester looked wistfully at his empty glass. "All right, all right. I'm just worried because you aren't happy, Gabe."

Sometimes, he could be sincere. "How many people are

happy, no matter where they are? Overall, my life is better in Japan than it was in America. Isn't that good enough?"

"If you say so." Lester squeezed her hand. "Now will you buy a round?"

Four

Rain bombarded the streets of Shizuoka, so hard that the rebound off the pavement was ankle-high. Under the eaves of the train station, the line for taxis tripled. As Alex, laden with luggage, fought to open his umbrella against the wind, he heard the Japanese version of his name.

"*Zone-san! Zone-san!*"

"I'm Thorn," he called. As he turned to locate the voice, the wind ripped his umbrella inside out, which pulled him one step into the gutter. In an instant, his sock was a swamp and his expensive leather wing tip shoe drenched. "Shit!" Immediately, he knew he had made a first impression, so important in Japan, about as good as his expletive. He withdrew the hand he habitually offered and tried to match the bow of the man in the bluish-black ink-colored suit, but he was hampered by heavy bags on both shoulders and a stiff back from standing for over an hour in the last car of a crowded bullet train from Tokyo.

The man in the dark suit didn't quite meet Alex's eyes when he spoke, but his eyes were set so far apart that eye contact might have been scarier. His shaved head and small nose, with no bridge, emphasized the effect. "I'm Marubatsu. The university sent me to meet you. I knew your son. I'm very sorry." His voice was a flat recital indicating no sorrow.

"Thank you," Alex said. So this was the man Cody had called "Carpface" in his letters.

Professor Marubatsu guided Alex into the taxi queue. "The weather was fair until you came. You must be *ame-otoko,* a man who brings rain wherever he goes."

It sounded like Marubatsu was blaming him for the storm; that he owed it to the City of Shizuoka to go back to Seattle so their skies would clear. "Doesn't it usually rain in June?"

"*Tsuyu* starts in June, yes." Marubatsu stood in line, his hands empty, his tiny fingers pressed close together. Under his inky suit was a beige mesh polo shirt. His shoes were khaki slip-ons. "You don't have *tsuyu* in America."

Alex half-smiled, feeling the squish of his soggy shoe as they moved up in line. "Actually, Seattle is famous for its rainy season."

"But not like we Japanese have."

In only three days, Alex had heard so many speeches starting "In Japan, we" or "We Japanese" that the words angered him at once, those little red flags of superiority, recitations of the Great Japanese Myth of Uniqueness. He had to get rid of his anger; anger was destructive, would go against his goals. "Oh, no, of course not." He worried about sounding too flippant, but Marubatsu gave a slight nod of pleasure.

They moved up one place in line. Marubatsu stood on the inside, dry and well protected by the overhang of the station. Alex, on the outside, was just under the edge, one nylon bag flanking the brunt of the downpour. The straps cut into his shoulders, but he didn't want to set his bags on the wet tile, flooded by an inch of moving water. If their situations were reversed, Alex would offer to carry one of Marubatsu's bags, but Marubatsu stared forward serenely, hands cupped in the formal posture of vocal recital.

At least Marubatsu was not asking for his impressions of Japan. Alex shifted the bag straps and moved up in line. Except for the smell, a thick wet stench of sulfur and burnt sugar, Shizuoka seemed the same as Tokyo. A generic concrete-box city, suitable for purposes of general despondency.

Abruptly, Marubatsu broke the silence. "Our university is not so rich. You understand our hospitality is under financial constraints. I will speak frankly; our assistance is purely courtesy. The university lost face with your son's death. I would not ask so many favors."

This came across like a reprimand. What favors had he asked? Alex said, "I'm very grateful to you for meeting me at the station. As you know, I wanted to see the city where my son . . . lived."

Marubatsu showed no expression. "I imagine your lecture fees in Tokyo were generous. There is a lot of money in Tokyo."

"I have no complaints." In fact, the total had barely covered his discount airfare. For everything else, he was using his own money, and he'd already discovered that American savings didn't last long against Japanese prices.

A pause. Then, "In Japan, foreigners are paid more than we Japanese are. Unfair, isn't it?"

Irritated, but unsure why, Alex answered with the Japanese *ng,* which means only, "I heard you."

After another pause, Marubatsu asked, "Did they pay in yen or dollars?"

"Ng."

The next taxi was theirs. The driver pressed a button and the trunk sprang open. Alex put his bags in, unburdened at last. He climbed into the cramped backseat. Water squeezed out from his shoe and made a conspicuous puddle on the cab carpet. Marubatsu got in front on the left and spoke Japanese to the driver. The flag went down at five hundred yen, and the tires spun spray as they drove off.

Alex peered out the window at rain-blurred buildings lurching with every turn. He imagined how different it would be if Cody were introducing him to Shizuoka, pointing out the sights, telling anecdotes in his raspy-teen tenor. "Isn't it a rush, Dad?" Of course, that was the sixteen-year-old Cody's voice, not the long-distant twenty-year-old he had lost. He allowed himself to close his eyes. He had to keep himself accurate. Keep himself from reinventing the past. Perhaps, for a few seconds, he fell asleep, because Marubatsu's voice startled him the way only voices that wake you can.

"Introduce yourself in Japanese."

"I beg your pardon?"

"Because we are *in Japan*." This was forceful.

"I'm sorry, but I can't speak Japanese," Alex said. "I thought everyone knew that."

The taxi driver, glancing in the rearview mirror, seemed sympathetic to Alex.

"Something simple. *Watakushi wa Amerika no shinri-gaku no sensei desu. Namae-wa Arekusandaa Zon. Douzo, yoroshiku one-gaiitashimasu.*"

"What?"

"That would be sufficient. Repeat, please."

"I'll look up something in my phrase book."

"Phrase book," Marubatsu muttered.

In the following silence, Alex again succumbed to closing his eyes, but this time the taxi stopped before his mind drifted.

Marubatsu leaned over the seat. "One thousand three hundred fifty yen."

Alex pulled two thousand-yen bills from his wallet. Marubatsu intercepted them and handed them to the driver himself. Some Japanese was spoken, and the driver wrote a receipt, which Marubatsu put, with Alex's change, into the breast pocket of his own jacket. Alex withdrew his waiting hand. He flipped his umbrella back in shape, adjusted a spoke, and pushed it open. Meanwhile, the trunk opened, and Alex's bags were drenched again before he hauled them out. The taxi backed into a gravel alley and hovered with the engine on.

The hotel looked like a large, two-story Western ranch house. Marubatsu kicked off his shoes in the entry and stepped into blue vinyl slippers with the hotel name written on the toes. Alex set his wet bags down and untied his shoes. The key to success in Japan was loafers. He joined Marubatsu at the reception desk, where a clerk bowed fast and often, like a pigeon.

Cultural differences, Alex reminded himself.

"You have room 203. I'll wait while you get ready. After your lecture, there will be a dinner." Marubatsu handed Alex the room key.

"Thanks. Um, my change?" Alex asked.

Marubatsu looked blank until Alex gestured toward the coins showing through his pocket. Marubatsu shook his head. "We are not finished with the taxi. Please hurry."

"What kind of dinner will it be?"

"Not so formal."

"On the floor?" This determined which pants he would wear.

"Japanese-style, of course. Do you know sushi?"

"Raw fish."

"Have you tried it?"

"*Ng.*"

Marubatsu checked his watch. "I'll wait in the taxi."

Alex went up one flight of stairs and found his room. He was lucky; he had his own bathroom this time, a one-piece molded pink fiberglass shell inset a step higher than the bed area. When Alex walked on the bathroom floor, the walls buckled slightly. To use the shower, you had to hook up a hose from the sink and hold the showerhead in your hand. Alex, finding no water glass, cupped his hands and drank from the faucet. The water was clean, cold, and delicious. The bed was small and a bit hard, but a bed nonetheless. There was little room space, but a TV, telephone, and air conditioner were mounted on the walls. Compared to his Tokyo hotel, it was luxurious. Alex dropped his bags at the foot of the bed and peeled off his soggy socks. He lay on his back on the bed for a moment, feet dangling over the edge. Then he rolled over on his stomach and opened the phone book on the bed stand. This would take only a minute. He took from his wallet a small chart of *katakana* syllables translated into English. *Go* was a variation of *ko*, and *n* was separate, the only consonant without a vowel. He flipped through the phone book to the *go* section, looking for the combination *gon*. He found a block ad, in English, even:

Gone With The Wind

ENERGETIC   DEATH

CREMATION   RECEPTIVE

0542-49-4444

He was surprised at how easily he had found the funeral company that had sent Cody's body back home. There had been no telephone number on the bill, and his letters had not been answered. But this wasn't the time to call: Marubatsu was waiting in the taxi. He got up, splashed more water on his face, decided against a booster shave, and changed into his blue pants, which gave the most leeway to sit cross-legged on the floor. He put on a fresh white Oxford shirt and chose a bright red "power" tie to pep up the ensemble. Looking in the mirror, he realized he was dressed like the American flag. He changed to a purplish paisley tie and gave himself the thumbs-up. "Way to go, Mr. Zone."

At the hotel entry, he glanced at his ruined wing tips and returned upstairs to get a dry pair of shoes. He chose mesh loafers he'd bought in Tokyo to serve as slippers. Ugly, but he wouldn't mind if the storm wrecked them.

Marubatsu grimaced at Alex's shoes when he entered the taxi and collapsed his dripping umbrella. He gave the driver directions and turned back to Alex. "Have you prepared your introduction?"

"Perhaps someone else could introduce me?"

"We Japanese introduce ourselves."

"Then could you be so kind as to write something for me?"

"Can you read Chinese characters?"

"No, I'm afraid I need a Roman-letter version."

Marubatsu shook his head. "That's not real Japanese."

Feeling more himself in fresh clothes, Alex said, "So Chinese characters are real Japanese?"

"*Ng.* You had better learn them."

"Right now?"

The taxi driver turned up the radio as it began to play a Frank Sinatra song. He softly sang along in English: "Ando now—za endo is near." Marubatsu glared fish eyes at him. The driver said *"Gomen-nasai"* and shut up.

Marubatsu suddenly asked, "Why Shizuoka? This is not so big a city. You can sell your book in Tokyo, Osaka. Why do you come here?"

"For my son," Alex answered softly, amazed that Marubatsu would think his book promotion was the only reason he was here. "I need to find out how he died."

"It has been a year. You should be resigned."

Alex grit his teeth. "If anyone had answered my letters, I might be resigned, as you put it. But all I was told was that Cody died in a motorcycle accident. No details. Nothing about how it happened, or who was with him, or what was done to try to save him."

Marubatsu tilted his chin up and looked, not at Alex, but at the cab ceiling. "We Japanese believe in acceptance. It was his destiny to die when he did. Questions will not change this."

"He's my son. My only child. Surely I have a right to know—"

"He died *in Japan.*"

Alex wanted to reach over the headrest and strangle Marubatsu. It took all his willpower to change his approach. "Tell me, do you have children?"

"I have two daughters."

"What if one of your daughters died in a foreign country?"

"My daughters are good girls. They would never do that."

The taxi stopped in front of a large concrete building.

"One zousando, five hundredo yen, *kudasai*." The driver smiled broadly, showing a gold front tooth.

Marubatsu turned to Alex for the fare. Alex gave him a thousand-yen note. "And five hundred," Marubatsu prompted, pointing to the meter.

Alex pointed to the change in Marubatsu's shirt pocket. Marubatsu frowned, but took out a five-hundred-yen coin. As Alex got out, the driver half-saluted. "Zank you. Bye-bye."

Marubatsu opened a large tan umbrella and Alex stepped aside to avoid a spike in his eye. The rain pummeled his black umbrella. He jumped across the clear river racing into the storm drain and onto the steps of the building. Automatic doors slid open and air-conditioning poured out. Alex copied Marubatsu, taking a narrow plastic bag from a box, sticking his umbrella into it, and locking it in a self-service umbrella rack. Spotting five umbrellas like his own, Alex was glad the lock keys were numbered.

He pocketed the key and followed Marubatsu. The elevator girl bowed and motioned them in with a rehearsed gesture of her white gloves. Marubatsu said *"Go-kai,"* and she gave an elaborate reply in a voice higher than helium. She bowed again when they got out on the fifth floor.

A tall man with shoulder-length gray hair greeted Alex with his first firm handshake since he got off the plane. "How do you do. I'm Kaneko. I will translate your lecture. We are all looking forward to hearing about *Why Love Fails.* This way, please."

Alex glanced back at Marubatsu, who was already talking to someone else, before following Kaneko. He felt like a relay baton, tossed by one racer, snatched up by the next. "About my introduction—could you teach me something simple in Japanese?"

"Oh, English is fine. I'm here to translate. Anyway, I will introduce you, if that's all right."

Alex sighed. He was in good hands for this part of the relay race. "Thank you. Thank you so much." He followed the gray-haired Kaneko into a plain meeting room with about forty people and twice as many empty folding chairs. Men sat in a group in the middle, and women sat around them on the sides and in the back. The women, very young-looking, held open notebooks and pens poised for action. Next to one woman was a conspicuously tall man with blond wavy hair, the only other Caucasian in the room.

Kaneko stepped up to the podium. "*Mina-san komban-wa.* We are fortunate to have with us a psychologist from America, Dr. Alexander Thorn, the author of *Why Love Fails.* When we think of America, we think of freedom and individuality, romance and glamour. Yet this American writer recommends pragmatic approaches to finding a partner, including a modified version of our *o-miai,* arranged marriage. As more and more Japanese women want careers instead of husbands, and the birth rate has dropped to around one point five, his book is relevant to our culture and our times as well as his own. Let's all welcome Dr. Alexander Thorn." Kaneko then repeated his speech in Japanese, which took twice as long.

Alex was astounded by the accuracy of Kaneko's introduction, as well as his fine English. Cody had written that the only safe thing to expect in Japan was to have your expectations destroyed. Alex tried the Japanese for "Good evening, everyone" that Kaneko had opened with. *"Mina-san, komban-wa."* The audience clapped halfheartedly.

Alex kept his speech to thirty minutes, but Kaneko's translation slowed it down to an hour and a half. As in Tokyo, the audience rapport was dismal—no one registered any response to what he said. He guessed the note-takers were here on a class assignment. He tried to move his eye contact around the room, but found himself coming back to the blond man, whose face showed the most expression. He was relieved when Kaneko asked for questions and no hands were raised.

After Kaneko thanked the audience, however, the blond man came up to talk.

"Isn't it depressing, being practical about love?" The blond had a British accent.

"Not at all. I'm advising men to seek more substantial relationships, instead of haphazardly pursuing women with pretty faces or figures. The irony is that women aren't usually impressed with men who are primarily attracted to their looks, anyway."

"So what does impress women?"

Alex shrugged. "You'd get a different answer from each woman you asked."

Kaneko coughed, making the blond aware he was monopolizing the guest speaker. "Excuse me, Dr. Thorn has a busy schedule."

"My name is Lester. Here's my card," the blond said. "If you're free later, come to Nature Squib Bar. It's where the *gaijin* go."

"I'll keep that in mind." Alex stuffed the card in his pocket.

Kaneko escorted him back to the elevator. "I am sorry to rush you, but the dining room was reserved from six to eight and it's already six-thirty."

"Thank you for translating. I'm sorry the lecture didn't go over well." Alex stepped into the elevator, nodding to the girl with the white gloves.

Kaneko spoke briefly to the girl, who pushed the button for the fourth floor. "Oh, no, the audience was quite receptive."

"But no one laughed at my jokes."

"They were being polite. When an audience isn't interested, there is constant chattering. Silence means success. You did well."

The elevator opened directly into a restaurant, so the next task was taking off shoes and putting on slippers. As Alex placed his loafers on the shelf, he noticed most shoes were blatantly synthetic, favoring Velcro fastenings. All looked small compared to his.

He entered an alcove room that had been prepared for the party. Tatami floor, low table, platters of sushi arranged at each place setting—he had been walking into this room four days in a row, like a recurring time loop. He looked at the guests, all men. Like Marubatsu, they wore bluish-black suits, but with white shirts and skinny ties. Tokyo's classic styles and muted colors had seemed conservative, but Shizuoka gave new meaning to the word. Alex's blue pants and sedate purple tie made him a peacock among magpies.

Beer glasses were raised for the *kampai* toast, after which the meal began. Unlike Tokyo, the guests didn't try to speak English, but spoke Japanese to each other, leaving Alex alone to work on his food. Occasionally, Kaneko would tell him the names of the dishes or urge him to try a fish paste that was a Shizuoka specialty. The fish paste had fine bones ground up in it, but Alex managed not to gag. In addition to the usual sushi, there was a tofu-and-mushroom custard that Alex actually enjoyed, a soup with a rubbery hard-boiled egg bobbing up, and a fibrous, prickly vegetable that tasted like fermented weeds. Alex reminded himself it was the last reception dinner. From now on, he intended to live on ramen.

At the end of the meal, Marubatsu tapped his spoon on a glass and stood to make a short speech in Japanese. Alex noticed the guests sneaking glances at him. Some, including Kaneko, wore expressions of stoic disapproval. "What's he saying?" Alex whispered.

Kaneko shook his head slightly. "Don't worry."

This made Alex worry. He smiled when Marubatsu gestured in his direction, and nodded after a fragment of applause. Then Marubatsu announced in English that each guest owed eight thousand yen for the dinner. Alex took out his wallet, but Kaneko stopped his hand.

"Not you," Kaneko said. "You are our guest."

"But he used English," Alex said.

"Only to ask for money." Kaneko's mouth smiled but not his eyes. "Excuse me."

Kaneko walked over to Marubatsu and the two huddled in dispute. Gradually more magpies gathered around them. Although Alex understood nothing, the body language showed

Kaneko prevailed. The men now pulled thousand-yen notes or change out of their pockets to add to the eight thousand already tendered.

One loud drunk slapped Kaneko's back and said something using *maru* and *batsu* as separate words. Some kind of joke.

Alex stopped a young man who had owlish glasses and spiky cowlicks. "What does he mean?"

"Ah . . . difficult. It is . . . ah . . . Japanese humor. We Japanese like word play." The young man was trying very hard. He drew a circle with his finger. "The word *maru* means 'true.' *Batsu*"—he made an X in the air—"means 'false.' So the joke is . . . ah . . . sorry. I cannot speak English. Sorry." He bowed and made a hasty escape.

Kaneko returned. "Marubatsu is too busy to take you back to the university hotel, so I will escort you." Alex picked up some sarcasm on the word "busy."

The girl with the white gloves was gone, so they rode the elevator in silence. In the lobby, Alex unlocked his umbrella. Water had collected in the tip of the plastic sheath, like a used condom. He threw the bag in a trash can and followed Kaneko outside.

In the taxi, he and Kaneko talked about college education. Kaneko held the Japanese system in contempt. He raved about the demanding course work and wonderful library at Berkeley, where he had studied on sabbatical. When they reached the hotel, Alex automatically took out two thousand yen.

"No, no," Kaneko said. "I insist on paying. It's the Japanese way. I will continue home. Good night!"

Alex thanked him and waved goodbye. He stood in the gravel drive of the hotel listening to raucous crickets. The rain had stopped. The sky was all dark, no moon or stars, but occasional headlights twisted around streetlights on an even darker hill. Alex inhaled wet air, relieved to be alone. The book tour was done. The rest of his trip was only about Cody.

Five

Gaby woke to the boisterous churning of the washing machine on her neighbor's balcony, separated from her own balcony by a thin metal partition. When they both did laundry, she and her neighbor stood with their shoulders less than a foot apart, but the partition between them kept them from seeing each other, and they remained strangers. Privacy depended on context in Japan. It was all right to wear pajamas on your back balcony; even if your neighbors spotted you, they weren't supposed to look there. But you had to be fully dressed to bring your newspaper in your front door, the legitimate realm of public scrutiny.

Gaby belted her robe and slid open the glass door to her back balcony. At five in the morning, the sun was bright. Neon green algae flourished on the damp cement and Gaby's potted tomato plants already showed a few pea-size green tomatoes among yellow blossoms. She'd have to run now, before it got too hot. Gaby hauled her futon over the balcony railing to air out, and anchored it with large coil-spring clips. Then she changed into her running clothes, put on sunglasses and a Walkman, and tied her apartment key into her shoelaces.

Gaby ran along a tiny river that was slowly being eaten up by a cluster of tractors, cranes, and other heavy equipment that was converting the reedy banks into a cement-lined culvert. After four years, she still received hostile stares from the construction workers, but lately, one of the rice farmers whose small paddies edged her route would call out *gambatte* and she would wave in reply. *Gambatte,* an imperative verb habitually mistranslated as "Go for it!" really meant "Struggle!" As a former student once explained to Gaby, *gambatte* was the spirit of driving up a mountain in fourth gear.

An uphill stretch following the rice fields shortened her breath and forced her to slow to a walk. For months—no, almost a year—the same course had become increasingly arduous for her. Gaby chalked it up to aging; thirty-six was harder than thirty-five. But she continued to push herself. Even if her run depleted her, it was still the best part of the day.

Mount Fuji was mostly invisible in the summer, but on clear days she could see its grand and graceful silhouette dominating the northern sky. White herons gathered in the river, upstream from laundry suds pouring out of a city grate, and hydrangeas bloomed on the banks, dropping blue and lavender petals over soda cans and *bento* cartons littered beside the asphalt. Above the smokestacks of the Tamiya plastic model car factory, green hills arched back into the snow-veined Japan Alps. Gaby often thought how stunning Shizuoka must have been in the 1950s, before its beauty fell prey to construction and pollution. The city of Shizuoka expanded daily: green-tea bushes ripped out, wood frame apartments hammered up.

Gaby tried to jog on the down side of the incline, but couldn't muster the energy for it. Although she walked the rest of the way back, by the time she climbed the metal stairs of her apartment building, sweat soaked her shirt, her hair, even her socks. The rainy season had ended, and summer had arrived—a thick white blanket of intense heat.

Gaby's apartment consisted of two rooms flanked by front and back balconies, with a bath room, toilet room, and closet lined up on one side. She headed straight for the toilet room. Perhaps Mr. Eguchi was right; toilets told the truth about people. The sit-down-style toilet was the main reason Gaby had chosen this apartment. Despite the ugliness of the mustard-yellow throne, despite how it clashed with the red marbleized linoleum floor and wallpaper with diagonal grape bunches, it still beat squatting. Fortunately, living alone, she could use it with the door open so the decor didn't drive her mad.

Her back room, which had only her futon and television set, had a beautiful tatami floor. She enjoyed the aesthetic of empty space and left the drab sand-colored walls bare. The front room was larger and had a short counter, a half-size refrigerator, and a hot plate against one wall, leaving the rest of the room open for a pine table, two wooden chairs, and a long, low bookcase topped by her boom box, Walkman, headphones, and telephone. Above the bookcase hung her one treasure, a silk scroll painting of women tending a lotus field, purchased at great discount due to a small scratch in the fabric.

Gaby flushed the toilet and moved to the adjacent bathroom. She showered Japanese-style, sitting on a plastic stepping stool in the tiled area beside a small, deep turquoise tub. Today was Friday. If she stocked groceries, she could stay inside her air-conditioned haven all weekend without going out. She looked forward to two days alone with books and music. She vowed never to waste an evening at Nature Squib Bar again.

Clean and dressed, she turned on the radio. Opera. She switched to a tape of Debussy. She filled a large glass of water and swallowed two pills, her maintenance medication with every meal. Then she unwrapped her last triangular sandwich of steamed bread and sweet bean paste to eat with her coffee. After breakfast, she had time to do a load of laundry and hang the wash before leaving for work at eight-thirty.

The Gone With The Wind office was not at the crematorium and tomb site, but in a downtown office building. This office wasn't open to the public. Gaby used an elevator key to get off on the fourth floor and another key to open the unmarked office door. Inside, a small window looked out over a giant mechanical crab lifting its legs and claws in orderly rotation to lure customers into a restaurant below. From this angle, you could see grime streaks on its carapace and wires beneath the shell.

In addition to Gaby, Mr. Eguchi had two other salesmen, a bookkeeper, and a succession of secretaries who rarely stayed more than a month. Mr. Eguchi had just hired a woman who had a deformed foot. Since most companies wouldn't hire someone with a limp, claiming it to be upsetting to customers or bad luck for their business, Eguchi figured she might last longer.

The office was filled with cigarette smoke, radio talk show

voices, and protruding file drawers that threatened to bring down the cabinets whenever a file was tugged out. This casual atmosphere was attributed to Mr. Eguchi being *kansaijin,* a man from the Osaka region. Native Shizuokans snubbed *kansai* people for their relish of food and leisure activities, but Gaby enjoyed Mr. Eguchi's more relaxed style.

The new secretary, Rie, brought a piece of paper to Gaby's desk, saying, *"Excuse me. This letter is in English. Could you help me translate?"*

Mr. Eguchi intercepted the letter. He had dark skin and eyebrows that pitched a tent on his forehead. His short hair was rippled by a permanent wave and shellacked with gel. He had a weakness for designer clothes, especially Kenzo's wild patchwork sweaters. Many people mistook him for the popular actor who performed buffoonish antics in a ramen ad. *"Look at all those cute little squiggles! If it's English, it's not important. Don't bother Gaby-san with such things."* He crumpled the paper and tossed it, basketball style, into the trash.

Rie bowed repeatedly. *"Sorry."*

Mr. Eguchi sat on the corner of Gaby's desk, careful not to crease his double-breasted silk blazer. *"I have another client for you to visit. He is a strawberry grower. He is not very religious, so we have a chance. His name is Yamamoto."* Mr. Eguchi handed her a sheet of information that included a map to Yamamoto's house.

Gaby took the paper. *"Did he call us?"*

"Not exactly."

"Did you bribe him?" Gaby knew him well enough to tease him.

Mr. Eguchi smiled, showing three gold crowns. *"Oh, no, I merely persuaded him to hear what you had to say. With some financial assistance."*

"Well, I'm glad you didn't bribe him." This would be a no-sale. Only customers who were brooding about death bought a Gone With The Wind package. *"How old is he?"*

"Maybe sixty-five."

"Young!"

Mr. Eguchi shrugged. *"You are never too young to die."* He got up, slapping his pockets to find his pack of cigarettes. He lit one and headed out the door. He would spend the rest of the morning in a coffee shop.

The phone rang and Rie picked it up, pronouncing the company name Japanese-style. "Cone whizzer window." Her forehead creased. *"Excuse me, I don't understand . . . Excuse me, can you speak slowly? . . . I'm sorry, I can't understand English."*

Gaby guessed it was one of Lester's jokes and gestured to Rie that she would take the call. She pressed the extension on her desk phone. "Resutaa-*san?*"

Silence. Then, "Gone With The Wind?" Not Lester's voice. An American man.

"Yes, may I help you?"

"Wonderful! Your English is excellent!"

"Perhaps because I'm American."

"Oh. I'm sorry. It's just been so . . . I've been a living mess since I got off the plane. My name is Alexander Thorn."

Gaby shifted the receiver to her other ear. Alexander Thorn. The self-help author Lester went to hear last night. Maybe Lester set him up to play a joke on her.

"I'm calling about—it's complicated. Could I speak to someone in charge of transporting bodies overseas?"

Gaby motioned Rie to hang up her extension. "I don't understand. Do you want to fly in guests for a funeral?"

"No, this concerns a casket shipped to Seattle last July."

"I'm sorry, but you must be mistaken. We only handle cremation."

"I have proof you shipped a casket." His voice had a hostile edge.

If this was Lester's prank, it was an odd setup. "In any event, all information is confidential, released only to family members." Gaby waited for the punch line.

"I'm his father." A pause. "Or *was* his father."

This was no joke. Gaby swiveled her chair to face the window. She watched the crab lift its shortest leg. "Oh, dear. Forgive me."

"That's all right." His voice was carefully controlled. "How can I find out about my son? His name was Cody, Cody Thorn."

Gaby had a flash memory of a young boy, a college student, coming up the staircase as she went down to her English class. He wore a denim jacket and balanced a cup of coffee on a stack of books. Eyes wide and blue as bachelor's buttons. Brown hair in a rubber-banded ponytail, a conspicuous deviation from the Japanese standard mop-top. But her memory was from her former job, and his father was calling Gone With The Wind. "I'm afraid I can't help you. Gone With The Wind doesn't . . . um, serve . . . foreigners. Only Japanese customers."

A crinkle of paper. "Who's your supervisor?"

"Mr. Eguchi is the owner, but—"

"Put him on, please."

"He's out right now. Anyway, he doesn't—"

"Can you make me an appointment with him?"

Gaby knew Mr. Eguchi would not see him, but how could she explain that? The crab's claws grasped at nothing. "That's sort of problematic."

"What do you mean?"

"Well, for one thing, Mr. Eguchi doesn't speak English. If you want, I can take a message and—"

"No! I mean, no, thank you. Look, I don't know how to get through to this company. None of my letters were answered. Would I do better if I came to your office in person?"

Gaby began to wonder if he wasn't a grieving father but a spy. "It's a private office. You can't get on the floor without an elevator key."

"Terrific. Just my luck." His tone was bitter, not flippant. "What should I do, Ms. . . . . ah . . . ?"

"What is it that you want to know?"

A sigh. "Everything. How Cody got into a motorcycle accident, whose fault it was, who was with him, who was the doctor who treated him—"

"Have you tried the hospital that . . . I assume they also sent you a bill?"

"That's my first question. There was no hospital bill. I don't know which hospital he went to. You tell me; how do you get information in this country?"

"I'm not sure," Gaby said honestly.

"*You're* not sure?"

Gaby tried to explain. "Things work differently in Japan. There is no hard information as we're used to in the States. Here, what applies to one person doesn't apply to another."

When Thorn responded, his voice had lost control. "Okay— I have a lot to learn about cultural differences. But I have tried, for almost a year, to find out how and why my son died and I've come up against silence, silence, and silence! Even the U.S. Embassy had nothing to tell me. I came to Japan as a last resort, and you're the only American I've met. You've got to help me."

Gaby cringed at his plea. "Mr. Thorn, I can imagine, or rather I can't imagine, what an ordeal this must be for you, but I don't see how I can help. Gone With The Wind doesn't ship caskets. You need special licenses for that. It must be a mistake, some other company."

"It can't be another company. I'm looking at the letterhead on the bill. I sent a check and you cashed it. I have my canceled check to prove it."

Finally, some concrete data. Relieved to have moved from emotions to finances, Gaby uncapped a pen. "Okay, give me your check number, amount, and date. If you sent dollars, we'll have a foreign currency exchange record that should stand out in our books. I'll talk to our bookkeeper. Are you in town?"

He gave her the information and the number of his hotel.

"The university hotel?" You could only get a room there with the sponsorship of a Shizuyama University professor. Gaby wondered who was sponsoring Thorn.

"That's right. I gave a talk for them yesterday."

So his lecture had been a university event. "Oh, yes, I heard about it. Well, I'll do what I can."

"When can I expect your call?"

"That depends on the bookkeeper."

"After lunch?"

"I'm not sure." Gaby remembered how frustrated she'd been her first year, unaware of the ways of Japan. Thorn had the common false impression that Japan was efficient; ergo, *she* came across as evasive. She felt sorry for him, but what could she say? A Lester-like speech wouldn't change his orientation. Like her friends in the States, he would just disbelieve her. "I'll call you tonight whether or not I have an answer."

"Wait! I don't know your name."

"Gaby."

"Gaby . . . ?"

"Stanton." Gaby felt exposed, glad her home phone was unlisted.

"Thank you, Ms. Stanton. Goodbye."

Gaby set the phone in its cradle. It had been years since she'd been called "Ms."

Rie smirked as she looked up from a file drawer. *"Was that your boyfriend?"*

"I don't have a boyfriend."

"He has a sexy voice."

"I didn't notice." Gaby longed to go back home, crawl into her freshly aired futon. Obviously, Thorn wouldn't disappear after she discovered the inevitable error at Gone With The Wind. He'd probably expect her to spend hours interpreting Japanese for him, expect her to introduce him to every shipping agent in Shizuoka, unaware that introductions were favors that required payback. She couldn't blame him for this—after all, he was alone in a place where survival depended upon connections—but she'd be stuck with him, a Thorn in her side. She remembered the mess she'd gotten into helping Lester get his first apartment. His landlord had demanded translation favors from her for a

year and a half, until Lester moved out to his current place. Helping people in America was easy; in Japan, it was sticky business, racking up obligations you had to honor after the person you helped flew home carefree.

Gaby thought about the blue-eyed American student on the stairs. Could he have been Cody Thorn? Was he now dead? *You're never too young to die.* She sorted out the timing in her head. Thorn said his son's body was sent in July, the last month of the spring semester. Gaby had been fired during vacation in August, so she had still been at Shizuyama University at the time. Gaby didn't have to appear on campus much during the last two weeks of July, which were reserved for final exams, but surely she would have heard gossip if an exchange student had died.

But here was another memory: one of her composition students, Junko, in her office the week before exams, upset about a friend's motorcycle accident, no final paper to hand in. Since Junko was a diligent, overly conscientious student, Gaby had told her not to worry and to bring the paper in October on the first class of the fall semester—but by then, the class had become Michael's. Had Junko's friend been Cody? Gaby reminded herself Thorn would certainly have gone through the university if Cody had been a student. The blue-eyed boy had to be someone else, safe and sound.

The bookkeeper came in and draped his jacket over the back of his chair.

Gaby approached his desk. *"Good morning, Nishida-san."*

Nishida was fifty, hair threaded with gray, cheeks riddled with scar pockets from teenage acne. His left hand was missing a finger, which stirred rumors of gangster involvement. Nishida habitually showed up after Mr. Eguchi left for the coffee shop. Mr. Eguchi might scold him for this, but wouldn't fire him.

Mr. Eguchi said the only thing that held back the booming fantasy funeral market was the difficulty hiring employees. Funeral industry jobs were considered degrading, which caused Gone With The Wind to be staffed by unconventional misfits: gangsters, cripples—even a female *gaijin* could work here.

Nishida stared. His eyes appeared to have a matte finish. *"What is it?"*

Gaby asked, *"Could you please check accounts receivable for last July?"*

"Why?" He opened a package of cigarettes.

"An American customer. He claims he paid us to send his son's corpse back to America."

Nishida sucked vigorously to light his cigarette. It was a cheap brand that didn't burn easily. *"He is wrong. American idiot."*

"Probably, but I told him we would check our records."

Nishida snapped his lighter shut. *"I can't do it. I'm busy."*

"He's persistent. He won't leave us alone unless we show proof."

"That's his problem."

"It will only take a minute."

"I won't do it. Hiroshima, Nagasaki, and we Japanese are forced to bow and scrape for those white shits. No Yankee favors." Nishida blew a stream of smoke at her.

"Ah, so." Gaby left Nishida to savor his hostility. She would have to get at the books herself.

Rie sat motionless, blushing, aghast at Nishida's rudeness.

Gaby gave her a reassuring smile. *"Let me help with the mail, now."*

"I am not to bother you with mail," Rie objected.

"It's okay. The boss won't know." Gaby pulled a chair over and started opening envelopes. She made small talk about the change of seasons while searching for notices of bank transfer payments among the bills and junk mail. She found one and brought it to Nishida. One of Eguchi's quirks was to keep two sets of books: one on the computer and another in old-fashioned ledgers. Gaby suspected he was underreporting income for taxes and chose not to know about it. The computer records were the ones the government officials saw, so Gaby figured the truth was in the ledgers on top of Nishida's desk. *"Eguchi will want this recorded before the weekend."*

Nishida squinted at the pink carbon paper. *"Ng."*

Gaby casually circled behind him and pretended to read

a letter while she watched him. Nishida picked up the notice, read it slowly, put it down, and lit a new cigarette. He placed his cigarette on the edge of his ashtray and carefully selected a pen from his collection in a beer glass. Then he pulled a green notebook from the middle section of his desktop divider and set it on his large blotter. He turned pages and flattened the last one with a sweep of his white sleeve. As he entered the deposit in the ledger, Gaby looked at the notebooks on his desk. No other notebook was green. All she had to do was wait until he left for lunch.

But today, Nishida ordered a *bento* lunch delivered. Gaby would have only a minute or two to sneak a look at the ledger while Nishida met the delivery boy in the lobby. And when the delivery boy phoned up, Nishida sent Rie, limping, to get his *bento,* instead. Then Mr. Eguchi returned and insisted Gaby accompany him to a Chinese restaurant for lunch to celebrate her sale to Mr. Aoshima.

Gaby had lost her shot at the books anyway, so she left Nishida shoveling rice into his mouth and Rie sipping a soda and reading literature comics (a glance at Beth-*san* dying proved the cross-cultural appeal of *Little Women*), and followed Mr. Eguchi to the elevator.

Outside the building, Mr. Eguchi looked for a taxi.

"We could walk," Gaby suggested.

"No, no, walking is not my style." A taxi pulled up and Mr. Eguchi opened the door for Gaby, an unusual gesture from a Japanese man.

"Shin Chiyugoku restaurant, please," Gaby said, assuming her role as the subordinate who handled things for her boss.

The taxi driver waited for Mr. Eguchi and asked, *"Where to?"*

"Shin Chiyugoku restaurant," Gaby repeated.

"Where does she want to go?" the driver asked. *"I can't understand English."*

Mr. Eguchi laughed. *"You can't understand Japanese! She said Shin Chiyugoku restaurant, very clearly."*

"Oh, Shin Chiyugoku, yes, I know it." He started the meter. *"Where is she from?"*

"She is from America, land of the free," Mr. Eguchi answered.

"Such a beautiful woman. Is she married?"

"She is a widow." Mr. Eguchi winked at Gaby. He had learned winking from American movies, and practiced his context on her.

Gaby kept quiet. The same old questions. Next he'd ask Eguchi if she ate *natto,* a fermented bean specialty that smelled like athlete's foot.

"Does she eat natto?"

Gaby made a gagging gesture that amused her boss.

"Ask her yourself," Mr. Eguchi said. *"She knows Japanese."*

"Is she a student?"

"She is a university teacher." To Eguchi, this was her ongoing status regardless of employment.

"I can't speak English," the driver continued. *"Except for my first lesson.* I am a boy. This is a pen. I am a boy, not a pen. This is a pen, not a boy." He braked with a flourish. Mr. Eguchi paid the fare and waved away the change.

In the restaurant, the waiter ignored Gaby and asked Mr. Eguchi where she was from and if she was a student.

"I'll have the dai yung special." Mr. Eguchi looked to Gaby.

"Make that two."

"Two dai yung. And steamed pork buns. And Tsing Tao beer." Mr. Eguchi leaned back and lit a cigarette. *"So, how is my best salesman?"*

"We have a small problem."

"Don't worry about the little things. If you watch the ants, you will be eaten by the bears."

Gaby thought a minute. *"That's not a Japanese saying."*

"It is my saying! Do you like it?" Mr. Eguchi grinned.

"Of course, boss. But this ant problem could turn into a bear. An American man called claiming we sent his son's corpse back to America."

"Why does he think such a thing?"

"He says he has a bill on our letterhead and proof that he paid it. He will not give up." Gaby played her trump card: *"If he spreads his story, it could embarrass us."*

Mr. Eguchi frowned, brows knit. *"Not good, not good."*

"Perhaps if you asked Nishida to look in our ledger?"

Mr. Eguchi waved smoke away from his face. *"Telling him the truth won't make him believe it. What is important is that we convince him we are an honorable company. We will help him and then he will respect us."*

The food arrived, steamed barbecued pork buns, large omelets packed with mushrooms, onions, bamboo shoots, roast pork, and water chestnuts, rice, tea, and a tall frosted bottle of beer with two glasses.

Mr. Eguchi snapped his fingers and his face broke into a smile. *"You will have dinner with him, our treat. Be charming. He is man, you are woman. Yes, that's the answer."*

Gaby lost her appetite. The prospect of going out with a stranger, much less charming him, sickened her. *"Why me?"*

"You are both American. You will understand each other."

"But Americans . . ." How could she explain to a Japanese man that being American established no innate bond with other Americans? Thorn was determined. He wouldn't be charmed away from his mission, especially not by her. She remembered Michael McKenzie saying he hadn't come to Japan to date white women, and tried again. *"American men often come to Japan because they admire Japanese women. A Japanese woman might be more effective, I think."*

"You speak his language. You are the best choice."

Although workers were supposed to pour beer for their bosses, Mr. Eguchi broke tradition and poured Gaby's. *"Kampai!"*

"Kampai." Gaby clinked her glass. Her weekend was ruined.

Six

Although Alex was tempted to hover in his hotel room for Gaby Stanton's call, he knew that would waste the day. She'd made it clear she was going to take her time, and Japanese time didn't move through the clock the way American time did. Why was this so difficult? Why hadn't Gone With The Wind answered even one of his letters? His mistake, he thought, was sending the check. If he hadn't paid them, they would be the ones sending letter after letter to *him*. But he had paid, never dreaming he would need leverage to obtain information about Cody's death. This country was heartless.

Then he reminded himself that it was an American who'd put him off this time. Good—he didn't have to feel guilty about judging the Japanese on this count. But Gaby Stanton was probably telling the truth when she said that no one else at the company spoke English. This, he was sure, was his biggest barrier. He needed to speak directly to Eguchi, the Japanese owner. He thought of Kaneko, who had been gracious and generous the night before. Would Kaneko help him get an appointment with Eguchi?

Alex dialed the university phone number.

A high female voice let out a rapid patter of Japanese. A pause. Then, *"Moshi moshi?"*

"Ah . . . Kaneko, please. Kaneko-*sensei.*"

"Naisen wa wakarimasuka?"

Message from Mars. "Do you speak English?"

"Gomen-nasai. Eigo ga dekimasen."

She didn't speak English. He repeated, "Kaneko-*sensei.*"

"Muzukashii . . . e . . . to . . . eibun-ka ni otsunagi shimashouka?"

Alex hung up. He couldn't even get through a switchboard. He decided to visit the university in person. He opened his tourist map of Shizuoka and located his hotel by Kaneko's red ink circle drawn in the taxi yesterday. From the scale at the bottom of the map, the university was perhaps two kilometers away, not too far to walk. Since he had no more official business, he could wear shorts and a short-sleeved shirt to feel more comfortable in the heat. He was tempted to wear sandals, but didn't want to risk getting blisters. He carried a pair of tennis shoes to the lobby and put them on there. He left his key at the desk, awkwardly exchanging bows with the clerk. Bowing looked so easy, but his head resisted his shoulders, or vice versa, and his hands didn't know where to go. He began to understand why Japanese people didn't shake hands well.

Outside, Alex felt physically slugged by the humidity. Haze or smoke intensified the hot white glare, nearly choking him. It was only nine o'clock. He was tempted to return to his air-conditioned room and wait for Gaby's call after all, but today was Friday, and he wanted to nail down an appointment with Eguchi before the weekend.

He walked out the gravel drive to a narrow road lined with shabby concrete buildings and waist-high weeds. By the laundry hung out on upper balconies, he figured people lived over the few businesses and cafes. There were no street signs. He checked his map: no road names there, either. His map was useless. How did people find addresses with unnamed streets? Figuring the sun was in the east, he tilted the map to determine the university was to the southeast, toward the ocean. He would try to find his way by the shapes of the roads.

As he reached a four-lane street, schoolchildren in uniforms zipped past him on bicycles. Boys wore black suits with Nehru collar jackets and brass buttons; girls wore black jumpers over white blouses. A few boys called out, *"Gaijin! Gaijin!"* and made faces at him.

Alex turned south, looking for a racetrack to confirm the large oval on his map. He followed three men with slicked-back hair and untucked shirts who might be headed for the track. He was already sweating profusely and wishing he had a hat. At the next block, more men with shellacked hair got off a bus and headed in the same direction as his three guides. Several had tattoos and a few wore dark glasses. When Alex spotted a grandstand, he felt a surge of encouragement. He had finally figured out something on his own. The gamblers funneled up to the racetrack entrance, where a girl in uniform took coins and handed out programs and tiny pencils.

Alex noticed a row of vending machines off to the side and went over to them, glad to discover they had coin slots and knobs like American vending machines. At least he could get a drink without having to speak Japanese. He looked at the cans, most of them labeled in English: Coffee Bitter, Coffee Jo, American Coffee, Fruipy, Pepsi, Jolt, Peach Fizz, Carpis, and Pocari Sweat. Alex couldn't resist. He put in a hundred-yen coin and pulled the knob for Pocari Sweat. The machine played "Camptown Races" and stopped mid-phrase when the can dropped down. Alex popped the tab and drank. Pocari Sweat tasted like sweetened mineral water. He gulped it all and placed the can beside an overflowing wastebasket. Other vending machines sold cigarettes, candy, sandwiches, batteries, and beer. Beer from a vending machine! What a temptation for minors. Cody had never mentioned this in his letters, and Alex had no trouble guessing why.

When he came to the next main street, he turned left and was pleased to spot a building with a sign that had TAMIYA written in English underneath two white stars on red-and-blue squares. This also matched his map and gave him more confidence. After the Tamiya building, he veered right on a short street that led to an artificial pond coated with bright green scum. Men fishing from the surrounding concrete steps turned to stare at Alex. Alex kept walking, feeling heat coming through the soles of his shoes.

The road shrank down to one lane. After that came new apartment buildings, large old houses, patches of daikon radishes, their white roots emerging above the soil, and fields of green-tea bushes. Old women in straw hats and baggy blue work clothes trimmed the hedgerows with power saws rounded precisely to shape the bushes. Tea leaves spewed out in shreds, giving off a bitter, medicinal odor.

Alex stopped to peel his shirtfront a few inches off his chest and palpitate some air through the cloth. His head pounded. He looked for shade, but found only a tiny circling shadow of a hawk. He would have to buy a hat.

The curving roads near the university were confusing, but Alex saw students with book bags and followed in the wake of their bicycles. He recognized the campus from a postcard Cody had sent. The university was built on a hill, postwar concrete-block buildings interspersed with steps. On the stone staircase leading to the entry gate, a teenage boy in a white shirt, starched enough to hold rigid an inch above his shoulders, stopped Alex.

"Excuse me, do you speak English?" the teenager asked.

"Yes!" Alex answered, delighted.

"I would like to pray for the purification of your blood. Please shut your eyes."

Right, while you take my wallet, Alex thought. "I'm sorry, praying is against my religion. But do you know where I can find Kaneko-*sensei*?"

The teenager looked flustered. Apparently his come-on line was rehearsed, as his language skill deteriorated at once. "Sorry. I student not. University, don't know. Please shut your eyes. I would like to pray for you."

"Not now. Thanks anyway." Alex walked on up the steps. To get out of the sun, he entered the first building, which turned out to be a cafeteria.

Mid-morning, there were only a few students at the long tables, in the seats closest to electric fans lined up against one wall. Alex staggered to an orange plastic chair and sat, puffing. He had to stop postponing getting in shape. When he got back to Seattle, he'd get serious about exercise—if Japan didn't kill him first.

Two women with green aprons and paper hats watched

him from the cash register. He heard the word *gaijin* in their conversation. What was with all this staring, anyway? At least in Tokyo, *gaijin* treatment was only inflicted by drunks. Was there some Shizuoka law that required them to make fun of foreigners? So he was Caucasian: White guys had been in Japan for over a hundred years.

As he thought this, a white man entered the cafeteria and Alex caught himself staring. He was young, definitely under thirty, with short hair, freckles, and a confident stride. He wore a pink shirt that made Alex long for raspberry sherbet. Alex made eye contact and waved, a *gaijin*-to-*gaijin* acknowledgment. The young man bought a cold canned coffee and sat across from Alex.

"Are you new here, mate?" His accent was Australian.

Alex sat straighter. "Does it show?"

When the young man grinned, dimples set in. "It's the dress code. No shorts on campus."

Alex looked at his bare legs and sighed. "Well, I hope that's why everyone is staring at me."

"No such luck. They stare because you're *gaijin*. You get used to it. I'm Michael McKenzie." He offered his hand.

Alex shook it. "Alex Thorn. Do you work here?"

Michael nodded. "English department. I'm their token native speaker. It's a great job. The salary is fantastic and I hardly have to do anything. No meetings, no committees, and all the students fall in love with me."

"Sounds good," Alex said. "How many classes do you teach?"

"Six, but they only meet once a week."

"Isn't it hard to master a foreign language that way?"

"It is. The Japanese study English their entire lives, but they never learn it. My classes are fairly basic. Good thing, since I majored in business. I suppose you heard Japan was pretty much bilingual?"

"That was my impression before I got here."

"What a joke. Even Americans learn foreign languages better than the Japanese."

This put Alex off. "I can't agree. A lot of Japanese people in Seattle are totally fluent."

"Oh, well, if they go abroad, sure. Those are the cream of the crop." Michael tilted his head back to gulp his coffee. "So, are you looking for an English teaching job here?"

"No, I'm on vacation. Sort of."

"Working holiday?"

"Yes, but my work is personal. At least, now it is. I started out promoting a book, but that finished yesterday, thank goodness."

Michael snapped his fingers and pointed at Alex in one smooth motion. "Say, are you the chap Lester went to hear? About women finding husbands?"

"Men finding wives. But I think I met Lester. Blond hair, nose?"

"That's him. He's been here two years; he knows everything and everybody. Including a lot of cute Japanese girls." Michael winked.

Unwilling to engage in male bonding with Michael, Alex changed the subject. "I came here to visit Kaneko-*sensei*. Do you know him, by any chance?"

"I've met him. He teaches American history and culture."

"Could you tell me how to get to his office?"

"At the top of the hill, same building as the English department. He's on another floor, though. Third floor, I think." Michael finished his coffee and checked his watch. "I'm on my way up. I'll show you."

"I'd appreciate it." Alex stood and followed Michael. The women in green aprons giggled as they passed, covering their mouths with their hands.

"Although I wouldn't count on finding him." Michael pushed through the door. "Most professors aren't here on Fridays. I get stuck with the Friday classes because I'm new."

"A universal hierarchy. The newest teachers get the worst schedules."

"It could have been worse. The person I replaced told me they used to have Saturday classes. Of course, they made her teach them, because she was a woman."

Outside, the heat slugged him again. "That's terrible."

Michael shrugged. "Not for me."

As they ascended the hill, the buildings were fewer and the steps got narrower, until they could no longer walk side by side. Alex hiked behind Michael up a path shaded by cherry trees full of whirring insects. Smashed cherries and pits underfoot forced him to keep his eyes on the ground. A brown snake slithered off the path into wild grass. Cody had probably preferred this wildness to the manicured campus of Central Washington.

"How long have you had this job?" Alex tried not to pant.

"Since last October."

So he wouldn't have met Cody. "Who had it before you?"

"Gaby Stanton. She was *really* qualified. I heard she has a Ph.D."

Alex stopped at the name. There couldn't be more than one Gaby Stanton in Shizuoka. Why would a teacher from Cody's college switch to a job with the funeral company that had sent Cody's body home? There had to be a connection. Whatever the reason for the silence about Cody's death, Ms. Stanton was involved.

"Are you all right?" Michael asked.

Alex stammered. "It's . . . uh . . . the heat. I'm not used to it."

"Here's the building. You'll feel better inside."

They entered a seven-story U-shaped building at one tip of the U. A heavy door opened onto a staircase. Michael walked past the stairs through a propped-open door leading to an unlit hallway of offices. Before Alex's eyes adjusted, he tripped over a tall wrought-iron doorstop, bruising his shin. The black linoleum floor had the familiar institutional odor of disinfecting detergent. At the end of the corridor was an elevator with a water fountain next to it. Alex drank and drank, the water colder and better the longer he stayed.

Michael looked at a map of faculty offices posted by the elevator. "I'm not positive, but it looks like Kaneko is in room 314. I'd go with you, but I have a class right now."

Alex wiped his chin. "Thank you. Nice to meet you." They shook hands and Michael turned the corner down the middle section of the U. Alex looked at the map. McKenzie's name was in English under room 245; everyone else's was in *kanji* characters. He pressed the button with an upward arrow and the doors opened at once with a ping. Inside, he pressed 3. Nothing happened. He pressed again. The doors held open. The non-numbered buttons were marked with *kanji*. He tried one and an alarm bell sounded. Fortunately, it ceased as soon as he released his finger. The next two buttons had no effect, but the fourth one closed the doors and the elevator rose.

On the third floor, he walked an empty hallway until he found 314 and knocked. No answer. The window above the door was dark. As he looked for a posting of office hours, a man in a white shirt and black tie and slacks breezed by.

The man pointed to Kaneko's door and said, *"Imasen."*

"Imasen?" Alex repeated, puzzled.

"Hai. Kyo Kaneko-san wa Tokyo ni imasu."

Alex repeated the one word he understood. "Tokyo?"

"Hai, so desu."

"Doumo," Alex said as the man went on. Kaneko must be in Tokyo. Just his luck after climbing a hill in hundred-degree heat. But now he had a new project: to find someone to tell him about Gaby Stanton. Marubatsu was part of the English department and probably knew her. Alex felt sick to his stomach. Perhaps Gaby's involvement in Cody's death was the reason Marubatsu had warned him not to ask favors of the university. Marubatsu could be covering up the wrongdoing of a former teacher. Except *what* could have happened? What could an English teacher have to do with a motorcycle accident?

Alex took the elevator to the second floor. If Michael McKenzie's office was 245, the other teachers in the department must be nearby. Only one window above a door showed light. He hesitated. After yesterday's treatment, he didn't want to have anything more to do with Marubatsu, but Alex's letters and faxes to the president of the university had been answered, weeks later, with superficial courtesy: "The university is very sorry about your situation. We have forwarded your letter to the appropriate personnel." They had never named "the appropriate personnel" and he'd received no further response—eight times. Marubatsu was the only name he had.

He decided to appeal to Marubatsu's egotism. He would sacrifice his own pride and flatter the man. He took a deep breath and knocked.

Professor Marubatsu opened the door and his face immediately went into a frown. His head only came up to Alex's sternum. Alex was sure he had shrunk overnight.

"I'm sorry to bother you," Alex said. "But I don't know who else to go to."

"I am busy."

Alex heard television voices from his office and glimpsed a TV showing *sumo* wrestling and a leather sofa with crease marks on the cushion. Marubatsu's office, unlike the corridor, was air-conditioned. "Then who else might be able to tell me about Gaby Stanton?"

Marubatsu opened his mouth to speak and shut it again. A lot of thinking went on in his wide-set eyes. "If you must talk to someone, you had better talk to me. Come in."

"Thank you." Alex entered and sat on the folding chair Marubatsu gestured to. Besides the usual wall of books, there was a computer, printer, and fax machine on a large oak desk, a cassette player on the windowsill, and a video player underneath the television. It didn't look like this university was under the financial constraints Marubatsu had mentioned the day before.

Marubatsu resumed his place on the sofa and muted the television sound with a remote control. "Why do you want to know about Gaby-*san*?"

"Did she know my son?"

"I have no idea."

"Would he have been in any of her classes?"

"*Gaijin* students don't take English classes."

"Why did she leave the university?"

Marubatsu was silent for a while. When he spoke, he averted his eyes. "She did not resign. She was fired."

Alex shivered slightly. The air-conditioning was set to re-frigerator temperature. "What was she fired for?"

"That is confidential."

"But why?"

"That is our concern, not yours."

Alex persisted. "She's working for the funeral company that sent my son's body home. According to Michael McKenzie, she left—was fired—shortly after Cody died. I can't believe that's coincidental."

Marubatsu's neutral expression changed ever so slightly. He was interested, even if he wouldn't admit it. "Unfortunately, we cannot prevent teachers from taking shameful jobs after they are fired. I encouraged her to go home to America and find a husband. But"—he shrugged, tiny fingers palm up—"she did not take my advice."

Alex chose to ignore that tidbit of sexism. "Why would an English professor take a job with a funeral company?"

Marubatsu looked steadily at him. "I hear there is much money. Many *gaijin* come to Japan to steal our wealth, not to learn from our culture."

"That's sad."

"*Ng.*" He looked pleased.

"It's the timing that bothers me," Alex said. "Are you sure she had nothing to do with Cody's death?"

Slight patches of red appeared on Marubatsu's cheekbones. "I cannot say. I would not like to think such things of her. But she is independent. We cannot be responsible for her."

"But what happened? What did she *do*?"

Marubatsu frowned and folded his hands together. "Let us say she did not fit into this department."

Alex was getting nowhere. Maybe he would get further if he asked about Gaby Stanton as a person. "What about her character?"

"*Ng.* I would not trust her." Marubatsu stared out his window. A bamboo grove swayed in the gravel courtyard below. After a while, he added, "Of course, all women are deceptive, but she is more difficult. I think because she has no husband, no children." He stood. "I must prepare for class."

Alex reluctantly got up, chair seat squeaking. "I appreciate your time."

"If you have more questions, come to me. You do not understand our Japanese ways. It would be better if I went between you and the university."

"Thank you, I'll do that," Alex said, knowing he wouldn't. He turned to bow or shake hands, but Marubatsu had already shut the door. If Marubatsu didn't trust Gaby Stanton, Alex thought, she couldn't be all bad. Then Alex made himself reconsider. Cold fish that he was, Carpface had offered to help. Marubatsu couldn't truly be as awful as he seemed; cultural differences had to be part of it. Perhaps Alex had been pushing too fast and that was why he'd gotten so much resistance. He would have to give up on American efficiency and stay in Japan until he got the answers he needed, however long that took. He only hoped he could afford it.

He walked down the hill of the campus, feeling the strain on his knees. As he passed the music building, bits of scales, a Beethoven sonata, a Chopin waltz, and wrong notes floating out simultaneously, he felt nostalgic for Cody's amateur but passionate piano playing. There was a piece with tedious scale-like passages designed to cause nervous tension that Cody had played over and over, hitting his fists on the keys when he missed the same note for the third time. It had driven Alex insane. The things he missed, now that Cody was gone.

The walk back to his hotel felt like a stroll inside a pizza oven, even though it was all downhill. When he turned left after the racetrack, he couldn't find the gravel drive to the hotel, and had to walk back and forth on the block several times until he recognized it. As he untied his shoes in the lobby, sweat dropping off his forehead onto the floor, the clerk, bowing and blushing, handed him a piece of paper.

"*Doumo.*" Alex took it: all in Japanese. He looked up the word "who" in his pocket dictionary. Pointing to the note, he asked, "*Dare?*"

"*Gebi Sutanton.*" The clerk bowed more, like a yo-yo on a short string.

Gaby Stanton. His surprise at her prompt return call was mixed with wariness. She had been an English professor when Cody was a student at Shizuyama University. Shouldn't she have recognized Cody's name? In his room, he took off his shirt and wiped his face and chest with cold water before calling Gone With The Wind.

"Cone whizzer window," said the secretary.

"Ms. Stanton, please."

Gaby's voice came on the line. "Hello?"

"Alex Thorn. Did you find my check?"

"Not yet. I was thinking we should meet in person. Are you free for dinner tomorrow night?"

Alex sat on the edge of his bed. "Would Mr. Eguchi be there?"

"No, just us."

Her voice had a resigned tone. What was up? "I want to meet Eguchi."

"His schedule is full. Anyway, as I told you, he doesn't speak English."

"What if I brought someone to translate?" Alex hoped he could reach Kaneko.

Gaby sighed. "Do you mind if I ditch the formalities for a moment?"

"Please do!" Those were words he'd been wanting to hear since his plane landed.

"This is Japan. Talking to the owner is a real long shot. You have to work your way up through underlings first. Because I'm American, Mr. Eguchi assigned me to handle your problem. Maybe I can coax him to meet you later, but for now, you're stuck with me."

Alex didn't want to waste time with underlings. "I need to talk to Mr. Eguchi directly."

"Mr. Thorn, I would love for you to talk to Mr. Eguchi directly, too, but it's not going to happen. Unfortunately, I'm a necessary step in the process. Are we on for dinner?"

It was clear she wished she weren't a necessary step. What made her so reluctant to fulfill her boss's orders? Maybe, at least, he could speed up the process. "How about dinner tonight instead of tomorrow?"

"Well . . . all right. What time?"

Alex's stomach rumbled. "As early as you can."

"Six-thirty, then. I'll pick you up at your hotel."

"Um, is it possible to have dinner here without *sushi*?"

Gaby laughed, a pleasant alto laugh. "Yes, it is. We can have chairs and silverware, too, if you'd like."

"That," Alex said, "will give me something to look forward to." He hung up the phone.

He liked the way Gaby laid things out. Thinking it over, he realized she was the first person who'd given him a clue as to how this country worked. Maybe this dinner wouldn't be a complete waste of time, after all. She might not tell him much about Gone With The Wind, but she could tell him about Shizuyama University. And he'd sure like to hear why she'd been fired.

Of course, Alex reflected, she wouldn't want to talk about getting fired to a total stranger. He would have to establish some bond between them. Quickly. Just for tonight, he would have to put aside his frustration and anger and try to be charming.

Seven

Gaby was aware she hadn't been charming on the phone. Neither she nor Thorn wanted to dine together, and nothing would be accomplished by it, but that's what Mr. Eguchi wanted. Americans wanted results. Japanese wanted relationships, coded into a hierarchy of favors and obligations. Doomed to frustrate each other.

Gaby glanced up when Nishida stretched and got up from his desk. He left the office without a word. His jacket remained draped over his chair; he'd return, but this might be her only chance to sneak a look at accounts receivable. Eguchi was at a nearby bar and Rie, at her clean desk, had nothing to do. *"Go home, Rie. No one will mind if you leave ten minutes early."*

Rie shook her head. *"I must keep this good job. It is difficult for me to find work. Mr. Eguchi is very kind."*

That Rie felt her job was a good one was a sad statement about Japanese discrimination. Gaby wasn't sure what to say. *"It's hard, isn't it, for women to find work these days?"*

"Yes, but I meant my leg." Rie looked down at her foot. *"I often wish I were American. It would be easier to be different if I were a foreigner."*

Gaby sat on a corner of Nishida's desk. This was a daring conversation, way beyond the scope of acceptable topics. *"Easier? To be gaijin?"*

Rie nodded. Her face matched those of women in old Kyoto wood block prints, rectangular with a high forehead and pale skin, but her black hair was permed into tiny spirals, not wrapped in a traditional bun. *"When Americans do something wrong, they are called crazy foreigners and that is that. But for us, there is no excuse."*

Gaby scooted closer to Nishida's green notebook. Maybe she could do this in front of Rie. If she kept talking, Rie might not ask questions. *"I don't think I get away with much because I am a foreigner. People always let me know I'm wrong."*

Rie looked doubtful. *"Really?"*

Gaby idly flipped open the notebook cover and turned pages. *"For example, when I ignorantly put empty bottles out on a wet-garbage trash day, one neighbor lectured me about bad manners and another put an angry note on my door. But when Lester—a male foreigner—made the same mistake, one of his neighbors removed his empty bottles and put them out on recycling trash day for him. It's harder to be a woman in this country. Japanese or not, women are judged by different standards. Like the disapproval I suffer for not being married."*

Rie's face suddenly beamed. *"Oh, you, too? Of course, in my case, it is obvious that no one would marry a girl with a limp, but they still point fingers and say, 'You should get married!' It's so embarrassing."*

"In many ways, Japanese people are quite rude." Gaby was back to July of last year in Nishida's records.

Rie giggled, delighted at the idea, and repeated Gaby's words, imitating Nishida's voice. *"Japanese people are RUDE!"*

Gaby quickly scanned ledger pages. A dollar/yen exchange would stand out amid the routine bank transfers, but she continued past July through August and September without finding any sign of an American check. When Nishida entered the office, opening a package of Mild Seven cigarettes, Gaby slammed the book shut and hopped off his desk. *"Well, goodbye, Rie. See you Monday. Goodbye, Nishida-san."*

"Ng," Nishida grunted.

Gaby caught the elevator Nishida had taken up and got out at the parking level. Her battered gray Honda played Cinderella to gleaming white Toyota stepsisters. The one American car in the lot, a 1971 pink El Dorado, belonged to the wild and crazy Eguchi. At first, Eguchi thought Gaby should drive a luxury car, to impress their clients, but she had argued a small old car gave a thrifty image that contrasted favorably to the huge profits routinely ascribed to Zen priests. *"We can emerge hard-working and humble while our competition seems greedy."* Eguchi accepted that, but the truth was Gaby hadn't wanted to squander her savings on a new car.

Gaby started her car and turned on the radio. News. She considered listening for the weather, then turned it off. She knew the weather: hot and humid for the next eight weeks. She wondered what she would talk about with Thorn after condolences and the bad news about Nishida's accounts. It occurred to her that Thorn might want to end the protocol dinner as quickly as she did, which could limit the amount of time she'd have to spend "charming" him.

She parked in her assigned space and went up the resonant metal steps to her apartment. Kicking her shoes off inside the door, Gaby experienced relief, similar to that of landing on your own property in Monopoly. Every outing felt like rolling dice through a game board of other players' hotels. After tonight, she promised herself to spend the entire weekend inside.

She unbuttoned her blouse and ran a wet washcloth over her face and chest. Since Thorn was American and probably wouldn't care whether or not she wore her formal business outfit, she changed into a blue seersucker dress with a large white collar and short-sleeved cuffs. Although the V neck was a trifle low for Gaby's taste, the pleated skirt almost reached her ankles, so she could get away without wearing nylons. Anything to be cooler.

The university hotel wasn't far from her apartment and she arrived promptly at six-thirty, asking for Thorn-*san* at the lobby desk.

"Are you his wife?" the clerk asked, ringing his room.

The clerk knew she wasn't Thorn's wife, or she'd be staying in his room with him. He was either offering a polite cover for an illicit affair or fishing for gossip. Gaby said, *"I am his translator this evening."*

"Ah, I see. Is he famous in America?"

Here was a chance to place a small deposit in Thorn's obligation account. *"Very famous. Everyone knows his books."*

Alexander Thorn appeared on the stairs, holding shoes in one hand and a briefcase in the other. He was about six feet tall and slender except for his protruding stomach. He had inquisitive blue eyes, a long slanted nose like a playground slide, and a thatch of gray hair in a trim-but-not-too-short presidential cut. He had the face of a man who could win the election, but not this year. Not until he had purged the self-consciousness from his smile. When he slipped on the hardwood stairs in his socks, the clerk rushed over to steady him. "I'm fine, really, just fine. Thank you, *doumo.*"

Gaby realized Rie was right about his sexy voice, reedy but not raspy. "Mr. Thorn?"

"Alex," he said, shaking her hand. "Nice to meet you."

Gaby wasn't used to a firm handshake and direct eye contact. It unsettled her. "Likewise. Shall we go?"

Alex handed his key to the clerk, who bowed low and often. Outside, Alex asked, "Why is he giving me special treatment tonight?"

Gaby laughed. "I boosted your status by telling him you were famous. Do you mind?"

"That depends on what I'm famous for." He said it playfully.

"Your books."

"Then I don't mind. But how did you know I write books?" Alex opened the door on the right side of her car. Gaby thought he had meant to open the passenger door for himself but when he saw the steering wheel, he held it open for her as if that had been his intention all along. Smooth.

Gaby got in. "Actually, I found out yesterday." He crossed the front of her Honda and took his seat to her left. "A friend of mine went to your lecture. I guess you specialize in marital relations?"

"Well, professionally. Not personally."

Gaby found this an odd remark. Why would he want to push the conversation in a personal direction? This was a business meeting, not a date. She went back to small talk. "Is your book getting a good reception in Japan?"

"I don't think so. I seem to keep learning the old saying,

East is East and West is West. Every day—no, every *hour*—something comes up to make me aware of how much I don't know about Japan. Isn't it frustrating to live here?"

Back to personal territory again. Perhaps psychologists habitually mined for feelings. "Sometimes. Not all the time." Gaby pulled into a right-turn lane behind four cars and prepared to wait for the second light. Alex listened so attentively, Gaby felt obliged to say more. "It's like the James Bond book in which Bond asks an Australian agent if Japanese life is difficult for him, and the agent says, 'The first ten years are the worst.' I love that line. Japan can be hard—intense—but it grows on you. A lot of *gaijin* end up staying longer than they meant to."

"How long have you lived here?"

"Almost five years."

"What brought you over here?"

Gaby glanced to her left and into Alex's direct eye contact. Blue eyes. Startling. "I accepted a professorship at the university."

"Really? How did you come to work for a funeral parlor?"

His tone of voice struck Gaby wrong. He was too interested. Why would he give a damn? She edged closer to the bumper of a Nissan sports car. "Oh, just the way things happened."

"What happened?" Alex prompted her.

"It's not worth getting into." Gaby got through the yellow light on the bumper of the Nissan. "I thought we'd go to Yaizu for an ocean view. There's a cliff-side restaurant with semi-French cuisine. Is that all right?"

"Sounds good. But how did you—"

"You live on the West Coast?" Gaby interrupted.

"Seattle."

"I used to live in Portland."

"Do you miss the U.S.?"

"Sometimes, of course, but not really." She had answered before she realized the conversation had turned to her feelings, again. She should get Alex to talk about himself, but as cars funneled into one lane of the curved mountain road, she had to concentrate on driving.

He continued his questions. "You don't have trouble fitting in over here?"

"Oh, I don't fit in: no foreigner ever does," Gaby said cheerfully. "You can stay twenty years, speak like a native, marry, have children, and you'll still be an outsider in Japan."

"And that doesn't bother you?" Alex probed.

"Not the way it bothers other expatriates." She braked after a curve to avoid hitting a truck turning off onto a dirt road. "You see, in America I never fit in, either. I've been a loner since—well, childhood." She felt her cheeks flash hot. Why had she revealed that to a stranger?

"So was I," said Alex. "And that's when being a loner hurts, when you're a kid. Was gym class a particular torture for you?"

"Oh, yes. Last to be chosen, first to be teased."

"Not to mention the horrors of the locker room," Alex added.

Gaby felt uneasy with his empathy. She wasn't used to personal questions. "Well, who enjoys childhood, really?"

Alex shot back: "People who can't remember theirs."

Gaby couldn't suppress an appreciative chuckle. Under other circumstances, she could like this man. She stopped at a small promontory with four cars crammed at the side of the road and waited for a white Toyota to leave before jockeying into its space one meter from the drop of the cliff. Alex followed her to a rectangular restaurant with porthole windows— a boxcar mated with a submarine. In America, the entire roadside pull-off would only have room for one trash can. Smoke twisted out of two pipes in the roof, circulating a fishy, spicy odor.

Alex held the heavy wood door open for her. She paused before going through. His arm seemed too close. She said, "You know, men don't open doors for women in Japan."

"Is it a bad thing to do?"

"No. I just thought you'd like to know it's not expected."
They ducked under blue curtains printed with white characters
and Gaby greeted the hostess, an older woman in a brown kimono whose purple hair advertised a botched dye job. *"Two
people."*

"Two people?" the hostess repeated. *"Please come this way."*
She led them down a narrow aisle beside the portholes, carpeted
with a garish flower pattern. To the right were side alcoves flanked
by spindly potted wisteria, each with its own picture window
facing out to sea. *"Our most romantic table has become available."*
She left them at an empty table at the end of the boxcar.

"What did she say?" Alex asked.

"Meaningless formalities." Gaby stood between two wood
chairs. Their view looked over the bay back at the coast of
Shizuoka City. High-tide waves crashed against piles of concrete
tetrapot shoring up the coastal highway. Above the city, the
barely discernible dark blue tip of Mount Fuji poked through a
cluster of clouds at the horizon. "You should have the view,"
she said, taking the chair that faced a hedge of palm bushes and
a dwarf pine. Alex held her chair and pushed it in. He did it
well. Gaby gestured toward the table. "You see? Forks, knives,
chairs, and a table taller than one's kneecaps. Will this do?"

Alex sat and picked up his cloth napkin folded into the
shape of a crane. The crane fell apart and flattened on his lap. "It
certainly beats raw fish on the floor."

"I gather you've been getting the honored-guest treatment."

"Well, I'm not an honored guest now, am I?" Alex's smile
didn't hide his meaning.

This was where the blind date ended. Gaby regretted what
would follow—Alex's questions and her lack of answers. She
wished she could have met him for another reason. A waitress
in a white blouse with a black ribbon bowed and handed them
menus.

"I recommend their Chicken Doria. It's chicken breast in
a sauce over—"

Alex folded his menu before looking at it. "I'll have that."

"For vegetables, they have—"

"I'll have whatever you have. With a beer."

Gaby ordered two Chicken Dorias, mixed salads, a Kirin Extra Dry, and a glass of red wine. The drinks came quickly, with a plate of soy-flavored rice crackers.

Gaby took a sip of wine and plunged in. "I'm sorry about your son. I don't know how people survive the death of their children."

Alex said nothing for a moment. Then, "I don't know, either. I hope finding out about Cody's death will help."

"I hope you can find whatever you need." She waited for Alex to speak.

Instead, he pulled out his wallet and withdrew a well-worn photograph, which he handed to Gaby.

Gaby picked up the snapshot and spilled a few drops of wine on the tablecloth. It was the blue-eyed boy she had seen on the staircase. "Oh, no!" she blurted.

"So you knew him," Alex said quietly.

Gaby shook her head. "I saw him once or twice at the university. We never said more than hello. It's just—he had a quality about him. He seemed like such a bright, intense kid." The picture of Cody looked like a young Alex but with a fairer complexion and a loose, irregular mouth, the kind that only opened in a slanted letter O.

Alex took the photo back. "Who would have known him?"

Gaby thought. "Exchange students mostly take Japanese classes. Mrs. Sakura teaches those. Where did he live? Did he have friends?"

"He rented a room in a boardinghouse to save money. I'm sure he had friends—he had his mother's knack for meeting people—but he never wrote about any."

"He's very good-looking. There must have been girls."

"I don't have any names."

Gaby stopped herself from offering to inquire among her

former students. She wished she could help him without getting entangled in the Japanese obligation game. She looked out the window. Out of sight, beyond the back wall of the restaurant, the sun was descending. The palms and pines cast long shadows toward her. "Wait a minute," Gaby said, "if Cody was a Shizuyama student, you could get the university to help you."

"Don't think I haven't tried." Alex let out a long breath. "As a matter of fact, I talked to a Shizuyama professor today."

"Did you learn anything?"

He hesitated, as if he weren't going to tell her. "I learned that you were fired from the university the same time my son died. Can you explain that?"

Gaby was puzzled, then hurt. "You think I had something to do with Cody's death?"

His face looked pained. "Well, the timing is disturbing. Would you mind telling me why you were fired?"

The ironic question of the year. It didn't surprise her that Alex knew—getting canned was gossip good enough to circulate for years—but she was surprised and hurt that he somehow suspected her. Gaby shook her head. "I honestly don't know. The best I can come up with—and I have thought a lot about this—is that Japan in general doesn't like women professors and one professor in particular doesn't like me."

"You can't be fired without a reason," Alex objected.

"This is Japan," she muttered. "Expect the unexpected."

Alex looked startled, even shaken.

"Alex?"

"That's exactly what Cody said," he murmured.

The waitress interrupted the moment, placing a sizzling *doria* in front of each of them. While the waitress fussed over arranging smaller salad and roll plates, Gaby looked out the window, twisting back to see Alex's view. "The clouds have moved. You can see part of Mount Fuji." She pointed to the dark blue outline of the squared-off tip and sharply flared left side of the mountain, more distinct now that the sky had paled to aqua at the horizon. While Alex looked out the window, Gaby removed a foil-backed sheet of pills from her pocket, pressed two out, and swallowed them with her wine.

"Beautiful," Alex said. "No snow on top?"

"Not in July and August. In winter, it's totally white. It looks bigger in the winter."

The waitress bowed, backing out of their alcove.

Alex stabbed a few bites of salad. "I'm sorry. I don't want to doubt you. Please try to understand. All I have is one letter from the university informing me of Cody's death, eight letters expressing sympathy and saying nothing, and my bill from Gone With The Wind. I'm at a total loss here."

Gaby moved her plate aside. "Show me the bill."

Alex took his briefcase from under the table, opened it on his lap, and handed her a manila folder. "My canceled check and copies of all my letters are there, too."

Gaby began to read. She felt him watching her. "You may as well eat," she suggested. Alex picked up his fork and she looked at the bill. Something didn't look right. The billing format was the one they used. Was it the font? Gaby suddenly knew what was different. "It's in English!"

Alex paid close attention. "So?"

"We never send bills in English."

"Even to Americans?"

"We don't serve foreign clients," Gaby said. Alex narrowed his eyes, and Gaby hurried to explain. "Even if we did, no one at the office knows English except me. Someone else wrote this bill. Someone outside the company. It's a fake!"

Alex reached across the table and held up his check. "Well, this isn't a fake check, so Gone With The Wind has my money."

"I'm afraid not. I checked our accounts receivable today and didn't find any foreign checks." Gaby turned the check over. "Aha! You see? This went to Ninka Bank. Our bank is Mitsubishi."

Alex grabbed the check. "Where does it say that?"

Gaby pointed. "It's in *kanji*. These two characters read *ginko,* bank. The other two are *ninka*. It means . . . hm . . . approval, as in they'll approve your loans. It's sort of a credit union. Oh, Alex." She wondered how he would react. Not only was his son dead, but he had been defrauded.

But Alex didn't seem to take it in. He was fixed on the bill. "The address is in both Japanese and English. If you only serve Japanese, as you claim, why is the address translated into English?"

"It isn't," Gaby said. She looked at the bill again. Underneath the Japanese address was a typed translation where the phone number should have been. "This is wrong. The Japanese reads 3-3-801 Nishimado-cho, which is true, but it's translated as 1-24-13 Kitanumi. Look, you can see an outline. This was pasted on over our phone number and photocopied." Gaby's voice was gaining volume. "Someone got hold of our letterhead and dummied this up. I can't believe this!"

Alex ate more of his chicken dish. "My check was written to Gone With The Wind. No one else could have cashed it."

"Not necessarily," Gaby said. "You see, checks aren't used in Japan. Everything's done by electronic transfer or cash. To cash a foreign check into yen, all you need is an *inkan*. An official hand-carved stamp that's used in place of a signature." She pointed to a circular red stamp on Alex's check. "That's the *inkan*. It reads 'Gone With The Wind' in *katakana,* the alphabet that's used for foreign words."

"I'm missing your point," Alex said.

"My point is that, unlike a signature, an *inkan* can be stolen or copied." Gaby adopted her patient-teacher tone. "For example, I have a personal *inkan* with my name carved in Japanese syllables. If you borrowed my *inkan* and knew my bank account number, you could legally withdraw all my money. They don't require signatures or any other identification, just the *inkan*."

"So this check was cashed at Ninka Bank with a Gone With The Wind *inkan*."

"Exactly. It's the wrong bank—not our account."

"Then your story is that someone, for whatever reason, stole your company's letterhead and stamp, sent me a false bill, and cashed my check. Is that a fair summary?" Alex continued at Gaby's nod. "Well, I don't buy it. If it were a rip-off, why would they have shipped Cody's body home? Why not just keep the money and forget—"

"Because they expected you to demand the body." Gaby leaned forward, speaking more softly. "The Japanese feed on scandal. When someone dies, there is no shortage of mean rumors. Parents are expected to try to hush the inevitable gossip, to protect their children's reputations. If they poked around for details, the speculation would get worse. The idea is, the less said the better. What's important is possession of the body, not possession of the embarrassing details."

Alex pushed his chair away from the table. "Gaby . . ."

"Yes?"

"You're telling me I've been deceived. Which bank your company uses and what the Japanese translation says are both a matter of your word. You've admitted you're the only one who knows English at Gone With The Wind. What proof is there that you . . . that I should believe you?"

"You don't believe me?" Her throat got tight.

Alex looked out the window. "It's not that I don't believe you as much as I can't allow myself to believe you. I need proof."

She watched him stare at the ocean, which grew darker as an orange glow stained the undersides of the clouds. His expression was inaccessible, as if his mind were busily padding his pain, holding himself in or blocking her out. He was *gaijin* in its literal sense, an outsider, beyond the reach of friendly arms. This man was permanently wounded. Gaby couldn't blame him for suspecting her. He was clueless about Japan.

The waitress came by and lit a candle at their table, glancing at their plates. Alex and Gaby both looked away. *"Is something wrong with your meal?"*

"Nothing." Gaby took a bite of her *doria*. It had cooled to

room temperature. *"I'm not very hungry."* She indicated they were finished.

The waitress cleared their plates. *"Where is he from?"*

"He's American," Gaby said. She figured she might as well get the drill over with. *"He's not studying Japanese and he doesn't eat natto. We are discussing important business."*

"I'm sorry." The waitress quickly moved away, bowing even though she carried a stack of plates.

Alex was still watching the sky. The clouds glowed in streaks of bright pink and salmon.

"I'm sorry you don't believe me." Gaby faltered. Eguchi wouldn't be pleased with the way this dinner had gone. Instead of charming Alex, he had charmed her: got her to care about his problems only to accuse her of causing them. He had a right not to trust her; it was her job to behave professionally, not emotionally. "You could hire any outside translator to verify my translation. As for Mitsubishi Bank, they'd keep their client accounts confidential, so I don't know how to prove that." She put her napkin on the table. "I'll try to persuade Mr. Eguchi to see you, if that would help. Is there anything else I can do for you?"

Alex slowly faced her. "Hear me out. Give me a chance to explain."

Eight

But Alex found he had no words to explain himself. In an hour, Gaby Stanton had given him more information than he'd been able to pry out of anyone else in Japan for an entire year. His rational mind questioned whether he was believing her out of the sheer relief of hearing something—anything—at last, but his intuition told him to believe her. Her reaction to Cody's photo and the Gone With The Wind bill seemed completely forthright, uncensored. Her surprise at being accused of lying was the response of an honest person. A real liar might have acted annoyed, outraged—overdone it. Liars prepared themselves to be challenged. "I'm sorry I offended you," he said.

"Don't be." Gaby looked up with a rueful smile. "I'm the one who should apologize. I should have been more sensitive about what I was implying. I'm very sorry. It must be awful to lose someone so close."

Alex regarded her carefully. He'd anticipated meeting a young, aggressive, tight-skirted tough cookie. He'd pictured her with war-paint rouge wedges and a cynical mouth. He hadn't expected an attractive, graceful woman with dark brown hair and penetrating brown eyes. Gaby was brusque and to-the-point, but he liked that. She knew who she was and didn't have to please men to prove herself. Under other circumstances, she would be his kind of woman. "Cody and I weren't close," he ventured. "I can't pretend I was a good father. I wasn't."

"How can you know that?" Gaby asked.

"I was an unavailable workaholic. And after the divorce, things got worse. Our weekends felt staged, unnatural. I kept thinking I could get to know him better when he moved out of Jane's house, but he stayed with her through his first year of college. His sophomore year, he went to Japan. I had no idea I'd never see him again." Alex picked up his beer and swallowed steadily, proud of the dispassionate tone he'd achieved.

"You . . . you talk as if you were a case study."

Busted. He set down his half-empty glass. "It's been almost a year."

"Well, you're the psychologist, not me," she said, "but isn't there a reasonable chance you were a better father than you think you were?"

"No, I don't think so." He was touched that she would argue with him on his behalf. *Reasonable chance*—she even spoke his language.

"How about a slight chance, then?"

Alex raised his eyebrows. "That's good. I hope I remember that line to use on my clients. But I can't let myself off the hook. I should have done better." He looked out the window. At night, the ocean was distinguishable only by the absence of lights that crisscrossed the city and speckled the hills.

"We all should have done better," Gaby said gently. "Sometimes, you just have to forgive yourself."

As Alex began to wonder if Gaby was speaking from experience and what she had to forgive herself for, the waitress approached hesitantly, with a dessert tray.

"*Sumimasen?*" The waitress's voice was a whispered falsetto.

"Ah, dessert," Gaby announced. "There's ice cream, jelly roll, litchi nuts, crepes, and tough, gluey rice cakes. Anything strike your fancy?"

Alex patted his stomach. "I'll pass."

"I'm going for the tough, gluey rice cakes." Gaby pointed and the waitress set down a plate of three unbaked globs, white, pale pink, and pale green. "I've come to like these a lot. Tea?"

"Coffee." Alex remembered McKenzie's cold can of coffee. "Black and hot."

Gaby ordered his coffee and waited until the waitress brought it, the tiny blue cup trembling on its saucer, before she picked up a rice cake with her fingers. "Sure you don't want to try *mochi?*"

Alex looked at the thick white wad of dough. "No, thanks. So, now that you know my situation, what do you think? How should I approach this to get the best results?"

Gaby avoided eye contact, taking her time pulling the gluey rice cake in half. "I don't mean to discourage you, but I'm not sure it's possible to get 'results.'"

Alex took one sip of his coffee—weak and instant—and set the cup down for good. "Is it because I don't speak Japanese?"

Gaby chewed awhile, and her expression became guarded. "Even if you did, you'd have a lot going against you. It's not the language as much as the culture. You don't have any connections and you don't have any obligations to call in. Maybe you should hire a professional detective. A bilingual one."

"I checked into that long ago. The cost for overseas private detective work is phenomenal. Everything I own wouldn't cover the bill."

"You've written to your congressman and senators to drum up a government investigation?" Gaby started her second rice cake, the pink one.

"I don't have enough to get them interested. They gave me sympathy, but they didn't see anything amiss. Even missing organs didn't—" Alex stopped abruptly. He'd blurted out his last secret when only his instinct had made him rule out the possibility Gaby was involved in Cody's death. The first rule of *Why Love Fails* was not to rely on instinct. He hoped he wasn't gravitating toward Gaby merely because she was attractive or because she was another American in Japan.

"Missing organs?" Gaby's eyes opened wider. "Oh, my God."

Mistake or not, she knew it now. Knowing that, she might as well know everything. Alex placed his voice in lecture mode. "You see, Cody considered himself a Buddhist. That's why Japan interested him in the first place. When he learned Buddhism prohibits cutting into bodies, he taped a note on his driver's license to specifically state he was *not* an organ donor nor did he want to receive a transplant. And when his body came back, there were scars in his—" Out of nowhere, tears blurred his vision. Alex blinked and felt them trickle over his cheeks. He picked up his napkin to blot them. "His chest was all . . ." He tried again. "His heart wasn't— I can't get used to . . . I can't. I. Sorry. I don't . . ." As tears got the better of him, he threw the napkin down and hung his head.

"Come on," said Gaby's steady alto voice. "We'll get out of here." His free hand felt fingers close around it and squeeze. Strong fingers holding on to him. "Stand up, that's good. I'll handle everything. You just keep walking. Good."

As he struggled to regain composure, he heard her speak Japanese, watched the floral carpet move under his wing tip shoes. The sound of paper and coins. A heavy door on his shoulder and muggy evening heat. Gravel, a gray car door, a rubber mat with dirt streaks and sand. When the door shut against his left shoulder, he lost control and began to sob.

Gaby got in and started the engine. "That's good. You cry and I'll drive. I've got a full tank, so take your time."

Alex cried. He was aware of lights jolting through the car and the pull of curves and hills, but nothing else except salt water in his face and racking in his ribs. Later, Alex would marvel that he had followed her instructions. His professional training taught him it was all right for men to cry as a general principle, but only Gaby Stanton had offered *him* explicit permission to cry through ten gallons of gas. When he entered the snuffling phase, he discovered they had stopped in a dark parking lot.

Gaby offered him a pocket-size package of tissues.

Alex blew and wiped. "I didn't know that was still in me. I'm awfully sorry."

"No problem," Gaby said, opening another tissue pack. "Here, I've got tons of these. People give them away at the train station."

"What time is it?" Alex asked. "Where are we?"

Gaby handed him a plastic bag for the used tissues. "Nine-thirty. We're at Nihondaira, the top of the hill that belonged to the first *shōgun*. Kind of a lovers' lane." She quickly added, "Of course, that's not what I had in mind, but it's about the only place you can avoid stares."

Alex peered up through the windshield at a blank, black sky. What he thought was a star turned out to be an airplane. Two greenish-white streetlights shone on the empty center of the parking lot. Other cars were parked in the murky fringes. Music drifted out of one, an old pop song: Karen Carpenter singing "Close to You." "What is this parking lot for?"

"During the day, they run a tram from here to the shogunate fort. You get the best view of Mount Fuji here, too, when it's visible. Which isn't often."

"I didn't mean to take up your whole evening."

Gaby grinned. "We were both going to make this brief, weren't we?"

"This is work for you," Alex remembered. "You've done more than your duty."

"Ah, you're learning the obligation game." Gaby's voice was light, teasing. "I bought the dinner, so, as Mr. Eguchi intended, you owe Gone With The Wind favorable treatment. If I told him you broke down in public you'd *really* owe us. But I won't tell him."

"Then I owe *you.*"

"Technically, yes. But since I'm American, you can renege on me without reprisal." Gaby said this as a joke, but there was a resigned undertone in her words.

Alex rolled his window down all the way. "I don't know what to do. There are so many unanswered questions and you've just added more."

"May I ask one you won't like?"

He was glad to have her take the initiative. "Go ahead."

She wet her lips with her tongue. "Do you think Cody was murdered?"

Alex had lain awake many nights over that one. "I can't imagine that. Cody was just a kid. No one had any reason to kill him. Because of his Buddhism kick, he didn't get involved with drugs, so we can rule out dealers or gangs. I got a full coroner's report in Seattle. There were skull fractures and burns and internal bleeding. No knife wounds, no bullet wounds, no trace of poison. I read the report so many times I have it memorized. The only mystery is why his heart was removed, 'as if for transplant,' the report said. But he had so many injuries that a transplant wouldn't have saved him. They assured me nothing could have saved him." Alex was relieved he didn't start crying again. For the most part, his emotional armor held up.

Gaby let a moment pass before speaking. "What worries

me most is that you never received a hospital bill or doctor's report. There are very strict regulations in Japan about operating on patients. Nothing is done without a family member present."

"This was an emergency situation," Alex pointed out.

"That's true. But never, *never,* would anyone attempt a heart transplant without family consent."

Alex didn't want to dwell on Cody's heart. Not at this moment. He thought over what Gaby had said. "Why do you think I didn't get a hospital bill?"

"Could someone else have paid? Cody's mother?"

"No, Jane didn't pay, either. It would have to have been someone in Japan, and we don't know anyone in Japan. I can't believe a stranger would pay my son's hospital bill. It just doesn't make sense." Alex felt choked by the heat. No breeze came through his open window, only the silly pop song from the other car.

Gaby gave him a light punch in the shoulder, a surprisingly masculine gesture. "Why don't I take you back to your hotel? There's only so much one can absorb in one night."

"No! Not yet." Alex caught her hand as she reached for the ignition. Her fingers were soft and, compared to his, cool. He saw a flash of fear in her eyes, which puzzled him. He followed her gaze to her hand in his. They had been getting along so well, it hadn't occurred to him his gesture might be unwelcome. He let go at once. "Tell me what to do," he pleaded. "You know how to get around in Japan. Where do I start?"

Gaby looked away. "I don't know what to tell you. This is a serious situation."

"Should I go to the police?"

"Yes, definitely. Although . . ." Gaby trailed off.

"Although what?"

"You'd need a good translator."

"Would you be my translator?" Alex asked hurriedly. "I'll pay you the going rate, of course."

"I don't feel comfortable with that." Gaby's fingers fidgeted on the steering wheel. "I can look into hiring a professional translator for you."

Alex, hurt by rejection, said nothing. The "Close to You" car roared to life. Its headlights shone on Alex and Gaby before racing off. Now it was so quiet he could hear the repeated sound of distant breakers collapsing against the shore. "Gaby, you've listened to me all through dinner. You've let me cry in your car. If you won't help me, who will?"

"I said I'd help you find a translator." Gaby looked straight ahead. "I better get you back to the hotel." She started the engine and moved out of their space.

As they wound down the hill, Alex acknowledged there was nothing in it for her to be his translator. All he could offer was money. A hairpin curve pressed Alex against the door. He couldn't make out much in the dark except some tall trees to his left and an open pasture to his right. The next curve threw Alex toward Gaby, and he leaned away to compensate.

In the dim light, Gaby looked like an Italian painting, her nose a shallow arch ending in a hint of a double bump, her skin faint gray, transparent. A del Sarto, Alex decided. Her thoughts were unreadable, complex. It would take more than tonight to pick her brains.

The bottom of the hill meshed into the city grid of lights. They said nothing while Gaby drove through the city. Alex couldn't recognize any landmarks at night. He was surprised when Gaby turned onto the gravel drive of the university hotel.

She jerked the brake and shifted into neutral. Her voice suddenly soft, she said, "I'm sorry. This must be very hard for you."

"Thank you. I appreciate everything you've done tonight." Alex was about to ask for an exchange of phone numbers when he noticed every window of the hotel was dark. "I wonder why the lights are out."

"Uh-oh," Gaby said. "You have an outside key?"

"I have no keys. I left my room key at the desk."

"Try the door."

Alex walked to the hotel. Gaby pulled her Honda around to shine its headlights at the hotel door. Alex tried the handle. Locked. He cupped his hands and peered in the adjacent window. No hall light. A paper notice was taped to the window. In Japanese, of course. Alex turned into Gaby's lights and pointed to the note.

Leaving the engine running, Gaby came up and joined him. She read the posted notice. "The hotel closes Friday night at ten for the weekend." Gaby traced her finger over the characters as she continued reading. "It reopens Sunday night after seven. The management regrets . . . extends apology."

"How can they shut me out like that? All my stuff is in there."

"I vaguely remember this. Since the university closes for the weekend, so does the hotel. It's not a regular hotel."

"What do they expect me to do? Why didn't anyone tell me?" All at once, fatigue clobbered him. Jet lag and the ongoing humidity ganged up on him, merged with his anger. Locked out of his own hotel room without warning, he had never needed a bed faster.

Gaby headed back to the car and Alex followed. "Calm down, it's not deliberate," she said. "It's a Japanese thing. Everyone assumes someone else told you. You need a hotel room for two nights. You have your money and passport?"

"Yes, but that's all I have with me. What will happen to my bags?"

Gaby fastened her seat belt. "Don't worry. They'll be here Sunday evening when you get back. Everything's locked up, safe and sound. What kind of hotel do you want: a hundred dollars, two hundred, three hundred?"

Alex sighed. "How about fifty?"

"Doesn't exist. Sixty-five, maybe—a cockroach special." Gaby drove out and slowly cruised the side streets until she found a phone booth. "I'll see what I can do."

Alex leaned against the open phone booth while Gaby

flipped through the yellow pages. The heat lingered and crickets rasped noisily. Gaby slid a card into the bright green phone and dialed. Alex kicked at a clump of tall grass as Gaby spoke Japanese. At least he had Gaby to make arrangements for him. He felt like a child, unable to do anything on his own. She hung up and dialed another number, talking with her eyes shut, fanning herself with her purse. She was tired, too. She made call after call until the phone spat out her card, used up. Then she delivered the bad news. "Everything's booked. There's a big soccer tournament in town. I could try other cities, but there aren't many trains this late. I suppose you could rent a room in a love hotel."

"A love hotel? You don't mean a whorehouse, do you?"

"No, no. Just a hotel they rent by the hour, for couples, usually. I've never been to one, but at least you'd have a bed. Other than that, I don't know."

Alex could see Gaby wasn't about to invite him to sleep on her sofa. And why should she? She'd only met him tonight. Funny how it seemed he'd known her longer. "I guess it's a love hotel." It sounded like the name of a television sitcom.

"I'll call a friend of mine. He knows where the love hotels are. In fact . . ." Gaby mustered a smile. "He owes me some favors. Maybe you could stay at his place." She rummaged in her purse for coins to put into the phone.

Alex offered a handful of change from his pocket. "I really appreciate this."

"Hey, it's my job. Appreciate Gone With The Wind." She picked a coin out of his hand, put it in the phone, punched a number, and waited. "He's not home. I bet he's at Nature Squib Bar."

Alex recognized the name of the bar from the Brit who'd given him his card. He was wearing the same pants he'd worn for his lecture. He pulled a crumpled card from his pocket. It was a Nature Squib Bar card with a name scrawled on top. "Is your friend Lester Hollingsworth?"

Gaby's mouth dropped open. "How did you know?"

Alex gave the card to Gaby. "He attended my last talk on *Why Love Fails.*"

"Oh, of course. He's the one who told me you wrote books." She chose another coin from his handful.

So the long-nosed blond was her friend. The man who had asked what impressed women, as if all women were alike. Alex resented this, though he knew he had no reason to.

"Lester gets around," Gaby said, punching in the number. "I think he enjoys being the *gaijin* who knows all the *gaijin,* even a recluse like me." After a moment, Gaby covered her other ear and shouted a few sentences. Then she hung up. "They said he just left. Which could mean anything." She glanced at her watch. "I don't know what to do. I guess we could go to my place and keep calling from there until he gets home."

Alex wondered why she sounded so reluctant. "Could I sleep in your car?"

Gaby shook her head. "You'd get in trouble. We both would. Well, come on." She motioned Alex into her car.

Alex leaned back in his seat, ready for a flash-nap, but it took less than a minute to reach Gaby's apartment. She parked behind a two-story wood building. From the back, Alex saw four patios topped by four balconies, each with a washing machine and clothesline. The upper balcony on the end had clothes hanging in the dark.

He followed Gaby around to the front, up reverberating metal steps and past three doors before the one she unlocked. "I take my shoes off," Gaby said. "Not to be Japanese, but it really does keep the dirt down."

Alex bent over to untie his shoes in the square meter of cement that served as an entry. The floor of the main room was hard straw, tatami. To his immense relief, the air was cool, without the frosty drafts usually generated by air-conditioning.

"Help yourself to water or juice," Gaby told him. "I have to bring my laundry in." She went into a back room, sliding a paper door shut behind her.

Alex went to a short, low counter beside a half-size refrigerator. No dishes in the dish rack, no stains in the sink. He opened an overhead cupboard and found a neat row of four glasses beside two coffee mugs. He took a glass, filled it from the tap, and drank. He set it in the sink, aware it was the one dirty item in the place.

He looked around the mostly empty room for a place to sit. There were two hard chairs at a wood table. No sofa, no cushions. The single nonfunctional item in sight was a water-color scroll hanging over a bookcase. By habit, he checked out her books: three different medical encyclopedias, various dictionaries, textbooks, and Norton literature anthologies on the bottom shelf. On the shorter top shelf were paperbacks: Austen, Brautigan, Carver, Chandler . . . alphabetical.

Gaby closed the sliding paper door behind her again as she emerged from the back room. "Oh, don't psychoanalyze me by my books. Most of them are in storage in Portland."

Alex rubbed his eyes. "When do you plan to move back to the States?"

"I don't know. Not for a few years. Not before I'm forty."

"I see." Alex tried not to sound surprised. Gaby looked his age, forty-five, not in her thirties. He slumped into a wood chair and stared at the luminous hands of his silver wristwatch. Eleven o'clock—the latest he'd stayed up in Japan. Jet lag torqued his mind. His body longed to be horizontal.

"I'll try Lester again." Gaby went for a black phone on top of her bookcase.

Alex wished she would invite him to sleep here. Obviously, she had no soft furniture, but even the floor tempted him. He put his elbow on the table and rested his head in his hand while Gaby telephoned.

"No answer," Gaby said. "We better put our shoes back on and try to find a love hotel on our own." Gaby massaged her shoulder and winced. Clearly, Gaby didn't want to go back out, either.

"Could . . . could I sleep here?" Alex ventured.

"On the floor?"

"I'm exhausted. Aren't you?"

"You can't spend the night here." Gaby was firm. "The neighbors would talk."

"Do you care what they think?" A yawn grabbed him.

"Yes, of course. Gossip is powerful. It can get you fired."

"Okay. Just let me rest for ten minutes. Then I'll get up." Alex stretched out on the tatami floor. "Ah, this feels good." He shut his eyes. The last words he heard were an agitated "You can't stay here!"

Nine

Mr. Aoshima unbuttoned his shirt and, calmly tearing into his skin with his fingernails, opened his chest to show her his Korean heart. Gaby saw bubbly red blood spurting around clear plastic vessels, but no heart. Aoshima glared at her. "Where is it? Where is my heart?" Electric amplified heartbeats came through a loudspeaker.

Gaby woke to her neighbor's pulsating washing machine. Five-thirty in the morning, and she hadn't fallen asleep until four, anxious about the presence of a strange man in her apartment, hot because the paper door between her and this man blocked air circulation. The hard knob of pain in the left side of her abdomen was all too familiar. She had no time to dress before rushing to the toilet. She slid open the door, glanced at Alex's prone body, grateful he was still asleep, and stiffly walked into the toilet room. She shut her eyes against the orange checked floor and diagonal grape walls in the suffocating cubicle, hoping Alex wouldn't wake up.

She'd had ulcerative colitis since she was sixteen: over half her life. Twenty years of experience with her illness had taught her to rest, exercise, watch her diet, and take sulfa drugs every day, but these were all partial modifications. The only cure for ulcerative colitis was removal of the entire colon: a drastic operation Gaby was afraid to undergo. Short of surgery, nothing prevented spontaneous bouts of diarrhea and intestinal bleeding that lasted from a few days to a few months. Sure enough, when she wiped herself, the toilet paper showed blood.

Gaby darted back into her bedroom and put on shorts and a big T-shirt. To stop the internal bleeding, she had to start taking corticosteroids right away. Unfortunately, today was Saturday, and she couldn't see her doctor until Monday. Gaby reminded herself that she would go into remission again sooner or later. The challenge today would be to get rid of Alexander Thorn without him noticing she was sick. Hers was not a disease anyone understood; he would only find her disgusting.

Footsteps in the other room signaled Alex was up. Through the wall, Gaby heard him pee loud and long in the toilet room. Damn! She'd forgotten to wipe the underside of the toilet seat, to erase the telltale splatters. She had to get him out of here.

Gaby hauled her futon to the back balcony and slung it over the rail. When she entered the main room, Alex was drinking water at the sink. "Hi."

His hair was flattened around his left ear, pushing up in mad-scientist spikes at the crown. "Good morning. Are you feeling okay?"

"Fine. Although I didn't sleep much. Did you?"

"Out like a light. I guess you put a pillow under my head. Thanks."

Gaby supposed she couldn't ask him to leave before breakfast and a shower. "Would you like some orange juice?" She opened the refrigerator and a cellophane bag of coffee beans fell out of the shelf in the door.

"Are those coffee beans? I haven't had a decent cup since I left Seattle."

Gaby set the beans on the counter. Nothing like uninvited guests to deplete your most expensive supplies. "Eggs or corn flakes?" Since corn flakes cost more, he'd probably choose those.

"Just coffee. I don't eat before my rational mind kicks in."

"Would you like to shower first?" Gaby felt a twinge in her gut and placed her hand below her stomach.

"Coffee always comes first." Alex cleared his throat. "Are you mad at me for sleeping here?"

"I'm not mad. I'm not happy about the situation, but I'm not mad." Gaby filled a kettle and lit the gas burner. As she ground beans, the aroma made Gaby long for a cup herself— but coffee was out of the question during an outbreak.

"What situation?" Alex was asking.

"Neighborhood gossip. If anyone sees you leave, they'll assume we had sex." Gaby stood over the kettle so he wouldn't see her blush.

"Oh, come on. It's the nineteen nineties."

"Shizuoka is a very conservative city."

"I see." Alex sat in the chair she usually used. "I'm really very sorry I crashed on you. After all, you only met me yesterday. I'd be irritated if I were in your shoes. Is there anything I can do to make this up to you?"

"What's done is done." Gaby caught the kettle as it began to whistle and poured water through the filter into a small glass pot. The next pang of pain was urgent. "Here. Take over." Alex, baffled, picked up the kettle as she hurried back to the toilet.

He'll hear this, Gaby thought, huddling over the bowl. At least Alex had put the seat down. She leaned forward to ease a spasm. It was impossible to keep her illness secret in her own home.

She could pass as normal in public—she *looked* okay, no matter how sick she was. It was better to take teasing about her need for privacy than to try to explain this humiliating affliction. Better to get the job than to admit to chronic illness in an interview. Better to have friends who didn't know everything about her than ones who held her in contempt, convinced she could heal herself "if she only wanted to." For the bottom line was that no one liked sick people. Overall, denial served her better than the truth.

When she returned to the front room, Alex had filled two cups with coffee. Gaby poured hers back into the pot. "No coffee for me today."

"I'm sorry." Alex combed his hair with his fingers. "Do you have the flu?"

Why couldn't he pretend he hadn't heard anything? It would be so much easier if he were Japanese. Now Gaby had to figure out the quickest way to end this line of questioning. "No, I'm, uh, often like this in the morning. Nothing contagious, I promise. Do you like the coffee?"

"You have IBD or something?"

Her head whizzed with helium. "What did you say?" IBD stood for irritable bowel disease, a broad category of intestinal ailments including her own. Dizziness forced her to sit down. This couldn't be real. No one knew that acronym.

"IBD. It's irritable—"

"Have you ever heard of ulcerative colitis?"

Alex winced. "That's pretty serious."

"That's what I have." Her voice sounded weak, childlike.

"Oh, no." Alex stared at his coffee. "Oh, Gaby. I'm sorry."

"No one knows this," Gaby hurried to say. "Please keep it to yourself."

"Of course."

Gaby couldn't bring herself to look at his face, so she focused on the tabletop. Why had she blurted that out? It was so unlike her. Alex stretched his hand across the bare wood, palm up. Not knowing what else to do, she clasped it, a warm hand with calluses at the base of his fingers. Had she really told him? Why had she done that? "How come you know about it?"

"Two of my clients had ulcerative colitis. It was a big challenge for them, coping with the unpredictability, the fatigue, the complications." Alex gave her hand a slight squeeze.

This unsettled her, and she withdrew her hand. In her life, the teasing of gym class prevailed; acceptance was not an option. But when Gaby ventured eye contact, his blue eyes held sadness, not suspicion or disgust.

"Well," Alex said. "I see why you don't want to get involved with my problems. You have enough of your own."

He was letting her off the hook. They could part congenially after breakfast and never see each other again. Last night, that would have been an ideal outcome. But a lot had happened since last night. Gaby cleared her throat. "I suggest holding off on the police until you've covered everyone who might have known Cody. Mrs. Sakura speaks perfect English, so you can see her on your own. Do you know anyone else at the university?"

"There's Marubatsu."

Gaby shook her head. "He avoids foreigners as much as he can."

"He was the one who sent the letter about Cody."

Gaby raised her eyebrows. "Why would he do that?"

"Why wouldn't he? Cody took a class from him, Zen and Western Literature." Alex got up and refilled his mug. "Cody liked the idea of learning from a Zen priest."

"Good for Cody," Gaby said. "Marubatsu and I don't get along, so it would be best if you didn't mention my name to him."

Alex sat and turned his coffee mug round and round on the table. "I already have. He was the professor I talked to yesterday."

"About me?"

"Well, yes."

"All bad?"

Alex broke eye contact. "He spoke in generalities. He told me not to trust you."

Gaby got up and took a glass from the cupboard. "That doesn't surprise me."

"Why would he say that?"

"Aside from general misogyny, I don't know. We never got along."

"What happened between you?"

Gaby left the refrigerator door open as she poured herself a glass of milk, cold air wafting against her thighs. "Small things that shouldn't matter but do. One time I taught my students a point of grammar that Marubatsu regularly misuses. Turns out they corrected him and he blamed me for making him lose face. I didn't find out about that until a month later. Another time I objected to one of his rape jokes at a faculty meeting. Apparently, that made the rounds and gave me a reputation. And I didn't wash his teacups for him in the faculty lounge. Stuff like that." Gaby came back to the table. "Since Marubatsu was my senior, I should have just apologized as a daily routine, but I didn't know any of this my first year. By the time I figured out the system, the grudge had grown beyond retrieval."

"Don't you have to demonstrate gross misconduct to get fired?"

"Not in Japan. Being different is tantamount to criminal behavior here. At one meeting, I'm not kidding, a professor proposed a policy to ban hiring unmarried female faculty. It was discussed as if it were a reasonable suggestion. Right in front of me, the only female professor in the room."

"Does Marubatsu have a lot of power?"

"You never know. I can't believe the dean would have fired me without a lot of pressure from Marubatsu."

"You had no recourse?"

"No." Gaby sipped her milk. "As Lester says, even if I can prove I was fired unjustly, the university would lose face by taking me back. All I have to gain is peace of mind, but I want to *know*."

Alex nodded. "I hear you. I'll never get over Cody's death. I'm just hoping to find out enough about what happened to carry on with my own life."

Gaby understood. Alex was the kind of person who

needed the truth. "I'll check with some of my former students to see if they knew Cody. And we need to visit the boarding-house where Cody lived—a phone call might scare them off."

"You mean, you're going to help me?" His smile made him momentarily handsome, despite wayward hair and puffy eyelids.

Gaby knew herself well enough not to waste time denying the inevitable. "That's what it looks like."

"I am grateful, but are you sure it wouldn't be too much for you?"

"No. But no one's sure of anything in Japan."

Alex nodded. "Expect to be surprised. That's what Cody used to say."

Outside, a truck with a scratchy loudspeaker played a re-peated snippet of a Swiss yodeling tune, which triggered a se-quence of barking dogs from block to block. The truck stopped, motor running, under Gaby's window.

"The milk truck," Gaby announced.

Alex grimaced. "Why so loud?"

"Who's still asleep at seven? Actually, it's late, but today is Saturday." Gaby rinsed her glass in the sink. "I'll show you how to take a shower."

Alex held out a stop hand. "I know how to do that."

"Are you sure?" Gaby slid open the closet door, took a folded towel off a stack of two, and motioned Alex to follow her into the bath room. "You flip this switch to get hot water. There's no hot-water tank, so it's heated as it runs through. Be sure to switch it off when you're done, or the pipes will fry. You shower in this area, outside the tub. Hold this thing for spray. Here's a stool, bucket, shampoo, soap. This is hot, that's cold. Okay?"

"I got it," Alex said. "I've done this before, except for the heater switch."

"Don't forget to turn it off with the water. No, wait! Leave the tap running. That way I'll go right after you and the neighbors will hear one long shower instead of two." Gaby shut the door behind her. He was going to think she was a nutcase. Maybe she was. Showering in the morning was radical enough for her neighbors—they might not be counting the times the water went off. The harder trick would be getting Alex out to her car unnoticed.

Meanwhile, he needed a hotel for tonight. She opened her phone directory and started calling hotels. By the time Alex emerged from the bath room, pink and wet and reassembled in the clothes he'd worn all night, she'd found out every bed in town was booked for the soccer tournament on Sunday. While she took a quick shower herself, she decided her best bet was Les. But he'd be more likely to let Alex stay at his place if she waited to call until his hangover had abated.

She put her foot through her shorts the wrong way and stumbled. She needed seven more hours of sleep. Although her abdominal pain had subsided to a mild ache, the elastic at the waist of her shorts dug in meanly. She guessed at parting her hair in the steamy mirror and opened the door to let some air in.

Alex was writing notes on a pad of paper in front of his open briefcase. "What do you think I could accomplish this weekend? The boardinghouse?"

Gaby nodded. "Don't expect much, though. Student tenants don't last long and it's been a whole year." She increased her air-conditioning a notch. "I'm worried about where you'll sleep tonight. The hotels are full. I'm hoping my friend Lester will put you up. His Japanese is good and he might be able to help you with translation, too, especially if it involves cute girls."

Alex, who had been rummaging for the boardinghouse address, put his pad down. "I thought *you* were going to help me."

"I will. The problem is, I can't risk you staying here another night."

Alex sighed. "I forgot. I swear, I used to be more considerate. I'm sorry. Is that my fourth or fifth sorry this morning?"

Gaby smiled. "It's dangerous to call Les before noon, so

I'll escort you to the boardinghouse this morning." She paused. "That may be all I'm good for today."

"I understand."

Did he? His acceptance was too new to believe. "Are you ready to go?"

Alex packed his briefcase and she gathered her purse, keys, and sunglasses. While he tied his shoes, she gave him instructions. "Don't talk on the balcony. Match your footsteps with mine, especially going down the steps. If we're lucky, no one will suspect you stayed overnight."

Alex looked doubtful, but agreed.

Gaby opened the door and peeked around it. She couldn't see anyone, so she motioned for Alex to follow her. This time, she looked into her neighbor's window instead of away, relieved to notice the curtains were drawn. Alex did a pretty good job of matching her pace, only one misstep on the stairs to give away their plurality. They circled the building to her car. Gaby unlocked the doors and hoped for a clean getaway, but a dog in the downstairs apartment started yapping, pushing its nose against the glass patio door. "Get in! Hurry!"

Alex, surprised, stumbled into the passenger seat.

Gaby started the engine and got the Honda in gear right as the dog's owner came to her patio door with a clothes basket. The woman stared as Gaby and Alex drove off.

"Damn! That was Fumiko. She'll gossip." Gaby shifted the towel she left on the driver's seat to get her bare thighs off the hot vinyl. She cranked down the window and turned the fan as high as it would go. It would cost a lot of yen to fix the air-conditioning, but she might not get through the summer without it.

Alex fastened his seat belt. "How would Fumiko know I slept over in your apartment?"

"Because she didn't hear footsteps going up the stairs before she heard ours coming down. But it's too late now. *Shikata-ga-nai:* it can't be helped. What's the address?"

"Room 4, Nakamura House, 23–27 Katayama—"

"The Katayama district is near the university." Gaby turned at the Tamiya building.

"It's not a street?"

"Streets don't have names. Well, only the big ones." By habit, Gaby reached for the radio, then withdrew her hand. Once Lester took custody of Alex, she'd go back to bed with her headphones. It occurred to her that part of her trouble sleeping might have been from forgoing her usual bedtime mellow jazz.

Ahead in the road, a middle-aged man slowly rode a girl's bicycle, his knees bumping the handlebars. He steered with one hand, holding a cigarette in the other, weaving around phone poles set inconveniently in the road itself. Gaby pulled up beside him. *"Excuse me, do you know where Nakamura House is?"*

He kept pedaling and Gaby idled along beside him. *"After the ABC Pachinko parlor, to the right."*

"Thank you very much." They stopped tandem at a light.

"Where are you from?" he asked.

"America," Gaby answered. *"I'm not studying Japanese, I use chopsticks, and I don't like natto. Goodbye."*

"What was that all about?" asked Alex.

"Asking directions." Gaby turned at the *pachinko* parlor and cruised a few blocks. "Well, that was a false lead." She flagged a student hanging up pair after pair of grayish boxer shorts and asked him directions.

He pointed in the direction they'd come from. *"Go to ABC Pachinko and turn right. Turn right again after the tobacco stand. Where are you from?"*

"America. Thank you." Gaby turned around in the next driveway.

Alex fanned himself with his notepad. "It's 23–27 Katayama. Can't we find it by the numbers?"

Gaby waved as she passed the student. "Only the post office and pizza parlors can find addresses by the numbers. The rest of us have to ask."

"Even Japanese people?" Alex asked.

"Yes! It's like their language—you feel your way around."

"But what about—oh, let's say, furniture deliveries?"

"I'm not sure, but I've seen van drivers stop and ask passersby."

"You're not kidding?"

"I'm not." Gaby braked hard as two children crossed the road without looking. Her Honda skidded and the kids stopped in front of her hood, motionless. Horns beeped behind them. Gaby honked back. The kids didn't move until she raced her engine, threatening to run them over. From the safety of the side of the road, they pointed and screamed, *"Gaijin, gaijin!"*

After talking to two more people, Gaby triumphantly parked in front of a two-story gray building. "Aha! There's even a sign: Nakamura House."

"I don't see a sign."

Gaby pointed to a small metal plate on the front gate. "Two *kanji, naka,* middle, and *mura,* village. Then *katakana* syllables for HA-U-SU. The Middlevillages own this place. Let's see if anyone's home." Gaby was at the gate before she noticed Alex still in the car, fussing with his briefcase. Then it hit her; this was the first time he had seen where his son had lived in Japan. She moved away from the gate to wait until he was ready.

Ten

Alex lingered in the car, pretending to have trouble with a clasp on his briefcase. His neck and shoulders ached from sleeping on the floor, and his shirt stank. Gaby's strong rich coffee had tasted wonderful, but now gave him the jangles. He wanted more time to get his questions together. He sensed Gaby was eager to finish this up and dump him on the British guy.

The handle scorched his fingers. He slammed the door

shut and joined Gaby. The gate, metal bars on wheels between concrete walls, was slid half-open across the gravel walkway. The house reminded Alex of cheap Mexican hotels: thin gray siding with no attempt to conceal clusters of pipes and meters. Six identical doors and windows, three downstairs and three up-stairs behind a balcony railing. An outdoor staircase connected the two floors. Some window screens were patched with mask-ing tape, and the lights beside the doors were bare bulbs. He had never imagined Cody living in a place like this. To the left of the apartment building, hidden from the street, was a tradi-tional Japanese house with large wooden shutter doors, a thick red tile roof, and a porch covered with pots of bonsai.

"As a courtesy, we should talk to the landlord first," Gaby said. "But I think we'd do better starting with the tenants. Col-lege students are much more open about talking to foreigners."

"Whatever you think is best." Alex noticed a broken wash-ing machine and stained futon by the side of the building. A pair of swallows swooped over his head.

No one answered Gaby's knock on the first door. A young man opened the second door, wearing only blue jeans. His plump, hairless chest seemed feminine, but his biceps showed the results of weight lifting. Gaby asked a few questions, to which he rubbed his eyes and repeated *"shiranai"* until Gaby bowed and he shut the door.

"He doesn't know anything," Gaby reported.

"Could he be lying?" Alex asked.

"I doubt it. When my students missed class, they told me that they'd slept in or that they hadn't done their homework. Remarkably guileless. None of the automotive crises or dead grandmothers that American students invent."

Gaby sounded fond of American excuses, not critical of them. He wondered why she chose to work for a funeral parlor in Japan instead of returning to America.

A tiny young woman with big glasses and a gray front tooth opened the next door on its chain. She kept the chain on while Gaby asked a question. After her high-pitched answer, Gaby bowed and left.

"She doesn't know anything. She moved in a month ago." Gaby headed up the rickety stairs and Alex followed, clutching the rail.

Unlike the ground-floor doors marked 1, 2, and 3, the first upstairs door had no number. The curtains were shut and no lights were on, but Gaby knocked anyway. "This is number four, *shi* in Japanese. But they call it *yon* because *shi* also means death. In hospitals, there are no doors numbered four because patients would be afraid." Gaby knocked again. "Well, death doesn't seem to be home." She glanced at Alex. "Oh, I'm sorry. Bad joke. I wasn't thinking."

Alex cupped his hands around his eyes and peered in the window. "This was Cody's room." He strained his eyes, but all he could see through the crack in the curtain was darkness. He kissed his fingertips and placed them on the glass. Then he heard cheeping. Above the window, daubs of mud made a trail of false starts to a swallows' nest, two fledglings inside. Well beyond the beaky bug-eyed phase, they looked large enough to fly on their own. A flicker of purple scissors in the air—an anxious parent. Alex moved away so the bird could return to its nest.

When a young woman answered door number five, she and Gaby spoke quickly, gesturing surprise. They knew each other. The woman's hair was brushed back long on top, but shaved close to her scalp below her ears. She had lively dark eyes and four silver hoops in each ear. She wore brand-new baggy shorts that had been ironed, and a man's white oxford shirt with sleeves down to her thumbs. An oxymoron: pristine grunge.

Gaby switched to English. "This is Junko Suzuki, a former student of mine. This is Alexander Thorn, Cody's father."

"Nice to meet you." Junko thrust her hand forward.

Alex shook her hand and part of her sleeve. "You, too. You knew Cody?"

"He lived adjacent." Junko pointed to number four. "Now,

no one lives. His room is very sad and lonely. He was my friend."

"Mr. Thorn would like to talk to you. About Cody. Do you have time?" Gaby asked.

Junko nodded. "Please, come in. I am sorry for a mess."

Alex hit his head on the doorway. He ducked and entered a single, square room. An orange-and-red futon hung out the back window. No kitchen or bathroom, only a sink. Shelves above the sink held teacups, a teapot, and cellophane packages of rice crackers and sandwich cookies. A mountain bike on brackets occupied most of one wall. Books and clothes lounged around a low table with an electric cord dangling underneath it. A synthetic disco beat eked out from a cassette player, which Junko punched off. She cleared an area around the table and plumped square pillows for them to sit on.

"Would *Zone-san* like green tea?" Junko asked. She formed her words deliberately, each one separate.

"No, thanks. Water would be nice, though."

Junko filled three teacups from the tap and set them on the table. She opened a box labeled "Pocky" and shook chocolate-coated sticks onto a saucer.

Gaby bit into a stick. "Mm. These are good Pocky. Caramel?"

"*Hai.*" Junko sat in a yoga position, bare feet crossed and resting on her thighs. "I mean, yes." She looked at Alex. "I am sorry my English is very bad."

"It's a thousand times better than my Japanese," Alex said. He tried to picture Cody living in a room like this. He wondered about toilets and showers.

"Junko is an excellent student," Gaby bragged. "Her major is Chinese. She knows four languages: Japanese, Chinese, English, and French."

Junko blushed. "No, no. Only Japanese. Ms. Stanton is the excellent teacher. And, she is very kind."

Alex smiled at their mutual excellence. "She's been kind to me, as well." Alex wondered if he should initiate his questions. An electric fan with clear pink blades slowly shook its head no in the corner.

Junko carefully launched the next topic. "I want to visit She-attle. May I?"

No one asked permission to visit a city. Did she mean visit his house? Well, why not. "Of course. Just let me know when you're coming."

Junko smiled. She had curvaceous 1940s lips and dimples in her thick cheeks. Alex wondered if she had been Cody's girlfriend. The thought made him feel old.

Junko said something in Japanese and covered her mouth with her hand.

"Go ahead," Gaby urged her.

"In Japan, we visit shrine on important occasion. *Fujiyama* is most sacred shrine. I want to climb Mount Fuji for one-year anniversary of Cody's death. I would be honored if *Zone-san* and *Sutanton-sensei* would join me." Junko glanced at Gaby as if to ask if her speech passed. Gaby nodded approval.

Alex recalled Mount Fuji was around twelve thousand feet high. "I would like to go with you, but I don't think I could make it. I'm not in good shape."

"It is not so hard. Old people do it. There is path all the way, and rest stations. We Japanese go at night, to greet sunrise from top."

"You'll think it over, won't you?" Gaby looked pointedly at Alex.

Junko sipped water. "I do not want to . . . how you say, inflict? my presence on your anniversary occasion. I am not family."

Why hadn't Cody written him about Junko? She had more quality than any of the giggly grungers who had shown up at his door on Cody-weekends. Out of a mix of curiosity, envy, and affection, Alex went with affection. "There are families of blood, and families of the heart. If you were Cody's friend, then you are also part of my family."

Junko, half-comprehending, looked to Gaby, who quickly

muttered several sentences of Japanese. Junko blushed, kneeled, and bowed her head all the way to the floor.

Embarrassed, Alex stuffed a Pocky into his mouth. Chocolate and bland crunch. His stomach rumbled, hungry from chewing.

Gaby took over. "Junko, Mr. Thorn wasn't given much information about how Cody died. In America, people find comfort from knowing as many details as they can. For his peace of mind, could you remember what happened last year?"

Junko said something to Gaby in Japanese.

Gaby answered in English. "He wants to know the truth."

Junko hesitated, spoke more Japanese.

"The day it happened," Gaby suggested.

Junko dabbed her neck with a handkerchief and then switched to English. "I saw Cody-*chan* leave Saturday morning with two men. They had borrowed extra motorcycle for him."

The university letter hadn't said anyone had been with Cody. On the other hand, it hadn't specified he'd been alone, either.

"... but no *herumetto*." Junko gestured around her head.

Alex remembered Cody had taken up dirt-bike riding after the divorce. Cody would ride off with the chin strap of his helmet unfastened, and Jane worried that he took it off as soon as he was out of her sight. Was their divorce to blame for his recklessness?

"Cody-*chan* did not return that night. I was upset." Junko twisted the kerchief between her fingers. Her fingernails had been chewed shorter than her fingertips. It hurt to look at them.

Alex asked, "How did you find out about the accident?"

"At school, next day, there were rumors." The handkerchief bandaged her fingers as she wove it between them. "I went to hospital, every hospital in Shizuoka, but Cody was not in. I could not believe."

How well Junko's faulty grammar put it: *I could not believe.* After twenty years as a psychotherapist, Alex had thought he was immune to shock, but his work hadn't prepared him for the unthinkable when it landed in his own life. Alex heard his own heart pounding, crowding his throat.

Gaby picked up a paperback book and fanned herself with it. Her face was pale and dark lines cradled her eyes. "Who were Cody's friends with the motorcycles?"

Alex realized he had to stave off his feelings in order to concentrate on what Junko was telling him. He was glad Gaby was there to ask the right questions. Finding himself close to tears, he fixed his gaze on the book she used as a fan. The cover showed cartoon girl faces with enormous purple eyes and yellow hair, balloons with Chinese characters coming out of their mouths. Incomprehensible.

"I don't know," Junko said. "It was first time I saw."

"They were students, I suppose?"

"They did not look like students."

"I wonder who they were, then," Gaby pressed obliquely.

Junko squirmed into a sideways kneeling position. "They were not so young. Maybe not so smart. Maybe drop out of high school."

"How can you tell if——" Alex began.

Gaby interrupted. "Laborers?"

When Junko tilted her head, her shiny black hair slanted out into a wedge. After a moment's hesitation, she said, "Maybe not so employed."

"*Wakatta.* I understand," Gaby said.

Alex said, "Well, I don't under—"

Gaby kicked his leg under the low table. It hurt. "Did Cody mention where he was going the day of . . . what day was it?"

"July ninth," Alex and Junko said together. Alex motioned Junko to go on.

"Cody-*chan* had a saying, 'Be open to the moment.'"

Junko imitated Cody's voice well. Alex had heard Cody recite that motto many times, as if he expected Alex to convert to Buddhism on impact. It had to do with enlightenment. The kind teenagers were sure they had over their parents.

"He was eager to climb Mount Fuji all year. His karate

circle was climbing in August, but he didn't want to wait." Junko paused. She continued cautiously, "I think maybe he should not have been open to that moment."

What a sensible young woman! If only she had persuaded Cody not to go. No, Alex reminded himself, no "if only" scenarios. Flirting with alternative pasts only made it more difficult to face the present.

Junko bent her head. "Sorry. I would rather talk about happy times."

"I'm sure Mr. Thorn would, too. It's just that—" Gaby stopped abruptly. While she thought, she picked up her teacup and drank water. "Mr. Thorn wants to be certain Cody didn't act wrongly. He needs to know whether it was Cody's fault."

Junko nodded. "Cody-*chan* had no fault. His death was unlucky accident. I believe this in the heart. The men he went with, he probably met at bar. He was friendly. Always meeting. Always invited."

Alex wiped sweat off his forehead. The pink fan moved the air but didn't cool it. Junko showed no sign of perspiration. "In a bar, huh? I guess they don't check ID, because Cody was only twenty."

"The legal drinking age in Japan is twenty," Gaby mentioned.

"Cody never told me that."

"Well, of course not; you're his father." Gaby went back to Junko. "Which bar did Cody like to visit?"

"Different ones," Junko said. "Japanese bars. And Nature Squib, sometimes."

Where the gaijin go, Alex recalled. Where Lester and Michael went. Alex, suddenly hotter, picked up a book to fan himself. A small brown cockroach that had been hiding under the book scrambled for cover beneath his pillow. "Gah!" Alex jumped up and the women giggled.

Junko grabbed a slipper, lifted the cushion, and swatted the roach. "Got it!" She scraped the sole of her slipper over a wastebasket and washed her hands. "I am sorry but I have to go. I have to meet someone soon."

Gaby looked at her own watch. "Thank you so much, Junko. Perhaps you could give Mr. Thorn your phone number? To arrange climbing Fuji-*san*?" While Junko wrote on a piece of scrap paper, Gaby wrote on the back of one of her business cards.

"This is Mr. Thorn's number, at the university hotel," she said, exchanging it for Junko's paper. "Are there any more of Cody's friends in Nakamura House?"

"No. I am oldest tenant. I mean, longest tenant. Students leave when they can afford, but I am poor, so I stay." Junko bowed to Alex. "It is nice to meet you. It is pleasure to see Cody's blue eyes again."

"Uh, thank you, you're, uh, too kind to an old man," Alex stammered. Her flattery was false. Cody had Jane's extraordinary sapphire eyes, not Alex's commonplace blue-when-he-wore-a-blue-sweater color. "I look forward to seeing you again."

On the balcony in the bright heat, Alex took another look at Cody's former room before following Gaby downstairs. The swallows were quiet in their nest. He hurried to catch up with Gaby.

"That was good luck, finding Junko," Gaby said. "Isn't she a remarkable young woman? She's actually putting herself through college, which isn't cheap, believe me, especially in a country that doesn't have student loans. She works two part-time jobs and lives in that dump, and she gets A's in everything."

"Even English?" Gravel ground under Alex's shoes.

Gaby put on sunglasses. "Keep in mind English is her *third* language. How many languages could *you* hold that conversation in?"

Alex put up his hands. "I didn't mean to insult your student."

Gaby unlocked Alex's door and went around to her own. "Well, she was extremely helpful. I'd say we made big progress today. Sort of."

Alex sat gingerly, bracing himself for the hot car seat. "We did?"

Gaby fastened her seat belt. "Junko flat out told us the men who took Cody for a motorcycle ride were a pair of *yakuza*."

The word *yakuza* brought to mind B-grade movies starring Chuck Norris in a black *ninja* costume. Alex had to laugh. "The Japanese mafia? You're kidding."

"It's not a joke, Alex. I wish they weren't *yakuza,* but that's what she said."

Alex placed his briefcase by his feet. "I didn't hear her say that."

Gaby glanced at the house before she pulled into the road. "You have to listen between the lines. Do you believe that she and Cody were just platonic friends?"

"Well . . . almost. Except she wanted to climb Mount Fuji for him."

"Very good. The key to mastering Japanese is understanding what's not said." Gaby braked and waited for a brown cat with a broken tail to cross the road. "I'm looking for a pay phone, to call Lester. We still have to get you a place to stay tonight."

Alex wasn't ready to be passed on. "Could we talk about *yakuza* before you call him?" His stomach rumbled. "And get lunch?"

Gaby blinked hard. Twice. "I guess so. Do you mind a Denny's-type restaurant?"

"No problem."

Parked cars in the street forced traffic into a single veering lane, caroming between open storefronts selling clothes, fish, vegetables, shoes, or liquor. Alex was struck by the grayness of it all—sky, road, cars, people; even a dry summer day had the look of rain. Next to a concrete-and-glass restaurant, Gaby pulled into an alley that ended in seven parking spaces, each occupied by a white car. Gaby squeezed her car into a gap next to several trash cans. "This is a chain called Skylark. Not the best food, but they have picture menus, and the booths cut down on the stare treatment."

A waitress seated them at a booth looking out at the street. She placed laminated menus on the table and handed them wet finger towels packaged in plastic. Alex dropped his, scalded by its heat. He pointed to a picture of fried fish and cole slaw. After Gaby ordered, they gulped what little water fit around a glass full of thick ice cubes. Piped-in music played a peppy, repetitive tune of squeaky girl voices alternating with whistling. The table was lower than what Alex was used to. It was, he decided, like going to a Denny's specially built for children: everything smaller and higher in pitch.

Gaby pressed her cold glass against her forehead for a moment. "You aren't reacting to the involvement of *yakuza*. That worries me."

"Well, let's talk about it." His towel had cooled quickly in the overblown air-conditioning, but Alex had to bite the plastic wrapping to get it open. He washed his face and neck. "Why would *yakuza* want to go biking with a foreign exchange student?"

Gaby shrugged. "I have no idea. Do you have any idea why Cody would want to go biking with them?"

Alex thought while the waitress set pale fried fish in front of him and arranged tiny dishes of rice, cole slaw, and pickles around it. Hungry, he bit into a piece of fish and crunched on a bone. The fish was barely warm. Gaby had a fragrant noodle soup with scallops and bok choy. He should have had her order for him. "Cody liked to socialize beyond the suburban range. He made a point of chatting with bums, drifters, drug addicts. His version of cool. Of course I worried, but I didn't want to make too much of it and cause him to rebel. We tried to teach him tolerance. I mean, what do you tell your kids, treat the homeless with respect but don't talk to them? In a way, I was relieved when he wanted to go to Japan. I thought Japan would be safe."

"Japan is safe," Gaby said. "No guns, hardly any drugs."

"But you say there are *yakuza*. What makes them dangerous? What do they do?"

"Gambling. *Pachinko* parlors, racetracks. And prostitution. What they call 'soap land,' bath houses that are actually whorehouses. Sometimes they own construction companies or love hotels."

"How could Junko know they were *yakuza*? All she got was one look at them." Alex realized the music had already looped back to the tune with girls and whistlers. A short tape.

"They have a certain look. Slick hair, tattoos, flashy clothes." Gaby lifted the large soup bowl to her mouth to drink the broth. "Missing fingers aren't too common, but you still see them once in a while."

"How would I go about finding these *yakuza*?"

Gaby set down her bowl. "You don't want to find them."

Eleven

Alex threw his chopsticks on his plate. "Don't tell me what I want! I didn't come all the way to Japan to politely back out if the going got rough! I came for answers!"

Alex's sudden anger assaulted her. The clash of blinding sun through the window and the darkness inside the restaurant intensified. It wouldn't be long before her next attack. Her familiar dilemma: eating or drinking triggered diarrhea, but diarrhea required her to drink more fluids, and if she didn't eat, she'd faint. Last fall, she'd passed out at a bus stop and hit her head. She had to get home and back in bed. "I'm sorry. I didn't mean to sound bossy," she murmured. "I meant this: If Cody got into an accident when he was with *yakuza,* the reason you heard so little about his death is probably that one of them did something illegal. They had to cover it up to save face. In which case, lifting the cover might get *you* killed." Not to mention herself.

Alex pushed slices of pickled ginger around the rim of his dish.

Gaby took out her packet of pills, punched two through the foil backing, and swallowed them with melted ice. She looked into eyes almost as blue as Cody's, shaped in impish crescents with convex lower lids. Alex didn't seem familiar with his own rage. Had he been angry before his son's death?

Alex finished his rice and pushed his plates to the side. "You know Japan better than I do. I guess I shouldn't underestimate the power of the Japanese mafia. Personally, I'm willing to risk anything. But I have no right to ask you to take chances on my behalf."

"I appreciate that." Gaby breathed deeply. The Skylark theme tune, with its baby-talk voices and whistling, seemed engineered specifically to discourage customers from lingering at their tables.

Alex continued. "I think I overreacted because of something Marubatsu said that I haven't got out of my system yet. He implied Cody got what he deserved. That his daughters would never do what Cody did."

"Meaning what?"

"Dying in a foreign country. He made it out to be a volitional act."

"I'm amazed that Marubatsu took such an interest." Gaby didn't want to start talking about Marubatsu, or she'd be the one losing her temper. She looked at her watch. Eleven. "Well, it's still early for Lester, but I'll call him anyway. Excuse me." She crossed the room to a pink pay phone on the wall and dropped in a large copper ten-yen coin.

Lester answered on the fifth ring. *"Moshi moshi?"*

"Lester? Are you awake?"

"Let me check. You're up early, Gay Bee *san*."

"I've been up all night."

"I'm shocked. Who's the lucky bastard?"

"No, no, it has nothing to do with sex—"

"Then I'm not interested," Lester interrupted. "I was going to ring you today. There's a string quartet at Watanabe Hall next Friday. Care to go?"

"Maybe." Gaby didn't know if she would be in remission by then. Sometimes it took days to heal, sometimes weeks. "I need to ask you an enormous favor."

"The answer is no. What is it?"

"Remember Alexander Thorn? The guy whose book lecture you attended?"

"Yes, yes, Mr. Why Love Fails. What about him?"

"He's staying at the university hotel, but they kick out their guests on weekends. He desperately needs a place to sleep tonight and every hotel is full. Could you put him up at your place? For tonight only. They'll let him back Sunday evening."

"Saturday night and you want me to baby-sit an old man?"

Alex old? He looked mid-forties, not much older than she and Lester. "Please, Les? For me?"

"How does Thorn suddenly rate a personal favor?"

A waiter bumped Gaby's back with a tray and she squeezed against the phone to make room for him. "It's a long story. Can you just say yes and hear about it later?"

"Absolutely"—Lester paused—"not."

Gaby scanned the room for Alex. His gray hair towered over the top of the booth, and his legs barely squeezed under the tabletop. He looked like a parent at a child's desk on teacher conference night. "Could you scout out a love hotel for him, then? I can't have him at my apartment again."

"Again? Gaby, surely you didn't say 'again'? You don't let anyone in your flat for ten minutes, much less overnight. No sex, you say?"

"None whatsoever."

"How on earth did you meet this chap? You never go out."

"I met him through my job." Gaby's intestines rumbled violently and she looked in vain for a place to sit. She breathed deliberately, four counts in, four counts out, to quell the urge. "His kid died here a year ago. He thought Gone With The Wind sent his son's body back, and had questions for us. Eguchi assigned him to me."

"He became your *o-nimotsu,* did he?"

O-nimotsu, or "honorable luggage," meant "burden" in Japanese usage. Gaby didn't want to slander Alex that way. It was more expedient, however, to insult Alex than to argue with Lester. "That's more or less the case."

"And now you want to check your luggage with me, is that it?"

"That's it. Please, Lester? I'm desperate."

"All right. I'll handle your baggage, and the string quartet on Friday will be your treat."

"Thank you. Should I drop him off at your place?"

Lester yawned. "I'll meet you. Where are you?"

"The Skylark on Route One. When can I expect you?"

"In a hurry, aren't you? Within the hour."

"Sooner is better." Gaby hung up and raced to the rest room. Her real reason for taking Alex to Skylark hadn't been the picture menus but the Western-style toilets, so she wouldn't have to squat. Fortunately, a stall was empty. She stayed longer than she needed, to ensure against being ambushed by a surprise second attack.

Thorn looked up anxiously when she returned to their booth, and she gave him a thumbs-up signal. "Lester will let you sleep in his apartment tonight."

"I appreciate your taking care of me. I feel like a six-year-old, unable to do anything on my own. Are you okay?"

Gaby shrugged. "Just the usual. I'm used to it." It was weird to mention her illness. If she'd been out with Lester, she'd have excused her lengthy absence by claiming she needed to put on makeup. It was so much easier simply to stay home.

"You didn't tell him about Cody, did you?" Alex asked.

Uh-oh. Gaby slid into the booth and used her hand as a visor against the light from the window. "Well, only a general outline. None of the details."

Alex crumpled his paper napkin. "Why did you tell him?"

"To explain how I met you."

"Does Lester demand a full account of everyone you meet?"

"No. But unless it related to my job, he'd get the wrong idea." Gaby felt herself blush.

"In short, he's insecure. He doesn't trust you with other men."

"That's not the case," Gaby said. "We're, uh, we're not . . ."

"You're not in a relationship?"

"Right." Moving to Japan had accomplished one good thing: preventing her from having bad relationships. Of course, Japan screened out all men, not merely the witty, lethal ones she somehow fell for, but not having sex was better than having heartless sex. And as this morning with Alex had proved, she couldn't hide ulcerative colitis from overnight guests.

"That's a relief."

This roused her curiosity. "Why?"

"Oh, nothing, I guess."

"But?" Gaby prompted.

Alex glanced up at her. "I don't know. I don't know Lester, so I have no right to judge him. I just wish you hadn't told him about Cody."

"Les won't tell anyone—unless you ask him not to. He has this perverse streak." Like her ex-husband, Gaby thought. Which was why she had never told Lester about her illness. Ron, a literature professor, had found sneaky ways to attribute all their problems to her being sick. In fiction, after all, sick characters are always metaphorically sick as well, and Ron loved to equate her physical defects with psychological ones. During their marriage, he had compared her to Richard III, Mrs. Rochester, Captain Ahab, and Caliban. Anything to blame her and exonerate himself.

Alex drained his water glass. "He sounds difficult."

Gaby brought her thoughts back to Lester. "Not if you keep things light. Unlike me, he's gregarious and friendly. You'll have a good time."

"I'd rather stick with you." Alex held up his hand to stop her from answering. "But you're tired and you need to pass the relay baton."

"The baton? What do you mean?" A shadow fell through the window and Gaby looked out to see Lester, pale and blond in ivory silk pants and a silk jacket over a biscuit-colored T-shirt. He could have stepped out of *The Great Gatsby*.

"I'll explain later," Alex said.

Lester circled through the glass door to join them. "Hallo, love." He kissed her cheek. "You ate without me?"

"We ate before I called you," Gaby said. "I didn't dare interrupt your hangover any earlier."

"A wise decision." Lester shook hands with Alex. "How are you, Thorn? I hope our Gabriela won't end up a case study in your next book."

"Of course not. I never use friends as examples."

Lester squeezed in next to Gaby while Alex resumed his seat on the opposite side of the table. "Well, the burning question is"—his voice changed to mimic a Japanese accent—"what are your impressions of Japan?"

Alex didn't bother to smile. "I had a glimpse of Mount Fuji yesterday. Impressive."

"Oh, don't be coy about the scenery. The women, Thorn, the lovely, lovely women."

The waitress returned and while Lester ordered, Alex almost imperceptibly rolled his eyes to show his opinion of him. Nice to know not every *gaijin* fell under Lester's spell. When the waitress left, Gaby said, "Les, Alex hasn't seen Shizuoka yet. Maybe you could show him the sights?"

"What a bore," Lester said. "The best way to know Japan is to get blotto. We'll go to Nature Squib and check out the girls with the longest hair and the shortest skirts."

It was as if Lester were deliberately pressuring Alex into a macho pose. He was never this offensive with her. If she asked him to lay off, though, he'd get worse.

Alex, to his credit, changed the subject. "Thank you for putting me up tonight."

"No problem." Lester leaned back as the waitress placed a club sandwich in front of him. "I look forward to watching a man who's written the book on women in action."

Gaby nudged Lester's elbow. "I have to be going."

"I didn't excuse you," Lester objected.

Gaby pushed his arm until Lester got up to let her out of the booth. Alex was already on his feet again, hand extended for a farewell shake. "I'll call you Monday," she told him. "Think things over until then, okay?"

Lester interrupted, "What's this about?"

Alex ignored him. "I will. Take care of yourself. I hope you'll recover soon."

"Recover from what?" Lester asked, annoyed.

"From sleep deprivation." Gaby shot Alex a fierce glare, trying to warn him not to tell Lester about her health. "So long, Les."

Lester one-upped Alex's handshake with a peck on her cheek. "Don't forget about the concert on Friday."

"I won't. See you guys later." Gaby discreetly picked up the tab off the table. At the register, she saw the waitress had added Lester's sandwich to their bill. She'd pay. Lester was doing her a favor.

She pushed out the glass door into instant sauna, relieved to get out of Skylark's chill draft and whistling music. Glancing in the window on the way to her car, she waved goodbye to a morose Alex and a suspicious Lester. She briefly felt sorry for Alex, but brushed aside her sympathy. Getting drunk encouraged male bonding. By tomorrow, they might be best buddies.

After her Honda started, Gaby turned on the radio. Brahms's Fourth Symphony, an oft-repeated favorite of the Saturday orchestral program. She set the volume loud on the two-note phrases. Going without music was like a smoker without cigarettes. How long had it been? Gaby counted eighteen hours since she'd picked up Alex for dinner the evening before. Eighteen unmitigated hours in his company. How strange to spend that much time with a person she'd just met.

Stepping inside her apartment, alone, had never felt better. Unlike Skylark's, her air-conditioning took the scorch off the air without freezing it. Her back balcony railing cast a striped shadow across the tatami floor. She turned the radio low to finish the Brahms, lay on her futon, and shut her eyes.

In her dream, Alex was lying close beside her, but out of reach. She had a sense of floating, as if on a raft. The sun radiated through her eyelids, swirling patterns of magenta on brown. If he moved his hand, he could touch her thigh. She willed him to touch her, too tired to speak. Suddenly, she was following Alex up a rocky path at night. Alex climbed a steep rock and held out his hand to help her. She hesitated, afraid of losing her balance. "Hurry," he urged, "before they catch up." Gaby looked down and saw *yakuza* with flashlights moving toward them. She reached for Alex, but her fingers closed on air, and she was falling off the mountain, terrified, falling . . .

The doorbell jolted Gaby awake, pulse speeding. Her dim room indicated the sun had crossed to the other side of the building. A man's voice carefully enunciated the news through the radio. She squinted at the red numbers of the digital clock on her television. Five-thirty already. The bell clanged three more times in a row. She stumbled to the door.

"Are you Sutanton-san? Here, please." A stout woman in a blue uniform thrust a bouquet of pink peonies at her.

"Doumo." Gaby placed them on her table. It was the first time she had received flowers in Japan. Perhaps Lester was trying to impress Alex by pretending they were a couple. She flipped on the light to read the card. "To the lady who let me cry in her car and sleep on her floor—your secret is safe with me. For everything, THANK YOU—Alex." The peonies were the exact shade of pink of the lotus blossoms in her Chinese scroll.

She folded the card, put it back in its envelope, took it out and read it again. She had never liked the word "lady." She threw the card in the wastebasket. Then she retrieved it and read it for a third time, uneasy about having divulged her humiliating illness to a man she barely knew. Lester was no fool. Alex might clue him in inadvertently, and then Lester would have a brand-new venue of harassment. On the other hand, Alex didn't lack brains, either. As a psychologist, he must be skilled at keeping confidences.

But why the bouquet? It was too extravagant, too romantic. Her dream about him began to haunt her. On an impulse she didn't understand, she grabbed the peonies by the stems to throw them out. But then she chided herself for wasting perfectly good, and quite expensive, flowers.

Okay, she thought, these are obligation flowers, not affection flowers. They don't mean anything. On that basis, she could keep them. She smiled at the meaningless flowers and put them in an empty mayonnaise jar with water.

She returned to her futon and covered her ears with headphones. Still news, but it would soon be time for the evening symphony program. Through the open paper door, she could see the creamy pink petals of Alex's peonies.

How could she help him? The police would have to assist Alex if it came to gangsters. And the horrifying absence of Cody's heart pointed to Japan's underworld. The only thing she could do was investigate the falsified Gone With The Wind bill.

Gaby wondered how to track the bogus billing statement. Alex had sent his check to the wrong address—the one in English—so someone must have received it there in order to have cashed it at Ninka Bank. She could try to find the Kitanumi address for him. All she knew about Kitanumi was that it wasn't one of the better neighborhoods; none of her clients lived there.

Then whoever cashed Alex's check would need a Gone With The Wind *inkan*. Gaby could try to find out if the company *inkan* had been reordered since last July to replace one that might have been stolen. She'd have to search Nishida's records again.

The obvious culprit was Nishida himself. Nishida could borrow the Gone With The Wind *inkan* whenever he wanted or, better yet, create a new, different Gone With The Wind *inkan* to open the Ninka account. It wouldn't need to match the real one as long as he avoided using it at Mitsubishi Bank. And not only did he handle the books and banking, he was rumored to have *yakuza* connections. Maybe Nishida was using Gone With The Wind as a front for some deplorable body disposal system. The single flaw in her theory was that Nishida didn't know enough English to translate a billing order. Then again, he could have hired an outsider to translate.

Gaby began to worry about her boss. Mr. Eguchi was a spirited *kansai-jin* with a trusting nature. Nishida's betrayal would break his heart. She couldn't accuse Nishida without proof, but maybe she could show Mr. Eguchi a copy of Alex's bill and the Ninka Bank stamp on Alex's check. Also, the *inkan* stamp on Alex's check might not match theirs. Since Gaby's job had nothing to do with banking, she didn't know what the real *inkan* looked like. She'd ask Alex for copies.

By the time Schubert's Unfinished began, Gaby was satisfied there was nothing more she could do until Monday. Tomorrow, Sunday, she would finally have a day to herself, and the pleasure of staying at home.

Twelve

As the Skylark tune repeated, Lester's iced tea arrived with two foil-topped cups bearing the brand name Creap. "Non-dairy creamer," Lester explained, allowing the white rivulets to thread around the ice in his tea. "Did you put on that show for Gaby?"

"What show?"

"Feigning disinterest in Japanese women." Lester bit into his sandwich, chewing with his mouth slightly open.

"Actually, I don't find them attractive. The little-girl stuff with high voices and ankle socks and hands covering their mouths doesn't turn me on."

"I take it you go for older women?"

Was this an unkind reference to Gaby? Alex chose to ignore it. "If you mean women who act like adults, yes." The baby-voice song reached the chorus, and Alex pointed to a speaker. "*That,* I don't like."

"That's only the wrapping paper. Japan is a culture of wrapping, don't you know? Underneath their girlish surface, Japanese women are frightfully competent. They have the real power in this country, controlling their husbands and children."

Alex knew the fatal flaw of that common argument. "What about women who don't have husbands and children?"

Lester had no answer. He chewed off more sandwich, his pointed Adam's apple wobbling. "What's your connection to Gone With The Wind?"

Alex rattled ice cubes in his empty glass. "Didn't Gaby tell you?"

"She mentioned your son died. My condolences."

"I thought her company sent his body back, but—"

"But they didn't," Lester finished. "Who did, then?"

"That's what I'm trying to find out, with Gaby's help."

"I see. She said Eguchi foisted you off on her, but she didn't tell me why."

The word "foisted" stung. "She's been very generous. In fact, I'd like to send her flowers, to thank her for putting me up. Could you translate me through that?"

Lester stabbed a straw in his glass, watching the creamer and tea blend into a mushroom color. Lightly, as if a joke, he asked, "Is that how you impress women? Sending flowers?"

"I'm not trying to impress anyone," Alex said. "This is

common gratitude. She let me spend the night on her floor when I couldn't get a hotel room."

Lester pointed at him, a skeletal Ichabod Crane finger. "You like her, don't you?"

Alex resented his tone. He had as much right to like Gaby as Lester did. "That's beside the point."

"Good. Keep it beside the point," Lester said. "Where's the check?" He beckoned the waitress over and talked to her at length before standing up. "It's been taken care of. Shall we go?"

So Gaby had paid. Alex picked up his briefcase. "I'll leave the tip."

"One doesn't tip in Japan. Come on."

Back into the glittering gray incinerator of Shizuoka, Alex felt the sun press on his head. "You know, I need a hat. If we could stop at one of these shops?"

Lester walked briskly through a cement courtyard packed with carelessly parked bicycles and Alex struggled to keep up with him. "What kind of hat?"

"The cheapest possible."

"A discount store, then." Lester turned down a narrow side street and led Alex to a store named Pleasure Fist. Open to the street, Pleasure Fist wasted a lot of energy attempting to air-condition the entire prefecture. There were boxes of jumbled clothes under tables of folded clothes under lines of clothes on hangers. Squeezing his way down an aisle, Alex spotted many shirts with English phrases printed on them: "Let's Think Tomorrow," "Bad Boy Tradition Succeeded to Men," "You Became Significant to Yourself," and, in small letters, an entire paragraph of directions off a shampoo bottle.

"Here's an American head covering." Lester dropped a baseball cap on Alex's head.

Alex took it off. The black-and-orange cap of the San Francisco Giants with a Y instead of SF. "What is this?"

"The Yomiuri Giants." Lester found an exact replica of a Cincinnati Reds cap. "Do you prefer the Hiroshima Carp?"

Alex chuckled. "Good enough. How much?"

Lester showed him the price tag.

Alex estimated the exchange rate. "That's over fifty dollars! That's absurd."

A clerk moved beside them, a tiny woman with thin white hair whose glasses magnified her eyes to Godzillan proportion. She spoke Japanese to Lester, smiling at Alex. Alex rummaged through more hats. A cotton green-and-pink painter's hat sold for two thousand yen, but looked embarrassingly juvenile. He heard the word "American" used first by the clerk, then Lester.

Lester turned to him. "You're in luck. She thanks you for bestowing democracy on her country and wants to give you a ten percent discount."

"I wasn't part of the war." Alex thought about the atomic bomb with discomfort. "I wasn't even born then."

"Who cares? You're American. She likes Americans. Take the discount and pick out a hat." Lester folded his arms, impatient.

The woman sorted through the hats and presented Alex with a straw fedora, with feathers dyed hot pink and purple stuck into a red ribbon band.

Alex shook his head and kept looking. The old woman pushed the hat into his hands and pointed to an unframed mirror mounted on a support post. Tawdry as it was, Alex realized this hat was the only one large enough for his head. The price was three thousand—two thousand seven hundred after his discount. Too much, but he doubted Lester would take him to another store. Anyway, he consoled himself, when Japanese stared at him he could pretend it was because of his tasteless hat instead of his Caucasian face. He paid the clerk, who clipped the tag so he could wear it out of Pleasure Fist.

"I remember seeing a florist in the basement of a department store," Lester said. "I warn you, it's bound to cost more than five thousand yen."

"I'll spend it," Alex said. "I'm over my price resistance now."

They reached a large intersection and waited for the pedestrian light to change. When the red man with folded arms turned into a white man with bent knee and elbow, a mob of people stampeded the street, bicyclists weaving dangerously between the walkers. One bicycle came at Alex head-on. To keep from getting hit, Alex caught the handlebars. The rider, unhurt, jumped forward off his seat to stop, then spat on Alex's shoe and wrested his bike away.

"Unbelievable," Alex muttered. The walking white man flashed on and off and turned into the standing red man. Cars and trucks surged forward, barely missing Alex as he jumped to safety on the curb where Lester waited.

Alex panted, mopping his forehead with his shirtsleeve. "Did you see that?"

"I believe it's not their fault, once they have the light."

"Are you serious?"

Lester resumed his fast pace. "The needs of the group prevail over the needs of the individual."

Had Cody been hit on a street like this? Was a green light a green light to kill anyone in your way? Anger surged through him, helping him keep up with Lester's gait.

Lester glanced at his watch and turned right. "This is the main artery of Shizuoka, Gofukucho Street. I remember it by thinking 'Go fuck and choke.' Behold the Westernization of an ancient Eastern empire!"

Alex puffed past boutiques, restaurants, banks, and high-rise office buildings. Unlike Pleasure Fist, these stores were upscale—mannequins in show windows instead of stacks of clothes on tables. The mannequins, oddly, were Caucasian, and primarily blond. One wore a pea-green suit with large buttons down the front and a matching hat fashioned like an upside-down teacup, handle and all. He passed a restaurant with elaborate models of food, including a stack of pancakes with a pitcher suspended over them through a plastic strand of syrup. One store displayed toilets out on the sidewalk. These toilets had pan-

els of buttons on armrests and an electric cord to plug in. Another store displayed a human-size pink stuffed rabbit wearing
a Harley-Davidson leather jacket and ski goggles.

Lester walked up to a department store that covered an
entire block. Multiple glass doors slid open automatically, and
women in navy blue uniforms and white gloves bowed them
into cool air and Chopin preludes coming from a Plexiglas
grand player piano. Lester breezed through the perfume and
handbag sections to the descending escalator. The basement had
a complete supermarket and deli, separate butcher, bakery,
candy and liquor shops, and an imported-food shop stocked
with such delicacies as Shredded Wheat, Doritos, and Chips
Ahoy. Near doors that led to an underground mall, a florist displayed pots of bonsai, big horseshoes of carnations, and a few
plastic buckets of wilting carnations and chrysanthemums.

"Ask if they have anything else," Alex said.

Lester sighed. "Don't be difficult." But his query to the
clerk brought them to a chilled glass case that had crisp blue
irises, white lilies, and pink peonies. The peonies reminded Alex
of the flowers in Gaby's scroll. He pointed to them and worked
on the card while Lester gave the clerk Gaby's address. Alex
could let Gaby know he hadn't missed her cue to shut up about
her illness in front of Lester. Beyond that, how could he thank
her? He wrote the words in capital letters and signed it. He enjoyed tweaking Lester's jealousy by sealing the card before
Lester could read it.

That done, Lester checked his watch. "Nature Squib is
open now. You weren't keen on visiting shrines and what-not,
were you?"

Alex asked casually, so that Lester wouldn't refuse him just
to be perverse: "I'd like to see a place called . . . let's see . . . Kitanumi?"

"Kitanumi? That's nothing. A district on the edge of town,
up in the mountains." Lester's face showed interest. "Why Kitanumi?"

Alex shrugged and lied. "Cody—my son—mentioned it in a letter."

Lester raised a blond brow. "What did he say about it?"

Alex made up an answer based on the truth. "Not much. I know he liked mountain climbing, but I had the impression it was a street in town."

"Well, it's not." Lester's interest dropped. "Come on, then: to Nature Squib."

Lester wheeled around and Alex followed. Lester's energy never flagged, but Alex's arms and legs were turning into stone. In the sun, his hat exuded a grassy scent Alex disliked. Large circles of sweat spread from his armpits halfway to his waist. The side streets seemed shabbier than Gofukucho, perhaps due to the comparative sanity of the shops. Alex noted another measuring-instrument store, a bread bakery, and a tailor. After a few more blocks, foot traffic dwindled. Red lanterns clustered on both sides of the street. It was similar to the bar district in Tokyo, but in the daytime, without lights and people, it felt like a ghost neighborhood. A quiet hole of abandoned squalor in the middle of a crowded, noisy city. Litter gathered in stairwells and door-ways. From a dark corner bar, its doors propped open, impas-sioned dialogue and organ music of a soap opera blared out.

Lester stepped in a narrow entry between buildings and went up a flight of steps. "Duck," he said at the top, stooping to fit under a short curtain hung over an open door. Alex ducked just in time to avoid smacking his forehead on the beam over the door.

Entering Nature Squib, Alex was immediately disoriented by a prominent wall poster of a Japanese Elvis. Directly under-neath, the words "King of Beers" advertised Budweiser. Also dec-orating the walls were Hard Rock Cafe T-shirts, with the names of various cities misspelled: Shicago, Rondon . . . even his home-town, Sheattle. The small black tables with metal chairs were empty except for one, at which two middle-aged women flanked by big shopping bags talked intensely over untouched martinis.

Alex followed Lester up to the counter where three men sat, heads tilted toward a television mounted in a corner near the ceiling. On screen, a dark-complexioned young man with permanent ripples in his hair slapped a frail woman and tore her yellow blouse. The sound was turned off—words didn't matter for this kind of program.

Behind the counter, a woman with a tightly wrapped bun of black-and-white hair and deep wrinkles fanning out from the corners of her eyes and lips chopped potatoes and tossed them into a large pot of stew simmering on a hot plate. Her expression indicated nothing could shock her and nothing could please her.

Lester spoke to the woman, who said something sharply and watched for his response. Lester answered in Japanese and opened his wallet. Alex thought Lester was going to pay and reached for his own wallet, but the female bartender merely squinted at the bills Lester exposed and nodded her head curtly.

Lester motioned Alex to a table. "Don't mind Chieko—she adores me, really."

Alex thought otherwise. He shoved his briefcase under the table and scraped out a chair. "So this is where the *gaijin* go." He wondered if this was where Cody met the *yakuza* bikers. He glanced back up at the television: the man was flinging the sobbing woman to the floor.

The bartender slapped down a plate of green crackers and two tumblers. She returned a moment later with a quart bottle of Kirin beer, then went back to chopping potatoes.

"Hold your glass while I pour." Lester filled Alex's tumbler, then his own. *"Kampai!"*

"Kampai," Alex echoed. "Do students often come here?"

"Oh, yes." Lester's mood had improved with his first sip of beer. "At night, it's a Mecca of gorgeous young girls. Better than Soap Land." He waited for Alex to say something. When he didn't, Lester went on. "Soap Land is what the Japanese call bath houses, which are really—"

"Whorehouses," Alex said absently. He was still trying to

picture Cody drinking here, legally, at the age of twenty. He couldn't place the memory of his son in this room.

"Did Cody tell you that?" Lester seemed miffed that Alex already knew.

"Not Cody, Gaby. I asked her about *yakuza*."

"Don't tell me Cody got mixed up with *yakuza*."

"He might have."

Lester stopped. "And you've got Gaby involved?"

Alex didn't know what to say. Lester's reaction caused him to rethink his perception of *yakuza* as a fake Hollywood cliché. "Not really." He added lamely, "No more than she would have been through Gone With The Wind."

Lester shut his eyes and shook his head. "I knew she shouldn't have taken that job."

Alex found his throat was dry and swallowed some beer. "What do you mean?"

"How could a funeral company be a legitimate business? Anything dirty and degrading that involves big money involves *yakuza*." Lester glanced around. "Oh, look at what just walked in."

Alex saw two slender young women, dressed alike in tan miniskirts and short-sleeved pink blouses. One's arms were so thin, he wondered about anorexia. The thin woman had hair down to her waist, parted in the middle. The thicker one had short, permed curls. They noticed Lester and their hands went up over their mouths.

"Excuse me," Lester said. "Can't ignore my students. They come here to practice English." He picked up his beer and walked to them.

Alex was glad to have a moment alone with his thoughts, but the moment was quickly interrupted by the youngest of the three men at the bar, approaching his table.

"Hallo." The young man with slick rippled hair could have been the brother of the actor on the TV. A scar ran through his upper lip to the edge of his nostril. His face was as pink as his half-buttoned shirt. Scar Lip slumped into an empty chair, legs wide apart, stretching the crotch of his black pants. He pointed to Alex's head. "Groovy hat."

Alex smiled uneasily. "Thanks." He took if off and set it on the table.

Scar Lip pulled his chair closer. "Where are you from?" When he belched, the odor was toxic. He'd been marinating in beer for several hours. His eyes were semigloss enamel.

"America." Alex looked to Lester, whose back was turned to him, engrossed in talking to the young women.

The drunk continued. "I talk you. I speak English. Can you eat chopsticks? Do you like *natto*?"

"I've never had *natto*."

Scar Lip nodded. After a while, he said, "Za bartender is ugly bitch. I don't like. She is fuckermother." He grinned, impressed with his command of the English language. He snatched Alex's hat and put it on his head. It fell to his nose and rested there. "I like za hat. I keep?"

"Sorry. I need it myself." Alex was planning to get up and join Lester when he decided to stay, instead. Scar Lip was drunk, but he was willing to talk, in English, no less. For all he knew, his son had drunk with Scar Lip at this same table. "Have some beer?" He lifted the quart of Kirin on the table.

Scar Lip slapped his back, hard. "Okay. I like. We make friends, *ne*?" Over his shoulder, he spoke to the bartender, who begrudgingly brought a fresh tumbler to the table.

Alex poured for both of them. "My name is Alex. What's your name?"

"Haneda. Like za airport." Scar Lip/Haneda blew air and tilted his hand to suggest an airplane landing on a runway. Then he picked up his glass. *"Kampai!"*

Alex raised his glass and took a sip. "What do you do, Haneda?"

Haneda thought for a moment before tapping his glass. "I drink beer!" He was pleased to have come up with the right answer.

"I mean, your occupation. Job. Work." He'd have to keep it slow and simple.

Haneda pointed to the ceiling. "I work for boss."

Alex was taken aback. "You mean, God?"

"No, boss. BOSS." Haneda lifted his glass, but missed his mouth and poured beer on his chin. He wiped his mouth on his pink sleeve and went on. "I speak English, *ne?* I learn English. I like to speak. I come to *gaijin* bar to speak."

If only Alex spoke Japanese, maybe he could get somewhere. Lester, he noticed, had ordered another bottle and remained with the women, standing between them while they sat at the counter. "Why do you learn English?"

"To talk to *gaijin,*" Haneda said. His attention was distracted by jumpy light from the television. The actor had pulled off the sobbing woman's brassiere and was now rubbing his hand over her underpants as if rubbing out a stain. Haneda turned back to Alex. "You like bike?" He squeezed air handles and made engine starting noises.

Alex felt prickles in his stomach. Junko's words came back to him: *The men he went with, he probably met at bar. . . .* "You ride a motorcycle?"

Haneda put his finger on his scar. "This from bike." He turned his lip inside out to show the scar had split his lip all the way through.

Alex recoiled. "That must have hurt."

Haneda nodded, and kept nodding, like a bobbing dashboard ornament. Alex began to suspect brain damage. It couldn't be long before this guy would pass out. Still, he had to ask him: "When was that accident?"

"All za time."

Alex tried to sip more beer, but found he couldn't swallow. "A year ago?"

"Every year akushidento," Haneda said. "Four in one year."

"That's a dangerous hobby."

"Not so hobby. Job." He poured more beer, half of it going over the side of his glass. He rested his elbow in the puddle on the table. "*Kampai!* Go ride. High speed." He imitated a motor again, dropping and rising the pitch to change gears. "Akushidento. *Doun-Doun!*" He rammed his glass against Alex's.

Alex moved his glass out of Haneda's reach. "And then?"

Haneda's eyes rolled up beneath his upper lid, then came back, bleary. "Then, boss pay me. You want to ride?"

Alex became aware of his heart keeping time beneath his sternum. "No. Too dangerous for me."

Haneda slung his arm around Alex's neck and breathed dead beer in his face. "We go hobby ride. Not so dangerous. No akushidento, *ne?*"

Suddenly, Alex put it together. Haneda was paid to get victims into motorcycle accidents. He'd been hired to kill Cody. He wanted to punch Haneda in the face, strangle him, kill him. It took every atom of his willpower merely to pry Haneda's arm off his neck. He could feel the ropy bulk of Haneda's relaxed muscles, much stronger than his own.

The next instant, Haneda's head crashed onto the table with an audible crack. Out. The bartender, finished with the potatoes, rinsed her knife under the tap. From her poisonous expression, Alex wondered if she was going to kill him. She came over, wet knife in hand, and spoke sharply to Alex.

"Lester!" Alex kept his eyes on the bartender.

She spat more Japanese at him. Alex shrugged to indicate he couldn't understand.

Lester came to the table and started talking. The bartender spoke to Lester without looking at him, fixing her glare on Alex until he felt cursed.

Lester sighed, throwing yen bills on the table. "Chieko's mad and booting us out. Go. I'll meet you outside after I say goodbye to my girls."

Alex picked up his briefcase and hurried out the door, down the steps, and back into the hot, empty street. A trace of danger began to radiate from the vacant sidewalks and red lanterns. His throat hurt and tears welled in his eyes. He clutched his briefcase to his chest. He hadn't expected his answers to come this quickly, or to hurt this much.

Thirteen

The sidewalk cement shimmered with tiny sparkles under the white, hazy Shizuoka sky, and Alex yearned for a hat, again. He had no hope of retrieving his feathered hat from the drunken Haneda. He trudged downhill from Lester's apartment, head throbbing from an entire night of drinking. Quart after quart of beer in various bars with various friends of Lester's, and he was fairly sure a bottle of Four Roses had drained around one table as well. But he didn't mind the hangover. Physical pain was a welcome distraction from the emotional kind, and he doubted he could have slept last night without the assistance of inebriation. What he had concluded yesterday—that Haneda was hired to cause motorcycle accidents—convinced him Cody's death had been a malicious act. It was bizarre to think that his son had been deliberately endangered, but he was all the more determined to find out who hired Haneda and why.

Alex looked around at the first intersection, where Lester said there was a liquor shop. He unfolded the paper on which Lester had drawn the *kanji* for "liquor" to match up with a sign. He hated his incompetence in Japan. Traveling in Europe, he got by with pocket dictionaries, but dictionaries were useless for ideographs unless you knew how to pronounce them, and if you knew the pronunciation it was because you already knew the meaning. The only other way to look up *kanji* was to match the character from a chart of characters with the same stroke count. If there were only four strokes, it was feasible, but if it took twelve strokes to write the *kanji*, the list covered pages.

Counting strokes in itself was an art, as only Japanese knew when you should lift the pen and when you shouldn't. *Kanji* made him blind in this country. Blind and stupid.

He spotted a sign with an approximation of Lester's drawing over a drab, concrete box building across a four-lane street and waited for the light. On the other side, a group of schoolgirls, marked by identical black-and-green-plaid uniforms, stared at him, and their hands flew over their mouths like a pack of speak-no-evil monkeys. When the light changed, a sound like a cuckoo beckoned pedestrians into the crosswalk. In the middle of the intersection, the tallest of the green-plaid girls bravely taunted *"Gaijin!"* while the others giggled behind their hands. Alex kept walking.

A loud buzzer sounded when he pushed through the glass door of the liquor store. He saw a cooler on the back wall and made his way down a narrow aisle, carefully stepping over boxes of whiskey set up like an obstacle course. At the cooler, confronted by infinite brands of quart bottles of beer, he realized he hadn't asked Lester which kind to get. Curiously, the labels were in English, but choices of super dry, extra dry, original lager, premium lager, and summer blend, to name only a few, overwhelmed him.

He closed his eyes, reached into the cooler, and grabbed a bottle at random—Original Kirin. As he studied the picture of a red dragon on the label, someone tapped his shoulder.

"Hello, mate. Did you find Kaneko last Friday?" It was the Australian teacher he'd met at the university, sunburned and wearing a "You're No Goo" T-shirt.

"McKenzie, isn't it?" Alex set down the beer to shake hands. "Kaneko was in Tokyo. I'll try again tomorrow. Do you happen to know if this is the beer Lester likes?"

Michael laughed. "Lester likes any kind he doesn't pay for."

"Then these should do the job." Alex hauled out four quart bottles.

"Did you lose a bet?"

"No, I'm thanking Lester for letting me sleep on his sofa."

More than that, he was thanking Lester for getting him out of Nature Squib and getting him drunk instead of asking him questions.

"If that's how you thank people, please stay at my place!"

Alex smiled. "Be careful. I might take you seriously. The university's hotel closes every weekend."

"How long will you be in town?" Michael took a quart of Foster's lager off the shelf.

"As long as it takes."

"To do what?"

Alex hesitated. Telling people widened his net of information, but he wasn't sure whom to trust. Still, it was hard to suspect the buoyant, boyish McKenzie, hired after Cody's death. He said, "My son died here a year ago. I'm trying to find out how and why."

"I'm sorry." Michael looked down at his sandals.

"I guess you didn't know him? Cody Thorn?"

"No. Sorry." Michael led the way back to the counter. The cashier, a skinny young man growing his first sparse moustache, nervously asked a question. "Why do they ask questions?" Michael grumbled. "Why can't they just ring it up?"

The clerk blushed and stammered something.

"Hai." Michael turned to Alex. "When in doubt, I say yes." The clerk worked the cash register and tore off the receipt, which he handed to Michael. "Oh, he put our beers together." Michael passed the receipt on to Alex and rummaged in his pocket for coins. "Japanese is a bitch to learn. D'you know it takes them eight years to learn their own language? Think about it; no one can read until the age of thirteen."

The receipt read 3,600 yen. Michael isolated his beer bottle and placed eight hundred yen on the counter. That left 2,800 yen for Alex to pay. Alex took advantage of knowing the exact price to lighten his pocket of change. Japanese coins were heavy. He pushed a pile of coins toward the clerk, who had put the other bottles in a plastic bag with handles. "Well, see you later."

"I'll go with you," Michael said. "I was on my way to see Les myself. This time he can't claim to be out of beer."

When they reached Lester's apartment, Alex's arm ached and his fingers were swollen from the heat. Through the window, he saw Lester on the phone. Lester hung up quickly and opened the door, hair still wet from his shower, tucking his white shirttails into khaki pants. Alex envied his clean clothes. His own, on their third day, had gone rancid. Lester looked past Alex to Michael. "McKenzie! Thought you were in Kyoto."

"I got back a few hours ago."

"Sit down and tell us about the temples." Lester took the bags and arranged the beer bottles in his refrigerator while Alex and Michael took off their shoes.

Lester's apartment was the same size as Gaby's but cheaper-looking. Mildewed white wallpaper curled away from the mold-spotted ceiling, and deep black scratches marred the lime-green linoleum floor. The draperies, a black-and-brown dead fern pattern, sagged on broken hooks. Dirty dishes overflowed the sink onto the green counter. Laundry slumped over an electronic keyboard. Above the sofa Alex had slept on was a poster advertising *sake,* showing a naked Japanese woman in a mountain hot spring reaching for a tiny cup off a floating tray. Her skin was ghostly white, her nipples bright pink, and her black hair swirled into dark blue water that obscured her body below the waist. Alex sat on the sofa, rubbing his sore bicep.

Michael lifted a wet towel off the sofa and sat on the other end. "The gold one with the big pond was the best."

"You mean Kinkakuji. Thoughtful of the Yanks not to bomb it, eh?" Lester popped the cap off a Kirin. Beer frothed over the top. "Damn."

Michael went on. "I wanted to see the one with the Silent Garden, where a tourist vanished last year."

"A tourist vanished?" Lester asked.

"You didn't hear about it?" Michael gloated. "Lester Hollingsworth, the resident expert on things Japanese?"

"I probably did. Tell me."

Michael absorbed more space on the sofa. "Well, you know how they edge the temple paths with boards and put up signs forbidding you to go off the path? So you're in a line, trudging along, unable to stop if you want to look for a while?"

Lester wiped the spilled beer with a sponge. "An old Zen custom."

"Zen, my ass! Those monk chaps took their time observing nature."

"Mostly with their eyes shut." Lester searched for clean glasses.

"May I tell the story?"

"Then don't narrate with questions," Lester grumbled. "When I hear a question, I answer it." He rounded up a tumbler, a jelly jar, and a plastic cup, set them on the coffee table, and sat cross-legged on the floor, pouring beer.

Alex, amused at how obviously Lester sulked while Michael reveled in the spotlight, gave all his attention to Michael.

Michael put his hand around the tumbler to claim it while Lester was still pouring. "Well, last year, a tour group was allowed to visit the Silent Garden, which is usually off limits to the public. The guide warned them they must not talk for any reason and they must never go off the path." Michael lifted his glass. "Cheers."

Lester poured into the plastic cup and took a sip. Then he filled the jelly jar.

Michael continued. "Well, they got to this place where there was an amazing view of Mount Fuji. To get a better photograph, one tourist took a step off the path and disappeared. As if the earth had eaten him up. Everyone was surprised, but they said nothing. They waited awhile, but, as none of them were allowed to talk, eventually they moved on. When they got back to the temple, they alerted the monks. The monks searched and searched and couldn't find the tourist. His body was never found, either. He had disappeared, like magic. What do you think of that?"

"I think you made it up." Lester sipped carefully. The plastic cup was thin and his fingers dented the rim.

"I did not! I heard it from the tour bus driver himself."

Alex raised the jelly jar. When he drank, a faint scent of strawberries cupped around his nose. "I believe you. I bet the tourist was killed."

"By Zen monks? Hardly," Lester said.

"Why not?" Alex replied. "Didn't some religious group release nerve gas in a Tokyo subway? So why not kill tourists at a temple? Doesn't seem to be any point to it, though."

"That's the point," Lester declared. "We Westerners require a motive for every crime. Here, crimes are a matter of fate."

Alex sensed this speech was directed to him. "What about the victims?"

Lester looked straight into his eyes. "The victims are fulfilling their destinies."

Michael broke in, "My point was that Japanese follow rules no matter what. They could have called out to the tourist or searched the woods, but instead they kept silent and stayed on the path."

Lester pointed at Michael. "I lived here last year. If there was any truth to your highly unlikely story, I'd have heard about it. It's a classic ghost story. I bet it never happened."

Michael squinted suspiciously. "How much? Five thousand?"

"Ten," Lester countered.

Alex pursued the former subject. "If murder is fate and nothing can be done, why have police?"

Lester shrugged. "A mere formality. Most police work is a matter of procuring confessions. They wait a long time before making any arrest, make sure their suspect doesn't have strong connections to defend himself, and jail him until he admits his guilt. Which he usually does, because any appeal would cause the police or the judge to lose face. There is no jury system in Japan, you know."

Alex felt his stomach crinkle from the beer. "I didn't know."

"That's right," Michael said. "A student of mine wrote a

paper about court trials. The judge determines guilt or innocence. She favored it. Said a jury wouldn't have the wisdom to
make that kind of decision."

"I'd think judges would be bribed, then," Alex said.

"Routinely," Lester affirmed.

"It's barbaric," Alex said.

Lester's cup was empty and he poured himself more beer,
adding two inches to Michael's glass and a token dollop to Alex's
jar. "Ah, but consider how barbaric they regard your justice system. With deranged killers going free on technicalities, or phony
insanity pleas, or sob stories about how wretched their own
childhoods were. If the American—"

The phone rang, cutting off Lester's speech.

Alex rested his sweaty forehead in his hands, palms over
his eyes, willing a fresh wave of hangover to subside. He needed
to see Haneda again, to find out for certain if his boss paid him
to kill foreigners in accidents. Cody's death might still have been
an accident. But Cody's heart hadn't been removed without a
reason. Someone had a motivation for that. Alex knew from the
autopsy that Cody's heart had been surgically removed, "as if
for transplant." That operation couldn't be done by a basement
mafia doctor. Whether or not Haneda crashed into Cody, a major hospital and heart surgeon were undeniably involved. Pin-
pointing the hospital was crucial. Their mistake—Junko's as
well—had been assuming Cody would have been hospitalized
in Shizuoka. Why not Tokyo? Alex would check every hospital
in Japan, if necessary. Maybe Gaby would help him do this—it
was safer than tracking down *yakuza*.

Lester was prodding his elbow. "Alex?"

Alex roused himself. "What?"

"Gaby's on the phone. Want to talk to her?"

"Yes!" Alex quickly revised his response. "Sure, why not?"

Lester passed him a black cordless phone.

"Hi." Gaby's clear alto was a welcome voice. "Has Lester
been tolerable? I realize you can only answer yes or no."

"Not really. How are you?"

"Thanks for the peonies. They're lovely, but you really shouldn't have. I'm not on your obligation list."

"I hope you like them." Alex watched Michael pull a piece of paper from his pocket and show it to Lester.

"Oh, I do. Thanks." She hurried into her next question. "Lester said you got into trouble with a *yakuza*?"

Alex lowered his voice. "I got into trouble with a bartender, not a *yakuza*. He passed out and she stood with a knife and yelled at me."

"Did she think you hurt him?"

That possibility hadn't occurred to him. He replayed the scene in his mind. "I don't know how much she saw. But Haneda passed out. I didn't touch him. Her reaction was extreme."

"She probably thought you hit him."

"Why would she assume the worst of me?"

"She doesn't know you."

Alex snorted. "And to think the Japanese have a reputation for being so polite."

"Now, now. Americans don't treat foreigners well, either. Shouting at them as if they must be deaf or stupid."

"At least we try to communicate," Alex objected.

Gaby switched topics. "I want to hear more about the *yakuza*."

Alex casually walked away from Michael and Lester so they couldn't hear him and lowered his voice. "The *yakuza* was drinking at Nature Squib. Where Cody might have met him. He said his boss pays him to get into motorcycle accidents. I don't know the motive or the method, but that's a definite connection." Alex was impressed at how calmly and rationally he said that. Sometimes, emotional repression paid off.

After a pause, Gaby asked, "Are you sure about this?"

"He was too drunk to lie."

"It doesn't sound plausible."

"So? Is a hotel that closes on weekends plausible? Is a nation without checking accounts plausible? This is Japan, right?

Or so you always say." Alex glanced over his shoulder. Michael gestured at him, pointing to the phone and then to himself. Alex nodded and turned back to face the wall. The *sake* poster girl's nipples glowed at his eye level.

"It just doesn't sound like normal Japanese insanity," Gaby said. "Did he tell you whom he worked for?"

"He passed out before I could ask. I'll have to find him again." Alex felt a tap on his shoulder. Alex held up his hand to ask Michael to wait.

"Alex, foreigners are especially vulnerable to trouble. If he's dangerous—"

Michael grabbed the phone out of Alex's hand. "Gaby, it's Michael! I need your help . . ."

Alex blew out his breath. Michael might be nicer than Lester, but he was sure a spoiled brat. "Pass her back when you're done."

Michael held a sheet of paper in front of his face. "Gaby? I got a note from Marubatsu. He wants a file of medical records of exchange students from *my* desk. By eight-thirty tomorrow. The note was under my doormat when I got home. . . . Right, my apartment. Anyway, do you know why that would be in my desk? . . . Oh, you did? . . . Well, where are they? . . . I can't read *kanji*. Could you drive me to the university and find the file for me? . . . Please? I wanted to sleep in tomorrow. . . . You're no fun! . . . Wait, Alex is pestering me."

"I want to come along," Alex said, loud enough for Gaby to hear. Exchange student medical records might include Cody's. Maybe the name of the hospital would be there.

"What? I can't listen to two people at the same time. . . . All right . . . All right. You're a good sport, Gabe. Bye." Michael turned the phone off.

Alex threw his hands up. "I wanted to talk to her again!"

"Oh. Sorry." Green eyes blinked. "Anyway, she'll pick us up in twenty minutes."

"How did you get her to leave her flat, with no notice, on a Sunday, to help your sorry ass?" Lester asked.

Michael grinned. "Must be my devilish good looks."

"Gaby's too old for you," Lester said pointedly. "She's thirty-six."

Michael shrugged. "They say older women—"

"Don't even think about it," Lester stated.

"Take it easy, mate," Michael said. "I was joking."

Alex made a brief inventory of his briefcase and pockets. "I'll ask Gaby to drop me off at the hotel. That way, I won't have to impose on you anymore."

"Why do you want to tag along?" Lester asked. His tone suggested he planned to needle Alex about seeking Gaby's company.

Alex borrowed his answer from Cody: "I thought I should be open to the moment."

Fourteen

Although campus was usually deserted on Sundays, Gaby couldn't wear shorts on the off-chance she might run into a former colleague. She changed into an L. L. Bean button-front shirt and cotton skirt in a color called "natural." If it weren't for international mail order, she'd be stuck wearing chaotic flower prints designed for Japanese women whose largeness was in girth rather than height. It was hard on a woman's ego to live where size ten made her a giantess. Sandals, at least, were no problem, since men's shoe sizes fit her feet.

On her way downtown to Lester's apartment, she turned on the radio (Peruvian folk music) and pondered Marubatsu's request for the student records in her old desk. She used to translate medical records of foreign students for the president's office. No one knew what to do with the originals in English, so she kept them in a file, afraid to throw away any official paperwork. Since the university took only three or four exchange students each year, the file was thin. Marubatsu had never asked to see that file when she worked there; why was he suddenly interested enough to leave an urgent note at Michael's apartment?

When Gaby pulled in front of Lester's apartment building, Michael and Alex were at the curb. Michael, with a newly sunburned face, looked peppy and casual as a soda commercial. Alex looked weary and grim. His pants and shirt were wrinkled and sweaty. Lester should have offered the use of his washing machine. Gaby couldn't; a man's pants on her clothesline would generate tendrils of gossip as hard to kill as a kudzu vine.

"Stanton Taxi at your service," she called through the open window.

Michael held the door open for Alex to crawl into the backseat. Gaby noticed Alex's hesitation. "Hey, Michael, let Alex sit up front."

Michael squeezed behind the seat. "There isn't enough room for a contortionist back here. I don't have wraparound legs."

"You're young. You'll live," Gaby said.

Michael objected. "You're not old enough to call me young."

Gaby turned to Alex, adjusting his seat forward to give Michael more room. "Hi. You okay? You don't look very good."

"It's called a hangover. I have only myself to blame." He smiled, and good looks flashed through his tired face. His direct eye contact, with eyes so blue, unsettled her. The last thing she needed was to get a crush on this doomed man.

She glanced in the rearview mirror at Michael. "What did you think of the temples?"

Michael groaned. "Is everyone going to ask me that?"

Gaby laughed. "Probably. You should memorize the names of the big four: Kinkakuji, Ginkakuji, Ryoanji, Daitokuji. Your colleagues will like it if you can recite them." She turned off the highway onto a less crowded two-lane road and picked up speed.

"Speaking of which"—Michael leaned over her neck rest—"have you heard about the tourist who vanished in the Silent Garden?"

"No," Gaby said. "I've never even heard of a silent garden."

"Damn!" Michael said. "I've lost ten thousand yen to Lester."

"It's generally not a good idea to take him up on his bets." The Honda jolted over pits in the road.

Alex gripped the dashboard with one hand. His face was pale. Gaby slowed down. Potholes and hangovers didn't mix.

Her route took them beyond the industrial south side of town to leveed roads through flat rice paddies and a different stretch of the stream Gaby ran beside. After the rice fields came student apartments and cheap noodle shops clustered on the outskirts of the university.

Gaby drove through the open university gate and up the winding road to the top of the hill. Sometimes she could see Mount Fuji from here, but today was too hazy. Only two white cars claimed spaces in the nearly vacant faculty lot; she wouldn't have to worry about meeting anyone. She parked in front of a wilting white hydrangea. "Here we are."

"Sure beats walking up that hill," Alex offered. He held open his door as Michael crawled out from the back.

"Speak for yourself," Michael said, stretching his arms.

The three of them walked to the U-shaped building. Michael swiped his card through the scanner and pushed open the door at the buzz. Gaby entered the dark lobby with a pang of nostalgia. How many times had she ridden this elevator with the faded sign warning students that only teachers had permission to use it? How many times had she got out at the second floor and unlocked the office Michael now had the key for?

She half-hoped to find students waiting for her in the hall, like the old days.

The way Michael held the door open, she had to duck under his arm to go in.

She didn't like the Australian travel posters Michael had put up, or the dartboard where her calendar used to hang. Instead of books, her shelves now held a coffeemaker, cups, a cassette player, and a paddle ball. The odor of stale tobacco lounged around the blue sofa she used to eat lunch on. A glass plate filled with cigarette butts lay next to a beige telephone on top of an otherwise empty desk.

Alex looked around as Michael switched on the overhead light and unlocked his desk drawer. "How come Marubatsu's office is so much nicer? Seniority?"

"And how," Gaby answered.

Michael gestured to the file drawer. "It's all yours."

Gaby sat in the familiar brown swivel chair and opened the drawer on the right side. It was eerily just as she'd left it nearly a year ago; half-filled with university files labeled in her belabored *kanji*. The folders lay slanted from the absence of the teaching files she'd taken with her. Apparently, Michael had no need for a file drawer. She found the exchange student folder and placed it on top of the desk.

"Is Cody's in there?" Alex asked, moving around behind her.

"Let me check." Gaby paged back until she found a sheet marked Thorn, Cody James. "Here it is. Look familiar?" She held up the sheet so she and Alex could read it at the same time. There was nothing unusual in Cody's medical profile. No major illnesses, no medications. Cody had no allergies and his blood type was AB. Then she saw a handwritten note in the bottom margin: "Patient requests no organ donation and no autopsy for religious reasons." She remembered translating this into Japanese two years ago; she hadn't known the Japanese for "autopsy" and had had to look it up—*kenshi*.

"Are you done?" Michael asked.

Alex turned it over. Nothing on the back. He had obviously hoped for something more. "I may as well keep this."

"Hey!" Michael objected. "You'll get me in trouble with Marubatsu."

"He won't miss one form," Alex reasoned.

"Make a copy," Gaby suggested. She handed the file to Michael. "To the mail room?"

As she and Alex followed Michael down the unlit hallway to the faculty lounge, she suddenly needed a toilet. She stood perfectly still, letting the men get ahead of her. She had twenty years of practice delaying diarrhea. If she could stifle the first urge, she might be able to dash to the bathroom before the second. The trick was in the timing. She drew a deep breath.

Alex, turning back, asked, "Gaby?"

"Excuse me!" Gaby bolted across the corridor into the women's bathroom. She pulled her skirt off over her head before entering the stall, but she felt herself lose control before she could position herself over the squat toilet.

Afterward, she began the cleanup. She laid her skirt over the top of the stall partition. Thanks to her quick thinking, it was spotless. Her underpants washed out easily with hand soap and cold water. Then she grabbed a stack of paper towels and cleaned a few spots off the floor tiles. She was grateful it was Sunday, so no one would come in and find her naked from the waist down. She wrung her panties as hard as she could, rolled them up and stashed them in her purse. Then she put on her skirt and headed out the door. Wait! She checked the bottom of her sandals. Yuck. She used the toilet brush on the soles.

Alex and Michael stood waiting outside the faculty-lounge door.

"What took you so long?" Michael asked.

"The toilet was broken." She'd rehearsed a list of lies for times like these. "Did you make a copy?"

"Couldn't. The machine was broken," Michael reported.

Gaby looked to Alex.

"I left Cody's history in the file," Alex said. "After all, it didn't tell me anything I didn't know."

"So we're done?"

"We're done." Michael made a fist and popped the elevator button. "On to Nature Squib?"

Gaby shook her head. "I have work to do before tomorrow."

The elevator opened in front of them. Michael got in first, holding the door back with his hand as Gaby and Alex followed. "I forget. What is your job, anyway? All I know is that Lester always wants you to quit it."

"I sell fantasy funerals. Catering and cremation with special effects."

Michael grimaced. "Sorry I asked."

"No one wants to hear about it."

Alex glanced at her curiously. She purposefully faced the elevator button panel while Michael asked, "Can you make a living from that?"

"Oh, yes. You see, for a traditional service, you not only pay the Zen priest for the ceremony and afterlife name, but you pay separately for the funeral banquet, for hotel rental, kiln rental, crematorium space—it adds up to quite a bundle. Our price is cheaper, and we handle all the annoying details, so sales are increasing. It's a booming new business." She stopped herself from babbling on. Alex certainly wouldn't want to hear about the Japanese way of death. Especially not the part about family members tending the kiln, bashing Grandma's skull with a poker to speed up the cremation process.

The elevator stopped and they got out.

"I'd think they'd only hire Japanese," Michael mused, using his key card in the electronic slot. At the sound of the buzzer, Alex pushed open the glass door and held it until Gaby was outside. It dropped shut with a loud click when the lock kicked in.

Gaby put on her sunglasses as they walked to the parking lot. "I would, too, but people find this kind of work unappealing, so Mr. Eguchi hires anyone he can get."

"Don't *you* find it unappealing?" Michael asked.

Gaby unlocked her Honda. "The commissions are good and my hours are flexible. I don't view any corpses, if that's what you mean." Again, she realized her comment had been insensitive. It must have been awful for Alex to look at his young son's body, stiff and pale in a box. She turned to find Alex. He had stopped ten feet back, examining a hydrangea blossom. She hoped he hadn't heard her.

"Isn't all the grief and mourning a drag?" Michael fit himself into the backseat.

"Sh. Don't let Alex hear you." Gaby got in and cranked down her window, watching Alex as he walked toward the car. "I won't pretend I wouldn't rather be an English professor."

Michael squirmed into a cross-legged position, as if the backseat were a floor. "Lucky for me you got fired."

Alex got in the car. He said nothing. He looked exhausted.

Gaby craned her neck over the headrest to talk to Michael. "Do you have any inkling who fired me? Any gossip floating in the halls?"

"I wouldn't know. No one speaks English in the English department."

"I suspect Marubatsu." Gaby started the engine.

Michael laughed. "Well, if it was, you showed him, joining his competition."

"I hadn't thought of that. I guess I am his competition." Marubatsu's priesthood seemed more like a résumé-filler than an occupation. She couldn't picture him praying for the salvation of all living beings. He wasn't even vegetarian. She could, however, easily imagine him sizing up a family's wealth and charging a high price for a funeral service.

Gaby drove slowly down the curves of the hill. She stopped at the university gate and waited for a group of children to meander out of the crosswalk. One of them bounced a ball off her windshield. "Michael, where should I take you? Your place? Lester's?"

"Actually, my friend Naoko lives nearby. I'll see if she'll go to Nature Squib with me. Could you let me out a few blocks ahead? At that kiosk? I need to get more smokes."

If Naoko lived this close to the university, she had to be a student. Gaby was disappointed with Michael for dating a student, but reminded herself it was none of her business. "Here you go," she said, pulling up next to the tobacco stand.

Alex got out to free Michael from his backseat entrapment.

"So long, Gaby," Michael said. "Alex, if you need a place to crash next weekend, let me know."

"Thank you, I'll do that." Alex shook his hand and got back into the car.

Michael lit a cigarette while Gaby waited for traffic to let her into the street. He waved when she pulled out, smoke cutting a Z in the air.

"You were quiet," Gaby commented to Alex.

"I was thinking. Was I rude? I didn't mean to be."

"Not at all." Gaby glanced at the clock in the instrument panel. "I'm afraid it's way too early for the university hotel. I could drop you at a coffee shop—"

"Your apartment," Alex said decisively. "I need to talk to you. Privately."

"If you're seen at my—"

"It's the safest place. Please." Those blue eyes, again.

Gaby sighed. "Okay, but this is the last time." Her apartment was the safest place for her, as well.

Fifteen

Two nights ago, Alex had found her apartment sterile and sparse. Now its emptiness enhanced the cool and quiet—a refuge from heat and people. Alex watched the tilt of Gaby's brown hair as she bent slightly to take off her sandals, watched her thin tan arm stretch back to hang her keys on a hook by the door. He was standing too close behind her, having quickly entered and shut the door to minimize the chance of a neighbor glimpsing him. He had an urge to hold her. Confused by this impulse, he did nothing. In less than a second, she had stepped barefoot onto the tatami floor, leaving him room to remove his shoes in the tiny cement entry.

Gaby took glasses from her cupboard. "Ginger ale or water?"

"Water is fine." Alex unlaced his shoes. They were dusty and hogged too much space beside her sandals. He felt like an intruder. Perhaps that's how she regarded him. Once again, he had forgotten that she was sick and he had forced her to host him here. Creep Alex. He resented the way Lester and Michael took advantage of her and now he was acting like them.

He sat on one of the hard wood chairs. The table was bare except for the vase of pink peonies he had sent her. They put out a tangy rose scent. Gaby set his water on the table and poured a ginger ale for herself. She put her ear to her glass before drinking.

Alex liked that; that she listened to hear if it had gone flat instead of looking at the bubbles pushing up. "I need to talk to you about medical matters."

"My specialty," Gaby said. "What do you want to know?"

"I was hoping Cody's Shizuyama medical record would tell me about treatment he got here in Japan. I'm sure he went to a hospital, and it must have been outside Shizuoka."

Gaby tapped her fingers on her glass. Her nails were

painted the palest pink. "I hope you're right, but . . . well, the Japanese mafia is keen on cutting off body parts. Initiates cut off their own fingers to prove themselves. They have their own doctors. . . ." Her brown eyes checked his face before continuing.

"It wasn't a butcher job," Alex interrupted. "The coroner in Seattle said it was skillfully done. As if to receive a transplant. It's not something you can do in a garage. You need bypass machines, specialized cardiac surgeons. My question is, which hospitals in Japan do heart transplants?"

"I don't know. Not many. Maybe one or two in Tokyo or Osaka."

"Could you find out?"

"I'll ask my doctor," Gaby said. "But if Cody went to a hospital, you would have received a bill. Bills, you can count on. In that regard, I promise you Japan is no different from the States."

"I hear you. But the billing could have gone wrong." He added, "Like the Gone With The Wind bill."

Gaby gave a wry smile. "I can't argue that, can I?"

Alex gulped down his water. "Well, that's why I needed to talk to you. We need to concentrate on finding the hospital. Then we can find the doctor who operated on Cody and I can find out what happened."

"That makes sense. I'll talk to my doctor on Monday." She studied his face in a way that made him self-conscious. "Does this mean you're not going to pursue your *yakuza* theory?"

He sighed. "No, but I want to approach it from fact, not speculation. I can't think of a motive for the *yakuza*. What's to be gained from killing a university exchange student? I go crazy imagining the possibilities. I even thought it might be a Machiavellian scheme to kill foreigners for their organs, but motorcycle accidents aren't reliable. If it's body parts you want, you don't randomly push people in front of trucks. Can you explain why they would want to kill Cody?" Alex buried his face in his hands. Would this hangover never leave?

"Let's say Cody died in an accident," Gaby said. "But, for

whatever reason, the *yakuza* he biked with felt responsible, or did something wrong—like not giving him a helmet. They took him to a hospital, where a transplant was attempted and failed. When Cody died, the *yakuza* bribed the hospital into removing the record of having treated him."

"They'd do all that cover-up just for not lending him a helmet?" Alex thought: which Cody might not have worn, anyway. Should he and Jane have taken away his dirt bike back in Seattle?

"All that," Gaby confirmed. "There's a much stronger sense of social responsibility in Japan. With it, a stronger urge to hide your mistakes."

Alex wasn't in the mood to learn about Japanese culture. "Do you really believe it happened that way?"

Gaby hesitated. "It's the best I can come up with."

"We need to be sure. We need to check every hospital." He stood and carried his glass to her sink. He didn't want to argue with Gaby. He wanted to lie down with an ice pack. "Is it far to the university hotel?"

Gaby looked at him suspiciously. "Not really."

"Great. I'll walk back, then. You won't have to drive me."

"But can you handle the heat?"

"Hey, I'm a tough guy." He smiled at her. "Just mark the way on my map." He pulled his map from his pocket and laid it on the table.

"This doesn't show much. Let me get mine." She opened her purse and pulled out a small wet cloth . . . with lace trim. Underpants. She quickly put her hand behind her back. "Hang on a minute. Could you, um, turn on the radio? I guess I left my map in the closet."

Alex turned his back to her and crouched in front of her low bookshelves. Poor Gaby. Her illness really embarrassed her. Talk about hiding. He would do her the favor of not mentioning what he'd seen. When he found the power button for the radio, a familiar bittersweet tune unfolded phrase by trembling phrase. Tchaikovsky's *Romeo and Juliet* theme.

When Gaby returned, he pretended to be too absorbed in listening to the music to notice her take her map from her purse, not her closet, after all. She looked at his map spread out on her table. He handed her a pen and she drew a box for her apartment, filling in smaller streets from her map that weren't on his.

"This is the street I drove in on, okay? Turn left at the fig patch and keep going until Monkey Video Store—their sign is in English. Then left at the four-way intersection. After you see this racetrack—"

"I know the racetrack. I can take it from there. It looks very close, actually." As he said the word "close," he became aware of how close they were standing.

"It is." When Gaby handed him his pen, she looked up, slightly surprised by their nearness.

Without thinking, Alex tilted his head and kissed her lips. He felt an amazing stir as she began to kiss him back—and then she stiffened, and he let go.

Gaby stepped aside and snapped off the radio. She attempted a laugh that came out more like a cough. "That music. Makes you do the stupidest things, doesn't it?"

Alex could literally feel a pang in his chest, as if his heart had taken a stitch. One bizarre impulse had scared away the person he needed and trusted the most. What had come over him? "I'm sorry. I didn't mean to—"

"I know you didn't," Gaby said too quickly. "Let's forget about it." Her neck muscles weren't forgetting.

"Are you sure?"

Gaby flashed a strained smile. "It won't happen again, right?"

"Right," he promised. Perversely, now, Alex wanted to make it happen again. This wasn't like him. But it *used* to be, before Cody died, his former self, the man who felt things. "I can't undo anything, but if I can explain—"

Gaby crossed her arms in front of her chest. "You don't have to explain the obvious. You're in a crisis, you're in a foreign country, you don't know what's going on, blah, blah, blah. We don't have to talk about it. Could we please not talk about it?"

He opened his mouth to disagree, then changed his mind. "Whatever you want," he said. "Can I call you tomorrow?"

She nodded nervously. "Sure."

"Right. Take care of yourself. If there's anything I can do for you—"

"I will. Goodbye."

When Alex stepped outside and heard her lock the door behind him, he was smitten simultaneously by the scalding late afternoon air and a sense of loss. For a year, his willpower had been his lifeline, the rope he held through the wretched job of existing. At first, it was a matter of forcing himself to eat, drink, and sleep through the pain of losing his son. When the brunt of the anguish subsided, so had pleasure. His emotions were stuck in a range between frustration and despair, so he suppressed them as much as possible. He had made an arbitrary decision that when enough time had passed, his life would become tolerable; he had nothing else to sustain him. It was absurd that now, in Japan—under the very conditions Gaby described—he had made a pass at a woman he barely knew and tasted his first real kiss in over a year. To begin to feel desire was a tiny miracle.

He trudged down the metal stairs, each footstep clanging, thinking about Gaby's kiss. *It won't happen again, right?* It was confusing to feel yes and hear no, though Alex knew decent men acted on words, not lips. Why had Gaby been so quick to pull away? His mind promptly provided a list of answers. They'd only met two days ago, they lived five thousand miles apart, sex was complicated for people their age, and he planned to leave Japan as soon as he could. It was a good example of *Why Love Fails.*

There were no sidewalks in Gaby's district, only narrow concrete blocks covering waste water ditches by the sides of the road. These blocks were notched for lifting, and the toes of Alex's shoes kept tripping on the notches. Most of the blocks wobbled. He gave up and walked in the street, moving to the side whenever a car, hysterically beeping its horn, passed by him.

Alex stopped at the corner and wiped sweat from his forehead. Across from a motorcycle repair shop and a three-story concrete-block house was a small lot, about an eighth of an acre, covered with gigantic round leaves notched into five lobes. An odd place for a fig grove. He didn't see any figs among the leaves. He shaded his eyes and scanned the road to the left of the patch. Several blocks down, there was a sign that read MON EY VIDEO. Monkey with the K missing.

He passed a one-family house, a fabric store, a miniature rice field, a Mitsubishi plant, and an apartment complex. He wondered about Japanese zoning laws. Was it chaos or was he blind to whatever scheme prevailed? He suddenly thought of the measuring-instrument stores in Tokyo and Shizuoka. Japan organized itself differently. It wasn't like Europe, where a drugstore was a drugstore with a different word for it. You had to learn a whole new way of thinking. No wonder he felt so stupid here.

Although the four-way intersection at Monkey Video had no traffic, Alex waited until the pedestrian light changed the immovable red man into a blinking white man before he crossed. He wasn't going to risk his life in a crosswalk again, no matter how safe it looked.

The next stretch of road bordered a culverted creek, and insects ratcheted up their grating drones. A lone bee veered at him, twice the size of a bumblebee, with orange markings that looked like an electrical outlet. As Alex stood still, waiting for the bee to pass, an iguana darted out of the dry weeds at his feet and darted back. Sweat melted from his body as if he were a human Popsicle. He felt as though he had been dropped into some parched apocalpytic fantasy.

When he saw the racetrack ahead, he crossed the street to buy a drink from the vending machines in front. He put in a hundred-yen coin and pushed the button for Pocari Sweat. A riff of "Camptown Races" started, only to quit abruptly. Then frenzied pinball noises took over while red dots flashed. The machine spat out four coins along with the can of soda. Alex laughed. A combination vending/slot machine—and he had won! He popped the tab and stepped into the shade of the building as he drank.

A handful of motorcycles and scooters were parked haphazardly against the wall. Alex had somehow assumed the track was for dogs or horses, but now he considered it could be for bike races. Although there were no crowds or ticket takers today, the racetrack gate was open and the sound of motors echoed out from the stadium. Anything related to motorcycles might relate to Cody.

Cautiously, Alex ventured down the tunneled entry to the stadium. About thirty people sat in the front rows of stands that could hold ten thousand. Other small groups stood beside the track where three motorcycles churned the dirt of the oval. One motorcyclist broke away, gathered speed for a lap, and jumped off a ramp, cruising air for twenty feet before falling onto a second ramp. A scatter of applause rewarded this feat.

Alex leaned against the cement wall, watching. The spectators looked like a parody of gamblers with their tight pants, slicked hair, tattoos, even gold chains. One man, dressed in a wide-lapeled lemon-yellow disco suit, wore a straw fedora like the one Alex had lost to Haneda in the bar. The hat was too big for him; the brim covered the man's eyes and rested dangerously close to the glowing end of the cigarette he held near his ear. Alex looked again. The feathers were hot pink and purple in a red band.

This man was shorter than Haneda, but Alex struggled nonetheless to see if he could spot a scar on the man's lip. Another patter of applause and a cyclist came off the field, making his way through back-slappers toward the man in the yellow suit. Alex drew back into the shadow of the tunnel entrance. The rider turned his back to Alex as he pulled off his helmet. The man in the yellow suit stood up and punched the rider's shoulder, taking the fedora off his own head and placing it on his friend's helmet-compressed hair. When the rider turned around, waving his fingers in victory V's, Alex saw a white scar splitting his face from his teeth to his nose. And Haneda saw him.

Alex's heart began to pound. Haneda waved and ran up to Alex. "Hallo! Remember me?" He pointed to the straw hat, bowing and grinning. "You forgot hat."

Alex panicked. He'd had no time to prepare for their meeting, and this was mafia turf. "Uh, yeah. I did."

Haneda laughed and slapped Alex's back. "You were drunk, *ne?*" Haneda leaned closer and confided, "I was drunk, too." By his smell, he still might be.

"What are you doing here?" Alex asked.

"This is my job," Haneda answered. He mimicked motor-cycle handles. "Today is *renshu.*" His brow furrowed. "How you say *renshu*? *Renshu, renshu* . . . practice!" He bobbed his head happily at his own right answer. "On Tuesday, there is race. Will you come?"

"I . . . uh . . ." Alex stammered.

"And bring lucky hat." Haneda crowned Alex with the fedora.

The inner brim was greasy. Alex took it off and held it in his hand.

Haneda shouted to his friend in yellow, who came up and fixed curious dark eyes on Alex while Haneda chattered at length in Japanese. Alex attempted to bow, but the man in the yellow suit stretched out a hand. Alex shook it—and shook and shook. The man wouldn't let go, pumping for a full minute. Finally, Haneda spoke again to Alex. "*Buchou* invites personally to come Tuesday. To bring me luck."

"Thank you—*doumo*—Boo-cho-*san,*" Alex said.

The man in yellow exploded into laughter, showing three gold crowns on his upper jaw.

Haneda laughed, too. "*Buchou* is Japanese for 'boss.' My boss, not your boss. That is funny, *ne?*"

Haneda's boss pulled a business card out of a silver case and presented it to Alex with a bow, speaking Japanese.

"His name is Eguchi," Haneda translated.

Alex glanced at the card. He couldn't read the characters, but there was one line in English. That line read "Gone With The Wind."

Sixteen

箸 Dr. Ono's small waiting room was so full that Gaby could barely push open the door. Like most Japanese physicians, Dr. Ono saw patients on a first-come, first-served basis rather than by appointment. Mondays were usually crowded, so Gaby had arrived at eight o'clock.

Most of Dr. Ono's patients were elderly, their spines uniformly curled over. When Gaby entered, she looked down on liver-spotted scalps with tufts of white hair, and the backs of hands gripping canes, bones and veins showing through brittle, almost transparent skin. Mr. Eguchi said visiting the doctor was an old person's hobby. Maybe he was right, but it was that kind of comment that reinforced Gaby's decision to hide her chronic condition; it was hard enough to be sick without also being regarded as a hypochondriac. A handful of younger patients leaned against the white tile walls napping or reading, while toddlers crawled on the cement floor between their legs, screaming.

While some doctors were beginning to establish cooperative clinics, Dr. Ono followed the custom of owning his small clinic, staffed by himself, a nurse, and two clerks who ran the office and dispensed prescriptions. His office was near the university, above a bookstore whose signs claimed the parking lot spaces for Shizuyama Book Store customers only. Dr. Ono's patients were expected to park across the street in a field of bamboo stubble and cross the four-lane highway without a traffic light to help them. Gaby had yet to find out how his patients with canes managed that.

She squeezed her way through to the reception desk and dropped her national health care card through the slot in the window. *"Good morning, Ueda-san,"* Gaby said. As a regular patient, she knew Dr. Ono's staff well. *"How long is the wait?"*

Ms. Ueda ran her long pink fingernail down a stack of insurance cards. *"Maybe four hours. Maybe more."*

"Thank you. I'll return after lunch." Gaby hadn't figured out why she was the only one who left her card and returned later, instead of waiting all morning, cramped between coughers and sneezers, thumbing year-old comic books. Was this a favor they did just for her, an example of what Rie considered *gaijin* privilege? Or had it simply not occurred to anyone else to do it?

She went back home, dragged her futon out to the back balcony, and clipped it over the railing to air out. A few days of intense heat had doubled the size of her tomatoes and lightened them to a silvery green. She filled an empty juice bottle from the washing machine faucet and poured water on the plants, listening to the buckling plastic bottle make gulping sounds. The algae had dried into brown stains on the cement. She leaned her elbows on her futon and watched a pair of gray herons fly over telephone wires, past a persimmon grove and beyond the university buildings on the hillside, shrinking into specks in the bright cloud cover.

Through mundane moments of beauty like this, and maybe the edge that came from expatriate life as well, Gaby had grown attached to Japan. She couldn't claim to be "happy" here, but it would be hard to leave. She had an income higher than she could ever achieve in the U.S. She lived near the ocean. She lived in a city where trains ran on time and she could walk the streets alone without fearing for her safety. She was lonely, to be sure, but solitude had sharpened her senses, causing her to really observe what she saw and listen to what she heard. She had the luxury of taking a lot of time to think her thoughts.

A knob of pain tightened in her swollen abdomen, and Gaby breathed deliberately until it eased. She had to admit that she missed more things about America when she was in remission. When she was sick, she preferred Japan.

It wasn't just having health insurance, although that was an obvious advantage. In the States, she couldn't mention her disease without getting revulsion and disgust in response. She had to hide it or be judged by it. After she'd lived in Japan awhile, she'd come to realize it was an American notion to believe that every illness could be cured. It was American to blame a patient for not *wanting* to get well; Japanese had no trouble accepting the concept of incurable illness. The Japanese might be just as prejudiced against the less able, but it was a relief to have it out in the open. They didn't whitewash hardship by calling it "challenge." And they recognized the reality of illness by providing health care to all legal residents regardless of employment or preexisting conditions. Here, for the first time in her life, she had credibility.

She wondered if she could fit into America again. There would always be the Japan years of her life that no one could understand. Yet in Japan, there was no one to understand any part of her life. The only person she'd met in Shizuoka who even had the potential was Alexander Thorn, and after a few more weeks, he'd be gone.

Damn his kiss! Why had it been so intense? Was she pathetically starved for sex? Was she so miserably lonely? The answer was yes to both, but it was more than that. The truth was, she liked Alex. His being a terrible candidate for a relationship didn't prevent her from being attracted to him. She should read his book, *Why Love Fails*. She should be one of his case studies: *Women Who Move to Japan and Make Sure Love Fails*.

Gaby went back inside her apartment and called Rie, telling her she was sick and wouldn't be in the office today.

"It's the change of seasons," Rie said. *"Please take care of yourself."*

And that was all. Yes, Gaby loved Japan—no one to ask exactly how she was sick or to insist she take vitamins or get acupuncture. *"Thank you. Oh, Rie? Could you do me a favor?"*

"Of course. What?"

"Could you find out when we last ordered an inkan?"

"I'll ask Nishida-san."

"Well, I don't want him to know about this." Gaby wondered what she could tell Rie without revealing her suspicions about Nishida. *"It's a sensitive matter."*

"Ah?" Rie stretched the word as her pitch rose, an ascent to rival Mount Fuji. *"A sensitive matter? About an inkan? Is Nishida guilty?"*

Uh-oh. How could she explain this? *"It's very complicated."*

"I understand. You have no proof. I will help you secretly, like a spy!"

Rie's enthusiasm surprised Gaby. *"Are you sure you won't mind?"*

"I will enjoy it. Nishida is so RUDE!" Rie giggled with glee. *"What did he do wrong?"*

"I don't know if Nishida did anything," Gaby cautioned. *"So you must promise not to mention this to him or to Eguchi."*

"I promise, or I'll drink a thousand needles."

Gaby smiled at the Japanese expression, from a song schoolgirls sang when they made a friendship pact, linking little fingers. *"Thorn-san showed me a check he wrote to* Gone With The Wind *last year. It was deposited in Ninka Bank."*

"But our bank is Mitsubishi."

"Exactly. That's why I need to find out if our inkan was stolen."

"Nishida-san wouldn't have to steal it. He can use it whenever he wants."

"It might not be Nishida. It might be a thief."

"But a thief would need our account number as well as our inkan in order to steal our money."

Gaby was impressed at how quickly Rie caught on. If Eguchi had sent Rie to have dinner with Alex, everything would be different. Everything. *"It could be the thief isn't interested in steal-ing money from us, but from our customers. By using our company name* with his own account. You see, Thorn-*san* received a bill from Gone With The Wind, *but the bill had an address that wasn't ours."*

"Ah! Our company has an evil twin! Like a Time Man comic I read."

Could the villain have read the same comic book and copied the crime? You never know. Maybe the fictional solution was their solution. *"What happened in the comic?"*

"Time Man went to another dimension through his magic wristwatch and prevented the evil twin factory from starting up."

So much for fictional solutions. *"What if the thief created his own* Gone With The Wind *inkan, unlike ours, to use at Ninka Bank? Could we find out?"*

Rie was silent only for a second. *"We would have to investigate all the inkan makers in Shizuoka, and they might not reveal the names of their customers. I could try to sneak into their records. Like a heroine on a television drama!"*

"Rie, I don't want you to get in trouble."

"Yes, yes! Someone always says that before the excitement begins. This is great! Don't worry, no one suspects a girl with a limp. Because I am slow, people assume I am stupid. Japanese are so RUDE!"

Gaby now doubted her judgment, involving Rie in Thorn's mess, but it was too late to change her mind. *"Please be careful."*

"Someone is entering. I must hang up."

"Goodbye, Rie."

After Gaby hung up, she turned on the radio and put the earphones over her head. Over concert hall coughing and stray warm-up notes of violins, the program hosts were discussing the superiority of Bach over Beethoven. A sonorous male voice said, *"Beethoven's music is emotional, but Bach's music does not have this flaw. His music exhibits a greater maturity."* A female voice murmured assent. Women never said much on Japanese public radio except "ooh" and "ah."

Well, she, too, would exhibit a greater maturity and not succumb to emotion. She would be friendly but impersonal with Alex. She could do it. The past five years had taught her a lot about self-discipline.

When Gaby returned to Dr. Ono's office at two o'clock, there was only one patient waiting, a college girl in a denim jumper over a tan blouse. Her thick makeup failed to hide her acne, and her pale foundation gave her the look of a Kabuki actor. Her character would be the greedy concubine.

Ueda smiled at Gaby and motioned her to sit. But as soon as Gaby sat on the bench with the vinyl cushions, the nurse called her name. The college girl looked up, surprised that Gaby's name had been called before hers. Gaby took off her shoes in the antechamber and put on blue slippers with *Ono Clinic* written over the toes. The nurse held the curtain aside for Gaby to enter Dr. Ono's consultation room.

Dr. Ono stood at his desk, her medical file open in his hands. He was five feet four, three inches shorter than Gaby, so she always noticed the bald spot nesting in his short black hair before his round, serious face. Narrow eyebrows arched over black horn-rim glasses. He wasn't overweight, but his white smock fit snugly, molding to his slightly rounded stomach. *"Ah, Sutanton-san. What's the matter today?"*

"My ulcerative colitis has flared up, sensei."

Dr. Ono set her chart on his desk and took off his glasses. *"When did this start?"*

"Saturday morning."

He clucked his tongue. *"You shouldn't start having symptoms when my office is closed."*

Gaby laughed. Over the years, they had become almost friends. Unlike America, where her relationship to doctors had ranged from resigned to combative.

Dr. Ono motioned to the exam table. *"Over there, please."*

Gaby lay on the table and unbuttoned the front panel of her tan cotton skirt, pulling it down over her hips. This beat waiting in a room in a paper gown on a paper sheet any day—more straightforward and dignified. She left her underpants on.

Dr. Ono gently pressed the places in her abdomen that hurt most.

"Hard, isn't it? Your colon is inflamed." He listened with his stethoscope. *"Lots of goro-goro, too."* That was the Japanese phrase for intestinal rumbling. He listened to her heart and felt her glands. *"We should schedule a sigmoidoscopy. Meanwhile, I'll give you pink pills to take along with your orange ones."* He sat in his chair with his back to her while she buttoned up her skirt and took the chair by his side.

"You mean prednisone, right?" Gaby asked.

"Yes." Dr. Ono put on his glasses to write notes in her chart. *"And get plenty of sleep! This illness makes you very tired for a reason. Your body needs to rest."*

"I understand," Gaby said.

Dr. Ono shook his head. *"You understand, but you continue to go to work. You should get a husband to work so you can take care of yourself."*

Terrific. Now her own doctor was prescribing marriage. Definitely time to change the subject. *"By the way, where are heart transplant operations done in Japan?"* Seeing his astonishment at her non sequitur, she added, *"A friend of mine wants to know."*

Dr. Ono finished his notes with a sketch of her intestines, shading in the inflamed areas. He held his pen underneath his hand, like an artist. *"If your friend has a failing heart, I suggest he move to the United States. They have the best technology and experience. I would not recommend having the operation in Japan. Transplants are hardly ever performed here."*

"Oh, his interest is . . . intellectual. He has been studying Buddhism, how it forbids cutting a corpse and thus prevents organ donation, and so—" Gaby was glad when Dr. Ono interrupted.

"Yes, it's a pity. So many lives could be saved."

"Which hospitals perform the operation?"

"Tokyo Women's Medical College is the only one I know. It is the leader in the field. Of course, you understand it is not my field. I am a digestive man." Dr. Ono placed his pen in a bamboo holder

and closed the folder. *"You are having too many flare-ups lately. Schedule an exam this week. I will order Ueda-san to fit you in."*

"Thank you, sensei. Goodbye." She bowed and went through the curtain to take off the slippers and put on her sandals. Unlike office visits, procedures were by appointment. Ueda scheduled hers on Wednesday. After that was set up, she waited for Ueda to fill her prescription.

The pink prednisone pills came in a sheet with individual bubbles and thin foil backing to punch them out one at a time. This packaging kept Japan's humidity from eroding the tablets. Ueda put three sheets of pills into a white paper bag printed with a multitude of directions. Then she circled the appropriate directions and pushed them under the glass partition. *"Take care of yourself."*

Ulcerative colitis was one of the incurable illnesses accepted on the national health plan's official "hardship" list. This meant Gaby's treatment and medications had no co-payment. *"Thank you, Ueda-san."*

As Gaby unzipped her purse to put the pills in, the college girl spoke sharply to Ueda. *"When I see Dr. Ono, I must pay cash. Why does the gaijin get credit?"*

Ueda glanced at Gaby, who pretended not to understand what the girl said. Ueda whispered, *"She has special circumstances."*

"Because she is gaijin, right? Gaijin are treated better than Japanese," the girl complained. *"In Japan, no less."*

Gaby let the door fall shut behind her. She fanned herself with her purse as she went down the stairs. When she began to cross the street, a female voice called out her name. *"Sutanton-sensei! Matte, kudasai!"*

Gaby turned to see a girl in the doorway of Shizuyama Book Store, stuffing books into a canvas tote bag that read "Holland Nurse Extremity Team." The glare prevented her from seeing the girl's face. She stepped back to the curb and shaded her eyes. The girl had a shave-up haircut and a row of earrings. "Junko?"

"Hai." Junko ran up, nodding vigorously, earrings quivering. "I planned to call you. I have been guilty feeling."

Gaby used English to follow Junko's lead. "Why have you been feeling guilty?" Hard to break that teacherly rephrasing habit.

Junko stared at her shoes. Black canvas shoes with straps that opened two windows on the tops of her feet. "It concerns *Zone-san.*" A truck sped past, spewing grit from its high wheel wells.

Gaby put on her sunglasses to shield her eyes as the next truck roared by. "Do you want to go where it's quieter?"

"Sorry. I have to catch a bus to university soon." Junko turned her back to the road, and her hair lifted in the traffic wind. "I hope *Zone-san* is not upset with me."

"What is it, Junko?" Gaby asked gently.

"I did not tell everything." Junko blinked rapidly, as if she might cry.

"It's all right, Junko, whatever it is. Tell me, and free your heart." Gaby enjoyed the way she could say things like that in Japan and be taken seriously. No smug, ironic comeback. "I will take responsibility for telling or not telling Thorn-*san.*"

Junko looked up. "That morning, there was another person with the two men. He is Shizuyama student. He is with pressure—"

"Under pressure," Gaby murmured.

"He is under pressure and it is bad time for him. I did not tell *Zone-san* because I am afraid . . ." Junko went silent.

"It's okay to use Japanese," Gaby suggested.

"Sorry, I cannot in Japanese." She concentrated on finding the right words. "I am afraid this student might hurt himself. I am afraid *Zone-san* talk him and make him feel guilty. Already, he feels. And his grades are not so good. And if he can't finish at Shizuyama University, his family is not so understanding. Do you understand, *sensei?*"

"I think so." Gaby realized why Junko was struggling to use English; a foreign language made the words less real.

Junko rushed on. "But now, I feel pain of *Zone-san* and that is bad, too. I do not know how to do the right thing."

"Who is this student?" Gaby asked gently.

Junko hung her head. "Endo-*kun*."

"Kenichiro Endo? In my class last year?" Gaby remembered a slow, quiet young man who sat in the back row and slept with his head on the desk. Sleepy Mr. Endo said only "yes" or "sorry" in English. She had failed him, requiring him to repeat the class. McKenzie's class, this year.

Junko pleaded, "He is not bad person."

As another truck rattled past them, Gaby felt she'd failed him in more than one way. It was one thing to set a standard and another to push a student toward suicide. "I know. Maybe I could talk to him instead of Thorn-*san*."

Junko was visibly relieved. "It would be easier, I think."

"Thank you for telling me. It is important."

"About Fuji-*san*. I want to climb this Sunday for Cody's anniversary, but maybe *Zone-san* does not want." Junko kept a careful eye on her shoes, as if they'd walk off without her. She wore tan culottes and a black blouse, a step up from her peers, who dressed in denim and ankle socks. "Not when he knows I didn't tell him."

"He's a psychologist; he'll understand," Gaby reassured her. "He appreciated your invitation, I'm sure. I'll convince him to go."

Junko's face brightened. "Then *sensei* would come, too?"

"That would be difficult," Gaby said, meaning "impossible."

Junko checked her shoes. "If you do not climb Fuji-*san,* I cannot. It would not look right."

"I understand. You need a third person so that you and Thorn-*san* aren't alone." Gaby tried to think of a substitute chaperone. Rie? Her bad foot might prevent her from climbing. "Could you invite one of your friends?"

"*E . . . to . . .* there is problem."

Two motorcycles raced tandem in one lane and Gaby

edged farther back from the curb. Sweat broke on her neck and forehead. "Yes?"

"My friends don't speak English. It is hardship for them to be with English speakers." Junko's cheeks had flared bright red. "I am sorry, *sensei. Gomen-nasai.*"

"That's all right," Gaby assured her. "What if another *gaijin* went along? A man?"

"That is okay," Junko said. "But I don't know *gaijin* men. Only Cody."

Where a cute Japanese girl went, Lester would follow, even up a twelve-thousand-foot mountain. She felt uncomfortable, however, about putting Junko in a position of fending off advances from Lester. Would Michael be a better choice? Maybe all three men should go and dilute each other's effect. Assuming she could talk them into it. A white Toyota pulled out of the bookstore lot. Gaby had to step back to keep the car from running over her feet. "I'll try to find someone to go with you and Thorn-*san.*"

Junko looked dubious. "I am not so sure he will climb."

"Well, don't assume that. It would do him good, I think."

"I think, too," Junko agreed. A bus braked in front of them and the doors squealed open. "This is my bus. I must take. Goodbye!"

The bus honked twice and doused Gaby in exhaust as it took Junko away. Poor Junko, torn between protecting her classmate and helping her boyfriend's father. It wasn't easy to be Japanese. Difficult enough merely to cross the street.

Gaby was ready to retreat inside her apartment. From her safe haven, she could follow up on her two new leads: Kenichiro Endo and Tokyo Women's Medical College.

Seventeen

The university hotel breakfast was either broiled fish or fried eggs, both served with steamed rice, salad, *miso* soup, and green tea. Alex dreaded waking up and smelling the mackerel, but this morning turned out to be an egg day. He hoped that was a good omen—he needed one.

The night before, the clerk had put him into the same room he'd had before. His bags were exactly where he'd left them, nothing missing, and it almost felt like home. He had spent most of the evening staring at his telephone, fingering Eguchi's business card, unable to decide what to tell Gaby. If it weren't for Eguchi, Alex might have thought he had jumped to conclusions at Nature Squib Bar—that, in fact, Haneda's job was motorcycle racing and unrelated to Cody's death. He'd experienced Shizuoka traffic; it was insane. Accidents happened. But Eguchi was Haneda's boss, and Eguchi owned Gone With The Wind. Which could not be a coincidence.

He finished his egg and rice and went back to his room. He would have to think carefully before he broached this with Gaby. Eguchi's racetrack connection convinced Alex that her boss was *yakuza*. Did Gaby know? His intuition told him Eguchi had her completely fooled. Probably, on a subconscious level, Gaby wanted to be fooled, so she wouldn't have to face the fact that she worked for the mob. How could he expect her to help him go after her boss? The night before, he had lost her trust by kissing her. If he implicated Eguchi, she might reject him completely and close ranks on her boss's side.

Alex reminded himself of his resolve to locate the hospital that had treated Cody. Although yesterday's discovery at the racetrack had fired him up emotionally, finding the hospital was still the best plan. He would establish the connection between Cody's accident and Eguchi from the other side, the legitimate side. But he should get someone other than Gaby to help him.

He thought again of Professor Kaneko. It was worth a hot walk to the university to talk to him. In case Kaneko wasn't back from Tokyo, Alex could try to see Cody's Japanese teacher, Mrs. Sakura. Actually, he should try Mrs. Sakura first; unlike Kaneko, she had known Cody for a whole year. Plus, Gaby had assured him Mrs. Sakura's English was excellent. Mrs. Sakura might turn out to be a valuable ally.

Alex rummaged through the hotel's complimentary toiletry packet. There was a miniature tube of Etiquette Lion toothpaste, a flimsy plastic toothbrush, a cellophane shower cap, and a mysterious strip of paper marked Polish Boy that was too harsh for eyeglasses yet too fragile for shoes. He wondered why so many products bore bizarre English names, as if the purpose was to make fun of the English language.

Etiquette Lion tasted more like chalk than mint, but he let the foam linger, grateful to be using a toothbrush again after the weekend without. When he showered, he had to duck his head and hold the spray nozzle in his hand the whole time. No doubt the sprayer was intended only for rinsing off soap before you got in the tub. Still, Alex managed to shower with it, although the shifting of the one-piece fiberglass floor and walls under his feet hinted of potential hull breach.

This time he knew not to wear shorts on campus. He chose his thinnest short-sleeved madras shirt to go with his chinos and, despite the greasy rim, his straw hat.

A twanging sawing sound encased him the minute he stepped outside, as if the silvery sky were a metal roof over a stadium full of cicadas. The weeds beside the hotel's long driveway had opened out into large saucers of Queen Anne's lace. Their motionless shadows made the gravel look speckled. By the time Alex reached the road, his body felt cocooned in one of those plastic-wrapped burning wet towels at Skylark. He slowed his pace as rivulets of sweat clamped his shirt to his chest.

He turned on the street that led to the racetrack, but instead of reaching the racetrack, he came to a diagonal street crowded with small shops. Sidewalk bins, telephone poles, pedestrians, and parked cars all competed for space on each side of the road, narrowing traffic to one lane. Alex stood under the red-and-yellow-striped awning of a candy store and opened his map, looking for any street that cut a hypotenuse through the typical grid. He'd never take named streets for granted again.

"*Mushi-atsui, ne?*" An older man who might have been the owner sat on a stool behind barrels of peppermint and butterscotch hard candies. Missing teeth between dark gray ones indicated he ate plenty of his inventory. His head was wrapped in a wet checkered dish towel, no more than a few inches from an electric box fan.

Whatever his comment, it wasn't unfriendly. Alex approached him with his map to ask the way to the university. The fan flapped the map in his hand like a baseball card in bicycle spokes. "*Sumimasen*. University?"

The man ignored the map and pointed to the street. "*Hai. Basu wa asoko.*"

"*Basu?*"

The man got off his stool and gestured a pulling motion with his fingers, palm down. Confused, Alex followed him out to the sidewalk. The man pointed to a sign next to a bench, posting a schedule of times in black and red printing. "*Basu.*"

"Oh, a bus!" A nice idea, but he wouldn't be able to understand the candy store owner's explanation of which bus to take, much less when to get off. But instead of speaking to him, the candy man spoke to a stout woman using a tan plaid umbrella as a parasol, and when a large bus raced toward them and braked with a flourish in the middle of the road, completely blocking traffic, the woman collapsed her umbrella and motioned Alex to line up behind her at the back door. The relay system had kicked in again. Since he was lost, anyway, he had little to lose by accepting the role of the baton.

The stout woman took a slip of paper from a machine as she boarded the step. Through the windows, Alex saw passengers standing all the way down the aisle. He hesitated as the woman shoved two schoolboys, forcing them to stagger forward. The bus driver honked and the candy man physically pushed Alex onto the lowest step of the bus. The machine spat paper at Alex, and he took a slip as the woman had. The folding door tried to close, but his body blocked it. Everyone turned to stare at him. The driver said something over the loudspeaker, clearly annoyed.

Alex somehow crammed himself onto the second step and the doors shut. The bus took off with a jolt that rocked Alex off his feet. He reached for a ceiling strap, grabbing it over other passengers' fingers. The woman pointed to an electronic chart posted in the front of the bus, with boxes numbered from one to twenty and various numbers underneath them. With a ding, the lighted numbers changed: 240 under 1, 210 under 2, 190 under 3, and 170 under 4. The rest of the chart was unlit. Alex's white ticket was stamped with the number 4. What did this mean?

Alex hoped his current relay runner would guide him through paying and getting off. The loudspeaker delivered a taped announcement in a squeaky high voice. Soon, the bus stopped where two people waited to board. No one moved forward. Alex went limp and let the pressure on his back squeeze him tighter into the other passengers. His guide's shoulder was now embedded in his sternum. She wore a pumpkin-colored silk suit and gold button earrings. Her short black hair smelled like an orange lollipop. A teenager's cheek, ripe with acne, pushed into Alex's armpit the second he raised his arm for the ceiling strap. Finally, the bus turned up a hill and Alex recognized the buildings of the university. At this stop, the human throng slowly loosened into a line of disembarking passengers.

Umbrella woman showed him her ticket, also marked 4, and pointed to the chart again. She placed four coins in her hand: a hundred-yen, a fifty-yen (these were silver, with a hole in the middle), and two copper ten-yen coins. *"Wakarimasuka?"* She enunciated each syllable distinctly.

He must need to pay a hundred seventy yen. On the chart,

the box under number 4 still read 170. Aha! You matched your ticket number with the price listed when you got off. *"Hai, doumo. Doumo arigatō."* When he reached the front, he copied the woman and placed both his ticket and change in a clear slot. They fell onto a conveyor belt that rolled into the driver's till.

As soon as Alex stepped off, the woman's umbrella opened and spiked his nose. She set off at a brisk pace, unaware of what she'd done. Alex moved aside, rubbing his nose. Well, she'd got him to the university, faster than walking. Perhaps she could also show him to Mrs. Sakura's office. He hurried to catch up with her.

"Sumimasen."

"Hai?" She kept up her pace and Alex fell in step beside her.

Oh, to know Japanese. *"Sakura-sensei . . . ?"*

She said, without a trace of an accent, "I am Mrs. Sakura. Did you want to see me?"

Stunned by her perfect English, Alex wondered why she hadn't spoken to him in English earlier. She had held out on him, making such a lesson out of the bus ride instead of simply telling him. Sakura hadn't stopped walking, so Alex hastened to catch up to her again. "Yes. I'm Alex Thorn, Cody Thorn's father. I understand he was in your Japanese class last year?"

"All foreign students take my class." Mrs. Sakura's smile was a straight line extending between closed lips. "There is no escape."

"You knew him, then?"

"Of course. He was a good student. It was a shame he died." She said it as if it would be no loss if poor students died.

"Do you have time to talk to me?"

Mrs. Sakura shook her head, pointing to her watch. "I teach a class in three minutes. I must be on time so that I know which students are late. I deduct three points from their daily scores if they are tardy."

"How about after your class?"

"I have a committee meeting. What is it you wish to discuss? His failing grade? I had no choice but to give him an incomplete, since he didn't take the final exam." Mrs. Sakura opened the door to a brick building and Alex followed her inside. "Because he could not complete his work, it turned into an F after the following semester. I'm very sorry, but that is university policy. It couldn't be helped."

What kind of father would care about his dead son's grade point average? Alex remembered Cody's motto, "Expect to be surprised." No kidding. "I'm not concerned about his academic record."

Mrs. Sakura pursed her lips, continuing down the dark hallway.

"I want to know how he died, and what you knew about him."

"I only know that he died in a traffic accident." She pressed the elevator call button and the doors sprang apart at once, as if in fear of point deduction. "And you certainly knew your own son better than I did."

"I didn't know him in Japan." Alex stepped inside the elevator with her. "How did his classmates react to his death?"

She stabbed number three with her index finger and the elevator blasted upward. "He passed away during the first week of final exams. Classes had ended the week before."

Mrs. Sakura strode out of the elevator, Alex heeling after her. "Perhaps you can tell me who his friends were? You see, when Cody died, I hadn't seen him for nearly a year. I feel . . . incomplete."

She stopped at a classroom door. "I am very sorry about your situation, Mr. Thorn. Next week, I could visit with you, but now my schedule is so full, I restrict my sleep to four hours and eighteen minutes each night. If you like, you may sit in on my class. After attendance and the oral unit, I give a quiz. During the quiz, we can talk in the hall. I'm sorry, but that's the best I can do."

"Thank you," Alex said. "I appreciate it." Four hours and eighteen minutes of allotted sleeping time? IBM would love to hire this woman.

Mrs. Sakura closed the door behind them. The room had about fifty chairs attached to desks bolted to the floor in five deep rows parallel to a wall of frosted windows. Eleven students of various nationalities rose, bowed, and replied in unison to her Japanese greeting. Then they sat in the three front rows, in what had to be assigned seating. Alex chose the chair closest to the door. His knees wouldn't fit under the desktop, so he straightened his legs and slouched. His tennis shoes almost touched Mrs. Sakura's wooden lectern.

Mrs. Sakura opened a small black book and fired a question at the student who sat beside him, a lanky girl with bright orange hair and sandy freckles covering her thin face and arms. She answered quickly and shot a smile at Alex when Mrs. Sakura moved on to the next student, an Asian boy with sharp, pointed features. He hung his head and said nothing. Mrs. Sakura repeated her question. The student shifted his gaze to Alex's shoes. Mrs. Sakura asked a different question, slower. Still no response. She made a check mark in her book and shook her head slightly before moving on to a curly-headed boy whose baggy pants, torn T-shirt, and backward baseball cap advertised he was American.

Curly's answer caused the other students to giggle. Mrs. Sakura raised her pen and made two checks in her black book, to which Curly got up and knelt at her feet, bowing to touch his forehead to the linoleum floor in a manner that mocked ancient Zen homage. Alex would have guessed she'd be immune to class joker charm, but her lips twitched upward. She asked the original question again, and Curly's answer satisfied her enough to move on to her next victim.

After she went through the eleven students, she turned to Alex. *"Shumi-wa, nan desu ka?"*

He might have guessed he couldn't merely observe her

class. This question was obviously way below the level of the class, but Alex was clueless. "Sorry, *sensei*. I don't know how to answer that."

A few students made ominous "ooh" noises. Mrs. Sakura spoke in Japanese briefly and then in English to Alex. "English is *dame*—forbidden—during question and answer. Your punishment is three push-ups in front of the class."

Alex stared. Her prim face was actually serious. "I'm sorry. I didn't know English wasn't allowed."

Mrs. Sakura clucked her tongue. "Second offense. Now you must do six push-ups."

The students glanced at him sympathetically. Unbelievable. Was this a test of character? Was the right response to walk out of the room with dignity or indulge her sadism? But if he left, he lost his only chance to talk to her. Better to make a fool of himself before she doubled his punishment again. Alex untangled himself from his desk and lowered himself onto the black floor hands first, trying to keep his shirt and chinos suspended over dusty shoe prints and dirt smears. The first push-up told him he might not get through this. He did the next five shallowly to finish as fast as he could. Then he returned to his seat, rubbing his gritty hands and pursing his lips to conceal his rapid breathing.

Mrs. Sakura asked the redhead the same simple question.

Red answered, *"Shumi-wa . . ."* She pointed to Alex's shoes. *"Shumi-wa* tennis *desu."*

Mrs. Sakura turned back to Alex. *"Shumi-wa nan desu ka?"*

Alex spoke through clenched teeth. *"Shumi-wa* tennis *desu."*

Mrs. Sakura nodded and organized the class into pairs for dialogue. Since there were eleven students, she paired the redhead with Alex. The girl swiveled in her chair to face him.

"What was her question? What kind of shoes I wore?" Alex asked.

"No, no. She asked what your hobby is." The girl had a slightly British accent, but English was not her native language.

"*Shumi* is 'hobby.' *Wa* is a particle, to show the preceding word is the subject. *Nan* or *nani* is 'what,' *desu* is 'is,' and *ka* is a particle to make it a question. Verbs go at the end of the sentence, as in German. So literally, she said, 'Hobby, subject, what, is, question.'"

"You should be a teacher," Alex said.

"I hope to be. My major is linguistics, but there aren't many teaching positions for that in Germany, so if I can teach Japanese, it would help me obtain a job." She glanced at Mrs. Sakura, consulting with the silent boy beside her and his partner, Curly. "We should prepare our dialogue. It's worth ten points."

"I hope my incompetence won't lower your score," Alex said.

"No, she grades us separately. We just had a unit on comparisons. I could be a department store clerk, showing you this and that, comparing features. Whenever I ask a question, you say, 'I don't need it' and I'll try to sell you something else. Okay?"

"Fine! Except how do I say, 'I don't need it'?"

"Just one word: *Iranai.*"

"*Iranai,*" Alex repeated. "I think I can do that."

"Are you a new professor here?" Her eyes were Siamese-cat blue.

"I'm a visitor. I'm Alex Thorn, by the way. My son, Cody, studied here until last July. Were you here then?"

"No, I arrived in April. My name is Ingrid."

"Nice to meet you."

"How long is your visit?" Ingrid asked.

"I'm not sure. It looks like I'll be here awhile."

"Oh, you are lucky. Japan is wonderful. Everyone is so friendly and helpful! I'll feel very sad when I have to return to Germany."

Friendly? *Helpful?* Was she in an alternate dimension? Before Alex could ask for examples, Mrs. Sakura called them to perform their dialogue. It went well, thanks to Ingrid, who played up the role of an eager salesclerk. Alex acted resistant and said *iranai* each time Ingrid cued him. Even Mrs. Sakura joined in applause at the end. Curly and Silent used the same approach for their dialogue, Curly carrying the burden while Silent sneaked glances at the palm of his hand for his lines. As soon as the last pair finished, Mrs. Sakura slapped a quiz facedown on each desk. When she clicked a stopwatch, the students turned it over and began writing. Mrs. Sakura motioned Alex into the hallway.

"We have six minutes," she said.

Alex felt pressured to speak quickly. "It's like this. I received very little information about Cody's death. For my peace of mind, I need to know what happened. Can you tell me anything? His frame of mind? Anything he mentioned to you or the class? Any friends he hung out with? I'm a desperate man."

"That, I can see." Mrs. Sakura looked into his eyes, saying nothing for a while. She chose her words carefully when she spoke. "As for Cody, he was a good student, almost as good as Ingrid. Beyond that, I didn't know him. But perhaps I can help you in another way."

"Please."

"It is a matter of cultural sensitivity, I think," she said. "As an American, you are very direct. We Japanese are more polite; we discuss matters indirectly. It is our custom to communicate through mind-reading."

Alex protested. "But I'm not Japanese! How can I possibly be expected to read Japanese minds?" Or know her class rules, he thought.

"You must be patient. Most Japanese are not used to foreigners—we don't realize that Westerners don't think as we do. And, we are shy."

"So my style is the problem," Alex summarized.

"My first husband was American, like you. Japanese ways made him angry. His anger made people avoid him, which made him angrier. It was a vicious circle." Mrs. Sakura checked her watch. "I must return to my class. I am sorry about your situation, Mr. Thorn. Sometimes, one must accept what has happened without understanding it."

Mrs. Sakura bowed and slipped back inside the classroom door as her stopwatch pinged. Alex stood in the unlit corridor, absorbing her social analysis. He hoped he didn't make his patients feel as lousy as she'd made him feel.

Then he got upset with her. How dare she lecture him on sensitivity? She was the one who made him struggle on the bus when she spoke perfect English. She was the one who humiliated him in front of eighteen- and nineteen-year-olds, in a class he was merely visiting. She was the one who claimed to be too busy to talk to a former student's father except for six minutes during a test.

It wasn't as if he'd made a boorish tourist mistake. His son had left for Japan for a year of college study and returned in a body bag with his heart missing, and his son's teacher accused *him* of being rude for asking about it.

She was right about one thing; this was a matter of cultural insensitivity. Hers.

Eighteen

Alex marched out of the building, shoved open the door, and let it slam with a loud bang. A pair of students cringed and moved aside for him. "I hate Japan," he muttered. Then he said louder, "I hate this fucking country!"

Right then, he saw Professor Kaneko, no more than ten feet away, buying a drink from a vending machine. Alex hit his forehead with his fist. Why hadn't he looked around before cursing? He wondered if it was even possible to make amends for this blunder.

Kaneko scooped his can from the machine trough and glanced at Alex as if he just noticed him. "How do you do, Dr. Thorn? Miserable weather, isn't it?"

Kaneko had heard him say he hated Japan; he was obviously pretending he hadn't. Should Alex follow his cue and not apologize? Was that the polite—indirect—way of dealing with it? "It's certainly hot."

"And it will get hotter. August is known as the month of death because the elderly are especially vulnerable to the heat. The opposite of America, isn't it? I've been told your elderly die in the winter, when it's cold." Kaneko gestured to the vending machine. "Speaking of cold, could I buy you a cold coffee?"

Alex wished he had thought to pay for Kaneko's drink. "Thank you, but I should learn to do it on my own. My coin goes in here?" Alex dropped a hundred-yen coin in before Kaneko could insert his own. Alex pressed the button for what looked like a carton of orange juice. Nothing happened.

"They are out of mango drink. You may choose another."

Alex decided to try Peach Fizz. This time, a can plummeted into the gutter. "I'm glad I ran into you. I wanted to talk to you."

"Is everything all right at your hotel?" Kaneko asked.

"Oh, fine." No point telling him about being locked out over the weekend. "Actually, I wanted to thank you again for introducing me and translating my talk. You made it very easy for me. And for the map. I've used it a lot."

"It was nothing. You're quite welcome."

"And I wondered if I could get your advice about something."

Kaneko's face stiffened. "Nothing serious, I hope."

Once again, he'd pushed too hard, too soon. "I just . . . I don't know how to go about things in Japan. I'm always making mistakes."

"Perhaps it's not as bad as you think. Everyone knows you are not Japanese. If you forget to bow or take your shoes off, we make allowances." Kaneko motioned toward the cafeteria. "We might be more comfortable indoors."

"Good idea." Alex and Kaneko went inside and sat at the same table he'd used on Friday, next to the standing fan. Alex popped the tab of his Peach Fizz. It tasted like 7 Up mated with a Life Saver. It needed less sugar and more carbonation. He took several swigs, trying to find an indirect approach. "I don't know if you know about my son."

Kaneko's long hair immediately seemed more gray. He hesitated, and spoke reluctantly. "I heard. I'm so sorry. It must be a very hard loss."

"Death is never easy. It's not supposed to be, is it? But that's not what I wanted to talk about." Alex glanced at Kaneko, who looked notably relieved. "I wondered, would it be considered rude if I tried to talk to the doctor who treated my son? I've gathered Japanese are reluctant to discuss personal matters."

Kaneko chuckled, carefully peeling the foil tab off the teardrop-shaped opening of his canned coffee. "To your face, yes. But behind your back, there's no stopping them!"

English slang seemed weird coming from Kaneko, but he had, after all, spent a year at Berkeley. For the first time, Alex noticed Kaneko's glasses had subtle psychedelic tints on the thin wire frame. He also realized Kaneko was the only Japanese man he'd met with hair longer than his earlobes. Although he wore the requisite gray suit, white shirt, and shiny black tie, Kaneko might be a radical hippie by Shizuyama University standards. "What do you think? Would the doctor talk to me?"

"I can't see why he wouldn't. Does he speak English?"

"I don't know."

"There might be a language barrier."

Alex sighed. "And that's a big barrier. Even people who can speak English don't want to speak English." Oops. Another toad out of his mouth.

But Kaneko nodded in agreement. "We Japanese have an odd relationship with English. To old people, it is the language of the Occupation Army. To young people, it is the language they are forced to learn to get into college. It's become a sort of intelligence test among us. To other Japanese, if you speak English well, it looks like you are showing off. If you speak it poorly, you look stupid. It is a—what's your saying?—a no-win situation."

"I see," Alex said. Kaneko's explanation made much more sense than Mrs. Sakura's shyness excuse. "So speaking English isn't a matter of communicating in a different language. It's . . . it's posturing."

"Exactly!" Kaneko said. "Other professors are suspicious of me because they think my English is good. Of course, you know that's not true—"

"Your English is perfect," Alex objected.

Kaneko waved his praise away. "No, no, it's very bad. My field requires me to go abroad for research, and use English, but my Shizuyama colleagues would prefer me to study America from Japan, and write all my papers in Japanese. This year, I cannot travel at all because they have put me on committees that meet throughout the summer."

"To punish you? That is, to keep you in your place?"

Kaneko beamed. "Are all American psychologists so perceptive?"

"I wouldn't call myself perceptive." Deflecting praise was a contagious habit. "If the doctor doesn't speak English, what should I do?" Mrs. Sakura should be proud of his phrasing, his ambiguous "what should I do" instead of asking Kaneko if he'd translate.

"You could ask your son's sponsor to translate. In any event, it would be appropriate for him to accompany you."

"His sponsor?"

"All exchange students have a sponsoring professor. Your son's sponsor was Marubatsu-*sensei*. That's why he met you at the train station."

This was new information. "I didn't know that. That makes it difficult. You see, Marubatsu warned me not to ask favors of the university."

Kaneko smiled mischievously. Then he said, "Perhaps because he is the one who would be obliged to perform the favors."

That explained a lot. While Kaneko finished his cold coffee, Alex tried to imagine himself in Marubatsu's place. Would he begrudge assisting Japanese parents who came to Seattle after their son died? No, he wouldn't. Oh, he might be temporarily peeved if his schedule was busy, but he wouldn't brush off their pain and suffering. He would do what he could for them.

Kaneko pulled a cigarette package from his breast pocket and offered one to Alex. Lucky Strikes.

Alex shook his head and struggled again to be indirect. "Maybe I should ask another professor to help me."

Kaneko lit up and tucked his lighter back in his pocket. "That would be an insult to Marubatsu."

"Oh."

Kaneko pulled a white ashtray closer to him. English words in black letters on the edge read "Smokin' Clean and Tender Heart." "If you ask Marubatsu and he is too busy, you could try to find someone outside the university."

"Why outside the university?"

"It is not wise for university employees to appear to take sides against one another." Kaneko inhaled another drag. "Anyway, maybe the doctor himself speaks English. What is his name?"

"I don't know," Alex said.

"Do you have it written in Japanese?"

"It isn't written anywhere. You see, I never received a hospital bill." Alex stopped there. He did his best imitation of a neutral Japanese face.

The ash grew on Kaneko's Lucky Strike. At length, Kaneko said, "Well. That is unusual. I suppose it was a mistake in the post office."

"If so, Japanese hospitals are very"—Alex searched for a positive word—"lenient. American hospitals keep billing every month until they get paid."

"Here, too," Kaneko said. He smoked for a while, thinking. "Perhaps the insurance company paid for everything, so there was no bill."

"Cody was covered on my policy, and my insurance company was never billed. If he had Japanese insurance as well, wouldn't I have received a statement from them?"

"Yes, but if there was a postal error, they would not send you another."

Alex finished his Peach Fizz. Kaneko had offered him a reasonable explanation—if it weren't for the altered bill from Gone With The Wind. He wondered how to indirectly broach that subject. He decided to use Gaby as a transition. "Do you know Gabriela Stanton?"

"I know her name. She used to teach at the English department."

It occurred to Alex that maybe he could help Gaby find out why she'd been fired. Kaneko might tell him, a passing stranger, what he'd be too polite to tell Gaby to her face. "Why did she leave?"

Kaneko leaned back in his plastic chair. "I don't know."

"Marubatsu said she was fired around the time of my son's death." After a pause, Alex added, "And now she works for the funeral company that sent Cody's body home. I wonder if there's a connection."

Kaneko shook his head. "I'm sure that is mere coincidence. There were many rumors about her, of course, but nothing bad to my way of thinking. I also heard she was a good teacher. Some of my students were quite fond of her."

"Then why was she fired?"

Kaneko checked his watch and stabbed out his cigarette. "As I said, I don't know. There was gossip about misconduct in her personal life, which, frankly, means nothing to me, but Shizuyama is a conservative university."

"You can get fired for your personal life?" Alex asked.

"Oh, yes. Teachers are regarded as moral examples for students twenty-four hours a day. Unmarried teachers are expected not to have overnight visitors. It's not like Berkeley." He smiled knowingly as he stood and pushed his chair under the table. "I am afraid I must leave or I will be late for a committee meeting. Marubatsu is more devoted to his other job, as a priest, but he is not so bad a person. Talk to him. He is responsible for helping you."

"I'll do that. I really appreciate your advice." Alex walked out with him. He'd be pushing his luck to bring up Gone With The Wind. He'd have to be patient: save it for another conversation. At the door, Kaneko stopped Alex from throwing his empty can in a wire trash barrel.

"That is for paper trash only. Cans go in the blue bin, to recycle."

"Oh, thank you." Alex pushed in the hinged lid of the blue plastic container and heard a clank as his can hit others. He didn't even know how to throw away trash in this country. He shook hands with Kaneko. "I hope your meeting goes well."

Kaneko scrunched his face. "Japanese meetings are very long and very boring. I think they only exist for us to practice *nintai*. That is to say, endurance. Noble suffering."

Alex laughed. "I've been in meetings like that. Good luck, then. Thanks again."

"You're welcome. Goodbye, Dr. Thorn."

Alex watched Kaneko walk away, blending into a crowd of students. It had been his most productive conversation. Now he understood why Gaby was so paranoid about people seeing him at her apartment. The double standard was alive and well in Shizuoka. He was beginning to perceive Japan as an elaborate strategic game, based on invisible obligation ledgers, all interactions conducted in code and swathed in ambiguity. It was no place for a stranger who didn't know the rules.

Alex trudged up the hill toward Marubatsu's office. The noise of the cicadas seemed to drill the heat into his head. Under a cherry tree, a dark mat of rotten cherries coated the path. Before he knew it, Alex slipped on a cherry pit and grabbed at the lowest tree branch to keep from falling. When he steadied himself, his hand hurt. He saw a patch of bark shreds embedded in his palm. He couldn't get them out without a needle. He flexed his hand. It wasn't injured, but the splinters caused pain when he moved his thumb. He kept his eyes on the path the rest of the way up the hill.

His first stop inside the U-shaped building with the black floors was the water cooler. He couldn't get over how good the water tasted. Then he took the elevator to the second floor. The window above Marubatsu's door showed light behind it, but there was no answer to his knock. Alex pressed his ear against the door. He didn't hear the sound of television. He tried the handle: locked. He walked down the hall and found room number 245, McKenzie's office, at the end of the corridor. His office was dark, but Alex knocked anyway. No answer. Perhaps everyone was at lunch.

As he stood in the hall, a few students passed by, staring at him curiously. Then more, followed by a stampede of students pushing through the corridor to stairs at the end of the hall. Alex pressed his back against the wall and waited. When the throng eased, he saw Marubatsu unlocking his office, and stepped forward. "Marubatsu-*sensei*."

Marubatsu turned his head. His wide-set eyes registered no response to seeing Alex. "How are you, *Zone-san*?"

"Fine, and you?"

"*Ng.*" He entered his office and placed a folder of papers on his desk. "I asked my students to recite the first sentence of *The Raisins of Wrath*. No one could do it! Not one. When I was a student, I memorized the first paragraph of every American novel I read. Today's students are very lazy and spoiled. It is a shame, isn't it?"

Alex hesitated, then lied. "It certainly is." He'd never seen the value of memorization.

"You know the first sentence, don't you?"

"No, I don't." Why was everyone determined to make him a student?

Marubatsu didn't bother to hide his pleasure. "So Americans are no better."

"I'm sorry to bother you again so soon—" Alex began.

"I was going to call you," Marubatsu interrupted. "I am trying to gather all of the university papers regarding Cody-*kun*. I was able to copy his medical file. I have it somewhere." He lifted various folders on his desk.

So that was why Marubatsu had asked Michael for Cody's health record: to help him get information. Everything made more sense today. "I appreciate the trouble you've taken."

"Ng." Marubatsu handed him two sheets of paper. "You can keep this."

"Thank you." Alex looked at the form. "This is in English. Where's the copy in Japanese?"

Marubatsu blinked twice, slowly. "You cannot read Japanese."

"But I thought—" Alex realized it might be a mistake to divulge he knew Gaby had translated Cody's medical history. "I would think it would have to be in Japanese to be of any use. To doctors and nurses here."

"A Japanese version is with his admission file. It is locked up in the president's office."

"Do you suppose the president would release his admission file?"

Marubatsu's jaw hardened. "There are university rules."

Alex read what he already knew: that Cody's blood type was AB, that he had no allergies, illnesses, or current medications. What was Marubatsu's point in giving him this? It told him nothing about Cody's health after arriving in Shizuoka. He looked again. "This is strange."

"What is strange?"

"I don't see the note about not donating organs." Alex felt his throat thicken. "Cody didn't want to donate his body parts when he died."

Marubatsu sucked in a sharp breath. "You say he wrote a note?"

"Yes. It was important to him. Why isn't it here?"

"Perhaps Cody-*kun* forgot? Students are very forgetful."

"No, it was on this form. I saw it."

"You have seen this form?"

Alex recognized it was time for another lie. "At home, in the States."

Marubatsu took the paper from Alex's hand and studied it. He ran his finger over the edge of the page. "I don't see anything."

"I know. That's what's strange."

Marubatsu shrugged and handed it back to Alex. "Well, this is a copy of the original. If it is not here, it is because Cody-*kun* did not write it."

"I know he did," Alex insisted.

Marubatsu pressed his palms together, clasping each hand with the other. "I have only fifty minutes for lunch. Was there something else you wanted to say?"

Alex drew a deep breath. "Who is the doctor who operated on Cody? I'd like to talk to him."

Marubatsu said nothing. His dark eyes focused on a point slightly beyond Alex's shoulder. "I don't have that information."

It was Alex's turn to cast a blank look. "I don't understand. As my son's sponsor, didn't the doctor call you for permission to operate?"

Marubatsu sucked in another sharp breath. Alex could hear the air whistle between his teeth. "Perhaps you are not aware that I am a Zen Buddhist priest."

"I know that."

Marubatsu pointed at Alex, his forefinger close to Alex's nose. "In Japan, you do not doubt the word of a priest."

Alex stepped back involuntarily. "I'm not doubting you, I'm asking you. Did you talk to the doctor? You wrote me the letter—"

"I wrote what I was told. There is nothing more!" He wheeled around and busied himself with papers on his desk.

Alex stared at the back of Marubatsu's shaved head. Of all possible responses, he hadn't anticipated anger. "Who told you about Cody's accident?"

"The university." Marubatsu opened a briefcase and stuffed folders inside.

"*Who* in the university?"

Marubatsu turned around. His face was composed, his round chin held high. His voice was now calm and patronizing. "Perhaps you are seeking someone to blame for your son's accident. As a priest, I cannot encourage that pursuit. We Japanese are strong. We Japanese accept our fate."

It was the "we Japanese" that did it. Alex deliberately moved forward to intimidate Marubatsu, while maintaining a conversational tone. "We Americans are strong, too. We're brave enough to seek the truth. Who told you what happened to Cody?"

Marubatsu blinked several times and pushed a smile into his lips. "The department secretary. Are you satisfied now, *Zone-san,* or will you try to bully her? She will be frightened easily, by a big male *gaijin.* She doesn't speak English."

Alex shook his head and addressed the ceiling of acoustic tiles punched with tiny holes. "I don't want to bully anyone. I don't want to argue. All I want is a chance to talk to the doctor who tried to save Cody's life. Is that against Japanese tradition?"

Marubatsu held his office door open. "I will talk to the secretary and call you."

"I want to be there, too." He didn't know Japanese, but he knew body language. He could sense whether or not Marubatsu was mistranslating.

"No. You had better not."

Alex clenched his teeth. "Why not?"

"Because of misunderstandings like today. You do not understand our ways. I am forgiving. I can chalk it up to cultural differences, but not everyone has the tolerance of a Zen priest." Marubatsu pointedly looked at his watch. "Now, you will leave. I must eat before my next class."

"I'll be in touch."

As he was going out the door, Marubatsu called out, "By the way, you should have a doctor look at your hand."

Alex glanced, surprised, at his hand with the cherry bark splinters. It had puffed up pink around the abraded area. "It's not serious."

"It might be. You should be more careful." Marubatsu shut his door. The lock clicked.

Nineteen

After hours on the phone, Gaby found out Tokyo Women's Medical College had no record of Cody Thorn receiving treatment there, or any record of any heart operations on July ninth of last year, or the eighth or tenth, either. Several calls to the Endo family were answered by a machine, and she chose not to leave a message. She didn't look forward to telling Alex either piece of news.

She didn't have the energy to help him through this; it would be hard enough just to go to work tomorrow. She couldn't take another day off. Sick leave came out of her vacation days and she had only three left to last through September. If she called on Yamamoto tomorrow, she could pretend her sales pitch took all morning and not show up at the office until two o'clock. On the other hand, bathroom access on a strawberry farm was not guaranteed, and an unexpected burst of diarrhea would definitely lose the sale. If she worked in the Gone With The Wind office, she'd be within range of a toilet, but would have to stay from nine to six, breathing Nishida's cigarette stench all the while.

Maybe, she thought, Mr. Eguchi would allow her to clock her time spent on Alex. After all, Alex was business, despite the personal detour they had almost taken. This morning's phone time and Saturday's trip to Cody's boardinghouse added up to a full day's work.

She called Gone With The Wind. *"Rie-san? It's Gaby."*

"Oh, good. I have news. Are you feeling better?"

"About the same. I need to talk to Eguchi."

"Eguchi is at the racetrack."

Gaby was surprised. *"The racetrack? Did he tell you that?"*

"No. But my cousin works at the track. She sees a lot of Eguchi."

"And all this time I thought he went to a coffee shop."

"Oh, he does. But on race days, he is at the track. He is sponsoring one competitor today, and another in tomorrow's race."

Another likeness between America and Japan; the secretaries know more than anyone else. *"Are you alone in the office? Can you talk?"*

"Yes, and I have news. We haven't ordered a new inkan since the company began."

"Wow! That was fast work."

"I enjoyed having something to do for a change. But that's not all I found out. Your idea was correct. A Gone With The Wind inkan was made at a custom-order shop owned by a Chinese man, Wang."

"Rie-san, you're amazing. How did you find out?"

"It was easy. I called inkan makers listed in the phone book, saying I was the new accountant at Gone With The Wind and wished to order another inkan. If they said they had no account for us, I said I was so sorry for my ignorant mistake."

"And Wang had an account?"

"Yes! He made a Gone With The Wind inkan last September. He faxed me a photocopy of the stamp. They always keep a printed copy, for future orders."

"Good job! Does it match our inkan?"

"I don't know. I never handle our financial documents."

It occurred to Gaby that Nishida shouldn't see the copy of the new *inkan*. *"Don't let anyone in the office see that fax. In fact, could you bring it to me?"*

"I will stop at your house after work," Rie said. *"I am eager to meet this Mr. Sexy Voice."*

"You mean Alex?"

"So he is Alex now, not Zone-san?" Rie teased.

"I call you Rie, not Sato-san. It's no different."

"But he is a man. And you are a woman."

"He's grieving for his son. He's not interested in women right now." Gaby was confident this was the case. Alex's kiss had come out of confusion and frustration—whenever men didn't know what to do, they tried to have sex. She'd been the only woman around at the time. Her tough luck.

"Oh, he's given up on love! That's so romantic!"

"Only in the movies, Rie. At any rate, Alex won't be here when you come." Gaby deliberately changed the subject. *"How long do you think Eguchi will be out?"*

"I don't know. Maybe for the rest of the day."

Gaby shifted the phone to her other ear. *"Give me your opinion. I spent most of the weekend helping Alex. Do you think Eguchi would credit me with compensation time for that?"*

"I think," Rie said, *"it depends on how his rider does in the race."*

Rie was smart. Gaby hoped she would be discreet. *"I'll check in later. When I call, could you let me know if he won? With a code word, perhaps?"*

"Oh, yes!" Rie's voice rose with delight. *"It's so much fun to work with you! Let's see. If he is in a good mood, I will say* ice skates, *and if he is not, I will say* fever."

Gaby smiled. Obviously, Rie was still engrossed in her *Little Women* comic book. *"Those words won't sound natural if Nishida is listening. How about* blue file *for good mood and* red file *for bad mood?"*

"Ah, so ka. That is better. I can learn a lot from you."

"And likewise. You're an inspiration, Rie. Goodbye."

So an *inkan* had been made last September. The very month she had been hired by Gone With The Wind. Why did the timing link with hers? Was she being set up? There was no conceivable motivation for anyone to do this.

Gaby looked at her phone. She should get the call to Alex over with, practice being friendly yet impersonal. Report the news, wish him good luck, and hang up. That should be easy. So why was she staring at the phone?

When it rang, her heart lurched. "*Moshi*—hello?"

A pause was followed by a Japanese man's voice. "You say hello. Hello, hello?" It was Mr. Eguchi.

He was calling from a bar; Gaby heard voices in the background and a recording of a Japanese folk song. She wondered if he was in a blue-file or red-file mood. "*What can I do for you?*"

"*Will you be feeling well tomorrow?*"

She knew she wouldn't be, but if she said so, he might insist she take another day off and she couldn't afford to do that. "*I hope so. Why?*"

"*I have a special project for you.*"

What she least needed. "*What is it?*"

"*A goodwill campaign. I want you to come to the races with me and Zone-san. You will bring Zone-san and meet me there.*"

"*I don't understand. You met Thorn-san? When?*"

"*Yesterday, at the track. He is the friend of a racer, Haneda. I like this Zone. He is not what I expected.*"

There were more important questions to ask, but Gaby couldn't resist. "*What did you expect?*"

"*Bossy. Superior. Rude. You know, a typical American. But Zone seems sincere. I am confident he will soon understand we are honorable and unrelated to his hardship. Maybe he will win some bets. We can work it out.*" In order to speak a sentence in English, Mr. Eguchi had to have drunk a quart of beer. His English was restricted to Beatles song lyrics; but he used them well. Gaby believed he was much smarter than he presented himself to be.

Gaby decided this was a blue-file opportunity. "*Buchou-san,*" she began. It never hurt to use honorific titles when asking for something. "*I don't know how to classify my hours with Thorn-san on my time sheet. How should we handle this?*"

"*Ng.*" He said nothing more and in the background, the folk song floated through the telephone line. Someone clapped out of sync with the rhythm.

The pause indicated Eguchi regarded Alex as a volunteer project. She tried to think of a way to retreat from her request.

"Nishida won't be happy," Eguchi finally said, *"but I'll pay you a week's wages if you just take care of Zone. After all, you sold our first moon package, ne? You keep Zone happy, and I'll keep Nishida happy,* okay?"

"Thank you very much, Buchou-san." She caught herself bowing into the telephone receiver as the line disconnected.

She stared at the phone, knowing she should call Alex next. She silently rehearsed opening lines. Hi, this is Gaby, with my new impersonal tone. Hello, Alex, do you want the bad news or the bad news? Hi, Alex, aren't I doing well pretending you never kissed me?

This time, she was startled by the doorbell. She checked her watch. Rie must have left work early in order to deliver the fax. She hadn't heard Rie's moped brake with its unique squeal, but, after all, she'd been on the phone. She decided she could answer the door in shorts and a thin T-shirt for Rie.

The bell rang again. Gaby slid the chain off and opened her door.

Alex. In a straw hat with pink and purple feathers in a red band. Sweat on his face, shopping bag in his hand. "May I start apologizing inside?" he asked.

What could she say? It was her job to keep him happy this week. "Come in."

"I'm sorry for not calling first," Alex began, taking off his shoes in the entry. "I'm sorry to risk being seen at your apartment. I'm sorry to impose on you once more. I'm sorry I—"

"Stop! You might feel less sorry after you hear my news."

His blue eyes flicked up anxiously. "Bad news?"

"Well, good and bad." She gestured him to the table while she took out two glasses and filled them with ice. She glanced at the clock; she had an hour to talk to Alex before Rie might come. She didn't want Rie to find Alex with her. "Care for some iced barley tea?"

"Barley?" Alex made a face.

"It's good. Try it."

"I brought wine." Alex pulled a bottle of red wine from his shopping bag.

"I'm not drinking for a while," Gaby said. "But you go ahead."

Alex set the bottle down and wiped his sweaty forehead with the back of his hand. "I'm not drinking, either. It was a present for you. Another mistake. Do you think I have any chance of doing something right?"

Gaby remembered her own difficult initiation to Japan and felt sorry for him. "I think you already have. Eguchi likes you. He gave you the ultimate compliment. He said you weren't a typical American."

Alex shook his head. "You're kidding. He likes me?"

"Yes." Gaby poured tea from a plastic pitcher and brought the glasses to the table. "He told me he met you yesterday. With your 'friend' Haneda?" She sat and tugged at her shorts to cover more of her legs. She hoped Alex wouldn't notice she wasn't wearing a bra under her shirt. "At least we've found a benign explanation for Haneda's job."

"Maybe not. Did you know Eguchi sponsors bikers in these races?" Alex asked.

She didn't like the tone of his voice, as if he were testing her. "I learned that from our Wonder Secretary, Rie. Before today, I thought he spent his hours away from the office at a coffee shop." She hurried on. "Rie discovered another Gone With The Wind *inkan* was ordered last September. She's bringing over a faxed copy this afternoon."

Alex grimaced.

"Alex?" Gaby inquired. "That's the good news. Look happier."

He shook his head, pointing to the glass. "This tastes like liquid cereal."

"Oh. Should I get you some water?"

"I can get my own." Alex got up, dumped his tea into the

sink, and rinsed his glass. "Didn't you say racetracks are owned by *yakuza*?"

"Y-yes."

Alex came back with his water. "Doesn't that make Eguchi a *yakuza*?"

Gaby didn't know what to say. She thought of Eguchi's flashy clothes, his American car; they were *yakuza* fashion. She thought of Gone With The Wind's liberal hiring policy; that, too, was *yakuza* style. And the funeral business itself, like love hotels and *pachinko* parlors, lurked in the gray edges of respectable commerce. And Nishida kept double books. Lester had been telling her Eguchi was *yakuza* all along. She hadn't wanted to believe him because she liked Eguchi, but now she couldn't find a loophole to disassociate her boss from the mob. The racetracks were owned by *yakuza*. They wouldn't let anyone who wasn't one of them sponsor a racer. "Maybe he's an exception," Gaby said feebly. Reaching for her glass, her hand slipped and tea splashed over the rim.

Alex's blue eyes fixed onto hers. "Maybe you should quit this job."

Gaby looked at the puddle of spilled tea on the table. The room was too quiet. She longed to turn on the radio, to have something else in her head besides these words and thoughts. "You sound like Lester."

Alex sighed. "I didn't understand at first, but I really didn't mean to drag you into . . . I wish you weren't involved with Gone With The Wind. I care about you."

Gaby nearly swallowed wrong. Care about her? She cleared her throat. "Well, I'm not your responsibility. Eguchi made you my project this week. Tomorrow, I'm to accompany you to the races. Whether you like it or not." She escorted her empty glass to the counter and brought back a sponge.

"Naturally, I'd like it, but—"

"Good, because it's settled." Gaby wiped the table vigorously.

"You can't ignore this," Alex said. "If you confronted Eguchi, would he admit—"

"I wouldn't confront him," she cut in. "That would be the worst approach."

"You sound like Mrs. Sakura." His tone of voice was bitter.

Gaby hastened the change of subject. "You saw Mrs. Sakura today?"

"And how. She made me attend her class, and then made me do push-ups on the floor. A punishment for speaking English."

"No!"

"Yes! She lectured me about my evil American ways. But she couldn't help me with Cody. She claimed to know nothing about his life outside of class." Alex took a sip of water. "Look, Gaby, we've got to talk about Eguchi."

Gaby heard a motor and squeak of brakes. Then footsteps on the metal stairs that could only be Rie, followed by her doorbell. "Rie's here," she announced, a little out of breath. Saved by the bell.

Twenty

Rie's thick white cycle helmet made her look like a visitor from outer space. She pulled it off, freeing a globe of black ringlets, a permanent wave style called "macaroni." She kicked off her shoes in the entry and stepped up into the main room shod in pink ankle socks. Her bad foot, larger than the other and with a bulge at the ankle, stretched out the pale blue hearts printed on the cuff. In Shizuoka, it wasn't unusual to wear ankle socks with dressy office attire, such as Rie's navy blue skirt suit and white silk blouse. Spotting Alex, Rie's lips formed her signature smirk. *"So this is Mr. Sexy Voice."*

"I had no idea he would stop by," Gaby answered.

"What a surprise." Rie's voice oozed disbelief. *"He is handsome for a Big Nose, isn't he?"*

Gaby switched to English. "Alex, this is Rie Sato, a.k.a. Wonder Woman."

"Nice to meet you." Alex reflexively put out his hand, then withdrew it and bowed.

"Nice tomato," Rie said slowly, bowing deeper. She turned her curious face to Gaby. *"What did you say about* Wonder Woman*?"*

"My description of you," Gaby said.

Rie giggled, flushing. *"I can't even walk, much less fly."*

"But you searched an entire city to find an illegitimate inkan! In one day, no less. You brought the fax?"

Rie slung her backpack-style purse off her shoulders. She limped over to the table, unbuckled the leather strap, and took out an envelope, which she handed to Gaby.

Gaby passed it on to Alex. "Does it match the stamp on your check?"

Alex opened his briefcase and got out his copy of his canceled check. "It looks the same to me."

Gaby nearly snatched it out of his hands. "Aha! This is *not* our official *inkan*! Gone With The Wind isn't guilty!"

Alex held up his hand. "Not so fast. Eguchi is still a *yakuza.*"

Uh-oh. If only Alex had said "mobster" or "gangster" instead of using the Japanese word. Rie had heard "Eguchi" and *"yakuza"* in the same sentence. Gaby wondered how to keep Rie from getting alarmed.

But Rie laughed heartily. *"Is he afraid of yakuza?"*

"Well . . ." Confused by Rie's reaction, Gaby said simply, "Yes."

"Tell him no problem," Rie said. *"Eguchi has a high position. My father and brother are in the same family, so they know Eguchi*

is a good man. Zone-san has nothing to worry about. Eguchi will protect him."

Alex looked back and forth between Rie and Gaby. "She said no problem?"

Gaby, stunned by Rie's declaration, did her best to translate it for Alex. Rie nodded her head throughout, a curly black poodle, happy to reassure him. Gaby watched Alex's expression darken and then close off. He took the fax from Gaby and stared at it, saying nothing.

"I didn't know you—any of you—were yakuza," Gaby faltered.

Rie smirked. "How else would I have gotten this job?"

Gaby thought for a second. "So Nishida is also—"

"Everyone except you," Rie said cheerfully. "But you are gaijin. Gaijin always get special treatment."

"I wonder why I was hired," Gaby murmured.

Rie took it as a question. "For clients who do not like to talk to yakuza. Everyone knows gaijin can't be yakuza. Mr. Eguchi was smart to hire you. He even won a bet on you."

"A bet?" Her self-esteem plummeted. "A good bet or a bad bet?"

"Oh, good, good! Mr. Eguchi couldn't be more pleased. You are his number-one salesman. The bet was that you couldn't make a sale in your first month. The boss won five hundred thousand yen thanks to you." Rie must have read astonishment in her face, but misjudged the reason. "You wonder how I know this, since I was hired after you? My cousin told me. In fact, the bet gave me the idea to ask Mr. Eguchi for a job. He is a gambler. Who better to take a chance on a stupid lame girl?"

"You're smarter than all of us," Gaby said, relieved to focus on Rie instead of herself. "You are never to call yourself stupid again, Wonder Woman. Understand?"

"Understood." Rie giggled. She gestured toward Alex, who still stared at the fax on the table. "What's wrong with him?"

"A lot," Gaby said. "This fax is proof he paid a swindler to ship his son's body home. That is hard news to handle."

"*I suppose so.*" Rie tipped her head to regard him. "*I guess you are right—he's not romantic. He doesn't seem at all interested in you. Too bad, desu ne?*"

Gaby faked disinterest. "I really don't care."

"*Maybe I'll take him, then. What is his blood type?*"

"*Does it matter?*"

"*I think he is type B. Type B men are emotional and moody. They do not respect the social order. You are type A like me, right? That is the most common type in Japan. You pay attention to detail and co-operate. But type A women shouldn't marry type B men.*"

Gaby perceived no need to tell Rie she was, in fact, type O. "*Why is that?*"

"*The children might be type AB. That is bad, because AB children are not afraid of death. They are, as Eguchi would say, big dreamers. I think Eguchi himself is type AB, don't you?*"

Alex looked up from the fax. "What are we talking about? Algebra?"

"I'll explain later," Gaby said. She remembered Cody's blood type was AB. Maybe he had been unafraid of death. Too big a dreamer.

"*What did he say?*" Rie asked.

Gaby reminded herself never to apply for a job as an interpreter. "*He wants to thank you for your help.*"

"*Oh, it was fun! I would rather be a spy than a secretary!*"

"I'm lost," Alex stated. "Completely lost. What did she say?"

"I'll tell you later," Gaby said. Then she mock-translated for Rie. "*He can't thank you enough. He doesn't know how he can repay your generosity.*"

Rie raised her eyebrows flirtatiously. "*Maybe instead of my romantic boyfriend, he could be my English-practice boyfriend?*"

"*Do you want me to translate that?*" Gaby asked.

"*I don't think so.*" Rie checked her watch. "*I should go.*"

"*I appreciate this, Rie,*" Gaby said, following her to the entry. "*Now that we've matched the inkan, we need to find out who ordered it from Wang.*"

Rie sucked in a breath. *"That is difficult. Wang assumes we ordered it."*

Gaby didn't know what to say. *"A spy's job is not easy."*

"Ah, so ka. I must develop a plan!"

"That's your next mission," Gaby added.

"I'll report tomorrow," Rie promised happily.

"Thank you very much!" Alex called out. "Goodbye!"

"Bye-bye!" Rie said. She strapped her purse on her back, kicked on her shoes, and picked up her astronaut helmet. She winked at Gaby as she limped out the door. *"After I leave, try to seduce him."*

"Sayonara, Rie-san," Gaby replied. She chained the door in Rie's wake.

"Care to fill me in?" Alex asked.

Gaby told him everything, except the joke about Alex becoming Rie's boyfriend.

"How do you feel about the *yakuza* revelation?" Alex used the voice of a sympathetic shrink. To his credit, he wasn't saying "I told you so."

"Stupid. Really stupid. I knew there were rumors about Nishida. And Lester kept telling me all along, damn him. I hate admitting he was right."

"How did Lester know?"

"Simple association; if it's dirty work, it's mafia work." Gaby heard Rie's moped motor start up and putt-putt into the distance. She longed to turn on the radio to some music, but it seemed rude while Alex was there.

"I can't understand why you ever applied for this job."

"This is Japan." Gaby turned to face him. He needed a better answer. "I saw an ad. I knew getting hired without connections was a long shot, but the funeral industry is always desperate to find workers, and I was desperate to find work. It was August, and my work visa expired in September. I had to be employed to renew it. I didn't have time to land a teaching position; I only had three weeks to get a job. I was applying for waitress and clerk jobs all over the place, but nothing panned out. If Eguchi hadn't hired me, I'd have had to leave Japan."

"But why did you keep the job?" Alex persisted. "Why didn't you keep applying for teaching positions after your visa was renewed?"

"I did, but none of the colleges and universities I contacted had any interest in me. My record is tainted by being fired from Shizuyama." Gaby turned up her hands in a broad shrug. "And I still have no idea why."

"I have an idea," Alex said.

"You?" Gaby asked. "I mean, you do?"

Alex set his glass down and stretched his hand open, examining his palm. "Yes, I-who-know-nothing-about-Japan have a clue."

"What is it?"

"Dr. Kaneko said . . . well, he didn't say specifically, he offered a generality."

Gaby slid into the chair across from him. "Alex, this is big news! Kaneko would never have told me. You found out something I couldn't. What did he say?"

Alex's face was apologetic, uncomfortable to convey this news. "He said that unmarried female professors are expected not to have sex."

"And I certainly haven't!" Gaby blurted. Oh, great. Alex didn't need to know that.

"He said there were rumors. You've been telling me that's all it takes."

"Yes." Gaby trusted Kaneko; he wouldn't invent a disparaging rumor. But who would have started gossip so far from reality?

Alex's reedy baritone interrupted her thoughts. "Speaking of rumors, has Fumiko downstairs caused you any trouble about the night I slept here?"

Gaby shook her head. "I won't know for months. Then, out of the blue, I'll receive a new rental agreement with a special clause disallowing overnight guests. That's the way things happen. Or my neighborhood association will schedule me for post-garbage street-cleaning duty four weeks in a row. Or Mr. Eguchi will talk to me about image."

Alex held up a finger. "But he won't! Because he is a *yakuza,* outside the respectable social order. You know, it's fuzzy in my mind, but—"

"Fuzzy associations are fine. This is Japan. Go ahead."

"Okay. Your indiscretion that—"

"I wasn't indiscreet," Gaby stated.

"Your alleged indiscretion that made you unacceptable to the respectable social hierarchy was your passport into the disreputable hierarchy. You see what I mean? Getting canned earned you a 'bad girl' stigma that made you acceptable to work for the underworld. The moral equivalent of a tattoo."

Gaby leaned back as far as she could in the hard chair. "In the States, I'd laugh at you. But what you say makes sense."

Alex grinned. "Damn, I'm good."

Gaby thought while Alex went back to studying his hand. "I can believe the university would fire me for nonmarital sex. And Marubatsu could get behind it as a priest, for the cause of morality, pretending not to be the misogynist he really is. But I don't think he could start rumors about me without any hint of truth. At the very least, he'd need something or someone to support what he said."

"Is there any connection between Marubatsu and Eguchi?"

Gaby shook her head. "I can't imagine anyone who would know them both. Besides me, that is."

"You know, what Michael said yesterday really stuck with me."

Gaby blinked. Michael? The carefree young pup who was living out the life of a character in a textbook? "Did I miss something?"

Alex nodded seriously. "About Marubatsu. Michael said, 'You showed him, joining his competition.' Think about it,

Gaby. If you weren't thumbing your nose at Marubatsu by working for Gone With The Wind, maybe someone else was. Eguchi?"

"What on earth for? Anyway, no one knew I would apply for this job."

"Well, it's something to think about." Alex checked his hand again.

"Is something wrong with your hand?" Gaby asked.

He showed her a swollen pink mound dotted with splinters. "Me versus a killer attack tree."

"I'll get a needle and peroxide." Gaby went to the shower room and took a bottle of rubbing alcohol from the bottom basket of a plastic cart. She brought a pincushion from her bedroom closet. "Aren't you right-handed?"

"Yes."

"Then I should get them out."

Alex looked surprised. "You wouldn't mind?"

"Hey. It's part of my current job description." Gaby scraped her chair to the corner of the table and leaned over Alex's hand. She chose a thin needle and sterilized it. "You do like pain, right?"

"As much as possible, please."

Gaby went after the largest piece of bark first. "How did this happen?"

"On my way up the hill to see Misogynist-*san*."

Gaby steadily pushed the needle parallel to the largest splinter and pulled it up, popping a thin layer of skin. Then she poked the point under the tiny chip to prod it out. "Any news there?"

"Quite a bit." Alex kept talking as she freed more slivers from his scraped palm. "He said he was gathering all university paperwork regarding Cody, which does explain his asking Michael for the medical forms. He gave me a copy of Cody's form. But—get this—the note about not donating organs wasn't on the copy."

"He altered it," Gaby guessed.

"My thinking exactly," Alex said. "And there's more. It turns out Marubatsu was Cody's sponsor, something I didn't know until Kaneko told me. Marubatsu never mentioned that to me. Isn't that unusual?"

"That's Marubatsu. Avoiding responsibility whenever he can." Gaby looked closely at Alex's hand for her next target.

"But here's the strangest part." Alex winced a little as she picked at a sliver. "I asked for the name of Cody's doctor and he got all defensive, saying I must not doubt the word of a Zen priest and how I must accept fate without questions. He got really angry."

"That is strange," Gaby offered when he didn't say more.

"Well, that's all I have to report," Alex said. "How about you? Did you have a chance to talk to your doctor?"

"Hold still or I can't do this," Gaby warned him. "My doctor said organ transplants are only done at Tokyo Women's Medical College. But I called them and found out they did no heart transplants on the day Cody died, the day before, or the day after. On anyone. Cody's heart wasn't used for a transplant." Gaby lifted her needle, watching to see if Alex needed to make a fist and hit something.

Alex held steady. "Okay. But he was still operated on by a surgeon. I have to find Cody's doctor. Marubatsu said the department secretary told him all he knew about Cody. Do you think that's true?"

"I think he's using her as a scapegoat." Gaby went after a deeper bark shred. "Typical Marubatsu. Any hint of trouble, blame the nearest woman."

"Ouch!"

"Sorry." Gaby tilted his hand to catch the light better. It was a nice hand, large but graceful. A good holding hand. She pulled out the last splinter. "There. I'll put some ice in a towel for you."

"Thank you." He pressed the towel she gave him against his raw palm.

"I got another lead to follow." Gaby empathized with Junko's reluctance to tell Alex about Endo-*kun*. Alex was a tiger.

His relentless questioning could push a suicidal college student over the edge. All the same, she had to tell him. "Junko remembered someone else who came to Cody's room that last morning. Besides *yakuza*."

Alex looked up, immediately alert. "Who is he? I assume he's a he?"

"Yes. A former student of mine, in fact."

"Excellent! He'll speak English."

"Not a good student," Gaby cautioned him. "It's a tricky situation. I think I should talk to him in Japanese. Alone."

Alex went to her sink to rinse his towel. "Cody was my son. This is my quest."

"I know, Alex, but it's not your country." Gaby came behind him and placed her hand on his shoulder. "Remember your talk with Kaneko? He told you what he could never tell me. It's easier to speak to a third party. Let me talk to Endo-*kun*. Unless you don't trust me?"

Alex spun around. "I've told you everything about Cody. Every last detail. I've let you stick needles in my hand. And you have to ask if I trust you?" He caught her hand and pulled her a step closer to him. He looked down at her, waiting for a signal to kiss her.

The next ten seconds felt like minutes. She hadn't felt this churned up for a long time. Her instinct was to turn off her good sense and kiss him, to enjoy the sensation without interfering thoughts, but her reasoning mind prevailed, and she backed away.

Alex let go of her hand. "Should I apologize again?" he asked softly.

Gaby folded her arms in front of her chest and thought awhile before she spoke. She decided to be honest, even if it made a fool of her. Alex deserved honesty. "I'm not rejecting you, I'm preventing you." She glanced at him. She couldn't read his face. "A relationship isn't an option, is it? And I— I don't— I don't do casual sex." She could feel her cheeks grow hot.

"I understand your position completely," he said quietly.

Gaby watched as he dabbed the towel at his temples, down the playground slide of his nose, around his broad jaw and finishing with a single swipe at the sunburned triangle of skin at the collar of his plaid shirt. He had a beautiful mouth, she noticed. Long lips slanting inward, parted by an irregular curve. She weakened. Would it be worth a little heartache to kiss those lips? It had been more than five long celibate years. Years of being a person, not a woman. She reminded herself that he lived on the other side of the Pacific. If that weren't enough, he was—shudder—a pop psychologist. He had written a book called *Why Love Fails.* And he would never get over the death of his son. It would never work. Sheer chemistry couldn't conquer all. She forced her thoughts back to Endo and Junko. "Junko is worried you won't climb Mount Fuji with her. She's going this Sunday."

"That's a day before he died."

"The idea is to greet the dawn at the peak. It would be Monday, then."

Alex wrung out the towel and draped it over the faucet. "Gaby, I can hardly walk level ground in this heat."

"It will be cold on the mountain."

"You look after your students, don't you?"

Gaby felt defensive. "You can let Junko know last minute. Please—keep the option open. Don't rule it out because of everything else going on right now."

He looked at her. Another whammy look that got her thinking about sex. She was ruling him out because of everything else. But that was different. "Well," she faltered. "I guess I'll take you to the races tomorrow, around eleven."

Alex darkened his voice for melodramatic narration. "And so she sent him out into the sweltering dusk, locking the door behind him." He smiled at her, a resigned, complete smile. "Let's see if I've got Japanese protocol down. I enter with apologies and exit with thanks?"

"You don't have to thank me."

Alex moved to the concrete entry and bent over to tie his shoelaces.

Gaby looked down at his madras shirt straining over the arch of his back. A tiny patch of skin showed where the shirt had pulled out at his waist. He straightened up and tucked in the shirt. "See you tomorrow."

She felt self-conscious bolting the door after he left. He was starting to lower his guard, she thought—more angry, but also more of a sense of humor. She turned on the radio: a fast, flashy piano piece. The mood hit her wrong and she punched the music off. The room felt too empty.

Gaby went to her bedroom and lay on her futon, curling around a pillow. She felt worse now that Alex had left. Would one night of sex be better than nothing at all? Alex's presence in her apartment had made her aware of how lonely her body was, how starved for touch. He was the first opportunity to come along in Japan.

Not that America had provided much more. After she divorced Ron, there had been James, a predictable enough rebound: sweet, openhearted, six years younger than she, attracted to her because he was in love with the entire world. But she was a thinker while James was a doer, always going out to this art show or that restaurant, going skiing, going camping—going, going, gone. After James, there had been a few dates with stray musicians or carpenters, brief fantasies about men in line at the post office. Followed by Japan-inflicted years of nothing. While Japanese women collected foreign men as English-practice boyfriends, Japanese men uniformly shunned foreign women. And expatriate men, as Michael had put it so well, "didn't come to Japan to date white women."

That Alexander Thorn had dropped out of the sky, accepted her secret bloody illness, and wanted to make love to her ranked as a miracle. Gaby rolled over with a groan. Alex might be her last chance for sex for a long time, and she was afraid to let it happen.

Twenty-one

As Alex came down the stairs of his hotel, he saw that Gaby and the young female clerk in the lobby both wore thin hand towels around their necks, folded neatly under the collars of their white shirts. They couldn't have looked more different in white. The clerk's thick black hair and golden skin made her polo shirt look extra clean and cool, an antidote to the weather. Gaby's face looked paler than it had yesterday, while the lines under her eyes were darker. In her white blouse, she looked ready for surgery. Alex worried about her.

"Ready to go?" Gaby asked.

"Yes." Alex handed his key to the clerk and put on his shoes.

The heat outside was relentless. The white cloud cover seemed capable of burning his eyes. Alex watched the gravel underfoot until they reached Gaby's car. She opened her car door on the left. Alex stood beside the right door, waiting for her to get in. She came back and tapped his shoulder. "Are you driving?"

He looked down at the steering wheel on the right side of the car. "No, just used to passengers on the right." He went around the trunk of her Honda and got in on the left side.

"Things like that take a while," Gaby said, starting the car and holding her hand by the vents to check the fan. "You never forget to take your shoes off in Japan, but you do forget to drive on the left side of the road. Another reason the Brits adapt more easily."

It took less than a minute to reach the racetrack by car. Gaby drove through an open gate in a concrete wall that surrounded the racetrack parking lot. She paid a fee to a girl in uniform who waved an orange baton toward where she should park her Honda.

"We've got to find the connection between Eguchi and Marubatsu," Alex reminded her as they merged with a crowd of gamblers waiting to get in.

"I don't think Eguchi's involved," Gaby said.

"You didn't think he was *yakuza*," Alex replied.

Gaby glared at him. "Don't use that word in public. Especially here, of all places. Jesus, Alex, get a grip."

"Sorry! But I don't think anyone heard—"

"We're foreigners speaking English. They're paying attention to us whether or not they show it. Do you see any other Caucasian faces around?"

Alex could easily see over the top of the heads in the crowd. Another tall man's blond hair stuck out in the crowd of brown and black. "As a matter of fact, there's Lester."

Gaby cupped her hands over her eyes. "Oh, no! Did he see you?"

"I don't know. Is something wrong?" Alex was confused by her exaggerated reaction. It occurred to him her medication might be making her jumpy, snappish. Steroids did that.

"I don't want to deal with Lester today. It's bad enough being on my feet in this blinding sun without eating anything. To have to listen to one of his speeches or take his teasing would be the last—" She stopped. "Sorry. I didn't mean to rant."

"You should eat," Alex said, trying not to feel too pleased that Gaby finally had something negative to say about Lester. "I'll get you a sandwich from that vending machine." This, at least, was something he could do by himself in Japan.

"No, I can't eat."

The crowd pushed closer together as they neared the turnstiles.

"Why not? Gaby?" But he knew: something about her illness.

She laughed awkwardly, almost like crying. "I'm not used to talking about it. I have this procedure tomorrow, a sigmoidoscopy, and I can't eat today in preparation for it. There. That's it."

Alex took it in. How had he dared to feel superior to

Lester while he himself was forcing an ill woman to be his bilingual baby-sitter? "Look, you shouldn't be here."

"I have to," she insisted. "It's my job."

Alex couldn't agree with her priorities. "Your health is more important."

"My health depends on my job," Gaby stated firmly. "Everything depends on my job."

"Gaby—"

"I can do this. I've had twenty years' practice." Her expression warned him against saying anything to contradict her.

They had reached the turnstile. Gaby gave an attendant some coins and Alex pushed the bar down after Gaby went through. On the other side of the line of turnstiles, the crowd dispersed. Gaby made her way to another attendant wearing a large apron with programs in one pocket and pencil stubs in another. She bought a program and glanced at it. "It looks like Haneda is only in one race. Let's hope he wins it."

"He will."

"How do you know?"

Alex touched the pink and purple feathers in his hatband. "The lucky-hat system."

It was good to see Gaby smile. "I wouldn't put money on that hat."

Alex hadn't noticed Lester sneaking up behind Gaby until he ambushed her with a kiss on the cheek. "Gay Bee *san!* I didn't think you were the wagering sort, love."

Gaby turned to Lester. "I'm not. This is business."

Lester looked from Gaby to Alex and back. "What kind of business?"

Alex disliked the tone of Lester's question. "None of yours?"

"What is this? Why the cold shoulder? What are you still doing with this *o-nimotsu,* Gaby?" Lester was unusually edgy. His pastel clothes looked cheaper without his confidence.

"You're too sensitive, Les." Gaby said the words soothingly. "Our business is meeting Mr. Eguchi here, and knowing how you feel about him—"

"I'll vanish," Lester concluded. "But I'll expect a full report on Friday."

"Friday?" Gaby asked.

"Concert tickets ring a bell?"

"Oh! Right! Friday."

"Honestly, Gabe, how could you forget the social highlight of your week?"

Gaby waved to a man in a pumpkin-colored suit. "There's
Mr. Eguchi."

"I'm gone. Ciao." Lester wheeled around and took off
toward the stadium.

"Asshole," Alex muttered. "Calling himself the highlight
of your week."

"He's not that bad," Gaby said. "Just a typical *gai* in Japan.
It's why men come to Japan, you know—to free their inner jerk.
Start bowing." Gaby bowed as Eguchi approached.

Alex tried to bow, but as usual his shoulders and hands
didn't agree how to do it.

Eguchi bowed to Alex, pointed to Alex's head, and said
something.

"You remembered the hat," Gaby translated.

"Say whatever I'm supposed to say back," Alex said. The
less he spoke to Eguchi, the better he could hide his anger at
the man who'd gotten his son killed. Eguchi believed they were
in friendly cooperation, and Alex would find out more if he
could keep that pretense going. He forced himself to smile at
the man.

Gaby spoke a brief sentence in Japanese. This was followed
by a conversation between Eguchi and Gaby; a serious one,
from her expression. Alex kept his eye on Lester, who glanced
back at Gaby after he bought his tickets, and again as he studied a vending machine. What did Lester have to be anxious
about?

An announcement came over the loudspeaker and people
meandered toward the entrance to the stadium. Eguchi bowed
and hurried off. Alex was relieved to see him go.

"Eguchi went to visit the pit. Do you want to go sit in the bleachers and watch?" Gaby asked.

"Don't I have to bet on Haneda?"

"He's not in the first race. I wouldn't mind sitting down."

"Let's do it."

They went through the entrance tunnel and sat on a narrow metal bench a few rows upwind from the cigarette smokers pacing the concrete floor close to the track fence. Some people watched from the comfort of air-conditioned glass booths, but most sat in the benches close to the track. Alex figured the booths must cost a lot.

Gaby took a purple fan out of her purse and worked it in front of her face. "Bad news. Eguchi heard a message from Wang on the answering machine. He knows about the *inkan*."

"What did he say?"

"Not much; he was very upset. I'm not sure if it was because another *inkan* was made, or that I didn't tell him about it, or that Rie and I knew about it before he did. Maybe all three. He said he should know this kind of information first, and expected me to keep him fully informed. It was a serious reprimand. I think I'm on probation."

Alex thought quickly. "Does he know about Ninka Bank cashing my check?"

"He didn't mention you, but he must know. Except for you, I wouldn't know about a false *inkan*. I never deal with bookkeeping."

"Did he reveal anything to prove his guilt?"

"No. He was upset, but who wouldn't be?" Gaby turned her dark brown eyes on him. "I don't think Eguchi's guilty. You wouldn't either, if you knew him."

Her loyal defense of her mobster boss irritated him. "Charming men can be murderers."

"Alex, please don't—"

"Look, Gaby, Cody died on a motorcycle. Motorcycles and death: Eguchi's right and left hands!" Alex found he was almost yelling to be heard over motorcycle motors.

The racers cruised past the stands single file as the loud-speaker proclaimed garbled announcements in Japanese.

"I only ask that you take this one step at a time." Gaby spoke near his ear. "Can you do that? There's a lot at stake here. For me as well as you."

The flag fell and the bikers shot forward. Alex was glad it was too noisy to talk. He had overlooked Gaby's involvement in his quest for the truth—inadvertently, but selfishly all the same. For the first time, he acknowledged there would be consequences for Gaby after he proved Eguchi guilty. For starters, she would lose her job. He thought that would be a good thing, but Gaby didn't see it his way. *Everything depends on my job.* He assumed her visa would expire again in September, same as last year. Without employment, she'd have to leave Japan.

The heat of the metal bench radiated into his butt. He shifted position and took off his hat to use as a fan as sweat rolled down his chest. If Gaby had to leave Japan, he supposed she'd return to the States, but to what? Getting fired twice in a row would hurt her employment chances in the States, as well. From the looks of her sparse apartment and old car, she didn't have the money to pack up and establish a new residence in a different country. His agenda would trigger huge changes in her life.

Alex had told himself over and over that this trip was about Cody, but he knew that wasn't really accurate. His son was irretrievable. He knew he had come for himself, to get his life unstuck. If the years ahead held nothing but sadness and grief, he longed to grieve cleanly, to move beyond angry fantasies of one death scenario after another. But now, his long-awaited, longed-for truth would hurt someone else. Gaby would be the one to pay the price for his peace of mind. That wasn't fair. Was there any way around it?

The crowd cried in unison, and Alex looked at the track. A racer had spun out under his motorcycle into the oval grass center. The others kept going while the injured biker cradled his bent knee, unable to stand. Not until the racer with "5" on his jersey crossed the finish line, beating his closest competitor

by a meter, did two paramedics trot onto the track. As they
moved the hurt biker onto a stretcher, Number Five did hand-
springs in front of photographers.

"Let's get out of here," Alex said abruptly. "Let's go home."

Gaby placed her hand on his forearm. "It's not how it
looks. The winner is distracting attention away from the injured
man, to lessen his shame."

Gaby's hand was cooler than his arm. How could her hand
be dry in this inferno? "It's not that," he said. "It's everything.
I've had enough. I mean it."

"You've come this far," Gaby said. "Be strong." With her
purple fan, she kept up a slow rhythm, a butterfly wing beating
over her heart.

How did Gaby find it in her soul to help him, to encourage
him to be strong, when helping him could cost her so much?
Alex stared at her, overwhelmed by a feeling he couldn't name.

She must have thought he was staring at her fan, because
she stopped fanning and showed it to him. "It's a souvenir from
my favorite temple, Todaiji, in Nara. It's the one with the enormous Buddha with the hands."

"Don't they all have hands?" Alex was unsettled by the absence of Gaby's hand on his arm. She had touched him, all right.

"They're special hands, besides being big. His right hand
signifies the removal of human fears, like this." Gaby held up
her right hand, tilting her middle finger forward slightly. "And
his left hand signifies the hearing of people's desires." She set
down the fan and stretched her left hand out palm up, with her
thumb overlapping the base of her forefinger. "I get a sense of
genuine compassion from the Daibutsu. I wish you could see
Todaiji."

Alex tried to kid her. "Now who's telling me to visit the
temples?"

"Well, they *are* worth seeing."

Alex knew Gaby had come to terms with Japan, but he
hadn't perceived before that she had found things to like about
Japan. "Are you sure you want to stick this out?"

"Of course. It's my job, remember?" She checked the race program. "It's time to bet on Haneda. Let's go." She stumbled as she got up.

Alex offered her his hand, but she didn't take it. He followed her gaze to a crumpled can of Jolt cola by her feet. "Gaby?" he asked.

She glanced up and smiled to reassure him she was fine, took a step forward, and collapsed. Before she fell face first to the cement, Alex caught her and eased her down onto a bench. She had passed out. Alex sat with his back to the sun, and adjusted her head onto his lap where his torso made a tiny puddle of shade.

Spectators on their way back to the ticket windows changed their course of traffic to clear space around the two foreigners. Those who stared, stared from a distance where they wouldn't have to make contact.

"Help!" Alex called in vain. What was the Japanese word for "help"? He frantically scanned faces in the stands. In a crowded group, Alex spotted Lester, a head higher than the Japanese men. Much as he disliked Lester, his was the only familiar face.

Alex fixed on Lester, willing him to turn his way. He took off his silly feathered hat, ready to motion Lester in like an airplane. The crowd around him thinned, but Lester remained engrossed in his conversation with a Japanese man. A man in a pumpkin-colored suit. Could there be more than one suit that color? Alex wasn't certain the man was Eguchi from the back. The Japanese man, though six inches shorter than Lester, had an aggressive stance and calmly smoked a cigarette while he talked. Though Lester's face was unreadable at this distance, Alex noticed Lester's stiff posture and nervous foot-tapping. When the Japanese man flicked his cigarette on the cement, Alex could tell the conversation was about to end. He waved his hat vigorously in an arc over his head.

Alex was almost positive Lester caught his signal and pretended not to have seen him. He tried again. This time, Lester's

Japanese companion turned around. Lester had been talking to Mr. Eguchi.

Twenty-two

Alex felt Gaby stir in his lap. When she opened her eyes, her whole body startled. "Take it easy," Alex said gently. "You fainted."

"I know," Gaby said. "I had my fainting dream. I just didn't expect to come to in your lap. Are the betting windows still open?" She struggled to sit up.

"Not too fast, now." Alex kept his hands on her shoulders to steady her as she sat. "Eguchi and Lester are coming." He gestured toward the two men making their way toward them.

Panic flashed through her face. "No! Eguchi can't know I'm sick!"

"He doesn't know; I only waved to him. I was worried about you. I won't tell him about your illness, but you have to go home, Gaby. This is absurd, pushing yourself like this." Alex was afraid to let go of her shoulders. The empty can of Jolt rolled up to Alex's feet, scraping the cement.

"I do it all the time." Gaby shifted forward, out of his hands. "What am I going to tell Mr. Eguchi? That I— Is that Lester with him?"

"Know anyone else with that nose?"

"But Lester and Eguchi together?"

"Surprise, surprise," Alex muttered. The arrival of the two men prevented him from saying more.

Gaby rose to her feet and launched into a flurry of Japanese in an unnaturally high voice. Eguchi asked a few questions, watching her face like a terrier waiting for a special signal while Lester said nothing, looking trapped. Then Eguchi, bowing briefly to him and Lester, drew Gaby away. She looked back over her shoulder and made a tiny shrug.

With Gaby and Eguchi out of hearing range, backs turned, Alex regarded Lester. "So, how do you know Eguchi?"

Lester floated a smile, but it didn't anchor on his face. "Oh, everyone knows everyone in Shizuoka."

"Don't give me that shit." Alex spoke in a deceptively conversational tone. "Gaby is under the impression you don't know her boss. Why have you lied to her?"

Lester's Adam's apple made a sharp dip. "I don't answer to you, Thorn. It's none of your business."

Alex took in the blond curls, the waxy skin, the pastel garb. He hated this guy. "Is that what you're going to tell Gaby when she asks you? That her own life is none of her business?"

Lester brought his hand up to his forehead to shade his eyes. "Do you expect me to understand that absurd question?"

"Yes, I do. If you're going to play stupid, I don't mind spelling it out for you." Alex took a step closer, which made Lester step back. That told Alex he had the advantage. "One, you're a gambler. So's Eguchi. You know Eguchi because you gamble. Two, you're a liar, because you told Gaby you didn't know Eguchi. Three, you're acting guilty, no doubt because you are. So, what are you guilty of?"

"Cut the crap. You don't know anything about me."

But Alex, thinking over his three conditions, was smitten with a strong hunch about the cause of Lester's guilt. It was something Rie had said yesterday: that Eguchi had won a substantial bet concerning Gaby—against someone who bet that she couldn't make a sale in her first month. Who would make a bet like that? "Could there be a certain wager you don't want Gaby to know about? A bet about, oh, let's say, a job?"

Lester whispered, but with force, "Fuck you."

Alex stepped closer, only a foot from Lester's face. "What did you say?"

Lester stepped back again. "I said fuck you, you fucking prick."

Alex grabbed Lester's shirt. "You want to fight me? It'd be a pleasure." His heart pumped him up. Alex had studied and observed aggression, but hadn't fought anyone since junior high. It was his job to defuse conflict, not escalate it. Part of his mind recognized, with consternation, that he was actually enjoying the adrenaline rush.

Lester sputtered out a tense laugh. "You're insane, Thorn! Be reasonable, old man. Let go."

"Tell me the truth, then." Alex tried to make eye contact, but Lester wouldn't let him. "Never mind. I already guessed it, didn't I?" He released Lester's shirt with a shove.

Lester stumbled backward, nearly knocking over Eguchi, who was returning with Gaby. Eguchi asked Lester a sharp question, which Lester answered briefly. Alex smiled. Eguchi, probably the youngest of the four of them, was playing father to the three *gaijin*. Excluded from the language, Alex could still read the pattern. Lester had covered for him, not wanting to involve Eguchi. In Eguchi's presence, Gaby wouldn't ask what went down. He himself was the bad brother with the angelic smile, presumed innocent.

While Eguchi and Lester talked, Gaby moved up to Alex and spoke under her breath. "Here's the deal. Mr. Eguchi needs me to handle a follow-up house call. It has to be done today, or we could lose the sale. Meanwhile, you and your lucky hat stay here and bet on Haneda. Mr. Eguchi will get you back to your hotel. Is that okay?"

"No, it's not okay. You need to go home and rest."

Gaby sighed. "Alex, I appreciate your concern, but it's my choice. I'm used to it."

Lester came up and touched Gaby's shoulder. "Ready to go, love?"

Alex wanted to hit him. Just land a fist on his jaw. "He's going with you?"

Gaby looked puzzled. "I'm dropping him off on the way."

Lester smirked. "Calm down, old man. No need to fight about it."

"Then don't tempt me," Alex replied. Lester backed away. Alex moved close enough to brush his arm against Gaby's, and spoke quickly. "Lester is running away from me. You have to ask him about a bet he made with Eguchi. As soon as you get in the car. Don't give him time to think up a cover story. Ask him—"

Before Alex could say more, Eguchi broke them apart, one hand on each of their shoulders. He grinned and pointed toward the betting windows. He carefully pronounced his words: "We have a wrong shotto."

"A long shot," Gaby murmured. "It's almost time for the next race. You have to bet. I'm not sure how much, your bet can't be too small—maybe five thousand yen?"

"I'll do what it takes," Alex said hurriedly. "Call me tonight?"

Gaby nodded and walked over to Lester. As soon as Gaby turned, Lester looked back over his shoulder and flipped Alex the bird. Alex watched Gaby's brown hair and Lester's blond hair descend into the exit tunnel. He should be going with her, not Lester. Had she even understood about the bet? Her face hadn't shown any reaction. Reluctantly, he followed Eguchi to the betting windows.

There were no lines at this point, and five clerks watched him curiously to see which of them would sell tickets to the *gaijin*. Eguchi herded him to the booth of an overweight woman with a permanent wave that had gone mad scientist. A microphone was clipped to her pink shirt, which read "Rinse Twice" in large blue letters. A block of smaller blue letters below gave a series of laundering directions, with misspelled words like "bleech" and "luck-warm" thrown in. The clerk's prominent eyeteeth reminded Alex of Jiyuko in Tokyo. He wondered if Jiyuko had found an American penis for her novel research.

Eguchi stood to the side with a flourish, leaving Alex to make a fool of himself on his own.

Alex leaned over to talk into the speaker. *"Haneda-san."* Maybe that would do.

"*Ni-ban kara roku-ban desu ka?*" The clerk's voice was distorted by the intercom, but her manner was pleasant. She was speaking very slowly for his benefit, but he didn't know what she meant. He glanced at Eguchi, who gave a fatherly nod.

"*Hai,*" Alex said. He pushed a purple five-thousand-yen note in the slot below the glass.

Eguchi chuckled and made some joke to the clerk, who laughed on purpose, not spontaneously. She waited for the register to print Alex's ticket, then ripped it off and slid it under the glass. "Gouda raaku!"

"*Doumo,*" Alex said. It wasn't until he and Eguchi were back at the track that Alex figured out she had said "good luck." Even when Japanese spoke English, it wasn't English. He sat on the bleacher and felt it burn his butt.

Eguchi sat close beside him. His lively eyes darted repeatedly toward Alex as if he wanted to speak, but he said nothing.

The race began. Eguchi offered Alex a cigarette. When Alex declined, he lit one for himself. The smoke drifted across Alex's face. The motorcycles passed the first lap, zinging around the curve, wheeling up dust that hung in the air. Alex, unable to see the racers, studied Eguchi. Except for his rapid smoking, Eguchi seemed calm.

The spectators rose to their feet during the fourth lap. Alex stood, too. While others yelled or cheered, Eguchi remained silent, but smoke shot out his nostrils. Suddenly, Eguchi clenched Alex's forearm. Hard.

Alex breathed deeply, hoping bruises would be the only consequence of Eguchi's grip.

Then, the race was over. Eguchi grinned and slapped his back. Alex stumbled forward, tipping over an abandoned plastic cup of beer. Hot beer cascaded to the cement step below.

Finally, Eguchi spoke, in a perfect Paul McCartney imitation: "Baby, you're a rich man."

Alex, surprised, drew out his ticket. "Haneda-*san* won?"

鋒

Gaby waited until Lester fastened his seat belt. Then, as she backed out of her parking space, she asked, "What bet did you make with Mr. Eguchi?"

"What?"

Her Honda bounced over a pothole and she slowed down. "You heard me."

"You got this idea from Thorn. What did he tell you?"

Gaby squeezed past a blue truck. "You sound defensive."

"The man's a prick! He almost took a swing at me!" Lester sounded like a petulant child, not the suave, sarcastic Lester she knew.

"Calm down," Gaby said. "If you don't want to talk about the bet, I'll ask Mr. Eguchi, instead. No big deal." There was a line of cars waiting to get into the lot, but Gaby was the only one leaving early. She turned left to avoid the line and sped up. "Music?" She turned on the radio. Brahms's Fourth Symphony. Again.

After a few minutes, Lester turned the radio off. "I didn't tell you because I didn't think you'd understand. I didn't want to lose our friendship over this."

The words sounded familiar. This was what her ex-husband, Ron, had said when she had discovered his affair. "I didn't tell you about Courtney because I didn't want to lose you." As if that justified everything. As if she should be so impressed that he didn't want to lose her that she'd forgive his infidelity on the spot. But if she showed her feelings, Lester would clam up. She faked a smile. "Les, you don't have to tell me anything. It's not important, is it?"

"No! But I don't want Thorn to give you the wrong idea," Lester said.

"Oh," Gaby said.

"I wouldn't have made the bet if I hadn't been desperately short of funds."

"Of course not." Gaby paused a beat. "Why not?"

"It was harmless."

"It was?"

"But now that Thorn has stuck his nose where it doesn't belong—"

"Forget about Thorn. I just want to hear it from you, okay?"

Lester sighed. "It's like this. I went to a bar after the races. Eguchi was at the same counter, bragging about the fact that he had just hired a university professor. Well, after a while, I found out the professor was a *gaijin,* and when I learned what the job was, the bet sort of . . ." He trailed off.

"Sort of what?" Gaby prodded.

"Sort of coalesced on the spot. Spontaneously, you know?"

"You have such a quick mind," Gaby murmured.

"Exactly," Lester said, pleased. "I bet that you couldn't make a sale in your first month. I'm amazed Eguchi took me up on it. I wasn't betting against you, Gabe; I was betting against Eguchi's idiotic notion that a *gaijin* could sell fantasy funerals to Shizuoka's aged and ailing. You've got to admit his idea was crazy."

"Totally insane," Gaby affirmed.

Lester continued, relieved. "I'm glad you see it my way. The only trouble was, I lost. You and your damn competence cost me five hundred thousand yen." He tried to laugh, but she could tell it wasn't funny to him.

"Five hundred thousand? That's almost a year's rent!"

Lester glanced over sharply. "You're angry."

"Angry? Me?" Gaby considered, concentrating on turning right through a yellow light. "I'm surprised you haven't asked me to reimburse you."

Lester cautiously settled back in his seat. "Well . . . it was your fault that I lost."

"But I'm confused," Gaby went on. "All this time, you knew Mr. Eguchi was *yakuza.*"

"Yes. That's why I've been trying so hard to find you another job. I don't want you involved with *yakuza.*"

"Why didn't you tell me?"

"You'd ask me how I knew. How could I tell you I bet five hundred thousand against you? If our situations were reversed, wouldn't you have a hard time telling me that?"

"No, I wouldn't, Les, because I'd never make a bet like that." Gaby boldly went first in a four-way stop, causing two cars to creep backward.

"You're not a gambler," Lester concluded. "I am."

It was true, Gaby realized. Lester was always betting for drinks, or cash. She thought back to Nature Squib Bar and the last bet. What had it been for? Some trick translation project? If Lester had won, he would have taken her money. But he lost, she remembered. He lost, and then pretended the bet was a joke so he wouldn't have to pay her. He didn't like to lose. "It must have hurt to pay up."

"I'm still making payments," Lester said.

"So you got nothing out of it." Gaby began to feel sorry for Lester despite herself.

"Only the satisfaction of seeing Marubatsu's face when—" Lester stopped abruptly and started over. "I got nothing out of it. I lost my shirt and you became employed by the mafia."

Her Honda had almost veered off the road when Lester mentioned the name of her former colleague. "What was that about Marubatsu?" Gaby tried to sound casual. Alex's voice echoed in Gaby's head: "Is there any connection between Marubatsu and Eguchi?" How did Lester know Marubatsu? Why had he kept this secret, too?

Lester waited a little too long before saying, "Did I mention Marubatsu?"

Gaby took a quick left turn off course, toward the ocean.

"Gabe?" Now Lester was apprehensive.

"Scenic route," Gaby explained. From her morning run, she knew there was a narrow pull-off on this road that housed three vending machines, nestled against a tall wild gardenia hedge. She turned into the pull-off and parked with Lester's window a few inches from a display of Suntory drinks.

"Did you want a beer?" Lester asked carefully. "Because I can't get one through the window and you've parked so I can't open the door."

Gaby didn't know how to begin. Lester had led her to believe he did not know either Eguchi or Marubatsu when in fact he knew them both. He kept Eguchi a secret because of his bet against her, but why had he pretended not to know Marubatsu all the times she'd complained about him? She felt too weak to conduct an impromptu cross-examination. She dug in her purse for her purple fan and snapped it open.

"You are angry," Lester surmised. "Well, you have me trapped. You might as well let me have it."

"You're supposed to be on my side."

"I am, Gaby. I am."

"Then why didn't you tell me you knew Marubatsu?"

"Well, you know, you go ballistic when you hear his name."

Ron had used this tactic on her, too. Lester wanted to make her appear unstable in order to justify deceiving her. It was all right to lie to keep the little lady calm. "You were saying, the only satisfaction you got out of the bet with Eguchi was seeing Marubatsu's face *when* . . ." Gaby used her teacher voice. "Finish the sentence."

"All right, all right. It doesn't deserve this buildup. Marubatsu was livid to discover that you not only found a job in Shizuoka, but with a company that challenged his Zen Buddhist funeral monopoly!" Lester sneaked a smile. "You would have enjoyed seeing his face, too."

"Why couldn't you have told me about this?"

"I didn't want you to get all worked up."

"But you knew it was important to me."

Lester was stuck. "I can't argue that. What's your point, Gaby?"

"My point is that you've been lying to me all along."

"There's a difference between lying and saying nothing—"

"Stop, Lester. There's more." Gaby paused, trying hard to keep her voice steady. "Yesterday, I learned why I was fired."

She didn't have to go on. Lester's mouth instantly coiled up and struck. "This was Thorn's doing, wasn't it? He'd do anything to turn you against me."

"He was trying to help me."

"And he blames me, doesn't he? Well, it's not my fault. Marubatsu had already decided to find a way to can you. It would have happened with or without me."

Gaby leaned her forehead on the steering wheel. So it had been Lester. Lester had promoted the rumors of sexual activity that had cost her her job. She began to cry. "I trusted you, Les. I thought we were friends."

"We are!" His voice was genuinely anguished.

Gaby shook her head. "You lied to Marubatsu. You started rumors that got me fired. You!" Gaby grabbed a tissue, wiped her eyes and blew her nose. "You made me lose my job. My *job,* Lester! You cut my lifeline. My income, my sponsorship, my work visa . . . I nearly had to leave the country. How could you do it?"

Lester sat still, his long, pale fingers stretched out on his cream-colored pants. His voice got smaller. "Because I'm a colossal cad? Because I'm selfish and horrible? Go ahead. Call me whatever you want. I deserve it."

Gaby stared at him. "Why? Why did you do that to me?"

Lester turned away and cranked down his window. He explained himself to cans of Suntory Malt, Budweiser, and Beer Kenjo behind glass. "It wasn't something I did to you. It was something I did for myself. I know how upset you must be, but if you could try to understand *my* feelings."

Lester must be Ron's evil twin, Gaby decided, asking her to understand his feelings after he'd ruined her life. Next, he'd claim he did it for her own good—to send her back to America to find a husband. "I loved that job, Lester. You have no idea how much it meant to me."

"It's true, I didn't. I really didn't know how important it was to you until afterward." Lester's voice expanded back to its usual size. "I assumed with your experience and fancy-ass degree, you'd simply move on to the next position. I was the one who needed that job! Can't you see? There you were, on the hill, with the high-and-mighty professorship while the rest of us *gaijin* slaved in the Berlitz league. You were paid twice our wages, plus enormous bonuses, and you didn't even spend it. And there I was, overwhelmed with debt—"

Gaby cut in. "So you deserve to be a university professor because you gamble? And I'm unworthy because I live frugally? That's how you justify destroying my career?"

"I'm not justifying anything. I'm trying to explain how I felt."

"Oh, excuse me for neglecting my duty to understand you."

Lester faced her. He looked as if he'd been hit by a truck. There were tears in his eyes. "I never wanted it to turn out like this."

"Neither did I," Gaby said softly. Parked, the car was reaching kiln temperatures. Gaby worked her fan in front of her face. "Tell me exactly what you told Marubatsu."

"Must I?"

"Yes."

"It was his idea, Gaby. You've got to believe that. He'd seen us together, at films and concerts, and he wondered how close you and I were." Lester fanned himself with his hand. "I don't suppose we could continue this in a coffee shop? With air-conditioning?"

"Here is fine. Go on."

Lester searched his pockets until he found his white hand-kerchief. He blotted sweat off his temples. "Marubatsu praised my Japanese. Said the British were superior to Americans because they learned languages better. Then he said the English depart-ment should have a British professor instead of an American, and he should be a man instead of a woman because women were in-herently unreliable and stubborn. He asked for my résumé." Lester paused. "It boiled down to promising me your job if I could substantiate your moral turpitude. And I thought: You'd get another job, easily, and this was my only chance for a university position. So Marubatsu and I had lunch on campus a few times, and in front of various other professors, I worked it into the general conversation that we . . . I implied we were close."

Gaby exploded. "Implied? You mean, you lied!"

"Damn it, Gabe, I wanted it to be true!"

Gaby let out a laugh that sounded like a sob. "And that makes it all right?"

"I wanted you, Gaby." Lester repeated it softly. "You've hurt me, you know. We've known each other two years and I've never once been inside your flat. I get the perpetual brush-off."

"You get perpetual Japanese girlfriends. You can't con me that way."

"I hoped they'd make you jealous."

"That's sick. You're a sick man, Lester."

"Am I? Haven't you ever wanted someone you couldn't possibly have?"

Gaby thought of Alex and said nothing. "Let's get back to Marubatsu."

"There isn't much more. He broke his promise to me. McKenzie appeared out of nowhere and took your job away from me. So I lost. Then came the bet with Eguchi and I lost again." Lester threw up his hands. "End of story."

Gaby considered. "So you knew all along why I was fired. You made it happen. And your advice about accepting things and letting it go was all to protect yourself. And you knew, all along, Mr. Eguchi was *yakuza,* and you didn't tell me, again to cover your ass."

Lester winced. "Must you be so harsh? I didn't know how things would turn out. I honestly thought you'd merely move to another university."

"Rather like, you loaded the gun but you didn't mean to shoot me?"

"It's you who were killing me! You, with your vacation time and million-yen bonuses. You, who were too good to mingle with the *gaijin* at Nature Squib. And on top of that, I had to watch you flirt with McKenzie—"

"Oh, get real!" Gaby said, but she felt caught.

"—and then this obnoxious, arrogant Thorn shows up and you let *him* stay overnight after one dinner. Don't think I haven't suffered, too."

"Poor baby," Gaby replied tersely. "Is there anything else?"

Lester looked her straight in the eye. "That's it. All of it. You know, I do feel better, having come clean and all."

Gaby started the car. She collapsed her fan and put it back in her purse.

"Do you forgive me?" Lester asked.

Gaby adjusted her mirrors. "You've asked me to understand your feelings," she said, gritting her teeth. "But did you ever stop to consider mine? When you came here two years ago, who helped you get an apartment? Who walked you through immigration papers? Who got you into a Japanese class? And to repay me, what do you do? You conspire to make me lose my *job*!"

Lester tucked his handkerchief away, subdued. "I suppose this means no concert on Friday?"

"No concert." Gaby made a careful U-turn to head back downtown.

"So you'll take me home and dump me off and that will be that?"

"Not quite," Gaby said, stopping the car. "You'll have to get home on your own."

"What?" Lester looked at the rice fields on either side of the narrow road. "I spent my money at the track. I haven't got enough for cab fare. Not even bus fare."

"Then you'll have to walk," Gaby said. "Get out of my car."

"You can't mean this. It's a hundred degrees. This is joke, right? Ha, ha?"

"Out. Now."

Lester opened his door and put one leg out. "I've seen this in films. You drive a few blocks and then turn around and get me. All right, I'll play along. I understand you're angry right now, but I want you to know I still care about you."

Gaby shifted to first gear and moved forward. Lester quickly hopped out and slammed the door behind him. She stepped on the gas and didn't look back.

Twenty-three

Alex pushed his track ticket under the glass at the betting window. The clerk smiled broadly, stamped the ticket twice, and tapped something on her computer, which released the cash drawer. She counted out yen in bills, and counted them again as she spread them in front of Alex, and then pushed them through the slot. Alex picked up his money. He had won eighty thousand yen—enough to cover ten days at his hotel. The yen notes had the unreal quality of play money; he wasn't sure they would work.

While Alex waited for Mr. Eguchi to conclude his business at the track, he thought about Gaby and hoped she had confronted Lester right away. Maybe she didn't want to learn anything bad about Lester, the way she kept giving the bastard the benefit of the doubt. In his heart, though, he felt that Gaby was like himself: the kind of person who needed the truth.

Alex fanned himself with his hat, watching Eguchi approach him. He wanted Eguchi to drop him off directly at his hotel, so that he wouldn't have to smile and play along with Eguchi's agenda instead of pursuing his own. Without a translator, however, he couldn't confront this grinning man in a pumpkin-colored suit. He would present his professional face— the neutral, nonjudgmental mask he used on clients—until Eguchi set him free.

Eguchi came back and flagged them a taxi. A sign was posted on the back of the driver's seat, in both Japanese and English: 10,000 YEN FINE FOR VOMITING IN TAXI. Alex wondered how often these fines were collected. He sniffed. Only the oily upholstery smell of interior detailing and a faint bleach scent from the air-conditioning. Out the window, he glimpsed the road to his hotel. The taxi went past it, dashing his hope for a quick escape. Whatever Eguchi's plan was, he had little choice but to go along.

The driver kept looking in the rearview mirror at Alex, asking Eguchi questions in Japanese. Finally, he pronounced in English, "You are a pen. I am a pen. We are pens."

Alex didn't want to laugh, but he couldn't help it. It was the last thing he had expected their muttered conversation to be about. *Expect to be surprised*. The driver laughed, too, though his expression was uncertain. Eguchi playfully hit the driver's shoulder with a rolled-up race program and chuckled. *"Baka!"* Eguchi said.

The driver tried again. "You are *the* pen? I am *the* pen?"

Eguchi hit him again with the program, as if housebreaking a puppy. *"Baka, baka! Pen ja nai. Man desu."*

The driver, surprisingly, didn't back down. *"Kotoba-wa pen, so omoimasu."*

"Chigau! Man."

"Pen."

"Man!" Eguchi slapped his pockets until he found a ballpoint pen, which he brandished in front of the driver. "*Kore-wa* pen. Pen, pen, pen!"

Alex couldn't stop laughing while Eguchi and the driver continued to argue whether they were men or pens. Each line was a new punch line, striking Alex as funny all over again.

"I am the pen," the driver insisted.

"I am the man," Eguchi corrected him. "*Tatoeba* 'I am the egg man.'" He sang the line from the Beatles song to illustrate. "I am the egg man, *u-u, u-u.*"

Now Alex's ribs hurt from laughing. Especially at the way Eguchi's Liverpudlian accent vanished on the *"u-u, u-u"* part.

"A-a-a-ah, so desu ka." It seemed the driver was convinced.

"Hai, so desu. Itte, kudasai."

"You are the man," the driver recited. "I am the pen."

"Baka!" Eguchi roared, hitting the driver's ear with his program. Turning to Alex, Eguchi shook his head and pointed at the driver's back. *"Baka,"* he muttered. Then he smiled, showing his gold teeth, and started laughing along with Alex.

It was impossible to hate Eguchi as he had before. Alex reminded himself that a moment of comic relief in a taxi didn't lessen Eguchi's guilt, but he could better understand Gaby's persistent defense of the man. He didn't seem like the kind of mobster who could send drunken motorcycle racers out to hurt foreign exchange students. Perhaps Eguchi was not Haneda's only boss. Another *yakuza* might be the villain, instead.

Alex noticed the Skylark restaurant at a stoplight. They must be headed downtown. Perhaps, he thought, Eguchi was taking him to Nature Squib Bar to celebrate. Would Haneda meet them there? It would be a chance to discover more about Haneda's job outside the track, if it weren't for the language barrier. Alex doubted he could conduct a cross-examination in bar English.

Alex fantasized himself at Gaby's apartment, talking about their respective triumphs. Gaby would know how she got fired, and he would know how Cody died. Then . . . what? His fantasy fell apart at this point. He would fly home and she would lose her job? She deserved a better ending. If he dropped his quest, she could go on as she was—but was selling funerals for the Japanese mafia a happy ending?

"I am the egg man," Eguchi sang under his breath, for his own edification.

The taxi stopped, and Eguchi quickly peeled bills off his roll. The driver bowed many times, so Alex assumed Eguchi had tipped him, even though Lester had said it wasn't the custom in Japan. Alex left the cold shell of the car for the shimmering heat of the pavement and the stench of deep-fried oil.

Eguchi steered him to the source of the boiling oil, a take-out window under a sign with a cartoon of a brown octopus holding sticks with round balls in each of its tentacles. The octopus wore a blue baseball cap with the letter Q on it.

"Tako-yaki ga suki?" Eguchi paused and translated. "Like octopus balls?"

"I don't know," Alex said. He wished he could just say no.

"Turisto rikuwaiyamento," Eguchi said.

"I don't understand," Alex said.

"E . . . to, ne?" Eguchi frowned. "In Japan . . . turisto . . . must four things." Eguchi counted off his fingers by folding them in, starting with his pinkie. "See temples." He pulled down his ring finger. "Play *pachinko.*" His middle finger was next. "Buy tea set." His forefinger completed a fist. "Eat *tako-yaki.*" Eguchi grinned, relieved to have gotten through it. "Checklist *desu.* You must do, or Japanese police stop you at airport."

The concept of a tourist checklist was actually a good joke, but it came too slowly to be funny. Alex smiled and said, "I got it."

Eguchi ordered at the counter and handed a stick to Alex. Alex bit into a lukewarm fried morsel. The taste was mild, like a fish stick, but it was tough and rubbery. It tasted more and more like a tennis ball the longer he chewed, until swallowing proved a challenge.

"Anozzer?" Eguchi asked, already on his third.

Alex shook his head. "No, thanks."

Eguchi began the struggle to say something in English, but gave up before any words materialized. While he chewed his last bit, he busily wiped his fingers on a napkin and tossed it into a trash can. Then he beckoned to Alex to follow him down the street.

Alex thought it looked like the bar neighborhood, but

there were no red lanterns. Gray high-rises stretched up into a painfully bright gray sky. Fewer stores, fewer people, more litter. He looked for street signs before remembering only the biggest streets had names. Was it Gaby who had told him you had to feel your way around in Japan? This area looked nothing like a slum in an American city—no graffiti, no homeless, no malingering teenagers—but it had a dangerous feel. Alex wondered what data his senses were interpreting as danger.

His thoughts were interrupted by a car screeching to a halt at least ten feet before the stoplight in the empty lane beside them. Painted on the side of the white sedan were the words: "Flush You Driving School." Alex did a double take, and, in the backseat, three startled Japanese women, about college age, clapped their hands over their mouths. The woman driving had the same permed black hair and beige sweater as the others, but her face was strained. She clutched the steering wheel to make sure it stayed on the car. Beside her sat a middle-aged man, taking notes in a notebook. She let the car ease forward a smidgen in automatic drive before slamming the brakes again. She repeated this maneuver six or seven times until the car finally met up with the crosswalk. The instructor said something to her, and she shut her eyes and bowed her head while he spoke.

Alex was wary about crossing the street in front of a student driver with her eyes shut, but Eguchi sauntered across fearlessly. On the corner was a bar, an open mouth of darkness in a city of white glare. Eguchi waited in the doorway until Alex caught up.

Entering the bar, Alex forgot to duck and smacked his head on the beam over the door, knocking off his hat. Eguchi picked up the hat and brushed it off while Alex pressed his hand to his head. When the initial sting subsided, Alex looked around. It was not Nature Squib Bar. This bar was narrow and deep, with a box fan whirring at the far end. The bartender—a man with a narrow face and a crew cut—pushed through a beaded curtain with a tray of clean glasses. With his pristine white shirt and brand-new jeans, he looked like an American dream from the 1950s.

"*Daijobu?*" Eguchi asked, lightly touching his own head. "Okay?"

"*Hai,*" Alex replied. Without a translator, how could he say it throbbed with pain?

Eguchi ordered, and the bartender set two small glasses and a large bottle of beer on the counter. He added a chilled plate of what looked like lima beans, cooked in the pod. Then he busied himself wiping the clean glasses with a dish towel and putting them away.

Eguchi poured for Alex. "*Kampai!*"

"*Kampai.*" The beer was room temperature, but lively. They sat in awkward silence. Eguchi kept busy splitting open the cold green pods and popping the inner beans into his mouth.

Alex suggested another toast. "To Haneda-*san?*"

Eguchi grinned. "Haneda-*baka!*"

Alex remembered to pour more beer for Eguchi as soon as Eguchi set his glass on the counter. He didn't know what to say, so he waited for Eguchi to speak.

They drank the rest of the quart in silence. After Eguchi poured down to the last inch, the spiffy bartender immediately popped open a new quart and set it on the counter between them.

Alex thought he should pay, especially considering all the money he'd won. He reached in his back pocket for his wallet, and the folded photocopy of his Gone With The Wind bill came out with it and fell to the floor.

Eguchi was faster than Alex in bending to pick it up. He began to hand it back to Alex and stopped. Alex saw him looking at the Gone With The Wind letterhead peeking over his sloppy fold. He watched Eguchi's mouth turn downward in a slow-motion frown. He decided he should take the initiative.

Eguchi obviously understood more English than he spoke, and he already knew about the false *inkan*. "I suppose Gaby-*san* told you about my . . . situation?"

All of Eguchi's good humor withdrew, and he sat up stiffly. "Yes."

Alex took the paper from Eguchi and unfolded it. "Have you seen this bill?"

Eguchi didn't even glance at the paper. He called something to the bartender, who set two shots of whiskey beside their beers. "We can work it out."

"I'm glad to hear it. Have you seen this before?"

Eguchi seemed intent on not looking. He held up his shot glass. *"Kampai!"*

"Kampai." Alex drained his shot. Cheap whiskey on an empty stomach. Not a good combination for an amateur sleuth.

Eguchi signaled the bartender to set up two more. He faced Alex with an expression of sadness and finality. "Let it be."

"I can't," Alex said. "My son died. My only child."

Eguchi rubbed his thumb on the shot glass thoughtfully. "Boy, you're gonna carry that weight a long time. *Demo,* but . . . ob-la di, ob-la da, life goes on. Life is very short and there's no time for fussing and fighting, my friend. One-way ticket, yeah."

Stunned, Alex couldn't think of a reply. He drank more beer after his second shot. "Won't you please, please help me?"

The corner of Eguchi's mouth twitched and a dimple sprang into his cheek.

"Is this familiar?" Alex asked. He placed the copy of the bill on the bar.

Eguchi picked up the paper and began to hand it back unread when something caught his attention. He glanced down once, twice. He held the paper at arm's length and frowned. He ran his finger over some words, as if that would explain them.

Alex found himself encouraged by Eguchi's evident surprise. Gaby could be right about Eguchi's innocence. But if not Eguchi, who? One of Eguchi's employees turned traitor? He had to admit he liked the idea of an underling being responsible rather than Eguchi personally.

Eguchi folded the paper carefully and tapped it on the counter. He said something to the bartender, who brought over an entire bottle of Suntory whiskey. He poured shots for them both.

"I sent my money to that address," Alex said. "And I have proof that my check was cashed." Alex wondered how much Eguchi understood. A single unknown word in a foreign language could render a sentence meaningless.

Eguchi pretended not to hear him, and raised his glass. *"Kampai."*

Alex downed his third shot. Once he got back to the States, he was never going to drink again. He wished Japanese men could talk without getting drunk first.

Eguchi patted the folded photocopy on the bar and topped off Alex's beer glass.

Alex sipped automatically before setting it down.

Eguchi poured beer up to the rim again. "Who has seen?"

"Who's seen that bill? Me, you." Alex declined to mention Gaby and Rie.

Eguchi took that in. "And Gebi-*san*?"

"Oh, Gaby—yes." He hoped he wasn't getting her in trouble. He couldn't think of another plausible way to answer.

"And Resutaa-*san*?"

"Lester? No. He knows nothing."

"Good, good."

"Why?"

"Is Resutaa-*san* your friend?"

"No," Alex said bluntly. "He's not."

Eguchi, pleased by his answer, filled their shot glasses. *"Resutaa-san wa* Maxwell. Silver tongue *wa* silver hammer *no yoni.* Bang, bang, on Gebi's head."

Not understanding fully, Alex gathered Eguchi distrusted Lester as much as he did. Eguchi's metaphors were almost performance art. Anything that needed to be said in English had been written by Lennon and McCartney. Alex tried to think of what he needed to ask Eguchi. The booze blocked his brain synapses. His attention was on his stomach, inside of which a solitary octopus ball was awash in beer and whiskey. Oh, yes. "The address," he said.

Eguchi wrinkled his forehead. "Address? *Jyuusho?*"

"The address," Alex heard his voice begin to slur, "is Kita—" He forgot the word. All Japanese words sounded similar.

"Kitanumi," Eguchi filled in. *"Honto ni?"* Eguchi's sudden loudness startled Alex. Eguchi fumbled to open the paper, peeked at it, and folded it again. He sucked a long breath through his teeth and ran his hand through his short shellacked permanent wave.

"What is it?" Alex asked.

Eguchi startled, as if he'd momentarily forgotten Alex was there. Then he grinned, showing gold, hiding his feelings. "Let's go eat Mosburger."

"But that address—"

"My problem, not your problem. I handle." Eguchi signaled to the bartender.

The bartender picked up the half-empty whiskey bottle, shook it, and raised his eyes as if to say, "Something else?" Eguchi muttered something and the bartender closed the bottle and wrapped it in a paper bag. Eguchi got off the bar stool and pulled Alex out into the street. Alex blinked in the bright heat, glad he was a little drunk to soften the pain of whacking his cranium on the way in. What did Eguchi mean, it was his problem?

In the street, Eguchi opened the bag, took a swig from the bottle, and offered it to Alex. What the hell—he was going to be hung over tomorrow, anyway. Alex tipped his head back and gulped the bad whiskey. His throat stung. He handed the bottle back to Eguchi and belched. Had he just male-bonded with the man who had gotten his son killed? Unbelievable. Hello, Japan.

Eguchi clutched the crook of Alex's elbow and propelled him down the street. Alex stumbled into a bicycle leaning against a rack of bicycles. The bicycle slid, causing four more to collapse on the sidewalk, domino style. Alex looked at the tangle of spokes and handlebars. Alex began to right the bicycles, but Eguchi stopped him.

"Come on," he said, flagging a taxi. "Come on for the magical mystery tour."

Alex got in, hoping he wouldn't have to pay that ten-thousand-yen fine.

Twenty-four

Mr. Aoshima had canceled his order for a moon package that morning. Mr. Eguchi wanted Gaby to see him right away and save the sale. She was due at the Aoshima house within the hour, but she decided she had to stop at her apartment and take a shower first—her white blouse and tan skirt were blotched with sweat. Maybe she could wash off some of the pain of Lester's betrayal, as well.

How could she have been so blind? There had been clues all along; why hadn't she seen through Lester's façade of friendly concern? Since she'd moved to Shizuoka, her standards for men had fallen. It had taken Alex, fresh from the United States, to challenge Lester's character.

Fumiko's little dog barked and growled as Gaby pulled the Honda into her parking space. Gaby growled back, and the dog, alarmed by a new response, took shelter behind Fumiko's washing machine before venturing a single tentative yelp.

Gaby mounted the metal steps, using the rail to help pull herself up. At her door, her vision darkened, and she hurried with the key to get inside before she fainted again. She stumbled into her entry and bent over to lower her head. Made it.

When the churning sound of her heart abated, she slowly stood and slid the bolt behind her. After kicking off her shoes, she went directly into the shower room and undressed. Even her underwear had soaked through with sweat. She didn't bother turning on the heater. She took the water as cold as it came out of the pipes, and let it flow over her hot, sweaty scalp and down her body. Just when she was completely wet, the phone rang.

At first she ignored it, but on the fourth ring, she realized the call might relate to her appointment with Mr. Aoshima, so she wrapped herself in a thin towel and rushed to pick up the receiver. *"Moshi moshi?"*

"Oh, I'm glad you're there!" It was Rie.

"Rie-san? What happened?" Gaby looked at her track of puddles beading up on the tatami floor.

"It is about the inkan."

"Did you find out who ordered it?"

"I was trying to."

Gaby switched the phone to her left hand while her right hand clutched her slipping towel. *"Rie, I'm in a hurry to see a client. Please tell me what's wrong."*

"Wang is dead."

"Dead? Didn't you speak to him yesterday?"

"And today when I called his shop, a woman—his sister, I think—told me he died last night. Am I responsible?"

"Calm down, Rie. Did the woman say Wang was killed?"

"She didn't, but it is suspicious, isn't it?"

"Maybe not. Was he an old man?"

"I don't know. I never saw him."

"I suppose you couldn't have asked his sister how he died?"

No answer.

"Rie?"

"I think Nishida-san has a red file, perhaps."

"Nishida came in and you can't talk any longer?"

"Yes, that's right."

Just as well. Gaby didn't have time for the details. *"We'll talk about this later. Can you come by after work?"*

"Thank you very much." Rie hung up.

Gaby shook her head at the phone. What did that mean? She glanced at the clock on the kitchen wall. No time to finish her shower. She toweled off and combed her hair quickly before it dried crooked. With her abdomen swollen and sore, panty hose were out of the question, but she couldn't visit a client barefoot. She put on her long blue seersucker dress and rolled knee-high nylons over her calves. Good enough as long as no one watched her legs when she sat. She took a white umbrella from her collection at the door. As she opened the umbrella against the sun, she thought she must resemble Mary Poppins. If only there were any kind of breeze to lift her up through the clouds and blow her to a destined doorway. An assignment where she could be certain she could do some good for a change. But since there was no magic wind to power her umbrella, she drove to Aoshima's house in her battered Honda, instead.

Mr. Aoshima himself answered the door this time, shaking her hand at length while she struggled to kick off her pumps and maintain her balance. Mr. Aoshima initiated the conversation. "I'm fine, and you?"

"Fine, thank you." Gaby stepped into one of the many pairs of cloth slippers lined up on the tatami mats. The slippers were too small, and her heels lapped over the sole.

"You look terrible," Mr. Aoshima commented. "Are you ill?"

Gaby copped to a lesser plea. "I'm just tired—the change of seasons, you know."

Mr. Aoshima led her into the room with the big television. He was barefoot. His navy blue polo shirt and tan pants were casual, but with a designer cut. His belt might have been real alligator. He switched to speaking Japanese. *"My wife always gets constipated from the change of seasons. She is in bed today."*

"I hope she feels well soon," Gaby said politely.

Mr. Aoshima shook his snowy head. *"Never,"* he said. *"She will only find a different malady to complain about."*

"I'm so sorry," Gaby murmured. She lowered herself to the floor and tucked the hem of her dress under her knees.

After declining Mr. Aoshima's offer of refreshments the requisite three times, speculating at length whether or not the temperature was over forty degrees centigrade, and praising a watercolor scroll of black bamboo leaves, Gaby decided it was time to mention the lunar funeral. *"There is never a good time to discuss business, is there?"*

Mr. Aoshima sat casually in a half-lotus position. *"There is no need for more discussion. My wife insists on a traditional Zen Buddhist ceremony. It is she who will outlive me. She has put up with me for fifty-four years. I realize it is my duty to do what she wants instead of what I want."*

The sale was lost. Goodbye, half a million yen. *"And you want . . . ?"*

"The moon, of course! But I am—how do you say?—'a wild and crazy guy.' It is in my blood to go my own way."

"A big dreamer," Gaby said without thinking.

"Hai," Mr. Aoshima agreed, pleased.

Gaby recalled the reason Aoshima had originally called Gone With The Wind. *"Will your family tomb accept your Korean heart?"*

"Yes, thanks to you."

"To me?"

"I used your argument: that hearts are muscle, which burns away. Bones make ashes, not muscles."

"Did I say that?"

"It is true, isn't it?"

"Yours is such an unusual situation—"

"The only trouble is that I worry about the man whose heart I carry. A Korean might not want his heart burned in a Japanese crema-

torium. A Korean ghost might seek revenge on my wife. After he gave his life for me, I should consider his ghost, so desu ka?"

Perhaps she should try to convince him the Korean ghost would want him to buy a moon package, but she was exhausted and in pain and wanted to leave. *"That man didn't die for you. His death was accidental."*

"Ah, but now that I believe in God, I am not so sure I believe in accidents. I was given this heart for a reason." He shifted his legs and settled in for a long philosophical discussion, brown eyes sparkling.

He was lonely, Gaby recognized. He might have asked Mr. Eguchi to send her over so that he could enjoy a conversation while his cranky wife had taken to her bed. He might change his mind about the sale, but he would change it again and again, each time bringing her back to sit politely in his big house and listen to him. She felt sorry for him, but she had more important problems at the moment. She wasn't paid until the contract was stamped. If all Mr. Aoshima wanted was attention, he could hire a bar hostess. She spoke bluntly. *"What reason?"*

"I don't know, but there is a purpose for everything." Aoshima paused and checked her face. *"Don't you agree?"*

"It is hard to say one way or the other."

Aoshima changed the subject. *"About your husband's death. He died in Japan?"*

"Hai," Gaby said warily. She tried to remember the widow story Aoshima had invented for her.

"What did he die of?"

Had she mentioned an accident or an illness? She couldn't remember. It should be an illness, so Aoshima couldn't verify the specifics. He was already suspicious about the time it was taking her to answer. *"Cancer."*

"Oh, that is bad. What kind?"

Gaby tried to remember which cancer killed the fastest. Pancreatic cancer? But "pancreas" was a word she didn't know in Japanese, and if her husband had died of it in Japan, she should know the terminology. *"Skin cancer?"*

"You are asking me?"

"Is my Japanese correct?"

Aoshima lightly rubbed his bare forearm and his face. *"This is skin."*

"Yes. That kind of cancer."

"Oh, that is very bad. What did you do with his corpse?"

"Well . . . I cremated it."

"I thought Americans were buried."

"Most are," Gaby hurried to confirm. *"Are you interested in burial?"*

"No, no. I am interested in your story. Why didn't you bury him?"

"Well, he died in Japan, and, uh, shipping a corpse overseas is expensive. Besides, his body—with the cancer—wouldn't look presentable."

"I see. And what did you do with his ashes?"

She couldn't say they were at Gone With The Wind in case he asked to see them. *"Scattered at sea!"*

Aoshima drew back. *"Really?"*

"It is often done, for Americans," she explained.

"Gone With The Wind tosses ashes out like garbage?"

Uh-oh. She had to invent something else. *"I made a special arrangement. With the American military, you know?"*

Suddenly, Aoshima grinned in victory. *"Now I understand the reason for his death. Your husband was part of the American army. The American army was responsible for Hiroshima and Nagasaki. Millions dead with burned skin. So, your husband dies of skin cancer and is burned in Japan. It makes sense, ne? Me, I was supposed to die, but God made another man die to save me. So I must discover why God keeps me alive."* Aoshima fell silent.

In the quiet room, Gaby's intestines roiled loudly. Loud enough to break Aoshima out of his reverie and glance at her, startled.

"Excuse me. Please wait just a minute," Gaby said. She walked awkwardly to his toilet room, hoping the constipated Mrs. Aoshima wouldn't be lingering on the padded seat, paging

through magazines. Fortunately, the room was empty, and Gaby could use the flushing-noise feature of the Toto Home Sound Princess to mask her own sounds.

Aoshima would argue there was some purpose in her having ulcerative colitis. Well, there wasn't. She had drawn a losing gene in the genetic lottery, and she suffered for it. Her illness hadn't helped anyone, nor had it made her a better person, as far as she could tell. It was just her burden, her *o-nimotsu,* heavy luggage she carried around invisible to others. She often wondered if her burden would lighten if she could openly admit to being sick. But even the most discreet, minimal description of her condition involved the combination of the words "blood" and "diarrhea" and ignited instant reactions of "eew!" or "yuck!" or "gross!" to shut her up. Ulcerative colitis was unmentionable.

If she had to have a shameful illness, Japan was the place to have it. Where else in the world could she find a luxury toilet with sound options to hide her diarrhea noises? After she was done, she cupped her hand under the faucet to catch a few swallows of water before rejoining Aoshima in the main room.

In her absence, he had brought out a bottle of *sake* and two cups. *"Douzo."*

Gaby had to accept to be polite. She tilted a tiny drop onto her tongue and set the cup next to her knee, where Aoshima couldn't see how little she'd drunk. *"Perhaps we should talk another time. Together with your wife,"* she suggested.

"You are sick, aren't you?"

It wasn't polite to probe about her illness, but maybe that was part of Aoshima's being a "wild and crazy guy." Gaby thought quickly. *"Not really. I think I ate bad sushi for lunch."*

"You don't have to be polite. I can tell you are sick." Aoshima poured himself more *sake. "Will you see a doctor?"*

"I have an appointment tomorrow."

"An appointment! That is serious, then. Will you need surgery?" His lively dark eyes showed more curiosity than concern.

Gaby thought of Mr. Eguchi saying illness was an old person's hobby. *"I don't expect that to be the case."*

"If it is, you should go to my hospital."

"Thank you, but Tokyo is a bit far for me."

"My hospital is not in Tokyo."

But where else could he have received a heart transplant? Gaby thought of Cody and decided to press the point. *"It's not Tokyo Women's Medical College?"*

"No, no. I went to Tokyo Women's Medical College first, but they had a long list. They said I was seventy-six years old, I had lived long enough. I was too old for surgery. But I celebrated another birthday, thanks to my progressive doctor."

"Where did you receive your heart transplant, then?" Gaby asked.

"In a private hospital, for members only. Transplants aren't covered by insurance, so it cost me over ten million yen; but that was quite reasonable to save my life, I think."

"What's the name of this hospital?"

"Saishinkai."

"I have never heard of it."

"They prefer to keep quiet. If everyone knew about the miracles they perform, they would have too many patients. They would have to turn thousands of sick people away. They have the best surgeons, and a progressive philosophy."

"What do you mean?"

"If you are sick, they help you get well. It is that simple. They don't let Japanese thinking prevent you from getting medical care."

"Is it illegal?"

"Not at all. But because it is privately owned, they are free to do more. They are aggressive in treatment, and lenient in paperwork."

"How . . . interesting."

"You are interested?" Aoshima reached to fill her *sake* cup, and it overflowed into the tatami. *"Drink, drink!"*

"I'm sorry. I really shouldn't." Gaby bowed as she spoke.

"Sake is good for health," Aoshima argued.

Gaby raised the cup just enough to wet her lips. *"Where is this hospital?"*

"Near Fujiyama. I had a beautiful view from my hospital window." Aoshima clasped his bent knee and rocked forward and back. *"I plan to climb Fujiyama on the anniversary of my operation."*

"And when is that?" Gaby asked politely.

"This month," he said. *"July ninth."*

Her shiver was involuntary. She picked up the *sake* cup and drained it, bottoms up. Then she composed a smile for Mr. Aoshima. *"Please, tell me all about it."*

Twenty-five

On his way to Gaby's apartment, Alex noticed a large branch of bamboo mounted like a flag beside the door of Monkey Video. The branch was decorated with folded paper cranes and tinsel and long strips of paper with handwriting on them. He thought perhaps the store was having a sale until he saw two more bamboo branches flanking the gate of the Mitsubishi plant. These branches were plastic and bore heavier silver star ornaments along with handwritten tags. He'd have to ask Gaby what they were.

A white moped leaned against the railing of the metal stairway of Gaby's apartment building. Alex stepped around it, climbed the steps, and knocked on her door. He heard two female voices before Gaby opened the door.

Since that morning, Gaby had changed into the blue dress she'd worn when they first met. She was barefoot, and her forehead and neck were moist with sweat. As soon as he saw her eyes, he knew the news was bad, but Gaby spoke brightly. "Alex, you remember Rie?"

"Of course. *Konnichi-wa*." Alex took off his shoes and set them beside Rie's sturdy black lace-ups in the cement entry.

Seated at the kitchen table, Rie nodded her chubby face toward Alex in a modified bow. Her black hair was losing its permanent; the macaroni curls were longer and limper. She wore a polo shirt printed with brown teddy bears, a gathered pink skirt, and red ankle socks. Her bad foot turned inward at an odd angle. She had been involved with papers on the table beside her motorcycle helmet, and pressed her hands over them as if Alex shouldn't see what they were.

"Have I come at a bad time?" Alex asked. He meant to see Gaby earlier, but somehow it was already six o'clock. He couldn't explain where his afternoon had gone, although drinking with Mr. Eguchi was no doubt relevant, along with the blurry headache that was starting to emerge.

"You've come at a good time," Gaby said. "Rie had an idea how to find out who ordered the *inkan* from Wang. She suggested tracing the account at Ninka Bank where your check was cashed."

Rie sneaked a sideways glance at Alex and ventured a comment.

"If she could have a copy of your canceled check," Gaby added.

It was confusing to think about *inkan*s and checks, but easy to sense the emotions of the two women. Both were suppressing their feelings: Rie reining in eager enthusiasm, Gaby bottling up anxiety. Alex decided he might be drunk; alcohol had a way of numbing his rational left brain and leaving his intuitive right brain in charge. "Of course." He felt in his pocket for the folded photocopy of the Gone With The Wind bill and his canceled check. A crescent stain from a beer bottle marked the edge.

Rie took it, bowing, and whisked it into her leather backpack-style purse. Her lips moved nervously before she said abruptly, "*Sayonara, Gebi-san.* Goodbye, *Zone-san.*" Purse on her back, she pulled her helmet over her head and fastened the chin strap. If it weren't for the teddy-bear shirt, she'd look ready to fight germ warfare.

Gaby saw her to the door, where they took turns bowing for a while. Then Gaby fastened the chain and came back. Without making eye contact with him, she went to the cupboard and took down glasses. "Did Eguchi take you to a bar?"

"Yes. But we ate lunch afterward." He half-sat, half-slid into the chair Rie had vacated. The vase of peonies, he noticed, was no longer on the table. He looked up to the scroll of the lotus field. The field diminished into layers of mountains floating in mist. Did the absence of a horizon signify a cultural difference, or had this painter simply painted what he'd seen?

Gaby placed a large glass of water in front of Alex with two small white pills.

"Aspirin?" Alex heard his voice say "ash burn" instead. "I'm not drunk."

"Good," Gaby said. "Save them for later, then."

"What were you and Rie talking about?" He strove to enunciate.

Gaby took the opposite chair. "Well, Rie set out on a spy mission and accidentally made a sale for our company."

"I don't get it."

"Remember our friend Wang, the *inkan* maker?"

"Yes?"

"He died last night. He had a heart attack in the middle of dinner. Fried shrimp." Gaby paused to sip some water. "Rie reports that by the time his family mustered the courage to call an ambulance, he'd stopped breathing."

Alex's left brain began to kick in. "How old was he?"

"Fifty-seven." Gaby rubbed her forefinger over a tiny stain on the table, still avoiding looking at him.

"Was it *yakuza*?"

"I have no idea."

"Are you going to find out?"

"I think we should leave it to Rie. She's alarmingly competent. She sold them a budget oven-and-urn package without trying."

Alex shook his head. "Fifty-seven is too young."

"Mr. Eguchi says you're never too young to die." Suddenly, tears filled her eyes. She blinked, and they escaped down her cheeks. "I'm sorry. I don't know how to tell you, but you have to hear this."

The bad news. Alex found himself grateful to Eguchi for having taken him bar-hopping, so he wouldn't have to hear it sober. "Go ahead."

"This afternoon, I saw Mr. Aoshima, another Gone With The Wind client." Gaby ran her hand through her dark hair, side to back, and lifted it off her neck in a fist, looking down. "Mr. Aoshima had a heart transplant at a private hospital near Mount Fuji."

Alex took that in. He spoke cautiously. "Isn't that good news? We have another hospital to check for records, right?"

"The bad news is that we don't have to check." Gaby dropped her hair and finally looked at him. "Mr. Aoshima told me that the hospital performed his heart transplant on July ninth last year. And he told me his blood type is AB."

Static exploded in his ears. "Are you saying this man has Cody's heart?"

Gaby reached across the table and laid her hand on top of his. Her fingers were thin and even cool. "I don't know for sure. Mr. Aoshima was told that his donor was a Korean laborer, but—well, the date, the place, and the blood type all match." She lightly squeezed his hand. "I'm sorry. There's no good way to break this to you."

"It's what I came to hear," Alex mumbled. His own voice sounded odd. He listened to a vacuum cleaner next door attack and retreat, occasionally hitting the common wall. A large truck shook the building as it passed. In its wake, Alex heard loud hammering, workers shouting, and the tedious grind of locusts. Was Japan never quiet?

Gaby went on. "The name of the hospital is Saishinkai, and his doctor's name is Hayashi. Dr. Hayashi studied at Keio Medical School, one of the best. His specialty is cardiac surgery. Aoshima calls him progressive."

Saliva rushed to his mouth, and Alex pulled his hand out from under hers. "Excuse me. I think I have to vomit, please."

He shut himself inside the toilet room and knelt on the orange checked linoleum. When he lifted the mustard-yellow seat of the toilet, he saw blood splatters on the underside. Poor Gaby. Enough saliva gathered to drown him, but he spat it out without retching. The stuffiness of the cubicle weighed down on him. He was inside a pressure cooker lined with bunches of grapes. The diagonal wallpaper began to spin, and he hurled up the afternoon's bar crackers, beer, and lukewarm hamburgers. When he stood, he was surprised at how much cleaner he felt, physically and mentally.

He came back to Gaby's anxious brown eyes, and washed his face and hands at her kitchen sink. Cool water soothed his forehead. "Eguchi took me to a place called Mosburger," he remarked. "Can you believe that name? It used McDonald's red and yellow colors, sort of a Japanese copy. But my burger wasn't hamburger. It tasted like meat loaf." He took a beat. "Mostly loaf." Another beat. "In fact, it tasted distinctly like breaded bread . . . between slices of bread." He chuckled.

Gaby only looked more concerned. "I'm sorry, Alex."

"What happened to Lester?" he suddenly asked. "Did you confront him?"

Gaby bit her lower lip and let it slide away. "I did. You were right about him, but we don't have to talk about it. Would you like some coffee? I can make it iced."

"You think I'm drunk?"

"Well . . ."

"I'm not. Not really. I feel pretty good, actually, considering how much I drank this afternoon." He shrugged. "I'll analyze myself later. Am I correct in assuming you'll be seeing less of Les?" He laughed again. He wasn't usually this funny.

"That's for sure." Gaby got up and pushed him away from the counter. "I'm making coffee."

Alex caught her hand. "Don't. It's not effective, you know. I really feel all right. What you said—it's what I always suspected. In a way, what I'm feeling is relief."

"I don't know what to make of you." Gaby squinted at him. "Is this a shrink reaction?"

"I don't know."

She moved into him, wrapping her arms around his back and turning her head sideways on his collarbone. He held her, leaning his cheek against her head. He would have gone on holding her, but she broke away.

She took a deep breath. "I think the next step is to visit Dr. Hayashi, don't you?"

"Right." Alex pulled out a chair at the table to sit again.

"Maybe you need to be alone." Gaby nervously folded her arms across her chest.

"You want me out of here?"

"No, but—" Gaby worked hard to complete her sentence. "I have a sigmoidoscopy tomorrow and I have unpleasant prep work to do this evening."

"And *you* need to be alone." Alex retreated to the entry. He reluctantly tied his shoes and put on his feathered hat. "May I come by tomorrow?"

"I won't be home before noon."

"I'll see you then." Alex opened the door. "I want to hear about Lester, you know."

"Tomorrow." Gaby took hold of the door from the inside handle, pushing.

Alex pushed it back. "Oh, and Gaby?"

"What?"

He brushed his forefinger against the side of her cheek. "Thank you."

"You're welcome. Goodbye, Alex." She shut the door and chained it.

That was their pattern. Each time he intruded upon her

sanctuary and attempted a minuscule sub-survival amount of human contact, she closed him out and locked the door. Alex went down the stairs slowly, letting one foot drop after the other. Fumiko's dog cranked up barking. A jungle-size wasp U-turned in front of his nose.

He didn't want to be alone, but there was no one besides Gaby whose company he wanted, either. He thought of calling Jane, but was wary of how she'd take the news. Cody's heart was keeping a Japanese man alive. It made perfect sense. Why did he have to be alone tonight?

Outside the motorcycle repair shop, two men stood and smoked cigarettes. They wore bright pink coveralls that flared out at the knees and gathered in like pantaloons on top of black cloth work boots. The boots were notched to separate the big toe, like cloven hooves. Though the men were smaller than he was, they looked solidly built, and Alex could tell these guys were tough. They gave full attention to watching Alex pass. He nodded nervously and turned at the fig patch, sensing their scrutiny on his back. Was Aoshima like those men? Was Cody's heart keeping one of them alive?

In front of a fabric store, a woman with a full-length apron over a long denim dress mounted a two-step ladder. Two children in school uniforms waved strips of paper, shouting in high voices. The woman took a paper from the taller child first and tied it onto a green bamboo branch stuck in a crack between the store's concrete-block walls. Then she bent to take the paper from the younger child, who stretched on tiptoe on one foot, fingertips barely meeting the woman's. They were a family putting up decorations, and Alex was jealous for a moment. Was Aoshima their father?

He wished he could go back and ask Gaby what the bamboo meant. He wished he could go back for any reason. He made himself trudge past the Mitsubishi plant, but when he reached the creek, the heat brought him to a halt.

The chain-link fence on either side of the culvert was coated in toothpaste-blue plastic. Natural mud banks covered with grasses and hydrangeas stopped abruptly at new concrete walls flanking the stony stream. On the battle line of construction, two blue dump trucks, a skinny tractor, and a large crane were abandoned after the day's work. A long-legged bird picked its way through construction gravel blocking the trickle of the stream.

Alex looked up the scaffolding of the mechanical crane to the bright white sky, in which a giant hook balanced, poised and ready.

Twenty–six

箭 Dr. Ono turned a sheet of photos on the corner of his desk. A series of tunnel shots taken by the camera at the end of the scope. He pointed the end of his mechanical pencil to shots of pale pink walls, mottled with tiny red veins, like the red webbing of an irritated eye. *"Your transverse colon is in pretty good condition. The inflammation is mild. But your descending colon is worse."* He moved his pencil above a shot of a red-streaked tunnel. *"And your sigmoid colon has narrowed quite a bit with scar tissue."*

Gaby followed his pencil to a small, tortuous tunnel. *"What is this that looks like a red mushroom? I've never seen that before."*

Dr. Ono placed an X ray in her hands. *"That is a tumor, or polyp. That is why I continued with barium. Polyps show more clearly on X rays. There are two serious ones. Here"*—he circled a dark, stemmed protrusion on the film—*"and here."* He circled another that nearly blocked the white barium path. *"They have grown since your exam a year ago. They are causing your current flare-up."*

"So I need to have surgery?"

"Yes. This surgery is minor, but mandatory. We don't know how fast these polyps are growing. If they obstruct the intestine, it is very,

very dangerous." Dr. Ono slapped his glasses back up on his nose. *"You should have these polyps removed as soon as you can get home. The good news is that you'll feel much better as soon as it's done. The same day of the surgery, your condition will improve."*

"Home?" Gaby asked, bewildered. *"My home is in Shizuoka."*

"Your family home," Dr. Ono said. *"In America."*

"I can't go to America. I only have three vacation days." Why wouldn't Dr. Ono treat her? The Japanese health care system had worked so well for her, but now her favorite doctor wanted to abandon her to the horrors of the American medical system.

Dr. Ono retrieved the X ray she held and set it on his desk. *"Your husband—in your case, your father—must give permission for surgery."*

It was pointless to mention her father was dead; Dr. Ono would go through the patriarchal order of uncles, brothers, brothers-in-law, etc. But it wouldn't bother Gaby to forge her father's signature; her father would have applauded her for it. *"I can fax his signature to you."*

At this, Dr. Ono sucked a breath between his teeth and Gaby knew she wasn't going to like whatever he said next. *"The operation itself is easy—no incision, no anesthesia—but because of your ulcerative colitis, there is a slight chance of excessive bleeding. Then, you could need more serious surgery. There is also the matter of biopsy results. It is better to be with your family in America."*

"You think I have cancer?" Gaby knew what that meant: a colectomy. The operation American doctors were always trying to force on her. Disembowelment. A poop bag in her side, or her small intestine attached directly to her anus. Her body jerked reflexively at the thought. She couldn't have cancer—not now, not yet.

"I don't think so," Dr. Ono said soothingly. *"In ninety percent of such cases, it is a simple matter of removing polyps, and everything turns out fine."*

His words did help quell her panic. *"Please, sensei, can't you do this for me?"*

"Chotto muzukashii," Dr. Ono said. *"It is somewhat difficult."*

In Japanese, "difficult" meant "impossible." She was doomed.

Alex didn't call first. He showed up at noon, tan and sweaty, holding a white paper bag. "I'm sorry, I'm sorry, and I'm sorry. Here."

While he took off his shoes, Gaby lifted a plastic quart cylinder out of the bag. She pried up a corner of the lid and a hot rush of steam assaulted her eyelashes. The odor was salt and soy sauce.

"I managed that on my own," Alex said, wiping his forehead with the back of his hand. He wore a blue-and-green-plaid shirt tucked into khaki chinos. She could tell he'd lost weight this past week—his shirt was looser, and she could see a worn crease in his belt where he used to buckle it. "I waited until someone else ordered ramen to go, and then pointed. Lo and behold, it actually worked. So I guess the Japanese are capable of understanding gesture; most of them merely pretend they can't." His blue eyes examined her face. "What's wrong?"

"You're beginning to sound like Lester, making generalizations about the Japanese. They're no worse than Americans."

"Good point. But that's not what's wrong. You look like an earthquake victim cornered by a TV reporter. Besides, you're holding a hot water bottle on a hot day in July. What's really wrong?"

Gaby shifted the water bottle against her abdomen. "You seem in too good a mood after yesterday's news. Are you—what do you guys call it?—are you in denial?"

"No, I'm in Japan." Alex looked for a reaction, then shrugged. "Well, *I* thought that was funny. Where do you hide your bowls?"

Gaby opened a top cupboard, but stretching her arms up made her flinch.

"I see them." Alex took down two bowls, in a common Chinese blue-and-white rice-grain pattern, and portioned out the soup. "Spoons?"

Gaby pointed to a drawer beside the refrigerator.

Alex plopped a spoon into each bowl and carried them to her wooden table. He found her roll of paper towels and tore off two to use as napkins. "Let's see. Glasses for water?"

"How about wine?" Gaby bent over a lower cupboard and took out a bottle of red wine, the one he had bought her. Cheap wine would suffice. She twisted a corkscrew into the cork.

"No, thanks. Should you be drinking?" Alex asked, concerned.

"It won't make much difference at this point." She pulled at the cork, straining, but it held fast. "Damn it!"

Alex went over to her. "Let me try." His hands, as he took the bottle from her, were hot against hers. The cork was hard, but he managed to shimmy it out. *"Voilà."*

"Oh, great. Now I need a *man* to open a stupid bottle of wine for me."

Silence. Why had that toad fallen out of her mouth? She said nothing, regretting it but unwilling to apologize.

After a while, Alex ventured, "Gaby, are you mad at me?"

Gaby snatched a wineglass, one of two, from a lower shelf. "Believe it or not, Alex, everything isn't always about you."

Alex used his psychologist voice: "It sounds like you want to be angry with me. I don't know why. So I'm just going to eat my soup and say nothing. If you'll talk, I'll listen." Alex raised a spoonful of ramen to his mouth, but it was too hot to eat. He blew on it, tried again, and stirred it back into his bowl.

Gaby wet her lips with wine, ashamed of her childishness.

Alex began to eat his ramen, still too hot.

"You're allowed to slurp," Gaby mentioned. "In fact, you should."

Alex nodded, and slurped the next spoonful.

Gaby started on her bowl. The noodles were flavored with mushrooms, seaweed, and bits of fish cake. The first few swallows landed hard on her empty stomach, but the heavy salt tasted good and made her feel better despite herself.

When Gaby finally spoke, she addressed her nearly empty bowl. "I have tumors. Inside your intestine they call them polyps. Two are pretty big."

Alex pushed his bowl aside and reached his hand across the table, hers for the taking. "Oh, Gaby. Are they— I don't know how to ask. How serious are they?"

"You mean, is it cancer?" Gaby ignored his outstretched hand. "Well, you see, because they're inflamed and bleeding, they can't tell for sure until they operate and do a biopsy. Dr. Ono wants me to have surgery right away, but he won't do it."

"What's the problem? Insurance?"

"Nope," Gaby said. "*Un*like the U.S., Japan is civilized in that regard. No, the first problem is that I need a father or a husband to give consent."

"You're kidding." Alex held up his hand in a stop signal. "Sorry. I know the drill. This is Japan, right?"

"You said it," Gaby muttered. She raised her wineglass in a mock toast. The wine wasn't bad. She checked the label: a French pinot noir—not cheap, as she had assumed. Alex had spent too much on her. "And here I am, with my father dead and my husband divorced. No family, no surgery."

"What about your sponsor?" he asked. "Eguchi can sign for you, can't he?"

"I don't want him to know I have ulcerative colitis."

"But if it means getting surgery—"

Gaby shook her head. "It wouldn't matter. Getting consent is just the first hurdle. Dr. Ono insists on a family member to take care of me. It's a tiny operation, nothing for most people, but because of my long history of ulcerative colitis, I might have some annoying little glitch, like hemorrhaging. Dr. Ono doesn't want the responsibility."

Alex wiped his sweaty face with the paper towel. "What does Dr. Ono expect you to do, then?"

Gaby attempted a laugh that came out more like a cry. "He thinks I must have family and a doctor who'll do the surgery back in the U.S. He assumes I have family, no matter what I tell him."

"Is that a cultural difference?"

Gaby nodded. "No matter how long I live here, I'm regarded as a visitor. Dr. Ono doesn't realize I have no home in the States."

"You don't have anyone?"

Gaby laid it out for him. "My mother and her husband live in Brazil, saving the rain forest. She couldn't help me, especially not on short notice. As for Sophia—my sister—she's only twenty-six. I visited her Bronx apartment one time. She has these roommates—she has a lot of issues. It's not— Trust me, it wouldn't work."

"What about friends?" Alex was using his counseling voice, assessing her resources on the intake form.

"No one close enough for something like this." Gaby felt defensive. "You live in Japan, you lose touch. I've got to find another solution."

"Well, if you can't get surgery in Japan, won't you *have* to fly to America?"

"No!" She saw the surprise in his face and tried to explain. "I haven't been in the U.S. for almost five years, Alex. I can't just . . . *go* there."

"Why not? If money is the problem, I could—"

"It's not money! It's . . . I can't, that's all. I can't pick a city at random, hop a plane, fly ten hours, find a doctor—how? Out of a phone book? Who could give me an appointment within a week? For surgery, no less?" Gaby, tense, spoke faster. "Do you have any idea how awful the American health system is for people like me? I can't go through that, I can't—" Gaby stopped herself. If Alex had never had bad experiences with doctors in the U.S., he wouldn't believe hers. "The point is, I need to get this done soon, and that means I need to get it done here.

Somehow." Suddenly crying, she hid her face in her paper towel. "I'm sorry, Alex. You have enough on your mind. This isn't your concern."

"Of course it is," Alex said steadily. "Maybe we've only known each other a week, but we're friends. You can't deny that."

Gaby blew her nose and crumpled the paper towel in her hand. Her voice choked up nearly as high as the nurse's. "I'm scared, Alex. I hate being so powerless."

Alex stood and paced her kitchen floor. "Don't you have a right to health care, as a legal resident?"

He didn't get it; Japan didn't work the way America did. The rules were different for foreigners. Period. Gaby sighed. "In a word, no. Whatever the doctor says, goes."

Alex ran his hand through his gray hair. "There must be a way around Dr. Ono."

Gaby braced herself with the last of the wine in her glass. Wine worked well after a day's fasting. "Well, there might be one way for me to have this surgery. At least, I know of a private hospital that bends the rules."

"Where is it?"

"Near Mount Fuji, and I've heard . . ."

Alex stopped pacing. "No—"

". . . it has the best doctors." Gaby set her chin high and looked directly into his eyes. "I think Saishinkai is my best option."

Twenty–seven

Gaby had suggested a white shirt and tie. Alex put on a fine-lined plaid shirt that looked like graph paper. The lines were black, but the overall effect was gray. It was the closest thing to white he had. With a tie and cotton chinos, he looked like a dressed-up engineer or dressed-down businessman. Feet in socks, he carefully stepped down the slippery wooden stairs to the hotel lobby.

Gaby was talking to the desk clerk. Her cheeks were slightly bloated, and dark slashes under her eyes indicated she hadn't been sleeping well. All the same, it was a pleasure to see her, even if her deep brown eyes were upset and her mouth lined with tension. That morning, she wore a pale pink silk blouse and a nubbly linen skirt. He glanced at his own clothes; he was no match for her.

At the sight of him, the clerk started his nervous bowing routine, this time punctuated with a few words. Alex looked to Gaby while he put on his shoes.

"Bad news." Gaby waved a piece of paper the clerk had given her. "There's a university policy limiting guest stays to one week. Your time's up."

Alex set his briefcase on the floor and approached the counter. Just when he felt like this was his home base, his one secure spot in Shizuoka. "Does that include the weekend I didn't spend here?"

Gaby conversed with the desk clerk, whose eyebrows moved around in tortuous apology. Then she reported, "It doesn't make a difference. You'll have to settle the bill and leave by ten tomorrow morning."

Alex leaned against the counter. His firm narrow bed, his private pink shell of a bathroom, the air-conditioning, the fried egg and rice breakfasts—all to be cut off by one piece of paper. "I was going to stay with McKenzie this weekend, though I haven't called him yet. Can I check in again Sunday night and start a new week?"

The desk clerk had watched them like Ping-Pong, poised for his next cue to bow. Gaby talked with him for a while, after which she was the one who bowed. "They're very sorry, but there's a coral reef conference starting Monday and every room is reserved. I'll tell him you understand you have to leave tomorrow." She concluded formalities with the clerk and Alex added his own bow as they left.

As they walked to Gaby's car, Alex asked, "Did you know about that university policy?"

"No," Gaby said. "Maybe it only exists for this coral reef conference. If you spend Friday and Saturday night with Michael, you'll need a hotel starting Sunday night. Shall I try to get you one?"

"Maybe Michael could help me with that." He didn't want to ask her to do any more for him. The priority was her surgery.

"Rao-*san* doesn't speak enough Japanese."

"Who?"

"Sorry. Private joke. I'm not incapacitated, you know. So I have bleeding tumors—I can still use a telephone."

"You certainly have a way with words." Alex held the car door open for her. By the time he got in on the passenger's side, she had put on sunglasses and started the car.

The Queen Anne's Lace flanking the long gravel driveway came up to the Honda's window and brushed both sides of the car. Tiny white petals and bits of leaves scraped against the open window and snowed on Alex's lap. The car dipped into a pothole where the driveway met the street.

"How about a pop quiz before we get there?" Gaby asked. "Mr. Aoshima thinks my husband is . . . ?"

"Dead," Alex answered.

"Of?"

"Skin cancer. He was cremated and his ashes scattered at sea. Should I know his name, by the way?"

"Ron Esarey," Gaby said. "Unfortunately, I'll have to give him my name. We'll call him Ron Stanton."

"I hate him already."

"Oh, he's not so bad when he's dead."

Alex laughed. "He is really alive, right?"

"Last I knew. My ex-husband is ensconced in some English department, I'm sure, taunting his students and seducing his colleagues. Or vice versa." Gaby leaned on her horn through a four-way stop, cutting off two white cars alternately nudging centimeter by centimeter into the intersection. "And why have you come with me?"

"To get in touch with Dr. Hayashi, who I met at a medical convention in Seattle."

"Whom you met." Gaby turned onto an even narrower road and abruptly veered into a driveway. "Are you ready?"

"As ready as I'll ever be."

The first thing Alex noticed was an array of large rocks centered in a grove of pine trees with twisted branches. The house was merely the backdrop for the garden, and had no windows. As they walked closer, Alex realized the windowless house was a three-car garage. The real house was even farther back on the large lot, with windows too dark to see into, sheltered by a deep porch under a darkly glazed tile roof.

Gaby knocked on the double door. "Let's hope his wife is still constipated," she muttered. She crossed her fingers behind her back.

When a small, dark-skinned man with pure white hair opened the door, Gaby made introductions in Japanese. Alex bowed a lot, trying not to think about Cody's heart in this man's chest. He was grateful not to feel the resentment he feared he might. Mostly, he was surprised by the liveliness of the man before him; he didn't seem in his seventies.

As Alex struggled out of his shoes and forced his toes into house slippers several sizes too small, Mr. Aoshima thrust out his hand. "Nice to meet you, Dr. Thorn."

"You, too." Alex shook his hand and presented Mr. Aoshima with a copy of his book. "A gift for you."

Mr. Aoshima took it and brushed his hand over the cover. "*Why Love Fails.* Is it a romance novel?"

"It's nonfiction," Alex said. "Psychology. Self-help."

"Oh." Mr. Aoshima looked disappointed. "I will read it with great interest. Come in, please."

"How is your wife?" Gaby inquired.

Mr. Aoshima scrunched up his face. "Tired of me. Today she complains to our daughter and grandchildren."

They crossed the hall and arranged themselves around a low table on a tatami floor. Against one wall were two antique wood cabinets. The adjoining wall had an alcove in which hung a scroll painting of bamboo leaves. A gigantic television set bridged the corner. The remaining two walls were sliding paper screens, so the room could be entirely closed off without a visible door. Aoshima left the sliding screen half-open.

"Would you like some beer?" Aoshima asked Alex.

Alex, about to say yes, caught Gaby signaling him no. "No, thank you."

Aoshima was delighted with his answer. "*Sake,* then!" He explored a cabinet and pulled out three shot glasses and an opaque bottle with a *kanji* label.

After they had drunk a round, Gaby said, "I wonder if God caused us to meet."

Alex knew she had rehearsed this line. He glanced at his host to see if he could sense her lie. Aoshima had a shrewd expression that Alex didn't know how to read.

"I also wonder," Aoshima said. "I ask myself, why did I call Gone With The Wind? Why? Maybe God made me do it. There is a purpose, I think. And you?"

"I don't know," Gaby said. "But two days ago, you mentioned a hospital, and Dr. Hayashi."

"*Ng,*" Aoshima said.

Gaby continued. "Yesterday, I discovered I must have surgery."

"I am sorry."

"I was surprised," Gaby said. "But what surprised me more was that my doctor won't do the operation."

"Yes, I thought that would happen," Aoshima said calmly.

Gaby seemed as astonished as Alex. "You did?"

Aoshima poured more *sake* into the three cups. "It is how doctors are. It is because you have no family in Japan."

Gaby asked, "How did you know?"

Aoshima raised his glass for *kampai* and drank before replying. "It is not so hard. You are a foreigner and a widow, so you have yourself alone. Am I right?"

"Yes." Gaby bent her head and smoothed invisible wrinkles from her skirt. Alex perceived the words had somehow hurt her.

"That is why I went out of my way to mention my hospital. Do you want to go to my hospital?"

"Well . . . yes."

"Then, don't worry, please. No problem. Saishinkai will treat you, and you will be fine." Aoshima filled Gaby's *sake* cup.

"I couldn't find Saishinkai in the phone book. Could you please give me their phone number and address, Aoshima-*san*?"

"Yes, yes. But let's talk first. I enjoy speaking English." Aoshima fixed his dark eyes expectantly on Alex. "Let's talk about Hayashi-*sensei*. You met him at a medical convention?"

"That's right. I was impressed with his . . . case report."

"You had no trouble talking with him?"

"Trouble?" Alex coughed. "You mean, his English . . . ?"

Gaby attempted a rescue. "A lot of medical terms are the same in both languages. The more technical, the more similar, *so desu ne*?"

"English is no problem for Hayashi-*sensei*. It is talking." Aoshima cradled his foot in his hands, then looked up with an impish smile. "But he is a very important surgeon—why should he talk to an old retired businessman like me? What was his case study about?"

"Heart surgery," Alex said.

Aoshima touched his chest. "I know a few things about heart surgery. What was unusual about this case?"

Alex recited the coroner's report on Cody. "Well, the patient was in a bad accident. There were skull fractures, internal bleeding. Burns."

Aoshima asked, "Did the patient survive?"

"No. He died."

"If Dr. Hayashi could not save him, then nothing could."
Aoshima clucked his tongue. "Our friend Hayashi is a very good
surgeon."

"Do you have his phone number?" Alex asked. "I'd like to
look him up while I'm here."

"I don't have it. Dr. Hayashi is all surgery. I never called
him or saw him after. When Stanton-*san* goes to my hospital,
you can ask for him there. Tell me, are you as good a doctor as
he is?"

"I'm not a medical doctor. I'm a psychologist," Alex said.
"A therapist."

Aoshima stared awhile before resorting to Gaby as a human dictionary. She spoke a few sentences in Japanese. Then he
said, "We Japanese don't do much saikozerapi. It is not much
use to tell our problems to strangers."

There it was again: we Japanese. The national superiority
complex. "Maybe you Japanese would be healthier if you did,"
Alex suggested.

Gaby cleared her throat.

"*Ng*. But we Japanese are strong. Our ways have lasted
thousands of years. Even the atomic bomb, we survive."

Suddenly, Alex did resent Aoshima. Aoshima was in his
seventies; so what if he had died last year? No more *sake* to
drink? No more English to practice? It was Cody who should
be alive. What right had Dr. Hayashi to take the heart out of a
twenty-year-old boy to prevent an arrogant old Japanese man
from dying a natural death? "No one would deny Japan's
strength," Alex agreed. "Especially not the Chinese. Look at
Nanking."

Gaby glared at him.

Aoshima pursed his lips. "It is hard to say what happened
when the Japanese army visited Nanking. There are many different accounts."

"Visited? Is that what you call it? A *visit*?" Alex wanted to
punch his fist through his host's paper door. Why was his own
son's heart in this prejudiced man?

Gaby's voice rose to helium heights. "Thorn-*san*'s hobby is politics. He enjoys argument. It is an American trait. He doesn't mean to offend you. *Gomen kudasai,* Aoshima-*sama.*"

"But I like American argument!" Aoshima roared. "It is more interesting than polite-this, polite-that, *nani, nani, nani.* Let's drink more *sake.*"

Gaby's mouth fell open, silent.

Alex held out his tiny cup. "Bottoms up," he said contritely. He had to control his anger for Gaby's sake.

Aoshima chuckled. "Yes, yes, bottoms up. I remember. Oh, I miss America. I don't like retirement. Too much wife, *so desu ne?*"

"*So desu,*" Alex said. Wow. Was he the American counterpart of Mr. Eguchi, suddenly being able to speak Japanese under the influence of alcohol? Not that his word or two equaled precise quotes from Lennon and McCartney.

Aoshima, in half-lotus position, hitched his bare foot higher on his opposite thigh. "Tell me, Thorn-*san,* what is your impression of the A-bomb?"

"It's bad," Alex said without hesitation. "And it was wrong for the U.S. to use it. Now, if China had dropped the bombs on Hiroshima and Nagasaki, I might not think it was so wrong . . . but I would still think it was bad."

Gaby buried her face in her hand, shaking her head.

Aoshima's eyes sparkled. "*Ah, so desu ka!* You agree with nuclear weapon ban?"

"Absolutely." Alex drained his cup and set it on the table.

"But you like Chinese better than we Japanese?"

Alex drew a breath. What had he got himself into? "In the case of World War Two, yes. In all cases, not necessarily."

"That is very interesting," Aoshima remarked. "We Japanese believe Americans to be racist. You are against us Japanese because we are the yellow man, and white men feel superior. But the Chinaman is also the yellow man. Yet you like the Chinese. So it seems, Thorn-*san,* that it is not a matter of race, but of nations, and perhaps Americans are not so racist, after all."

Alex felt his rage retreat. He had always been a sucker for

logic. Now he felt compelled to cover the other side. "Well, many Americans are racist."

"Why do you say 'Americans' as if you were not American?" Aoshima asked innocently. "In English class, I was taught to say 'we Japanese' because I am Japanese. But you don't say 'we Americans.' Why is that?"

And just as suddenly as Alex had hated Mr. Aoshima, he stopped. Cody had warned him: Expect to be surprised. All the "we Japanese" that angered him so—was it all a result of one misleading English textbook? "I don't say 'we Americans' because it sounds . . . it sounds like a superiority complex."

"Eh?" Aoshima extended the syllable upward. "Very interesting. I never heard before."

Gaby carefully rose from kneeling to standing, keeping her legs together. "Excuse me." She bowed briefly to each of them and hurried out of the room.

Aoshima watched her go. Then he leaned toward Alex to speak confidentially. "She is very sick, I think. There was blood in my toilet after she used it."

Alex nodded. "She must have surgery as soon as possible."

"You will go with Stanton-*san* to my hospital?"

"If she wants me to."

"Of course she does, and I think it is good, but you should handle it carefully." Aoshima poured again from the *sake* bottle. "When will you get married?"

Alex wasn't prepared for this. "Well, I . . . we . . . we're friends. Just friends."

"Yes, I understand," Aoshima said knowingly. "But you should marry her, Thorn-*san*. It is better for women to be married."

Did Aoshima truly believe they were lovers who should tie the knot? "Our friendship is platonic." Alex tried to find another word for "platonic." "Our friendship is like brother and sister."

Aoshima chuckled. "You are not telling the truth, Thorn-

san. You came pretending to be Dr. Hayashi's friend, but Hayashi is a snob; he only talks to important doctors. No. You really came to be with Stanton. It is obvious you have feelings for this woman."

"It is?" Alex asked, surprised.

"Ng," Aoshima confirmed. "Why don't you marry her? Does it bother you that she married another man first?"

"Not at all. I was married before, too." Alex realized Aoshima had trapped him. He should stick to the buddy angle—the truth—and not give reasons for or against.

"Two widows! That makes a good pair. Is it a matter of children? She is too old to have your children, but there is more to life than children, *so desu ne?"*

Alex didn't know what to say. At last, he said, "I had a son."

"You have a son?"

"I had a son," Alex repeated. "He died last year."

Aoshima's smile vanished, and his face instantly aged ten years. "I am sorry. It is hard to lose a son. It is not the natural order. How old was he?"

"Twenty." Alex's voice was rough. Alex hoped Gaby would return soon. He wasn't ready to discuss Cody.

Aoshima poured *sake* until Alex's cup brimmed over and collapsed in a puddle on the table. "My son died at age eight. Would you like to see him?"

Alex, flabbergasted, had no words.

Aoshima twisted around and opened a cabinet drawer. He took out a silver frame and gazed at the picture before turning it around so that Alex could see it. The black-and-white photograph showed a small Japanese boy dressed in a traditional *yukata* robe and *obi* sash with wood platform sandals. His neck twisted and he squinted toward the photographer, clearly uncooperative. His hair was cut in a bowl cut, and one front tooth was missing. His eyes were alert, like Aoshima's, and he looked eager to run out of the photograph and play.

Alex noticed numerous fingerprints clouding the glass protecting the snapshot. "How did he die?"

"He was sick for almost a year," Aoshima said. "The doctors had no cure."

The little boy in the picture, emanating stifled energy, looked anything but sick. What kind of illness could kill such a vibrant boy? "How . . ." Alex could hardly believe he was asking this. "How did you get over losing him?"

Aoshima took the picture back and touched the glass over the boy's cheek. "I never did, in one way. I still miss him. But I no longer miss him with pain. Pain fades—you'll see."

"When does it fade?"

"When you decide so. Shinsuke was troublesome, but he made us laugh. My wife and daughter are sad by nature. I resolved to become the happy one in Shinsuke's place. I fought my grief." Aoshima's gaze flickered up. "In my father's day, every family had a child die—of birth, of illness, of accident. Unreasonable death is part of the human challenge, generation after generation, *so desu ka?*"

"I suppose so." It was too much to think about here, in this room.

Aoshima sighed deeply and laid the photograph back in the drawer. "Do you believe in God?"

"I'm not sure. Not in a traditional way."

"I am a beginner at it, but, as you Americans say, I think there is something to it. How does it go: When a door is closed, a window . . . what does a window do?"

"Opens," Alex said. "A window opens."

He looked up to see Gaby standing by the screen. She had been there for a while. She placed her forefinger over her lips and quietly stepped back into the hall. She coughed before reentering the room.

Aoshima startled and put his smile back on. "Are you all right, Stanton-*san*?"

"Fine, thank you," Gaby replied. "I hope Thorn-*san* hasn't bothered you with more arguments?"

"I insist you bring him again." Aoshima rose like a dancer, crossing one leg over the other and not using his hands. "We discovered we have much in common. Not so argument. I will go find the card of Saishinkai Hospital." He left the room.

Gaby gave Alex a hand and helped pull him up. "Overwhelmed?"

"To put it mildly," Alex replied. "How much did you hear?"

"I came back when you were looking at the picture of his son. I had no idea."

"I told him about Cody's death."

"Did you tell him . . . ?"

"No," Alex said. "I couldn't. There's no point to his knowing."

Aoshima returned and escorted them to the entry. While Alex laboriously tied his shoes, Gaby and Aoshima chatted in Japanese. Then came bows all around, and Aoshima gave a business card to Gaby.

When they were out the door, Alex felt sun scorch the back of his neck. Black pine needle shadows splintered the bright granite surface of a large vertical rock. He found himself thinking about Aoshima's words, "the human challenge, generation after generation." He wasn't the only man who had lost his son.

Twenty-eight

Cody began his life as bloodily as he ended it. Jane had been in labor nearly twenty hours, Alex by her side. Her fingers were nailed into his forearm, her eyes turned space alien, sapphire blue irises set in red from exploded blood vessels. Trapped in a pain that made it a struggle for her to breathe, she couldn't speak, only glared at Alex as if he were Satan incarnate. The doctors resorted to cesarean section. Cody was tangled up in the

umbilical cord and Jane was bleeding too much. In his state of
worry and exhaustion, Alex first glimpsed his son as a seven-
pound glob of mucus and blood, and feared him. Only after he
was assured Jane would be all right, after they cleaned up Cody
and set him on Jane's chest, did the miracle sink in, did he realize he would give his life for the red, wrinkled baby that
couldn't even see him yet. Jane said "never again" and she meant
it. Cody was their first, last, and only child.

And, like many only children, Alex had to admit Cody became a spoiled brat. Cody was the focus of attention that allowed Alex and Jane to ignore their marriage as it drifted from
adequate to disappointing and finally collapsed out of mutual
loneliness: separate bedrooms, separate private thoughts. Cody
had long hair that shone like a wheat field in the sun. He had
his mother's jewel-blue eyes. Strong, handsome, curious, he expected everyone to love him and most everyone did. Alex and
Jane had set him up to be a god; they could hardly blame him if
he acted like one, always zooming off to his next adventure,
throwing tantrums or sulking fits if anything got in his way.

After the divorce, Alex recognized that the lack of discipline was hurting Cody in the long run and tried to establish
limits when Cody visited every other weekend. At first, Cody
reacted by slamming doors, swearing, stewing in lethal moods
only teenage hormones can concoct, and blasting nerve-racking
music at top volume from his room.

When Cody was sixteen, and sauntered home one night
at two A.M., Alex grounded him for two weeks. Cody ran away—
to Jane, who canceled the punishment. It became a pattern, with
Alex cast as the Bad Cop while Jane hung on to—cherished—
her former role (his, too) as Santa Claus. Visits became scarce
and conversations scarcer.

Was it because Cody was closer to his mother that his
death was easier for Jane? That she had no unfinished business,
no need for future reconciliation? Or was it that she believed
Cody had gone "to another plane" and she would reunite with

him upon her own death? Alex wished he could believe in an afterlife, but he couldn't. Not only was Cody gone, but Alex bore the guilt of having failed his one and only son.

Cody was friendly, appealing, and had a fine questioning mind, but he was also impulsive and arrogant. Alex hadn't taught him to follow rules. He pictured Cody jumping onto a motorcycle and bursting forward, scorning a helmet, flaunting his immortality with his long, flowing hair. Alex should have protected Cody—from his own bad instincts.

He should never have agreed to let Cody spend an exchange year in Japan. At the time, he thought the experience might help Cody mature, but a small, guilty voice inside him kept asking if he had wanted Cody to go to Japan not for Cody's benefit, but for his own selfish motive: to get his son away from Jane as the first step in getting closer again.

Sometimes you just have to forgive yourself.

That was the moment he began to want Gaby, Alex decided. No one had ever told him that before. It was her compassion that drew him. A woman willing to let him cry in her car, through ten gallons of gasoline, if necessary. Gaby had learned how to accept hardship and bad luck. If he could learn from her, there might be a chance for him. He was beginning to express a few feelings in the safety of her presence. With her strength, could he move on, instead of endlessly going back over all the memories and mistakes?

"There's no answer," Gaby said. They were in her car, parked in Aoshima's driveway in the shade of a pine tree, windows rolled all the way down.

"There isn't?" Alex, broken out of his thoughts, had no idea what Gaby meant.

Gaby flipped her cellular phone shut and started the engine. "At the Endos'. The whole family wouldn't leave on vacation the week before final examinations. Something's not right."

"Oh, yeah, Junko's friend."

Gaby studied his face. "You haven't been listening, have

you? Alex . . . you just met a stranger who's alive with your son's heart. Should I take you back to your hotel, leave you alone to think things over?"

"No," he said with conviction, "I don't want to be alone."

"Do you want to talk about Mr. Aoshima?"

"Not really. At least, not now. Let's keep going, if it's all right with you."

Gaby smiled. "It's my job, remember?"

He longed to reach for her hand, to touch her shoulder, anything for more contact, but Gaby would probably interpret anything physical as another pass. "What's next? Calling Dr. Hayashi?"

"Or just going to Saishinkai Hospital," Gaby said. "I know you'd think phoning would be easier, but in my experience, they feel more of an obligation to help you if you're there in person. Plus, I miss the subtleties of what they're saying over the phone."

"Fine with me, but isn't it a long way from here?"

"Maybe two hours? We've missed the morning commute. If we leave from here, we could eat lunch in Fuji City and still have a few hours left at Saishinkai before five o'clock. I have nothing else to do today. Do you?" Her fingers tapped on the steering wheel.

"But if Hayashi isn't in today, we'd have wasted the trip," Alex objected.

Gaby wet her lips. "Well . . . I can't register as a patient over the phone. They have to see my national health card and green card. I was hoping if I could get the paperwork done to-day, a doctor might be able to see me tomorrow, before the weekend."

He'd forgotten that talking to Dr. Hayashi wasn't the only reason to go to Saishinkai. Gaby needed her surgery: the sooner the better. "Good idea," he said. "Let's go."

Gaby started the engine. "You're probably right; you couldn't see a cardiac surgeon without an appointment. I could go alone today, set it up, and come back again with you."

"I'd like to go with you," Alex said.

"Even though I haven't fixed the air-conditioning in this car?"

"Even so."

At first, Gaby had sped along on the Tomei Expressway, but an accident caused cars to thicken to a crawl, and she was forced to halt behind a tiny snail-shaped van. Trapped, engine idling, on the road from Kyoto to Tokyo. She glanced over at Alex, who hadn't even noticed they'd stopped, deep in his thoughts, his gaze far away, far inside himself.

This had once been the road ancient lords and traders walked for hundreds of miles, building castles and temples along the way. There had been fifty-three stopping points where travelers could eat and rest and admire striking views between the Pacific Ocean and the foot of Mount Fuji. What would a wood block printer today commemorate out of the clutter of power lines, billboards, and factories?

There was still the mountain. The phenomenal grace of Mount Fuji's curves was a privilege to see, a sight Gaby never took for granted. Even her students who had lived in this prefecture their entire lives would always comment in class if, on the morning train to school, they'd had a view of the entire volcanic peak. Gaby scanned the sky, peering up around a bug stain on her windshield. There was no mountain. Or was that one piece of it? A diagonal line of navy blue under the bright cloud cover?

Traffic moved forward again. Gaby saw flashing police car lights and two cars on the narrow freeway shoulder, one facing the wrong way with a sprung hood and broken windshield. "It's bad—don't look," she told Alex, who was already looking.

"How many accidents are there?" he asked as if it were a profound question, not small talk.

"On the Tomei? Three or four a day."

"How many are fatal?"

"I'm not sure. Does it matter?" What could she say to someone whose son had died in traffic? Through her open window, she heard garbled voices from the police radio. A handful of people were crouching in a circle over someone on the ground. She noticed a black high-heeled shoe on the pavement beside a shard of twisted metal.

To distract Alex's attention, she said, "Do you know what you're going to ask Dr. Hayashi?" She didn't look at him but concentrated on watching for the Fuji City exit.

"Pretty much. I'll start with what and how and see if I can—in an indirect Japanese way—lead him into why."

"Why there was no hospital bill?" Gaby tried to work into the left exit lane, but a white Toyota cut her off, beeping its horn.

"Why he didn't call me. Or Jane. I assume it was probably too late to talk to Cody, but Jane would have liked a chance to pray for him."

"And you?"

"I would have liked to have known he was dying. To mentally say goodbye before he was gone."

"That's important." Gaby escaped into the exit lane, letting the other cars continue to fight their way to Tokyo. The toll booth had no line. After paying her fee, she headed north on Route 139, directly toward the mountain she couldn't see.

Fuji City was a paper-mill town, and funnels of yellow smoke rose between buildings. Gaby recalled that peculiar thick, sulfuric stench from the old wigwam burners in Oregon. Environmental laws had closed them down on one side of the Pacific, but not on the other.

The air improved as they drove inland to Fujinomiya, a smaller city whose primary economy was tourism. Gaby found a rare parking space on a side road, rather than in an underground parking lot, and they got out.

Alex stretched. Crescents of sweat darkened the underarms of his checked shirt. Her blouse felt sticky and her hair was gritty and tangled from driving with the windows cracked open. They walked to a small restaurant shaped in an A-frame and painted like a miniature Swiss chalet. Once inside the door, the pungent fishy odor of *oden* canceled any illusion of Switzerland.

They sat at a polished wood counter and Gaby ordered bowls of noodles for both of them. "You know, Junko is serious about climbing Mount Fuji on Sunday."

Alex took a paper napkin and wiped the sweat off his forehead. "How can I get out of it? Nicely, that is."

"Her feelings will be hurt if you don't go," Gaby said. "She'll think you're snubbing her because she didn't tell us about Endo-*kun* right away and she'll carry that burden of shame for I don't know how long. It will make it harder for her to remember Cody, believing she angered his father."

"Gaby, that's not fair! This is supposed to be a road trip, not a guilt trip." Alex smiled—handsome, appealing.

Gaby caught herself wanting to touch him: just his shoulder or his arm would do. She reminded herself to listen to his words instead of watching his lips. "Why can't you go? It might do you good."

"How? For the exercise? I don't need exercise."

The noodles arrived in large shellacked bowls, topped with shredded meat, hard-boiled eggs, chopped green onions, and slivers of dried seaweed. Gaby blew on the hot broth. "Cody wanted to climb it, didn't he?"

"I'm not sure I *can,* Gaby. Have you done it?" Alex lifted out a tangle of noodles with chopsticks and gulped them eagerly, like a baby bird chugging a worm.

"Well, no. But every fall I get reports from students who went to the top during the summer. Including frail-looking students who don't work out."

"They're young," Alex countered. "Youth conquers all."

She couldn't argue that. "Junko will be disappointed," she murmured.

Alex didn't respond.

When they finished eating, Gaby asked the waiter for directions to Saishinkai.

The young man looked alarmed. *"Are you all right? Was the food all right?"*

"We're fine, and the meal was delicious. We're going to visit a friend in the hospital."

The waiter's eye began to twitch in a fast tic. *"Do you know Route 139?"*

"Yes, we came on it."

"Continue past Fuji Skyline Road, and e . . . to, continue to continue. It becomes long and winding. There is a turnoff road at a gas station, where there is a sign for Homei brand rice. That goes to the hospital."

"Thank you very much." Gaby bowed and left some change on the counter.

Alex watched. "Lester said you don't tip in Japan."

"You usually don't," Gaby said. "But he deserved it for enduring the torture of speaking to a *gaijin*. And not asking the usual three."

As if on cue, the waiter asked, *"Are you from America?"*

She'd spoken too soon. *"Yes, we are."*

"Ah!" The waiter laughed nervously. *"Ah, yes. You are Americans, then?"*

"Tourists," Gaby said, edging out the door. *"Thank you! Goodbye!"*

She and Alex got in the car and fastened their seat belts. It was easy to get back onto Route 139, and once they passed the intersection of Fuji Skyline Road, the road narrowed, buildings shrank into houses, and traffic all but disappeared. The road began to rise and curl around hillsides tiered with green tea bushes. The hills grew steeper and uncultivated, thick with wild vines, sumac, scrub maple, and bamboo.

Crowded onto the shoulder of the road was a brief row of

shops—wooden sheds on stilts with corrugated tin roofs: a bar, a convenience store, a rice and hardware store, and these were followed by an open lineup of vending machines tapering to a single gasoline pump. Gaby didn't see a sign for Homei rice, so she pulled as far off the road as she could beside the vending machines, where a man was tying a sack of rice on the rear fender of a girl's pink bicycle.

"*Excuse me, I'm looking for Saishinkai Hospital?*"

"This again," Alex said.

"No one knows addresses," Gaby reminded him.

"Only post offices and pizza parlors," Alex finished for her.

"*Where are you from?*" The man asked, sticking his head almost inside Alex's open window. If Ernest Borgnine were Japanese, he'd look exactly like this man.

"*America,*" Gaby said. "*Is this the road to Saishinkai?*"

The man pointed with his whole arm, twisting his torso. "*That is the road, right there. The gravel road. Stay on it until you see the hospital. Are you all right?*"

"*We're visiting a friend.*"

"*You have a friend in Japan?*" He couldn't believe it.

"*Our friend was in an accident,*" Gaby said. "*We must hurry.*" She let the car slip forward ever so slightly.

The man jogged beside the car, keeping his head in the window. "*You speak good Japanese. Are you a student?*"

"*I have to go. Thank you! Doumo!*" Gaby eased into first gear and the man dropped back, waving from the gas pump as they turned onto the gravel road. "Well," she told Alex, "I've avoided the issue of *natto* twice in a row. Maybe that's a good sign."

Alex laughed. It was good to hear him laugh. "I feel like we're off to see the Wizard of Oz. Are these yellow bricks we're driving on?"

The gravel was smooth but loud beneath the tires. She had to raise her voice to be heard. "I wonder how ambulances reach this hospital?"

"Slowly," Alex shouted back.

No doubt about it, Alex was getting funnier. Before Cody's death, he might have been described as "fun." Maybe he was one of those competent, carefree men she always craved but who never noticed her. It was nicer to be with him than to be alone, she realized, with a tiny jolt of surprise. Alone, she'd be brooding and anxious about her surgery. Sometimes, company was better than symphonies.

When the road widened, Gaby knew the round two-story building ahead had to be Saishinkai Hospital. It looked like a flying saucer that had landed smack in the middle of a clearing. Except for a low boxwood hedge skirting the foundation, no landscaping had been done to help the hospital blend into the slightly sloping field it had crashed on. Behind the building was a helicopter on a square landing pad painted with a red cross.

As she drove closer, she saw the curved concrete walls were embedded with tiny pebbles that created the appearance of gray sandpaper. Skinny slits of windows were spaced evenly around the outer wall. The windows were dark, as well as the entrance. The taxi port and bus stop were eerily vacant.

"Is this a ghost hospital or what?" Alex asked softly.

"I don't know." Gaby drove through a portal to an underground parking lot, reassured to find the ground level full, mostly with luxury sedans. She found a space on the second level down and parked. She looked at Alex. He looked back. They said nothing.

Then he got out. Gaby heard the echo of her door as she slammed it shut and locked up. She and Alex walked side by side to the entrance, where glass doors jumped apart to let them into a cement entry with wheelchairs folded up along one wall. A second set of doors opened into a lobby laid out like a bank, with plastic ropes marking where to stand in line. Rows of space-age black chairs lined up on spotless sand-colored tile. About half the chairs were occupied. The air was fresh and cool, faintly tinged with antiseptic.

Gaby felt her throat tighten. She had to make herself swallow. "Are you ready?"

"Yes," Alex said. "Are you?"

She nodded. "Here we go."

Twenty-nine

An hour later, Alex was waiting in the anteroom to the fourth-floor office of Dr. Hayashi, whose afternoon surgery had been canceled, due to the patient's death. Alex sat in a stuffed chair designed for shorter and thinner people: his knees higher than his lap, his elbows resting outside the chair below the armrests, the padded seat snug against his hips.

Gaby had negotiated his unscheduled visit by working through a hierarchy of referrals from desk to desk, office to office, bowing and launching into flurries of Japanese in an unnaturally high voice. Alex noticed her bows got lower and her voice got higher each step of the way, until she was practically kneeling on the floor and singing like Madame Butterfly. She knew her way around a hospital—perhaps from direct experience.

Since Hayashi spoke English, Gaby had left him alone to wait for the surgeon so she could go back to square one and begin all over again, this time for her polypectomy. They agreed to meet at the door in the front lobby.

Alex waited. Time passed. He looked at a stack of magazines on the end table, all in Japanese. He came across one titled in English: *My Wife.* The cover image of a young Japanese woman sticking out her tongue to lick cotton candy made Alex think it was a fashion magazine for teenagers. He opened it and saw the same teenage model wearing only a string bikini bottom, kneeling on a heart-shaped bed. She shoved her bare ass toward the viewer and coyly looked back over her shoulder. Alex set the magazine aside. It didn't seem right to have men's magazines in a cardiologist's waiting room.

A man in green scrubs and cap, feet wrapped in plastic bags, walked past Alex and into the office.

Was that Dr. Hayashi? He seemed too young to be a doctor, much less a cardiac surgeon. Alex waited, unsure. The man came back out carrying a clipboard.

"Dr. Hayashi?" Alex asked.

He froze at the sight of Alex, then shook his head. "Sorry. He is not in."

"Do you know when he will be?"

"I'm sorry. I cannot speak English." The man in scrubs bowed and rushed off.

Alex paged through a news magazine, then a comic book that alternated scenes inside a skyscraper penthouse and outside an archaeological dig. The Japanese characters had big blue, green, and purple eyes. He couldn't figure out the story.

Another doctor entered, dictating notes to a nurse at his side. The nurse wore an old-fashioned white uniform, complete with folded hat. Alex thought he heard the nurse murmur "Hayashi-*sensei*" while she scribbled on a chart and he looked more closely at the doctor in the white lab coat. He was in his fifties, with silver wings flaring back from the temples of his jet-black hair. His features were symmetrical, and he might be considered good-looking if his nose and mouth didn't seem too small for his round face. He had perfected the art of ignoring people in his waiting room. Was this the doctor who had operated on Cody?

"Mr. Thorn?"

"Yes!" Alex stood.

"I am Dr. Hayashi." He extended his hand. His handshake was weak. "I am sorry I have but a moment to talk to you. We're a bit busy this afternoon." His accent was British. He gestured Alex into his office, went around a large desk, and sat in the tall leather chair behind it, a king on his throne, backed by a glass-paneled bookcase full of medical references.

Alex took a chair in front of the vast desk. "I'm very grateful you could spare me a moment." How much of his precious moment must he waste in polite small talk? "On July ninth of last year, you operated on my son, Cody Thorn. A heart transplant. Do you remember?"

Dr. Hayashi frowned. He had the kind of frown that inspired fear in the innocent. "I did not perform surgery on an American."

Alex felt giddy: Saishinkai wasn't the right hospital, Aoshima had someone else's heart, maybe the Korean laborer's he was told he had. "Are you certain? I am sure my son's heart was used as a transplant."

Something began to click into place behind Dr. Hayashi's dark brown eyes.

Alex went on. "For a Mr. Aoshima?"

"Yes, of course. It was a very successful match. Type AB blood, as I recall. The boy—the boy was the organ donor, wasn't he?"

"So you only treated Aoshima, not my son?"

"Ah, your son." Dr. Hayashi thought for a moment. The frown melted; he looked only sad. "His injuries were severe. He was brain-dead on arrival. He had been hit by a truck. A motorcycle accident, wasn't it?"

"Yes," Alex said. "Was Cody wearing a helmet?"

"No," Dr. Hayashi said softly. "But it might not have been any better if he had. His spine." He said no more, as if the mention told the whole story.

"Did you try to save him?" The words blurted out. "Did you at least try?"

Dr. Hayashi nudged a box of tissues forward. His hand was notably clean and well manicured. "Your boy could not be saved. I am deeply sorry for your tragic loss." He sneaked an almost imperceptible glance at his watch. "Perhaps you could make an appointment for another time. Today is rather chaotic. I have a new emergency on the table as we speak, being prepped right now."

Alex hurried on. "Why didn't I receive a bill from Saishinkai?"

"Ah, that I can explain. The transplant recipient paid all costs. It is typical. There are so few organ donors in Japan—due to religious reasons—that patients are very grateful to organ donors' families." Dr. Hayashi rose and extended his hand.

Alex remained seated. "Why wasn't I contacted immediately?"

Dr. Hayashi was surprised. "Weren't you?"

"I didn't get a call until the next day."

Dr. Hayashi sucked in a breath. "I am very sorry. The boy's host father. I was told another doctor called you. I myself could not leave the OR at the time."

"Host father? Cody didn't have a host father," Alex said. "He lived in a boardinghouse, in his own room. He was a university exchange student. Who gave permission to use his heart?"

Dr. Hayashi paled. "You did. By phone."

"I didn't," Alex said. He saw a flicker of alarm in Hayashi's eyes before he composed a face immune to lawsuits.

"I sense your pain in this unfortunate misunderstanding, Mr. Thorn. I assure you I and Saishinkai Hospital acted in good faith in the interest of your son, as with all patients. I will have administration explore this matter, and perhaps we can talk again next week. Please, Mr. Thorn, I do not wish to be insensitive, but there is a patient awaiting surgery. Surely you understand I am obligated to . . ." He stopped there, opening his office door.

Alex reluctantly got up to leave. To his surprise, Hayashi left with him, locking his office door behind them. They said their goodbyes, shook hands briefly, and bowed, but as Dr. Hayashi strode toward the elevators, so did Alex. Hayashi pushed the "down" button a second before Alex arrived. The door opened at once, and they both got in.

Dr. Hayashi was clearly uncomfortable standing beside Alex, the two of them alone in the elevator after having said goodbye.

"One more question, a small one. Why did you tell Mr. Aoshima that his heart donor was a Korean laborer?"

"He was never told that," Dr. Hayashi said, watching the lighted numbers over the door. "It is Saishinkai policy never to mention any details about the donor to the recipient. We feel it is healthier if they do not know." The elevator stopped on the second floor, and Hayashi escaped. "We will talk again, Mr. Thorn? *Sayonara.*"

As the elevator shut its doors, Alex watched Dr. Hayashi, in his white lab coat, dash between nurses and doctors in green scrubs down an extra-bright corridor. The elevator bumped lightly at the bottom and let Alex out on the ground floor. He glanced around the lobby and noticed Gaby in the black plastic chair closest to the entry.

When he came up to her, he knew from her face that her news was not good. She had the stoic expression of someone determined not to cry. Her neck muscles were taut and her lips pressed together. She forced a smile when he came near. "Any luck?" she asked at the same time he said, "What's wrong?"

"You first," Gaby said. Even her voice was stiff.

"I only saw him for five minutes, but I got a few answers."

"Good. Shall we talk in the car?"

Alex looked at her and longed to comfort her. He didn't even dare touch her. "What happened?"

"Well," Gaby said too brightly, "Saishinkai might be open-minded enough to perform organ transplants, but they won't perform surgery on unmarried *gaijin*. Even in a progressive private hospital, it's still Japan." She turned her head into her shoulder as a tear escaped down her cheek. "Let's go. If we hurry, we can beat rush hour on the Tomei."

"Oh, Gaby . . ." Alex put his hands on her shoulders.

"No touching in public," she muttered, shaking them off.

They went through the automatic doors into the sweltering heat, a muggy blanket of suffocation. The gray cloud cover had darkened to the point where the field of dry grass nearly glowed in contrast.

"Looks like rain," Alex offered.

Gaby nodded without words, still fighting for self-control. She held it together as they descended into the cavernous underground parking lot and found her battered Honda, but once they were in her car, belts fastened, ready to go, she broke down. She clutched the steering wheel, sobbing, and huddled over it, unable to stop.

It was her turn to cry. Alex reached over and lightly stroked her back between her shoulders, to let her know he was there.

Thirty

Rain slammed against the roof of Gaby's apartment and dropped in a continuous transparent sheet off the eaves, while the wind buffeted the sliding-glass doors to the balcony. Lightning twitched in the sky only a second or two before the crack of new thunder.

Gaby's air conditioner was on, but the noise of the fan was lost under the typhoon. Alex sat across from her at her table with the lights off, sipping ice water in the storm-darkened summer evening. They had finished three boxes of take-out *bento* after the long drive home.

"I'll marry you," Alex said abruptly.

Gaby heard the words as mere sounds. "I should get you back to the university hotel. If you like, I can store some of your luggage here so you won't have to drag it all to Michael's over the weekend. Do you want me to get you a hotel starting Sunday or Monday?"

"I said I'll marry you."

"Thank you. Do you want to phone Michael from here?"
Gaby hesitated. Had Alex asked her to marry him? She must be
hallucinating. "What did you say?"

"I'll marry you." Alex shut his eyes and shook his head
slightly. "I finally understand what Mr. Aoshima was telling me."

"Mr. Aoshima?"

"While you were out of the room, he said, 'You should
marry her,' and 'It is better for women to be married.'"

Gaby nodded. "So he suspected his lenient hospital might
not be lenient enough."

"I had no idea he was talking about Saishinkai."

"What else could he have meant?"

"I thought—I thought he thought we were a couple."
Alex looked at her guiltily. "I'm sorry. I guess I should have told
you. I just didn't know."

Gaby couldn't blame him. It took more than a week to
hear Japanese as it was meant to be heard: one topic presented
near another topic, the listener expected to fill in the correct
relationship between the two. "It's too late now. They know I'm
single; we can't go back and pose as a married couple." She hastened to add, "But thank you, it's very generous of you."

"I mean I'll marry you," Alex explained. "Legally. They
can't argue that."

Gaby was unsettled. Maybe it wouldn't seem like such a
bizarre idea if she weren't attracted to him. The rain blew full
force, as if pummeling her glass doors thinner. "You would do
that for me?"

"Yes." He spoke emphatically. "I want to."

Gaby couldn't help asking, "Why?"

"Because I'm selfish?" Alex suggested. "I couldn't do anything for Cody, not one thing. If I can help you in some small
way, maybe I can redeem myself a little."

"Marriage isn't exactly small," Gaby pointed out. "It goes
on your permanent record."

Alex laughed. "Like a rap sheet? Prior history of committing marriage? We've both been married before. Think how easy and painless the divorce would be this time."

Gaby looked over Alex's shoulder out her sliding-glass door. Her clothesline jerked wildly in the air, as if it had caught a big, wayward fish. A marriage of convenience. The phrase conjured up the image of a romance novel cover, a violet-eyed heroine aswirl in a billowing pink gown, destined to fall passionately in love with the man she artificially married in chapter three or four. Getting married for medical care was a different story. One that would never get published; sick women weren't allowed to be heroines unless they died. "I don't know how to get married in Japan. Or divorced. Or how long it would take."

A sharp stab of lightning, followed by a broad flash. Alex waited to speak until the subsequent thunder rolled away. "I'll reschedule my flight. I'll stay as long as it takes."

A loud bang startled them both. The bang was followed by a sequence of scraping noises. Gaby got up and went to the glass doors. A tangled heap of bicycles blocked her neighbor's driveway, one front wheel spinning in the wind. A white plastic bag flipped and jumped along the side of the flooded road. Lodged in the gutter lay a large bamboo pole with tinsel and strips of paper stuck to its leaves. "Wow. A whole rack of bicycles fell over. And someone's *tanabata* branch blew down."

Alex left the table and came to the balcony door. "Someone's what?"

"*Tanabata* branch. July seventh is *tanabata,* the star festival."

She sensed him standing behind her. What would it be like to be married to Alex for real? Panic hit her. She barely knew this man. Could she even trust him to marry her on paper only? Would he go after a piece of her carefully hoarded savings? No, that would be Lester, not Alex. Alex was honest.

"I've wondered about those branches," Alex was saying. "I've seen them all over town. What are the strips of paper?"

"Wishes. If it doesn't rain on *tanabata* . . . well, you have

to know the whole story. It's about two stars, Altair and Vega."
Gaby remained facing out the door, talking to the raindrops on
the glass. She wanted to prolong the feeling of his body behind
her, backing her up, and postpone looking at his face. "The leg-
end goes that a cowherd and a weaver princess fell in love, but
their parents—or the emperor, or some god, or whatever superior power—forbade their union and caused them to be separated forever. But they could see each other one day each year,
the seventh day of the seventh month. So every year the two
stars travel across the galaxy to meet and pledge their love."
Gaby added the important condition: "If the sky is clear."

"That's a sad story," Alex said.

"It's a happy festival," Gaby said. "If it's not cloudy and the
lovers meet, your *tanabata* wish will come true."

"It doesn't look like a good year for wishes," Alex said. A
distant grumble of thunder backed him up.

"You never know," Gaby countered. "It often clears after a
typhoon. For a day or two, the air lightens up and you can even
see Mount Fuji." She turned around, ready to face him. "We
should make wishes. We have a shot at getting them."

"How many wishes do you get?"

"One." Gaby held up her pinkie finger. "Make it good."
She slid open her paper closet door, took out small sheets of
fancy colored paper and a pen, and brought them to the table.
"This paper is for *origami*. We can fold our wishes into cranes."

"What about the bamboo branch?" Alex asked.

"I'll use my tomato plant," Gaby decided. She drew two
characters on a square piece of paper. She pushed a sheet of
green paper at him. "Write your wish." She carefully aligned
two points of her paper and folded it diagonally. Then she folded
the paper smaller and smaller, remembering the pattern as she
went. She held the two points of the wings and blew in the tiny
hole in the middle. The paper turned into a crane. It was pale
pink, with gold threads running through it. She caught Alex
looking at her. There was no mistaking his expression; he
wanted her. It didn't make sense. She reminded herself there

was never a good explanation for attraction. It had to be a com-patriot thing—two Americans struggling in Japan, a man and a woman . . . Was this what Mr. Eguchi had anticipated when he assigned Alex to be her project? "What are you waiting for?"

"Does it work if it's written in English?"

"It's worth a try, isn't it?"

Alex used a ballpoint pen to write his wish on the edge of the green paper. He folded it into a triangle and gave it back to Gaby to make a crane out of it. Then she attached stout black thread to their cranes to hang them.

A gust of wind pushed rain inside as soon as Gaby slid open her balcony door. She reached for her tomato plant, but Alex stopped her. "Let me be the he-man, okay?" He bent down under the eaves, reached through the water line, and dragged the large pot under the eaves for her. Gaby tied the pink and green cranes to the stems. The green tomatoes now appeared to be festive ornaments, too.

Alex rubbed a hand over his wet gray hair. "Well? Should I call the airline tomorrow and change my flight?"

"Let me think about it." She knew she might not have an-other choice. In Japan, she had insurance but needed a husband. If she somehow managed a trip to the States, she wouldn't need a husband, but she'd have no insurance. What was the answer? Probably a trip to America. No. She dreaded the thought of throwing herself on the mercy of an anonymous gastroenterol-ogist, whichever one would give her the earliest surgery date. For that matter, she hadn't been too happy contemplating a brand-new doctor at Saishinkai. She wanted her own doctor, Dr. Ono. Gaby gasped.

"What?" Alex was worried.

"We don't need to get married!" Why hadn't she seen the solution earlier? "I said it earlier without thinking: We should *pose* as a married couple. Appearance is everything. He won't check our passports if you show up in his office with me."

"Who is he?"

"Dr. Ono. My doctor." Gaby began to laugh out of sheer relief.

"He doesn't know you're single?" Alex asked.

"He does," Gaby said. "But I'll come up with a story. Seeing you with me will be the key." She hoped she was right.

Thunder cracked loudly, and the rain poured on.

Thirty-one

When his luggage was packed, Alex glanced around a little sadly. He had gotten used to his university hotel room. The showerhead he had to hook up to the sink. The two-way toilet handle that, pushed up, delivered a big flush, and pushed down, a small one. The gargle of the air conditioner when he turned it on; the hiss of the TV when he flicked it off. The blinking telephone light that meant Gaby had called. He had been ready to marry Gabriela Stanton and almost felt cheated that he was merely pretending to be her husband instead. The point, however, was her surgery, not his assistance.

Alex settled his bill with his racetrack winnings and bowed to the clerk: the bobbing-headed young man this last day, not the serenely cool girl. He shouldered his bags and stepped outside.

The shock this time was that he *wasn't* flattened by the usual steam iron. Last night's storm had settled the dust, the sky was pale blue, the temperature merely in the eighties, and he made it all the way to Gaby's waiting Honda before breaking a sweat.

"Good morning, Mr. Stanton." Gaby unlocked her trunk for him to heave his luggage inside.

"Good morning, Mrs. Stanton," he replied. "How's my wife?"

Gaby placed a hand on her stomach. "Optimistic," she decided.

Alex remembered to get in the car on the left side. "Will I be talking to Dr. Ono?"

"He doesn't speak English. But he probably understands it, so watch what you say. Remember your name is Alexander Stanton and look concerned for me." Gaby drove out the long driveway and turned onto the main street behind an old pickup truck carrying crates of skinny purple eggplant. "Rie called last night, after you left."

"Any luck with Ninka Bank?"

"It's very hard to crack a bank." Gaby slowed as the truck ahead of her bounced on potholes. An eggplant flew over the side onto the road. "She couldn't get the name of whoever opened that Gone With The Wind account, but she did find out the address—the same one on your bill—and that the account was closed a month after it was opened."

Alex thought. "So I was the target. It's not a plan to defraud Eguchi. It's about me."

Gaby shot him a warning glance. "Don't jump to conclusions."

"I know, I know: this is Japan," he recited. But he was concerned about Eguchi. Tuesday, Eguchi had claimed the matter of the false Gone With The Wind bill was his problem. What had he done since then?

They parked in a field of stubble and crossed a four-lane street in two phases, pausing on the middle yellow line while cars whooshed by, whipping Gaby's skirt against her legs. How could anyone live a normal life span, dealing with Japanese traffic on a daily basis? And he used to think Californians were bad drivers.

Dr. Ono's office was above a store with a sign in English: SHIZUYAMA BOOK STORE. Alex could see it was a bookstore, from one look in the window. He didn't need a sign to tell him that. Why were the only signs in English redundancies, nothing

that could help a non–Japanese speaker? He trudged up concrete steps, following Gaby.

"This lovely weather could help us get in sooner," Gaby
said. "There's no line outside. Sometimes the line goes all the
way down the steps."

Alex held the door open for her and they entered a white-
tiled waiting room with a cement floor. Three patients sat on
benches reading comic books as fat as telephone directories.
Behind a glassed-in counter, a pretty, doe-eyed woman in a
white uniform stared at him. Her mouth actually hung open.

Gaby went to the counter and spoke Japanese to the
woman, who continued to stare past her at Alex. Alex smiled
and gave an abbreviated wave of his hand. She covered her
mouth with her hand, blushing.

Gaby faced Alex and crossed her fingers. No sooner had
they found places to sit than a nurse stepped out from a cur-
tained doorway, calling, *"Sutanton-san!"*

Alex did what Gaby did; took off his shoes by the inner
doorway and set them on a rack, taking in their stead turquoise
plastic slippers with white *kanji* characters on them. He chose
the largest pair, but his heels still hung over the edge.

"It's not even eight-thirty," Gaby whispered. "We're getting special treatment."

"Is that a good sign?"

"I don't know."

The nurse motioned them into Dr. Ono's office and
backed out of the room. Dr. Ono was short, his head below
Alex's shoulders, so that Alex looked down directly onto a bald
circle of scalp. Ono's head was round, like a Kewpie doll, but his
face had none of a doll's vapidity. The brown eyes behind the
black horn-rim glasses were intelligent, observant, wary.

They took seats around a small desk crowded with stacks
of paper, books, and charts. Anatomy posters on the walls
demonstrated three of the ways to map skinless humans: muscles, blood vessels, and the digestive tract. There were white cup-

boards, a sink, and an instrument tray. Compared to Dr. Hayashi's office, it looked almost funky.

Alex heard Gaby pitch her voice higher and knew the process had begun. She and Dr. Ono talked for some time. Now and then, Dr. Ono would regard him carefully, but no questions were directed his way. He listened to the Japanese flow past his ears, unable to determine from either Dr. Ono's or Gaby's face how the outcome was shaping up.

After about ten minutes, Gaby said, "Dr. Ono asks when is your return flight to Seattle."

"The eighteenth," he said. "In twelve days."

"Tu-we-ru-bu!" Dr. Ono sucked in a breath and spoke sharply in Japanese.

Bad answer. Then Alex realized Dr. Ono was saying "twelve." "No, no, eighteen." Alex caught himself raising his voice and started over. Dr. Ono wasn't deaf. With his finger, he wrote the numbers on his pant leg. "One—"

Gaby stopped his hand. She mouthed the words "he knows."

Dr. Ono scanned a calendar on his desk, tapping his pen. "*E . . . to . . . tabun ashita. Nantoka shite mimashiyou.*"

Whatever that meant seemed to please Gaby. She got up, bowing deeply, so Alex did likewise, until they were back in the waiting room, putting on their shoes. "Did it work?"

"I don't think he believed me, but he agreed to do it. He's going to try to reschedule another patient to fit me in tomorrow morning."

"Saturday morning?" Alex asked.

"Yes, Saturday morning. Doctors work half-days every other Saturday and Wednesday. Dr. Ono schedules minor surgeries on Saturdays to use the local hospital. He borrows the office of a hospital-affiliated gastroenterologist when that doctor is off." Gaby got up and went to the reception counter. "It makes sense after you've lived here a few years."

"I'll take your word for that." Alex waited while the receptionist handed Gaby a large brown bag and explained instructions. Now there were seven patients waiting, all looking at him. It was a relief to escape outdoors.

"What's in the bag?" Alex asked.

"You don't want to know," Gaby said. "Prep stuff, just in case."

"When will you know if you're going in?"

"Ueda-*san* will call me if they can change the schedule. Maybe Rie's right—there is some *gaijin* privilege, after all."

They had a chance to cross the street and ran for it, barely making it to the field that served as a parking lot. Gaby leaned against her car. Alex could see she was in pain, but she said nothing. After a moment, she unlocked the doors and they got in.

"I thought we'd go to Gone With The Wind next, to catch up with Rie," she said.

"Fine. But I want to know what you told Dr. Ono."

Gaby maneuvered around a luxury sedan that had parked carelessly, blocking her from backing out as she'd come in. "Well, I started by apologizing for never having told him about my husband before. I said we were separated and had some problems to work out."

"Problems? Why did you have to make it a bad marriage?" Alex objected. "I wanted us to have a good marriage."

"I thought a bad marriage would be more believable. If it's bad, it explains why I wouldn't talk about it, right? Plus, it accounts for your having written a book called *Why Love Fails.* I had you traveling constantly on book tours and not spending much time with me."

"Ouch!" Alex put on sunglasses. He recognized the highway to downtown.

"You get better," Gaby consoled him. "When I called you Wednesday night after my exam, you were so worried about me, you hopped on the next flight to Tokyo. I'm giving you another chance."

"You're too generous," Alex said. Her whole manner had changed. She was much happier since Dr. Ono had agreed to perform her surgery. "Why did he want to know my departure date?"

"Well, with you leaving in twelve days, he had to try to fit me in tomorrow morning. Otherwise, I'd have to wait two weeks for his next surgical Saturday."

"Great. But you don't think he believed you?"

"No, I don't. He's too smart. And I think my green card includes my marital status as single. But you're a white American man who came with me to see my doctor and what could he say? It would be rude to claim you were an impostor! I think he agreed because he thought you were my lover, though not my husband. In the end, he advised me to work things out with you, so we fooled him into thinking we have a relationship, at least."

"We do." At Gaby's look, he added, "We're friends, aren't we?"

"Yeah. Sure." Even that was hard for her to say. She drove into an underground parking structure. Cars were crammed into small spaces, and Alex had to hold the dashboard to keep from flinging into Gaby on the tight corners.

They took an elevator in the parking lot, and Gaby had to use a key to get off at Gone With The Wind's floor. The elevator opened onto a hallway no bigger than an American bathroom with three unmarked doors. Gaby unlocked the door on the left, and they went in.

"*Gebi-san!*" Rie greeted her cheerfully, curly black hair nodding in a bow. Her spirit subdued when she saw Alex. "*Konnichi-wa, Zone-san.*"

It was a small office, crowded and messy, steeped in the odor of cheap cigarette smoke. Three of the four desks were empty; Rie was the only worker there. A radio blared breathless voices singing a pop ballad. Alex knew it was sentimental crap, though it would take him a while to pinpoint how he knew. While Rie and Gaby talked, Alex looked out the dirt-streaked window. The motions of a giant mechanical crab mesmerized him. He only watched it because it moved, but he couldn't take his eyes off it.

"Look at this," Gaby said. She held the photocopy of his canceled check in one hand, and a paper with handwriting in the other.

Alex dutifully peered over her shoulder. It was all meaningless Japanese letters to him.

"This is the information Rie got from calling Ninka Bank: 1-24-13 Kitanumi, Shizuoka-*shi*, et cetera. But there's another line that reads *gi, zen, ji*. In *katakana*, the alphabet used only for foreign words. Or maybe Rie wrote it that way." Gaby asked a question in Japanese.

Rie answered with an expressive shrug. Alex knew what Rie was saying without translation: she heard the syllables and didn't know any Japanese words like that, so she wrote it in *katakana*, whatever, you know? When Gaby translated, she confirmed his impression.

If Dr. Ono pronounced "twelve" as "tuwerubu," what would "gizenji" decode into? Alex worked on it. "Givenchy?" That was his best guess.

Gaby frowned. "It sounds familiar. I don't know where, but I've heard it before."

Rie burst into a suggestion and looked up at Alex hopefully.

"Rie says maybe it's the name of a gang," Gaby translated.

"Interesting," Alex said. "A *yakuza* connection?"

Gaby had her own idea. "*Ji* is a suffix meaning 'time, hour, clock.' I don't know about *gi,* but *ji* as a prefix means 'self,' like self-service or self-operating. *Zen* means 'good' or 'whole,' unless it's referring to the Zen Buddhist religion. So *ji-zen-ji* might mean 'self-good-hour,' more or less. That might be a group of some sort. A service group."

Rie, who had been studying Gaby's face and listening hard, blurted out a word.

"Or a cult," Gaby translated for Rie. "We need a dictionary." Gaby looked around the office. "Where's Mr. Dictionary? *Jisho wa, doko?"*

Rie promptly went to an empty desk, crouched down, and pulled a paperback book out from under one of the legs. The desk wobbled slightly, and paper clips slid toward the edge, but nothing fell off. *"Douzo."*

While Gaby scoured the pages of the dictionary, Alex resisted the lure of the mechanical crab and compared Rie's neat, tidy handwriting with the printed *kanji* on his canceled check. Who had his money? Who had profited off Cody's death, hiding under the name of Gone With The Wind? "Hey!" Alex nearly shouted. "What about a reverse directory? Look up the name from the address?"

Gaby and Rie looked at him. Gaby shook her head and went back to the dictionary. Rie mumbled something in Japanese about "reberusu." So much for that idea.

"Here's something," Gaby said. "*Gizen* means 'hypocrisy.' Unusual word. This is only a pocket-type dictionary, but it's the only *gizen* entry in here. *Gizō* means 'forgery,' which certainly applies. It must be a made-up name. I wish I could remember where I heard it before." She closed the book.

Alex was still hooked on the idea of a reverse directory. "Could we go to the address and see what or who is there?"

"I suppose," Gaby said. "But you know how hard addresses are to find. And Kitanumi is on the outskirts of the city, in the hills. To ask directions, you'd have to trespass from house to house. If you could get inside the driveway gates."

"Well, the post office got my check delivered. Can Rie crack the Japanese postal service?"

Rie spoke impatiently, and Gaby took some time to translate what had been said. Then Rie said something to Alex.

"*Sugoi!* Brilliant!" Gaby said. "Wonder Woman to the rescue."

Rie giggled.

"What is it?" Alex asked.

"Rie suggests that we order a pizza."

Alex was baffled. It was too early for lunch and it hardly qualified as "brilliant" no matter how proud Gaby was of her co-worker. Then he got it. "We order a pizza delivered to 1-24-13 Kitanumi."

"Exactly."

"And follow the truck."

"Bingo."

Rie suddenly knit her brows. *"Bin-go?"* she repeated, as if it were a Chinese word. *"Bingo wa nan desu ka?"*

"Kankenai," Gaby assured her.

The phone rang and Rie hurried back to her desk to pick it up.

"Let's do it," Alex said.

Gaby bit her lip. "There's a problem."

"The pizza parlors aren't open yet?" Alex guessed.

"That, too," Gaby acknowledged. "If Ueda-*san* calls about Dr. Ono's schedule—"

"You have to be home to get the call." Alex felt ashamed. He wanted to put Gaby first; why did he keep forgetting about her agenda in pursuit of his own? The bad marriage Gaby had invented for them was uncomfortably realistic.

Gaby picked at her thumbnail. "Right." She looked at him and said, "Wrong. I lied. I have a cell phone. It's that— Oh, Alex, I'm sorry. You see, I'm afraid of being trapped in the country without bathrooms nearby. Isn't that selfish of me?"

"No, it's not. Listen, it's been ten months since they cashed my check," Alex said. "I don't have to rush out to that address right this minute. It can wait until after your surgery."

Gaby looked miserable. "I shouldn't be holding you back. I wish—I wish I were healthier for you. I'm not the right person to help you."

If Gaby had come to him as a client, he would have known she was speaking superficially about a deep issue. So many clients hid the truth with a lesser truth. She might be reluctant to call him her friend, but she was beginning to open up to him. As he was to her. They were just beginning to make this work . . . and if he were his own client, he would ask himself what he meant by "this"?

"You are the right person to help me," Alex told her. "You have no idea how right you are."

Thirty-two

In less than an hour, the surgery was over. There had been one tricky moment, when Dr. Ono had had to cauterize a bleeder, but she didn't hemorrhage. Overall, the procedure wasn't nearly as painful as the examination had been, and afterward she'd been wheeled to a regular hospital room to rest. In the States, she'd have been sent home, but Dr. Ono wanted to keep her under observation.

Alex had played the part of concerned husband beautifully, pacing in the waiting room and buying her a bunch of pink chrysanthemums sold from a pushcart outside the hospital. He wasn't allowed to see her until visiting hours began in the afternoon, but Dr. Ono reported Alex's behavior in detail to Gaby, concluding with a thoughtful, *"He is not a bad man. Perhaps you should go back to America with him."*

"Ng," Gaby had answered, busy writing a message for Alex. *"Please give him this message that I am fine and not to waste his morning in the hospital. Tell him to go home and come back at one o'clock."*

Dr. Ono chuckled. *"Spoken like a wife."*

Of the six beds in the cramped room, Gaby's was a middle one. The bed to Gaby's right, which had a view out the window, was occupied by an unconscious woman on a ventilator. The bed to her left, by the door, was taken by an overweight

woman in her fifties, with hair dyed Easter-egg purple, contin-
uously grumbling to herself. The bed on the other side of the
door held a thin young woman with long black hair, who lay
facing the wall. The opposite middle bed was vacant. The remaining window bed was cranked into sitting position, and a
nearly bald woman with tufts of white hair on her scalp and
cheeks stared curiously at Gaby. *"Where are you from?"*

The moon, Gaby thought. I am a lunar alien in Japan.
"America."

"Are you a student?"

"Not for a long time." Gaby knew what came next: could
she use chopsticks and did she eat *natto*.

But the old woman surprised her by asking, *"What's wrong
with you?"* She was missing several teeth.

"I had minor surgery," Gaby said. *"I'll be gone in a few hours."*
So don't get attached to me, she thought.

"Oh. I'm here until I die."

"I'm so sorry."

"Guess how old I am."

Gaby figured she was in her eighties. *"Seventy?"*

The old woman laughed. Her teeth were long and yel-
lowed. *"That was many years ago. I was a youngster, then. I am
eighty-four years old."*

"Really? You don't look it."

*"Well, I am. I don't know why I live so long. I'm so bored. Each
day is the same. Six o'clock, 'Good morning! Take your temperature!'
from the voice of God."* She pointed to the small speaker by the
head of her bed. Each bed had one. *"Then, bedpan and sponge
bath. Breakfast at seven. Rice and soup. Blood pressure and blood draw.
Dr. Hello and Dr. How Are You. Lunch at twelve. One main dish, one
rice ball. Afternoon visitors, talk, talk, talk. Greedy children wanting
my money after I die. Dinner at five. One main dish, one rice ball.
Nine o'clock, the voice of God, 'Turn off your lights and TV! Good
night!' Each night, I think maybe tonight will be special. Maybe I will
die. But I don't."* She sighed heavily. *"Eighty-four years has come
to this."*

Gaby didn't know what to say. She felt guilty, wanting to rest without conversation until Alex arrived. But a good person would pay attention to the poor dying woman. *"I'm so sorry. That's very sad."*

"I should have killed myself when I had the chance."

"Really?"

"Ng. Not seppuku. That is too masculine. But I would have liked to throw myself at a train, like Anna Karenina."

A romantic who read Russian literature and shunned Japanese tradition, Gaby thought. A big dreamer. *"Have you ever thought of doing something dramatic after your death?"*

"What could I do?"

"Oh, for example, you could have a funeral with a laser light show and fly your ashes to the moon."

The old woman stared out the window. *"The moon . . ."* Her mouth worked on silently, as if chewing on a thick *mochi*.

Gaby took advantage of the break to close her eyes. The euphoria of having accomplished the surgery was subsiding, and in its wake she felt weak and sore. She must have dozed, because the rattle of a cart and the humid smell of institutional food startled her. Noon. She sat up, and an orderly set a tray table on her lap and placed a covered dish, a cup of tea, and a saucer with a rice ball on top. The seaweed wrapping the rice ball was limp, not crisp as it should have been. Gaby lifted the plastic cover of the main dish. *Sukiyaki*. She broke apart her wooden chopsticks and began to eat. It was lukewarm, and faintly metallic-tasting. The watery tea, also lukewarm, tasted like spinach. She felt sorry for the old woman, clocking her life by these meals.

The purple-haired woman had fallen sound asleep, snoring, lunch laid out on top of her lap, anyway. The depressed young woman had set her food tray on the floor. She lay on her back, her hair over her face like a black veil. The octogenarian ate methodically, first the *sukiyaki,* then the rice ball, then the tea, until nothing was left.

After the trays were taken away, a bell rang and a soft female voice over a loudspeaker announced visiting hours. Almost immediately came the sound of footsteps in the hall, glimpses of faces peering in the door and apologetically backing out. One. One-thirty.

"You're still here," the octogenarian remarked. *"You said you would be gone."*

"I'm waiting for . . . my husband."

"Well, he's not here, is he?"

"Ng." Gaby wondered why. Maybe Alex had forgotten the way to the hospital. Her car was in the hospital parking lot, and she considered driving herself home. No; then Alex would show up at the hospital after she'd left.

"Your husband doesn't love you, does he?"

"Of course not," Gaby answered automatically. *"I mean, yes, he does."*

"He doesn't," the old woman concluded. *"Well, don't feel bad. Even if they love you in the beginning, they stop. Men are all the same. Beer and TV, they love. Women, they don't."*

"Your husband didn't love you?" Gaby asked.

The old woman grunted. *"Mr. Watanabe was a cockroach husband. I was glad when he died. I do not want my ashes buried next to his."*

This was an open invitation to make a Gone With The Wind sales pitch. She should try. She owed Mr. Eguchi that, at the very least, for giving her the week to take care of Alex. *"Then, are you thinking about flying your ashes to the moon?"*

"I would rather go by train," the old woman replied. *"First, a lavish, expensive funeral, to deplete my greedy children's inheritance. Then, send my ashes in a suitcase on the Trans-Siberian Express. All the way across Russia. I would like that."*

Gaby cleared her throat. *"I know a company in Shizuoka that could arrange that for you."*

"No! Really?"

"Really. The name is Gone With The Wind. To tell you the truth, I work there."

"You work? You are a wife. Your place is at home."

"Well, of course, but . . ." Gaby couldn't think how to finish her sentence.

"It must be your husband's company," the old woman volunteered. *"You work for your husband."*

Before Gaby could formulate an answer, a young woman in a white blouse and dark indigo blue jeans stepped into the room. She had a shave-up haircut and several silver hoops in her ears. Junko. She carried a foil-wrapped sweet potato, the kind sold from pushcarts on the hospital sidewalk. Gaby felt embarrassed to be seen in bed in a loose hospital gown by a former student.

Junko's face flushed solid red. *"Sensei! I am so sorry . . . I came to visit a friend. I didn't know you were in the hospital."*

"Why does she call you sensei?" the old woman asked. She looked suspiciously from Gaby to Junko and back again. *"Don't you work for your husband?"*

"She was my English teacher," Junko explained. She glanced around at the other roommates and said in English, "Were you in an accident?"

Gaby pulled up the starchy hospital sheet. "Merely a routine test. I'm checking out this afternoon."

"Oh, good, good." Junko didn't say more, but she didn't leave.

"I hope your friend is all right," Gaby ventured.

Junko looked down at the sweet potato in her hands. "I bought him potato, for health. I am worried. He is classmate."

Last year at this time, Cody had been the classmate Junko worried about. Who was it this time? She began to wonder how many students were hospitalized before final-exam week. Grades were too important, the stress too much. "I'm so sorry."

Junko lowered her voice. "He is Endo-*kun.*"

"Oh, dear." Gaby thought of all her calls to his family, the telephone rings cut off by the answering machine. "Did Endo . . . hurt himself?"

Mrs. Watanabe tapped on her teacup to get attention. *"Speak Japanese! We are in Japan!"*

"Excuse us; this is personal," Gaby said.

"I don't care! This is my country. You are being rude."

Junko, intimidated by Mrs. Watanabe's outburst, apologized and bowed. *"We were talking about a mutual friend. It is a private situation."*

"All the more interesting!" Mrs. Watanabe countered.

Junko looked in anguish at Gaby.

"Let's go for a walk," Gaby suggested. She put her arms into the sleeves of a robe—a sheet with blue flowers cut like a robe, at least—and swung her legs over the edge of the bed. In fluorescent lighting, her shins looked scrawny and pale. Standing was a little painful, but once she was on her feet, walking was no problem.

Mrs. Watanabe watched her and Junko leave, banging her plastic dish cover on the rails of her bed. *"Come back, you stupid gaijin! This is my room; I am entitled to hear conversations in my room. You are cruel to deprive a dying woman of her last chance for gossip!"*

Junko glanced back, but Gaby propelled her forward. They walked down a white-tiled, green-walled corridor to a waiting area and sat on a bench apart from other people. "Tell me about Endo-*kun*. Will he be all right?"

"I don't know," Junko said. "His mother told me nothing. That's why I am afraid. I don't know if I can see today, but I try."

Gaby breathed deeply. Suicide was honorable only if you succeeded. If Endo tried to kill himself, his family would never mention it. "How are his grades?"

"College is very difficult for Endo," Junko said. "And, he is not himself for a year."

"Since Cody died?"

Junko nodded. "Since then. He never says about it, but I can tell it bothers."

"Did he witness the accident?" Gaby asked gently.

"He came with two men that morning. I am sorry I didn't notice more. I had no idea it was last day." Junko set the potato on her lap. She carefully unfolded a handkerchief from her pocket and dabbed precisely at the corner of one eye.

"You're a good friend," Gaby told her. "I'm sure Endo will feel better after your visit. Would you call me this evening and tell me how it went?"

Junko shut her eyes and tilted her chin slightly.

"Thank you. I'll go back by myself." Gaby got up. Junko would be less embarrassed if she were alone in her grief.

"*Sutanton-sensei!*" Junko called.

"Yes?"

"Could you please . . . I would like if you came with me."

"To visit Endo?"

"As teacher and student together, it would be easier."

"All right." Gaby glanced down at her silly robe and gown. "But I'll get dressed first." Talking to one former student in hospital attire was barely tolerable; two, unthinkable. "Wait here."

Gaby went back to her room and found a nurse pulling a curtain around Mrs. Watanabe's bed. At first, Gaby feared the old woman might actually have died, but the sound of liquid hitting metal suggested she was using a bedpan. She drew the curtain around her own bed as far as it would go, leaving the gap positioned toward the patient in a coma. Then she changed into her underwear and brown mesh tank dress. This was a dress she hadn't worn since Lester had called it "a burlap sack" but it hung loosely and comfort was what she needed today. She felt stronger in real clothes.

"*Is the gaijin leaving?*" came Mrs. Watanabe's penetrating voice.

"*Please try to raise your hips,*" said the nurse.

"*She can't leave. Her husband hasn't come yet,*" the old woman went on. "*Her husband is probably getting drunk in a bar. He doesn't love her.*"

Gaby fastened her wristwatch. Two o'clock. Where was Alex? Waiting in another part of the hospital? Lost in the streets of Shizuoka? Had Michael pressured him into drinking at Nature Squib Bar? She pushed aside her curtain.

Mrs. Watanabe pointed at Gaby. *"This woman will put my ashes on a train to Moscow."*

"Is that so?" said the nurse, tucking a sheet around her.

"Watanabe-san has a romantic soul," Gaby explained.

"Oh, really?" the nurse murmured, picking up the bedpan.

Mrs. Watanabe beamed, missing teeth and all. *"I have a romantic soul,"* she confirmed, all previous rancor forgotten.

The nurse left the room, taking care to hold the bedpan level.

Gaby met up with Junko in the waiting room. As they went down the hall, searching for the right room, Gaby realized Dr. Ono might have a point in wanting someone to take care of her. She felt hollowed out, and walking was strenuous. As it turned out, Endo was in the same room number she had, but on the floor above hers. Gaby expected another six-bed room and was surprised to find it was a double. The patient near the door was an old man, leaving the young man with his head turned toward the window to be Kenichiro Endo.

In a chair beside his bed sat a middle-aged woman in a gray-plaid dress. She had a square face, deeply lined around her mouth and across her forehead. Her straight short hairdo was either a trendy fashion cut or clipped from under a bowl at a kitchen table. She wore large white earrings and clutched a white purse on her lap. She was the kind of woman who always went to church yet didn't believe in anything she couldn't see with her own eyes.

She looked afraid when Junko and Gaby approached.

Junko bowed and presented the roasted sweet potato. *"I am Suzuki Junko, a classmate of Endo-kun. This is Sutanton-sensei, our English teacher from last year. We hope this sweet potato will nourish his recovery."*

"Thank you very much. Kenichiro, wake up." Mrs. Endo

bowed and tapped her son's shin under the white hospital sheet. *"You have visitors."* It was a false, saccharine voice in any language.

The black glossy hair on the pillow tumbled around, and Gaby saw the same sleepy face that used to occupy the rearmost desk in her classroom. His face was almost paper white, and a long, thin cut puffed pink across his cheek. She noticed a plastic bag of blood hanging from an IV rack, tubed to a needle in the crease of his elbow. His left hand was bandaged from the elbow down and wrapped over his palm so that only the tips of his thumb and fingers showed. She thought: he slit his wrists.

Junko swallowed hard. *"Are you feeling better?"*

Endo said nothing.

"Shinohara and Sakano say hello," Junko said. *"They will visit, if you like."*

Endo had no response.

"Guess what," Junko said brightly. *"Tomorrow, I am going to climb Mount Fuji."*

Endo shut his eyes.

Mrs. Endo gestured Gaby aside. *"I apologize for my son's failure in your class. I hope you will give him a chance to take English conversation again."*

"I wish I could, but I no longer teach that class. I'm sorry." She felt worse than sorry; she felt guilty. Yet how could she have passed a student who didn't speak?

Mrs. Endo held her ground, gripping her purse in front of her. *"Perhaps you could put in a good word with Marubatsu-sensei. Marubatsu-sensei is pressuring my son beyond his capacity. My boy is in despair. He must get better grades."*

Gaby was surprised by her frankness. *"What class does he study from Marubatsu?"*

"He is not in a class. Marubatsu took an interest in him, and we are grateful for his mentorship, but he pushes Kenichiro. If you are a mother, you understand how it is. I want my son to work hard, but I think his grades would improve if he sometimes took time to sleep, to eat."

Why would Marubatsu take an interest in a student who

wasn't even in one of his classes? Marubatsu never did that. Gaby was too tired to conduct an investigation on Alex's behalf. But after he had posed as her husband to enable her to get surgery, she owed Alex that. If only there was a chair for her to sit on. Better yet, a bed to lie on. She leaned against the railing at the foot of Endo's bed. *"I understand Endo-kun had the misfortune to witness a fatal accident a year ago."*

Mrs. Endo shut her eyes dramatically. Two smudges of blue powder arched up toward her eyebrows. *"You know! Did Kenichiro tell you? He was not supposed to tell."*

"He said nothing." A summary of her entire experience of Endo-*kun.*

"How do you know? Does everyone know?"

Gaby spoke hesitantly. *"Endo-san, I'm sorry, but I don't understand why Endo-kun is not supposed to talk about the motorcycle accident. Many people think it helps to talk about traumatic events. That talking can ease despair."*

Mrs. Endo began to fan herself with her thick purse. *"Marubatsu-sensei will be angry."*

"Marubatsu didn't want your son to talk?"

"He said it would cause trouble in the university. And Kenichiro has caused enough trouble with his poor marks. If he can't graduate from Shizuyama, he will never have a college degree." Mrs. Endo's voice choked up. She quickly turned to face the window, fussing over opening Junko's sweet potato. She stepped in between Junko and Kenichiro and, in her saccharine voice, said, *"Would you like some of Suzuki-san's present? It was so thoughtful of her to bring it to you."*

Endo-*kun* said nothing.

"Did you thank Suzuki-san?"

He nodded slightly.

"I didn't hear you." Mrs. Endo's voice had regressed to baby talk.

Poor Endo! He had slashed his wrists to try to end his misery, and now not only did he have to deal with his failure to kill himself, his consequent shame and severe blood loss, but he had to endure his mother treating him like a four-year-old and be on display for an attractive female classmate and a former *gaijin* professor who had flunked him. It was too much for anyone. *"Endo-san,"* Gaby asked solicitously, *"have you had lunch?"*

"Oh, no. I couldn't leave my son alone."

"You must eat something," Gaby argued. *"He needs you to take care of yourself so that you can take care of him."*

"It doesn't matter. And hospital food is not so tasty."

"There are candy bars in a vending machine one floor down." Gaby could tell by the involuntary spark in her eyes that she had found Mrs. Endo's weakness. She wasn't sure there was a candy machine on her floor, but she'd seen one somewhere in the hospital.

"Well, maybe a little chocolate would keep my energy up."

"Junko and I will stay with Endo-kun until you return."

"Don't wear him out!" Mrs. Endo warned them. She brushed imaginary lint off her son's sheet and folded the top end down. *"Mother will bring you some candy. Won't you like that?"*

Endo-*kun* rolled his head toward the window. Mrs. Endo left.

"Endo-kun," Gaby said, *"I want you to know that if you ever want to talk about what happened to Cody, I will take responsibility for breaking your promise to Marubatsu. And I can give a message to Cody's father—or not—if you would like. Let me write down my phone number."* Gaby slid into Mrs. Endo's chair. The seat was still warm. It was a relief to get off her feet. She fished through her purse for her business card.

Endo looked at Junko—a pleading, desperate look—and spoke: *"You must hate me."*

"It was an accident," Junko said firmly. *"I know it. I feel it here."* She touched her heart.

"I am the one who deserved to die. Cody was the good student. I am the bad one. Cody would not wear my helmet, so I wore it. I was a coward. He was brave." Endo's dark brown eyes filled with tears. *"I can't stand it."*

Gaby felt like a voyeur. She regretted leaving the chair, but she wanted to leave her former students alone. She left her business card on the windowsill, next to the sweet potato. But when she quietly crossed in front of Endo's bed, he spoke to her.

"Please, sensei, tell Cody's father I am prepared to die for his son's death. Cody was my friend. I never meant to hurt him." Endo was struggling not to cry.

Gaby let out a long breath. She went back to the chair and hoped Mrs. Endo wouldn't return soon. *"Cody's father does not want you to die. All he wants is to know what happened. If you could tell him, it would ease his mind."*

"Maybe I should go." Junko stood with her feet together, head bowed.

"Please stay," Endo said. *"I want you to know what happened. You were Cody's close friend."* But he directed his story to Gaby. *"It was a beautiful day, like today, after a storm. I had finals to study for, but my brain was overwhelmed, chaotic. I decided to climb Fuji-san, the most sacred shrine, and pray for good grades. My Japanese friends needed to study and wouldn't join me. Cody never had to study, because he was so smart. He agreed to come with me, and I was happy. I thought we would be gone one day, that's all.*

"I like to go on my motorcycle because it is cheaper than the train and very refreshing. Cody used to go biking in America, but had no bike here. There is a motorcycle shop near my house. I went there to repair my bike from time to time. I asked if they could rent a motorcycle to a friend to go to Mount Fuji."

Gaby and Junko waited as Endo stared out the window, looking back in time to another July day. Gaby began to worry about Mrs. Endo returning. *"And they came with you to Cody's apartment?"*

"They thought an American might be too big for the motorcycle. They wanted to see him before they said yes or no."

"I saw them," Junko murmured. *"I thought they were yakuza."*

"I think so," Endo confirmed. *"But they were very helpful.*

They agreed to loan Cody a bike from their back room. Cody paid the fee, and I stamped my inkan on an agreement to take responsibility for the motorcycle."

Gaby thought of the mangled motorcycle. No doubt, Endo-*kun* had paid for that, too. She wondered how long his mother would hunt down a vending machine that might not exist. *"How far did you get before the accident?"*

"Almost to the mountain," Endo replied. *"We were going up-hill around a curve. Cody moved into the wrong lane of the road to ease the turn. The truck came so fast we didn't see it. The truck was in neutral gear to save gas, so we didn't hear a motor. I ran off the road, into the ditch. My bike fell on top of me, but I was all right. When I got up—"*

Gaby thought of the winding road she had driven only two days before to get to Saishinkai Hospital. She had almost run over a man on a bicycle. *"If this part is too painful . . ."* Gaby left her suggestion open.

Endo didn't seem to hear her. *"Cody was lying on the road, twisted. The motorcycle was on fire next to him. I didn't know what to do. The truck driver was Korean and frightened. He had a cell phone and he pushed it at me, saying, 'Call for help, call for help! I can't, I am illegal alien. Call for help!' I called 1-1-9. Then I remembered Marubatsu-sensei was Cody's sponsor, so I told the 1-1-9 operator. I was afraid to touch Cody. I sat with him, but he didn't wake up."* Endo finally looked at Junko. *"I sat with him. I was helpless. He didn't wake up. He never came back."*

Junko had remained in her schoolgirl posture throughout his story, absorbing his words in stoic silence, her face a stiff mask of neutrality.

Gaby was torn. Endo and Junko needed time to cope with their feelings, but Mrs. Endo could barge in at any moment. *"The ambulance took him to Saishinkai Hospital?"*

"It was the closest hospital. The Korean and I stayed. Then Marubatsu came and made everything better. He took over our responsibility. He told the Korean he shouldn't be deported for an unavoidable acci-

dent. He made me promise to say nothing, to protect the Korean man. The truck driver was very grateful. Then Marubatsu told me I shouldn't have to carry the burden, either. He was so kind. He said Cody's family would not understand it was an accident and blame me, so I should not tell them. He said if I didn't tell anyone, he would fix everything. He even loaned me money to pay the yakuza for the broken bike." Endo began to sob. *"I am not worthy of Marubatsu's generosity. I can't live up to his expectations. My guilt is bigger than I am."*

Gaby thought: that bastard prick, that asshole Marubatsu. How dare he ruin this young man's life. How dare he torture him with his threats. And why? What did Marubatsu get other than control, petty power over a student? Maybe that was enough for him. Before she could collect her thoughts, her cell phone rang. Alex, at last! She got up and moved to a corner of the room, facing into it for privacy. *"Moshi, moshi?* Hello?"

"Gebi-san!" It was Eguchi. *"Where are you? At home?"*

She didn't want to tell her boss she had had minor surgery for an illness he knew nothing about. *"I am visiting someone in the hospital."* It was even true.

"Zone-san has checked out of his hotel. Is he with you?"

Gaby felt her throat tighten. *"No, he's not. What is it?"*

"Has he called you?"

Something was wrong. *"We were supposed to meet at one o'clock."*

Eguchi drew in a breath. *"Then he is still gone."*

"Gone where?" She willed Alex to be all right. He had to be all right.

"I don't know, but Rie is hysterical. He called her this morning and said something about pizza. Does that mean anything to you?"

"Yes. He's gone to Kitanumi." Why hadn't she seen it coming? Alex had been on too tight a leash, too frustrated about his need for assistance every step of the way. He wanted to achieve something on his own, but he chose the wrong project to assert his independence on. Ironically, he would have learned more about Cody if he'd stayed in the hospital with her and listened

to Endo-*kun*'s confession. Instead, he dove into the realm of forgery and finance, where he could never hold his own without expert interpretation.

"Kitanumi—ah, so desu ka. The address of my enemy. It's 1-24-13, right?"

"Yes. The name is Gizenji."

"Gizenji? A temple of hypocrisy? Is it a cult?"

Gaby had forgotten the *ji* suffix was not only used for time, but also for temples: Kinkakuji, Ginkakuji, Ryoanji, Daitokuji . . . and then she remembered where she had heard the name Gizenji: at a faculty meeting at Shizuyama University. It was the name of Marubatsu's temple.

Thirty-three

During Gaby's polypectomy, Alex sat in a waiting room, trying to ignore the stares of the other people waiting, worrying about complications and what he could or couldn't do as Gaby's husband who didn't speak Japanese. When Dr. Ono came out, he simply gave Alex a thumbs-up signal. A few women giggled at this, raising their hands over their mouths, but Alex felt huge relief. Only afterward did he realize it had been the first time he'd been concerned about a problem other than Cody's death. There might be hope for him, after all.

After Dr. Ono handed Alex Gaby's message telling him to return to the hospital at one o'clock, Alex wandered outside, wondering where to go. He no longer had the university hotel as his retreat and he didn't feel like going back to Michael McKenzie's apartment. What could he do for three hours? The weather was almost as nice as the day before, though getting hotter. He looked up and down the street in front of the hospital. Unlike Saishinkai Hospital, taxis and buses arrived in a continuous flow. The sidewalk was crowded with pushcarts selling flowers, gifts, and food. Many of the pushcarts were decorated with *tanabata* branches, paper wishes and tinsel blowing in a slight breeze, more like a county fair than the entrance to a medical facility.

Alex decided to start by getting a snack. He crossed the street to a row of counter-service fast-food restaurants, no doubt catering to hospital visitors. A take-out ramen stand was empty, but McDonald's had a line for burgers and fries at ten A.M. Looking for a place to get a cup of coffee and a pastry, Alex passed a pizza parlor and got his idea.

He didn't expect to investigate his phony Gone With The Wind bill, but if he could order a pizza and get a cab to follow the delivery truck, he could at least check out the Kitanumi address. He could return with Gaby in a few days, after she'd had time to heal. He longed to carry out at least one tiny project on his own.

Of course, the first problem would be ordering a pizza. Maybe Rie could help him with that. There was a cluster of green phone booths at the end of restaurant row. A diagram on the phone showed a disembodied hand putting in two ten-yen coins and dialing. He could do that. He dialed the Gone With The Wind number. As the phone rang, he realized today was Saturday and was about to hang up when Rie's breathless voice said, "Cone whizzer window, *moshi, moshi?*"

So Eguchi made them work on Saturdays. "Hi, Rie, this is Alex Thorn."

"Ah, ah . . . hey row, *Zone-san!*"

But then he didn't know what to say. Maybe she understood English better than she spoke it. "I wanted to thank you for your idea of ordering pizza." Silence. "What do I say to order a pizza?" Silence. "Order pizza—how?" He simplified. "How—pizza?"

"*Gomen-nasai. Wakarimasen. Sutanton-san wa, doko desu ka? Issho ni?*"

Message from Mars. All he could recognize was "*Sutanton-*

san." "Sorry. I don't understand. I'll call again. Goodbye, Rie-*san."*

"Chotto matte!"

Maybe that was another way to say goodbye. *"Sayonara."* He hung up. He strode back into the pizza parlor. He could do this. There was no one in line to order, and a teenage girl in a starchy orange uniform covered her mouth defensively before he reached the counter.

She said something in Japanese, and a gangly teenage boy in the same ill-fitting uniform rescued her by taking her place. He had round black glasses that he kept swatting up on his nose. "May I herupu you?" His co-worker gazed up at him in awe.

"Hai," Alex began. The menu was on a board behind the counter, but also under glass beside the cash register. He pointed to the cheapest pizza on the list. He held up one finger.

"Cheezu pizza, *itotsu?"* The gangly boy seemed to get it.

"Hai," Alex said. Then he drew out his photocopy of the false Gone With The Wind bill and pointed to the Kitanumi address.

The kid swatted his glasses and sucked air. "Sorry. I don't understand English."

Alex pointed to the picture of the pizza on the menu. Then he used two fingers to walk over to the address on his bill.

The teenage girl burst into a laugh and cut herself short. Her hero scratched his ear. "Sorry. I don't understand."

Maybe this place didn't deliver. Alex pointed again, from the pizza to the address, this time mimicking driving a car in between. The girl thought he was a lunatic. The boy began to blush. Alex sighed. "Delivery?"

A cartoon light bulb clicked over the boy's shiny black hair. "Ah! Deriiburi!"

"Can you do it?" Alex asked.

The boy opened his mouth and shut it. He copied the Kitanumi address on an order slip and spindled it. He looked at the clock. "Dirty minutes, please."

"Thirty minutes?"

"*Hai.*"

Alex paid and got his change, triumphant. The next step was to get a taxi. He looked through his pocket phrase book to see if anything under the "transportation" heading approximated "Follow that car!" No luck. He looked up "follow" in his pocket dictionary and rehearsed what he would say: *Tsuzuku.* Since plenty of taxis delivered visitors to the hospital, he waited twenty-five minutes before flagging one down. The doors jumped open in unison, like chorus girls kicking out their legs.

Alex got into the backseat. His heart was beating faster, realizing he had a narrow window of time to make this idea work.

"*Doko made?*" asked the driver, glancing in the rearview mirror.

Alex opened with "pizza," waiting for the in-drawn breath of anxiety in response.

Instead, the driver delivered a short speech in Japanese.

Alex saw a man in an orange uniform carrying a pizza in an insulated bag. He pointed to him. "Pizza. *Tsuzuku.*"

"*Tsuzuku?*" He added a longer speech.

The pizza deliverer got into a white car with the restaurant's logo on the side.

"*Tsuzuku, tsuzuku!*" Alex cried out as the car nosed into the street.

The driver twisted around to face him. He was young, maybe in his early twenties, with smooth narrow cheeks and features that veered dramatically to the right, as if he'd skidded out of his mother's birth canal sideways, out of control. "Sorry, I don't speak English."

"*Tsuzuku!* Pizza *tsuzuku!* Follow that car!" Alex watched his hope of finding the Kitanumi address turn a corner and disappear.

"*Doko made?*" The driver blinked rapidly.

Alex slumped back in his seat. All this just to waste his money and send his defrauder an unexpected early lunch. Was there a remote chance the cabbie might know the address? Alex handed the photocopy over the seat. "Kitanumi?" he asked.

The driver looked at it carefully and handed it back. *"Shiranai. Gomen-nasai."*

He was saying he was sorry. Alex was about to give up and get out when he had one last idea. The name Rie had heard from Ninka Bank that wasn't written on his bill. "Gizenji?"

"Gizenji! Hai!" The driver sped out of the hospital turnout and got in the lane to make the same right turn the pizza delivery car had made.

Expect to be surprised. A cabdriver who didn't know an address but knew someone's name. Alex checked his watch: ten to eleven. Plenty of time.

The driver raced through city traffic, crowding other cars and honking his horn as if he were a New York City native. When streets thinned out, the driver turned onto a narrow one-lane road with no cross streets. Alex saw a continuous green hillside on his left and brief glimpses of a stream on his right.

The driver looked back curiously in the mirror. *"Doko kara?"*

"Gizenji," Alex repeated.

The driver looked surprised, then amused. *"Amerika-jin?"*

"Yeah, I'm an American." Alex tried to remember the usual three questions. What was next: whether he was a student or could he use chopsticks?

"Natto ga suki, desu ka?"

Straight to the *natto.* "I don't know," Alex said.

The driver didn't attempt more conversation. Soon he turned into a gravel road going up a steep hill. Alex, used to near-vertical roads in Seattle, knew the driver wasn't mustering enough speed in first gear to make it. The engine whined and bushes swiped against the doors. With a thrill, Alex saw the pizza delivery car coming down at them, head on. His cabbie had to back down to the bottom of the hill to let that car out. The two drivers bowed heads to each other, and the pizza car returned to the city while Alex's taxi tackled the hill again, faster this time.

The cabdriver hooked a sharp left at the top of the drive, where the gravel lane ended in a dirt clearing, with parking spaces for about three cars. There was a sign in Japanese above a rusty wire trash basket. What kind of place was this? He couldn't see a house from the parking area.

Alex struggled to think of a way to get the cabdriver to wait, before he realized all he had to do was not pay. He stepped out of air-conditioned vinyl into mountainside jungle. The taxi driver picked up on his message and began a sequence of cautious Y turns to park in the shade of a wild plum tree.

Alex took a dirt footpath that started at the trash basket and zigzagged up the hill. A firefly landed on his shoulder and hitchhiked a few meters before whirring off. He couldn't see a building until he was around the first bend. Smack up against a green hillside of crowded cypress trees, the house looked like a small fortress. The ground floor had no windows. Solid planks, as dark and heavy-looking as railroad ties, alternated with equally dark slatted sections that might slide open. An iron-studded door commanded the exact center. The second floor sat squarely over the middle third of the building. Two large windows were eyes over the great dark mouth of the door. The steep roof, old thatch so dense it looked like bronze, hung straight, as if a third story, but flared out sharply at the bottom to create wide eaves that shaded the eye windows.

When he looked at the house from the bottom up, the roof shaped itself into a porkpie hat. But if he looked first at the black timber beam capping the ridge of the roof, it looked more like the deep head of a medieval executioner's axe, blade poised to skim the front of the building and slice the ground.

The front yard was covered with black gravel, with clumps

of grass and bamboo poking through. Alex squinted at the upstairs windows. He glimpsed a round, white face in the bottom
corner of one—a Japanese girl in a red *kimono,* kneeling. When
she saw him, she quickly pulled an inside curtain shut. Black
cloth swayed, then settled.

It was creepy. Alex decided it was time to go.

A voice came from behind him. "*Zone-san.* I did not expect you."

Alex spun around to face Marubatsu. He wore a white
yukata robe held together with a scarlet *obi* sash. The robe
reached to his knees. Below, hairless legs came down to small
bare feet shod in tatami sandals. His smooth legs looked like a
boy's, but his face was locked into the disciplined tension of
masking emotion.

"Marubatsu," Alex said. "This is your home?"

"My home and my temple," Marubatsu stated. "Why did
you come to Gizenji?"

Alex hardly knew where to begin. "So it was you who
charged me for sending Cody's body home!"

Marubatsu's nostrils flared, but his face was otherwise the
same mask. "You cannot prove that."

"Don't count on it, you treacherous piece of sh—"

"Let us talk in the garden. Not here." Marubatsu glanced
up at the girl in the window, her frightened face pressed against
the pane. "No anger in front of children. This way."

Alex took a moment to compose himself. Marubatsu was
right. His fight was with Marubatsu, not his little girl. If Marubatsu was going to hide behind a Japanese mask, Alex would
hide behind his psychotherapist's mask. He could handle this
calmly. "All right."

Marubatsu gestured for Alex to go ahead of him. Alex had
to watch his footing on the dirt path and nearly walked into a
huge rock two meters high.

Marubatsu said, "You should pay more attention." He unfolded his arms. A square white sleeve unfurled. The tiny hand

at the end, fingers held close together, tilted to the left of the rock. "Is something the matter, *Zone-san?*"

"Nothing," Alex said automatically, though he suddenly felt at Marubatsu's mercy.

"The path is not arduous. The difficulty lies in finding it and keeping it." Marubatsu's lips flickered in a faint smile. "Is it your style to stop at the first obstacle?"

"No."

"*Sorekara, douzo.* Proceed."

It was ridiculous to fear a man a foot shorter than himself. How could he hurt him, after all? Alex moved around the rock to the left as Marubatsu had indicated.

He beheld a different world.

Thirty–four

A long oval lake appeared at his feet and stretched back the length of a football field to a wall of black boulders that, at their distance, mimicked a cliff. The lake was enclosed by sloping, wooded hills. Deciduous trees crowded at the lake's edge and hovered over the water, clutching the banks with contorted root balls. The water was opaque pea-green and looked like paint. The surface, perfectly still. A herd of tiny granite islands jutted up through the pea soup, some rusty with moss, others bare. Near the shore, the submerged rocks gradually blended with rocks on land that gradually became embedded in weedy, mossy gravel up to the path. It was a masterful visual transition. The path underfoot was unclear, although the distant, overall view showed signs of a path tracing the perimeter of the lake. No ropes or signs marked the path. It was not the way Michael had described temple paths in Kyoto.

Alex turned back to Marubatsu. "Tell me how it happened."

Marubatsu looked pointedly at Alex's feet. "That is a sculpture, not a stepping-stone. A sculpture that cost thirty thousand yen, and another thirty thousand to bury it."

Alex reminded himself to keep his temper. He stepped onto a lower rock.

Marubatsu shook his head. "You have no respect for Japanese tradition."

Alex perceived the game Marubatsu was playing: force the *gaijin* to make mistakes and then accuse him of insensitivity—unless, as Mrs. Sakura had said, Japanese truly expected foreigners to be capable of mind reading. Alex studied the rocks. A few vertical ones were obviously sculpture, but most were one to eight inches above the ground, scattered within an outcropping designed to look natural. He decided the ones with moss were sculpture, and moved onto a smooth one, expecting another reprimand. "Is this all right?" He was unable to keep a tone of sarcasm out of his voice.

"Why don't we talk as we walk around the garden? After you."

Alex wasn't going to let Marubatsu choreograph their confrontation so that he could never see the priest's face, so that he would be struggling to speak over his shoulder. "Here is good enough. Your daughter can't see us."

Marubatsu raised his chin. "There is much to be learned from following a path."

"Too bad." The noon sun was beginning to burn, and Alex swiped his face with his handkerchief. "I've waited long enough. Tell me how my son died."

Marubatsu stood in full sun with no sweat, not even a sheen, breaking his face or bald head. "You Americans come to Japan not to learn from us, but to insult us. Not to respect our customs, but to rob us of our new wealth. And you say 'too bad'?"

"Oh, please. I'm responsible for the sins of America?"

Marubatsu shook an angry finger. "You insult me, even now! But you will pay your karmic debt. The sins of your ancestors, the angry souls of those you killed. You cannot escape your destiny."

Alex decided to treat him like a delusional patient and fish for information to clarify the delusion. "My destiny?"

The priest regained his composure. "That is in the hands of the gods. As it was for your son."

Alex briefly lost his footing on the smooth rock and felt a twinge of pain near his spine. He stared down Marubatsu. "Cody wasn't destined to die."

"His death was a punishment for his selfishness and arrogance." The priest had resumed his impassive face, not making eye contact.

Selfishness? Arrogance? This had to be a case of projection. Fresh sweat rolled down Alex's face and chest. "If that's so, what's your karmic punishment?" he asked the priest. "For cheating me, lying to me, and hiding your lies!"

Marubatsu replied evenly, "I did not believe you wanted to know the truth. Are you so certain yourself?"

Alex couldn't read the priest's blank expression. He hated the way Marubatsu didn't answer directly, but turned the question back to Alex. It hit him; that was what *he* did, as a psychotherapist. For a moment, the concept of karmic debt spooked him. Then he decided to beat Marubatsu at his own game. "Why do you think I wouldn't want to know?"

An enigmatic smirk brushed the priest's lips. "Parents like to think well of their children, don't they?"

Alex needed to break the pattern of questions. Throw out bait Marubatsu couldn't resist. "Tell me, *sensei,* how am I like my son?"

"You disrespect Japanese tradition. *In Japan,* no less."

He could ignore Marubatsu's bait for him. He was a professional. "How did Cody disrespect you?"

"He called himself a Buddhist. Pretended to meditate. Ate no meat when others were watching. Here, as a guest in my country, as a student in my university, he mocked me. Me, a Zen Buddhist priest!"

It was working. He had hooked this carp. "How humiliating. What else did he do?"

"In my own class, he showed off by speaking Japanese. Trying to appear smarter than his classmates who struggled with English."

Cody probably *was* smarter. Alex said nothing, letting Marubatsu go on.

"He was a selfish boy. Other professors were fooled by him, but not me. He applied for another exchange year, against my advice. He did not know when it was time to leave. It was his arrogance that caused his death."

Marubatsu had shifted directly in front of the sun, so Alex had to squint hard to look at him. "Was he arrogant to try to climb Mount Fuji, *sensei*?"

"From the first day he arrived in Shizuoka, Cody wanted to climb Fuji-*san*. I told him he had better be patient, and wait until summer."

Alex remembered Junko had said the mountain was open for climbing only in July and August. No one needed advice about when to climb it—there was no choice. Marubatsu was taking credit for nothing.

"But he was not willing to learn from me. His sponsor, no less! He went off the week before examinations, alone, American-style."

Why did he say Cody went alone? Junko had said there were two men—no, three—who showed up at Cody's door on July ninth. But Alex only murmured, "Please go on, *sensei*."

Marubatsu stood still for a moment. "Your son was so egotistical, he did not even wear a helmet. He thought himself invulnerable as a god."

Alex's throat felt thick and his hands wanted to tremble. He made fists and held them tight. Alex had heard Cody boast about his dirt-bike adventures, acting tough after the divorce.

These words hurt because of the truth embedded in the priest's exaggeration.

"As his sponsor, I was telephoned by the hospital," Marubatsu said matter-of-factly.

Marubatsu sprouted a clear aura—perhaps a heat mirage, perhaps some moisture in Alex's eyes from straining to see into the sun.

"The surgeon said he had been hit by a truck, head-on."

Alex shut his eyes. The sun against his eyelids made him see painful scarlet blotches. He pictured the grill of a truck, a motorcycle vacuumed under it, and Cody slamming onto the pavement, no helmet but his own skull. He shielded his eyes with his hand to stop the scarlet torture.

"He was not dead, but he was not aware. He had no last words." Marubatsu paused. "Are you satisfied, now?"

Alex squinted at the priest. "I want the whole story."

"All right." Marubatsu held his pose like a statue. He folded his arms, his square *yukata* sleeves dropping down in front of his chest like overlapping white flags. "Dr. Hayashi said your son could not be saved. But there was another man who could be saved, with Cody's heart." He stood straighter, pulling his shoulders back. "I do not regret my decision to save a Japanese man's life."

Marubatsu savored this moment, Alex thought. Telling the unholy *gaijin* how he really felt. After a brief silence, Alex spoke softly. "It wasn't your decision to make. You should have called me or his mother."

Marubatsu replied indifferently. "Americans donate organs. It's what they do. How was I to know the eccentric request of a pretend-Buddhist *gaijin*?"

"You should have asked for our consent whether or not you knew. We deserved to know at once when our son was dying!"

"Why? So you could choose to make a Japanese man die along with your son? There was no reason to let that happen. Cody had the same rare blood type of the man who needed a transplant. Your son's death was fortunate."

Alex wanted to strangle him. "Did the university know about this? Did they cover up for you? My letters that were never answered?"

"Your letters were referred to me, as Cody's sponsor. I had nothing more to say to you. I told the university as much as they needed to know. I wrote a letter to you with as much as you needed to know. I even returned your son's body to you. I was generous."

"You sent me a bill under a false name."

"I paid for shipping with my own money. I was entitled to recompense."

"But why under a false name? Why did you bill me as Gone With The Wind? The company Gaby Stanton joined after she was fired." Alex stopped himself before he mentioned Marubatsu's collusion with Lester to get Gaby fired. His goal was to get information, not give it.

"She is American, same as you. Any trouble about an American boy should be her trouble." Marubatsu's face held a rigid passivity. "I did nothing wrong."

Alex couldn't take any more. "Fine. Think that when you're in jail."

Marubatsu smiled slightly. "A priest? In jail? On the word of a *gaijin*?" He shook his head. "This is what comes of your Western superiority complex. You white men believe you can get whatever you want from Japan. But we Japanese are children of the emperor, descendants of gods. We will rise again as a people and make the world acknowledge our superiority. Let me be your lesson, *gaijin,* to respect Japan as you should."

"It's not just my word." Alex stepped closer, deliberately standing on a mossy sculpture rock. "I have the bill you sent and the check you cashed. I have proof of your phony bank account at Ninka Bank and phony Gone With The Wind *inkan*."

Marubatsu had stopped listening. "This is my temple, *Zone-san*. You are no longer welcome."

As if on cue, two men suddenly appeared from behind the large rock at the entrance of the garden, flanking Marubatsu.

The men were dressed in identical dark pants, white shirts, and dark glasses. They were stocky and their arms were nearly as thick as their necks. A tattoo dragon tail curled up under the taller man's ear. Each man held a knife. And of all the things that should have been running through his mind at this moment, what bothered Alex was imagining Gaby in a hospital room, wondering why he was late. He had to meet up with her at the hospital.

Alex thought quickly. He was no James Bond, but an out-of-shape, middle-aged man. No amount of adrenaline could make him beat up two men and then get back to his taxi before they caught up with him. He couldn't fight knives with words. He had to run. Since they blocked the only exit, he turned and ran on the path that circled the lake.

He heard Marubatsu laughing as he ran scattershot between the stones. His back had developed extra nerve endings, anticipating the touch of a hand or a sharp blade. After a while, a dirt path was more evident and Alex sped up. He heard no footsteps behind him, but didn't dare look back and lose his head start. The black boulders were getting closer, and he burst into a fountain of perspiration. He couldn't run all the way around the lake ahead of them. His heart would split open and he would die. The heat was too heavy for him to fight. Heart pounding, he slowed to a walk, bent over.

No one had followed him. He looked across the lake. There, at the entrance, the three men stood, positioned in a triangle, talking to each other. The tattooed man glanced across the lake at Alex and pointed at him with his entire arm. Alex saw a gleam of reflection off the blade of the knife he still held.

Of course: The path was a circle around the lake. They didn't have to waste their energy chasing him, for he'd end up at the rock by the entrance, where he'd started. He was trapped. He looked around wildly—sloping banks of trees, sticky mud, deeply embedded rocks; nothing in the natural world offered a way out. He craned his neck and looked up. No plane, no helicopter, not even a hawk to break the broiling pale blue sky.

Alex leaned against a boulder, catching his breath. He longed to splash himself with lake water, but something about the opacity of the green put him off. For a second, he hallucinated it was an artificial lake, made of thick green latex. The three men would wait for him, however long it took.

What were his choices? Complete his circle or go back the way he came? Either route delivered him to the same point. He could try to climb the steep bank, but where would that get him? Wilderness? They could find him sooner than he could find his way back to Shizuoka. Especially since he carried no water. Swim the lake, underwater? It might confuse them for a while, but the lake was too big to cross without coming up for air several times. They could easily spot a human head bursting up through the green surface.

But they had knives, not guns. They had to get close to hurt him.

Alex began to walk slowly, resuming the path, looking for a water route around the jutting rocks. One thing about the surface; they couldn't see him under the water. He stopped almost halfway back, where a hardened mud patch served as a shore. It was solid under his feet. He squatted at the water's edge and stuck his hand in. The water was mildly warm, which meant the lake couldn't be very deep.

He looked at the entrance. Marubatsu was gone. His bodyguards remained. One had sheathed his knife and was smoking a cigarette. The other was using his knife to clean his fingernails. They weren't leaving.

The shortest route would be to swim in a diagonal line directly to the feet of Marubatsu's henchmen. He decided to swim in a line that would take him six or seven meters to their right. He would come up for air enough for them to follow his line and move toward his exit point. For the last lap of his swim, he would sharply veer back to the garden's entrance. If he could get a head start, he might have a chance to run as hard as he could to his taxi. Alex didn't like the plan, but he couldn't think of a better one. If he tried to sneak through the woods, his footing would be difficult and the guards would hear him. The green lake was the best option. He took off his shoes, tied his laces together, and hung them around his neck. He made sure all his pockets were securely buttoned. Then he waded in.

At first, the water was shallow, but as soon as it reached his thighs he took a deep breath and dove under. He couldn't see well underwater; bottom dirt swirled up and his hands and feet grazed rocks. He came up for air. He had swum only a few meters. He looked at the bikers; they had seen him and their mouths were open with laughter. He took another breath and tried again. The water got cooler and began to clear a little as he swam deeper. He was glad for the weight of his shoes around his neck, which helped him keep his head fully submerged. When he came up next, he saw he had drifted off course. The next time, he was able to make a slight correction. He eyed the bodyguards. As he had expected, they had walked over to where they expected him to come out. They couldn't see him under the water, only when he came up for air.

He drew another deep breath, aimed himself toward the big entrance rock, and went back under. This time his eyes began to sting a little. He bumped against a few rocks and tried to keep his sense of direction intact as he maneuvered around them. Then his feet scraped bottom. It was too shallow to swim any farther, and he needed air.

Alex put his head up. The large rock was about five meters ahead and to his right. The bikers were more than eight meters to his left, intently watching the water where they expected him to emerge. If he could get behind that rock, they wouldn't be able to see him. His drenched clothes and the shoes hanging around his neck made it twice as hard to totter to his feet, but at least the bottom of this part of the lake was lined with rocks instead of mud, so he had firm footing. He flung himself onward, his back bent over, dripping water on rocks and moss. Step by step, the path lurched under his feet. So far, so good.

At a sudden cry of *"Maa!"* he knew he had been spotted. The two men started toward him. Alex charged through the clumps of grass and gravel in front of Gizenji. He had to keep his momentum or he had no chance of escape. He hurtled himself down the path to the parking strip and banged his knee on the wire trash barrel at the end.

Gasping, dripping water, he lunged toward his taxi. The driver was gone; the car was empty. He pulled at the door handle—locked. Two black motorcycles were parked close by, handles arched high in the air. No time to stop and think. He half-hopped, half-skidded to the crest of the driveway.

The men behind him cried out *"Chotto!"* and *"Zone-san!"* One grabbed his shirt. Alex twisted free, but in the process he slipped on loose gravel and fell. He rolled down the steep grade, folding his hands close to his chest, using what strength he had left to hold his head up from the road.

As the men's voices got fainter, an engine noise got closer—a car in low gear. Alex stopped rolling at the base of the temple driveway and pried his eyes open, squinting hard. Marubatsu's men stood at the top of the driveway, looking down on him. But a shriek of brakes and an instantaneous shadow brought a car right on top of him.

His entire life flashed through his head and made sudden sense to him in a way it never had before. He lost all fear. All the while, in slow motion, he saw the dirt-streaked underbelly of a front bumper loom over him and brush his shoulder as it bounced to a stop. He smelled gasoline and rubber and felt the hot breath of the car's engine.

And he thought: *I've got to meet Gaby at the hospital.*

He wriggled sideways out from under the car, pulled himself up on the hood, and leaned over the windshield.

Staring back at him through the glass, mouth agape, bone-white knuckles clutching the steering wheel, was Mr. Eguchi.

Alex clutched the pink Cadillac, feeling his way into the backseat, while Eguchi got out and bustled around him.

"Hurry," Alex rasped, between the rapid slams of his heart.
"Step on it."

Eguchi looked around, confused. "*Zone-san* is hurt-o?"

Alex slumped in the backseat, dripping lake water over
the clean upholstery. He pointed to the bodyguards perched at
the top of the driveway. "They're after me!"

Eguchi broke into a gold-toothed grin. He tried to say
something to Alex, but couldn't find the words. Finally, he said,
"They are eggs. I am the Egg Man!"

"They're . . . your men?" Alex's mind reeled with possibilities. How could Eguchi have known where he was? Why
had he sent two *yakuza* after him?

Eguchi doubled over laughing, slapping his knee. "*Hai, so
desu!*" He waved his arm, and the *yakuza* on the hill waved back.
He lightly punched Alex's shoulder and winked, a broad and
phony wink. Then he scrambled into the driver's seat and
backed the Cadillac onto the road.

Thirty-five

Gaby met Mr. Eguchi in the hospital corridor leading to
the emergency room. "*What happened? Are you all right?*"

Eguchi seemed surprised. "*You worried about* me?" He
looked her over, down and up, his gaze resting briefly on her
wrist before returning eye contact. "*Maybe I should ask what happened to you.*"

Gaby checked her wrist and discovered she was still wearing the hospital's plastic bracelet. "*Nothing.*" She tried to rip the
bracelet off, but the plastic was tough and stretched without
breaking. "*It's unimportant. Is Alex all right?*"

"Minor scrapes and bruises. They're cleaning him up in there. He's fine. You can see him in a moment." Eguchi tilted his head toward the emergency room. Then he actually took her arm and propelled her down the hall. *"Come with me. I need a smoke."*

It was odd to be walking shoulder to shoulder with her boss, his hand on her bare arm. Japanese didn't touch. Never in public. He led her first to an enclosed waiting room designated for smokers. The smoke was so thick inside, she could see a gray cloud suspended under the ceiling. Eguchi clucked in disappointment and pushed through an emergency exit to get outside, where they found a concrete bench set against the hospital wall. It was a dead-end outlet, facing a tall hydrangea hedge and a patch of rubble. Numerous cigarette butts in the gravel indicated this was an escape hatch for smokers. *"This is good,"* Eguchi said, placing a broken roof tile in the jamb to keep the door from closing completely. *"I need to talk to you privately. It is a very complicated situation. This business about Zone."*

Gaby sat on the warm bench. She had to end this day, get home, and lie down in bed. *"Don't you mean, this business about Marubatsu?"*

Eguchi slid a cigarette out of his pack of Lucky Strikes and tapped the pockets of his red paisley blazer until he found his lighter. After he got his cigarette going, he visibly relaxed a notch. *"Other people prefer to think of it as this business about Zone."*

"Other people," Gaby repeated.

"Do you know when Zone is going back to America?"

The same question Dr. Ono had asked. *"The eighteenth, I think. Why?"*

"Not long—that is good. I can use that." Eguchi held his cigarette between his thumb and index finger, making the "okay" signal when he took a drag. *"Tell me, Gebi-san, do you think you might be interested in teaching English again?"*

Gaby looked up in alarm. *"Are you . . . am I fired?"*

His anguished expression confirmed her fear. *"It is a very complicated situation. This whole business about Zone-san."*

"*I see.*" Gaby smoothed her dress hem over her knees. "*You hold me responsible?*"

"*Not me, no,*" Eguchi hurried to say. "*My business associates are concerned. They were not aware I had an American on my payroll. It is not their policy to hire Westerners.*"

"*So I am fired.*" This was it: the end of her life in Japan. She wouldn't be able to find employment after getting fired twice.

"*Not fired. Quit,*" Eguchi said. "*With an excellent recommendation.*"

For what? How many fantasy funeral companies were hiring sales staff? And wouldn't they all be run by *yakuza*, after all? Gaby doubted a recommendation from a *yakuza* could help her in the legitimate job market. On her lap, a blotch darkened the weave of her dress to the color of coffee. A drop of water had fallen on it. A tear. Hers.

"*Oh, don't cry. Please don't cry. I don't like to make women cry.*" Eguchi produced a large maroon handkerchief with a flourish and handed it to her. "*You must understand it was not my idea. You are my Number One. You do good work, Gebi-san. Because you are foreign, you get our clients to accept foreign ideas. I don't want to lose you. Please, stop crying. Oh, I can't stand this.*"

Gaby couldn't stop. She sat stiffly on the bench, stone quiet, tears streaming out of her eyes. She held Eguchi's perfect silk handkerchief at her knees, unable to use it and ruin it.

Eguchi paced back and forth in front of her. "*Try to understand. I am just a poor boy from Osaka. My family had no money to buy me an education, so I didn't bother to study in high school. If I had only studied—*" Eguchi threw his butt on the ground and twisted his shiny black loafer over it. His socks were maroon, too, matching his handkerchief. He spoke with his back to her. "*I was so stubborn! If I had passed a college entrance exam, maybe—but I didn't even try.*"

Gaby only half-listened. Eguchi was firing her. This was the end. She would have to leave Japan. Her tears kept coming while the handkerchief stayed dry in her hand. Why was Eguchi revealing his life story? He was her boss; he had nothing to explain. It couldn't be helped—*shikata ga nai.*

"After high school, I worked as a bartender in a karaoke house. Then a nightclub. Those young Philippine girls—it broke my heart, those girls, sixteen, seventeen years old. I despised the corporate salary men who came to the bar. I didn't want to be a salary man in an ugly gray suit, drinking whiskey and humiliating pretty young girls. Work in a gray building twelve hours a day, get drunk, go home drunk in a gray train. Pass out at midnight in front of an angry wife. Wake up at five-thirty and do it again, day after day, year after year. Never see daylight. Finally, die of overwork, u-u-u-u! on the floor. That is the Japanese way. I did not want that life." Eguchi made a fist and slammed it into the palm of his other hand. *"I vowed I would never become a gray man."*

Gaby had stopped crying. His story moved her. He trusted her more than she had ever imagined, to tell her something this close to the core. Japan wasn't easy, even for the Japanese.

"So when 'Ikki-Ikki' Ito offered me a job, I said yes. In his world, I was smart again. I was allowed to do more than mix drinks. I could work my way up in management. First, an air-conditioning company, then a pachinko parlor, then a loan to start Gone With The Wind, my own company.

"Now I have money, a classic American car, clothes. I am not trapped in a building. I have coffee, go to lunch, go to the races, make friends, date women. Life is good, except—" Eguchi stopped. He wheeled around. Gaby hadn't seen his face like this before: tired, anxious. *"Listen to me, Gebi. I don't want you to get hurt in this whole business about Zone-san."* His dark eyes scrutinized hers. The intense way he looked at her was disarming. *"What do you want? Tell me directly, American-style."*

"I want . . . I want to keep working for Gone With The Wind."

"Forever? Until you retire?"

Gaby was caught short. *"I hadn't thought that far ahead."*

"You don't want to teach English again?"

"Of course I do. But that's not realistic. Shizuyama University fired me; no other university in Japan will hire me after that."

Eguchi scanned her face to catch any nuance. *"What about America?"*

Gaby's throat cramped. *"There are no jobs. Even if there were, I wouldn't have much of a chance to get one. I've been in Japan almost five years. An American university would regard me as being out of touch."*

"I can tell you are afraid," Eguchi said gently, *"but I am asking what you want."*

"Why?" Gaby countered. *"Why ask me this?"*

"To know what to do," he replied. *"This whole business about Zone-san."* He studied his cigarette butt on the gravel. *"Do you think . . . is it possible . . . you might go home to America with him?"*

It was one of those moments when the earth paused on its axis, and infinite futures hovered in place, waiting for the next tiny move to trigger the outcome.

And Gaby said the first thing that came into her mind: *"America's not my home."*

Eguchi's eyes widened. *"Japan is your home?"*

"No," Gaby said thoughtfully, taking her time, *"but I live here."* As she spoke the words, for the first time she clearly understood why she stayed. In Japan, she was accepted for who she was: an outsider. In her native country, her ulcerative colitis made her just as much an outsider, but an inadequate and incompetent one. In the States, it was always her failing that she wasn't healthy, that she didn't fit in. Ironically, in a country where conformity was crucial, she'd been let off the hook. As a *gaijin*, she was expected not to fit in and her illness was—at last!—irrelevant. And while she attracted too much attention, a lot of it unpleasant, she also attracted Japanese nonconformists. The refreshing, buoyant spirit of Eguchi, Rie, or Aoshima; she had never found people like them in America. *"I live here,"* she repeated. *"Of course I want to teach, but I'd take any job to stay in Japan."*

"So what you want is to teach at a university in Japan?" Eguchi concluded.

"Yes." The teaching, the students—they had made Japan

worthwhile. It was only after Gaby got fired that she had become reluctant to leave her apartment, hiding under cordless headphones, numbing herself with constant music. Alex had disrupted her routine, forced her out of her insulation. She had gone a long time with the radio off.

"Only in Shizuoka or anywhere in Japan?" Eguchi asked. *"For example, would Osaka be acceptable?"*

Gaby brought herself back to attention. *"Osaka would be better than acceptable. The Osaka style is relaxed, not as conservative as Shizuoka. I like kansai-jin."*

Eguchi was taken aback. Then his expression softened. *"Do you really?"*

Gaby realized the lack of plural/singular differentiation in Japanese could have made *"kansai-jin"* sound like she'd confessed to liking Eguchi, personally, instead of Osaka folk in general. It wasn't appropriate to use the familiar "like" with one's boss. She blushed.

Eguchi sighed. *"Ah, Gebi-san, if only you were Japanese."*

Gaby didn't know what to make of that remark. She folded his handkerchief and gave it back to him. He tucked it into his breast pocket and kept his hand over it a moment. He looked as if he were about to launch another difficult subject, but when he spoke, all he said was, *"Well, then. It is time for us to return to Zone-san."* He opened the heavy hospital door and kicked aside the broken tile. Gaby got up and trailed after him down the corridor, around a corner to the emergency ward.

Eguchi knocked on a door, bowed, said a few words to a nurse, and then stepped aside to let Gaby into the room. *"Zone-san is fine. Keep him company while I make a few phone calls."* He shut the door behind him as he left.

Alex sat on an examination table, pants rolled up, watching a doctor clean shallow cuts and scrapes on his leg. His left hand was wrapped in white gauze. When he looked up, his blue eyes looked bluer than ever, like turquoise coins. She moved closer and he took her hand, clasping her fingers tightly. "I'm so sorry I'm late. I was worried about you. How are you?"

"I'm fine. How are you?" She sounded like lesson number one in English conversation.

Alex winced as the doctor dug tweezers into a gash below his knee. The doctor lifted out a tiny piece of gravel. "Were they . . . were the tumors . . . ?"

"Dr. Ono couldn't tell from looking at them. He'll get the biopsy results in about a week. Why are we talking about me? Alex, Eguchi called saying—" Gaby's throat wasn't working right. She ended in a whisper. "I'm glad you're all right."

The doctor stopped poking at Alex's wounds and let the nurse finish up with sterilized gauze and tape. To Gaby, he said, *"We are finished now. His injuries are all very minor except for his wrist. He should use a bandage and antibacterial ointment for a few days. Will you explain to him?"*

"Yes, of course, thank you very much, sensei." Gaby bowed as they left the room. Alone with Alex, she asked, "How did you get hurt?"

Alex blurted out a laugh. "I decided to check out that address on my Gone With The Wind bill. You won't believe who our villain turned out to be."

"Marubatsu," Gaby said.

"Eguchi told you?" She nodded, and Alex continued. "I had a stupid adventure eluding the *yakuza* Eguchi sent to save me from who-knows-what and nearly ended up run over when Eguchi drove onto the scene." He mused, as an afterthought, "You know, I never paid my taxi driver. I wonder what happened to him."

Gaby walked around the table to the window. It looked out on a dense hydrangea hedge. She and Eguchi might have been right behind that hedge when he had fired her. She decided not to tell Alex she'd lost her job. She had to work that through on her own. She leaned against the window, facing him. "I found out what happened to Cody."

Alex looked at her with amazement. "But you've been in the hospital all day."

"So has Kenichiro Endo. The student who went with Cody on the ride to Mount Fuji." Gaby drew a deep breath. "Alex, it was an accident. Pure and simple. It got complicated afterward—"

"—when Marubatsu showed up at Saishinkai and started running the show." There was no anger in Alex's voice. He sounded like a counselor reporting someone else's story.

"Marubatsu actually confessed?"

" 'Declared' is more like it. He's proud of what he did. He believed Jane and I would never have agreed to a transplant, so he took it on himself to make that decision. He went on to decide how much I should know and how much the university should know without a single qualm of conscience. He wasn't even ashamed that he sent me a bill under a false name. In his mind, it was all right to exploit Gone With The Wind because you worked there and you, like Cody, were American. Marubatsu believes in Japanese superiority so fully that, to him, anyone believing in equality is deliberately acting up, defying the natural hierarchy." Alex rolled down his pant legs and stood to deliver the conclusive findings of his case study. "Yet he's a man of contradictions. On the one hand, he's all for traditional Japanese ways, but on the other, he's a priest willing to overlook the Buddhist ban on harvesting organs."

"If they're *gaijin*," Gaby amended, "and to save Japanese lives."

"And he has no remorse for not answering my letters."

"In Japan, silence is often regarded as an acceptable way to avoid conflict."

"The cruel joke is that his whole elaborate cover-up was for nothing! If he had called me when Cody was in Saishinkai, I would have agreed to organ donation. I would have said yes, let one good thing come out of this tragedy. If he had asked me for money to ship Cody back, I would have paid him. But instead, he didn't give me a choice. He manipulated me, controlled me, didn't let me in on my own son's death." Alex shook his head. "He's way beyond arrogance. It's hubris. Mixed with projection and paranoia."

Gaby assumed Alex was playing psychologist as his own defense mechanism. Maybe she should postpone telling him Endo-*kun*'s version of the story. "I'm sorry, Alex. It must have been horrible to listen to Marubatsu."

Alex smiled, alarmingly handsome. "I rather enjoyed it."

Mr. Eguchi entered the room bearing three cans of cold coffee, two in one hand and one in the crook of his elbow. *"We must vacate this room. They have a bus accident on the way. There is no one in the doctors' lounge; we can go there."*

Gaby went with the two men to a small lounge. This lounge was stocked with three vending machines, and also had a small counter and sink, which was full of dirty teacups without handles. There were four padded chairs and a short sofa Gaby longed to lie down on. At least she could lean back on some padding.

Eguchi sat beside her and played host by popping the aluminum tabs on their cans of coffee. *"I saw Fuji-san a while ago. Head in the clouds, feet on the ground. That is the way to be."*

After Gaby translated for Alex, she asked, *"Is that a Japanese saying or your own?"*

"My own." Eguchi winked. *"But don't tell."*

Gaby smiled.

Alex looked wary.

Eguchi's leg jiggled.

They each took a polite sip of cold coffee.

"Yesterday," Eguchi began, "all my troubles seemed so far away."

"Yesterday came suddenly," Alex chimed in.

Gaby wondered how long Eguchi and Alex could communicate through Beatles lyrics.

Eguchi shook a cigarette from his pack and looked around.

Gaby passed him an empty glass tumbler to use as an ashtray. *"Douzo."*

Alex raised his eyebrows. Gaby ignored him. Eguchi was trying to help him. She wasn't going to force him to do it without nicotine.

Eguchi lit up and checked his watch. *"Gebi-san, I must meet Ito and Murabe in thirty minutes. That leaves me no time to be polite. Would you explain this to Zone-san and tell him my desire is to negotiate a deal for him preferable to what my associates have in mind?"*

Alex looked to Gaby for an interpretation.

"Bad news," she summarized, setting down her can of coffee. It was too syrupy and made her stomach queasy. To Eguchi she said, *"Go ahead. Zone-san is very blunt himself. It is truly okay to come right to the point."*

Eguchi inhaled a deep drag. *"It is unlikely Marubatsu would confess to his crimes against you. It would be difficult to prove Marubatsu guilty in a Japanese court."*

Gaby translated: "No way in hell is Marubatsu going to confess in court, and it's impossible to send him to jail without a confession."

"There's hard evidence," Alex argued. "My bill, my check, the Ninka account with the name Gizenji, the *inkan* maker Wang—no, he's dead."

Eguchi's foot tapped nervously. *"As for fraud and forgery, my associates prefer to pursue other means of justice. That is between Marubatsu and Gone With The Wind."* Eguchi paused after each sentence to give Gaby time to translate. Alex kept his focus on Eguchi regardless of who was talking. *"My men questioned Marubatsu about your conversation at Gizenji. I am speaking of his unforgivable crime of signing away your son's heart. And in this matter, it is one man's word against another's. Marubatsu will claim Zone-san gave verbal permission over the phone. Zone-san will claim he was never called, never informed. It would be the word of a gaijin against a priest. Zone-san could end up disappointed if he pursues this with the police."*

"How disappointed?" Gaby asked. Images of bloodsplattered corpses lying on remote beaches filled her head.

Eguchi observed the ash crawling up the cigarette between his fingers. Then he spoke apologetically to the tumbler as he knocked the ash inside it. *"It's like this. My associates believe it could be useful to have a Zen priest indebted to us. If Zone would return home quietly, no one would stop him from taking his case through the usual channels after he is back in America."*

"Through the embassy that can be put off with paperwork?"

"Exactly."

Gaby turned back to Alex. "The *yakuza* want to hold this over Marubatsu's head. They want you to shut up, go home, and take it up with the embassy."

"I want Marubatsu in jail," Alex insisted.

Eguchi dropped his cigarette into the glass. It landed folded like a broken insect, smoldering. When he faced Alex, Eguchi looked like the older man, though he was Gaby's age, or younger. "You say you want a revolution."

"I want justice—"

"You say you want a revolution," Eguchi repeated calmly. "Well, you know, we all want to change the world."

Alex leaned back in his chair, quiet. The cooler of one of the vending machines woke with a rumble and hummed loudly.

"Let's take a sad song and make it better," Eguchi proposed.

Gaby closed her eyes in disbelief. The juxtaposition of lyrics from "Hey, Jude" on top of a vague threat from *yakuza* who wanted to blackmail a priest instead of sending him to jail was downright surreal. Utterly, thoroughly Japanese.

"I intend to persuade my associates to recognize that our recent gain of income and influence is due to Zone-san's inquiry, and we are deeply beholden to him." Eguchi checked his watch and made a face. *"Here is what I propose. Marubatsu will retire from Shizuyama University. He will remain a priest, but not a professor. And, as part of his early retirement, the university will apologize for their misunderstanding in firing Gebi-san. That way, she can get another teaching job, and you can have the satisfaction that Marubatsu was required to make*

a big sacrifice for what he did to you." Eguchi studied Alex's face as Gaby translated his words. He added, *"It is not what you want, I know, but it is something. Would Zone-san prefer something to nothing?"*

After Gaby translated, Alex said, "It's not enough." He looked at Gaby. "Don't get me wrong. I want you out of this mess, but there are other ways."

Gaby turned to Eguchi. *"You have the power to make the university apologize?"*

Eguchi grinned, a veneer of his old self over his new sadness. *"Well, not really. But I do have power over Marubatsu now. My men made him aware of Wang's untimely death and he thinks I caused it. He is afraid of me. As he was behind firing you, he can rescind his position. He will lose a lot of face, but the university will not lose face if they claim firing you was a mistake caused by a professor who no longer works for them."*

That explained Eguchi's hint of looking for a job in Osaka. Asking Shizuyama University to take her back would be too much, especially with Michael McKenzie in place, but with her record purged, she might be able to find employment in another prefecture. *"You thought of all this since we talked?"*

Eguchi shrugged. *"A poor boy from Osaka does not have the luxury of thinking slowly. So, what do you say?"*

"I wish I could say yes, but it's not my decision." She knew Alex couldn't compromise over something of this magnitude in his life. *"I don't think you understand how Zone-san feels. His son's death nearly destroyed him. Zone-san wants to go to the police, whatever the consequences."*

"Ask him to reconsider," Eguchi insisted. *"Not just for himself, but for you."*

Gaby looked to Alex. "He wants you to reconsider."

Alex shook his head.

Eguchi scowled at his watch. He appealed to Alex one last time. "And in the middle of negotiations, you break down?"

"I'll think it over," Alex offered. "But if I have to answer right now, my answer is no. Sorry, but no."

Gaby thought of all the obligation Eguchi had shouldered for Alex, obligation that Alex would never pay back, never even fully understand he owed, only to have his plan rejected. Eguchi was a good man. Certainly a brave one. *"Buchou-san, he doesn't comprehend the situation. Please, could your associates give him some time?"*

Eguchi sighed pessimistically. *"Well, they are businessmen. I will try to keep them thinking financially, not emotionally. But I could do better if I could promise Zone-san's compliance."*

"I don't want you to get in trouble."

"But I like trouble," he joked. *"I ask for trouble, don't I? I'm late; I must go."* He left without bowing, with a curt *"Sayonara"* at the door of the doctors' lounge.

"He's angry," Alex surmised.

Gaby emptied the cigarette butt into a wastebasket and washed the tumbler at the sink. She set it upside down over a paper towel.

"You're angry?" Alex asked.

How could Alex know how much Eguchi had done and continued to do for him? Gaby couldn't blame Japanese for disliking Americans; they required so much baby-sitting and never repaid the debt they incurred. Maybe that's what Rie meant about "special treatment." "You've had a hard day." Gaby chose her words carefully. "But I want you to do something that might be harder still."

"Whatever you want, Gaby," Alex hurried to say. "I'll do anything for you."

"I want you to visit Kenichiro Endo," Gaby said.

Thirty-six

Alex wasn't sure how he would feel meeting the boy who had accompanied Cody to his death, the one who came up with the idea of motorcycling to Mount Fuji. When Alex saw the desperate dark brown eyes of Kenichiro Endo, his pale cheeks, the long razor slash on his face, the thin tube of blood curling down from a nearly empty transfusion bag, he looked into the eyes of a tortured teenager who needed a lifeline. But this kid was the last person to have seen Cody alive, and Alex found himself guarded and oddly jealous, with no lifeline to offer.

Then Endo told the story and Gaby quietly translated. The borrowed motorcycle. Cody refusing the helmet. Uphill toward Mount Fuji. Cody swerving into the wrong lane. The truck speeding downhill, engine off. Alex felt his face contort with tears, but Endo went on. The frightened Korean driver. The cell phone. Saishinkai Hospital and Marubatsu. Endo stopped, tears pouring from his eyes, his voice choked.

Alex didn't know what to say. His long-awaited truth did nothing but hurt. He raised his hand to swat a tear off his cheek and Endo did the same. In that moment, Alex saw Endo's heavily bandaged wrist—his left, mirroring Alex's left wrist with its fresh gauze and tape—and what he saw was his own anguish materialized in human form. Looking up at him from a hospital bed was the face of a full year's guilt. He knew what Endo needed. "It wasn't your fault. You must forgive yourself."

Gaby said, almost inaudibly, "He can't. You have to do that."

Deliberately, though he didn't fully believe what he was saying, Alex told Endo: "I forgive you." Something flitted through his chest once the words were spoken. Something released.

Alex didn't want to wake Gaby when dinner was ready, so he turned off the gas hot plate and waited. At dusk, a truck went by slowly, repeating a mournful phrase of a tune over a loudspeaker. He heard Gaby rouse. She appeared in the doorway, blinking, brown hair tousled.

"I must have slept," she said. "That's the sweet potato truck making rounds."

O-imo-o-o. O-ya-ki-i-mo. The musical phrase rose twice like two questions.

"What are the words?" Alex lit the burner to heat their food.

"Honorable potato. Honorable roasted potato."

They both laughed.

"Come and eat," Alex said.

Dinner was spaghetti topped with a sauce made of tomato paste and canned tuna, and steamed peas out of a box from the freezer. Alex had wanted to show off a little more of his cooking ability, but other cans and boxes in Gaby's well-stocked cupboard were unrecognizable. Gaby didn't complain about the food. In fact, she cleared her plate. They lingered at the table, Alex with his ginger ale, and Gaby with a glass of iced barley tea.

"You know," Alex mused, "the more cover-up Marubatsu did, the more he exalted his own actions. The more powerful he felt."

Gaby nodded in agreement. "Who knows? Maybe Marubatsu is so paranoid that part of his cover was to fire me from Shizuyama. If I'd stayed on, with Endo-*kun* repeating my class that he failed, I might have learned the truth on my own. If I'd stayed, I'm sure your letters would have been directed to me, as the only American professor."

Alex felt sick. "You mean, Cody's death cost you your job?"

Gaby looked up in alarm. "No, no, I'm sure that's not the case. Marubatsu never liked me. He was always looking for a way to bring me down. He conspired with Lester long before Cody's accident. I think it may have triggered the timing, that's all."

Alex thought: after visiting Endo, she was anxious not to add to his load of guilt. "Don't worry, Gaby. I'm all right."

"Are you?" Gaby inquired. "Since we left the hospital, you've been awfully calm. Is this okay? After what you've been through today?"

Alex was touched by the concern in her face, the tilt of her chin, the way her brown eyes penetrated his. "I feel different, now that I know what happened." He thought for a moment. How was his new knowledge different from any of the scenarios he'd recited to others or imagined to himself over the past year? Only that there was one story now, instead of thousands. Giving up all the versions of Cody's death but one was like exchanging an avalanche for a single rock. A rock he could shoulder, like Atlas, no matter how heavy; it was the avalanche that overwhelmed him, that he couldn't carry through his life from one day to the next. "I'd say everything's changed, but I guess that means I've changed."

"How?" It was a real question; she wanted to know.

Alex turned his glass around, watching bubble trails rise. "Because when I arrived in Japan, my life was something to endure and get through. But today, when I ran from Eguchi's men and rolled under his car, I fought for my life—one hundred percent, no hesitation. I physically proved I didn't want to die."

"And the difference is . . . ?"

"I can't explain it well. It's in knowing I want to live, instead of telling myself I have to want to live." He could tell his words hit home with her.

"Is that enough?" she asked.

Alex paused. "It's enough for today. I'll let you know if it's still enough tomorrow."

"I meant, is it enough to . . ." Gaby bit her lip. "I guess I'm being selfish."

"You? Selfish? What do you mean?" Alex regarded her curiously.

"Nothing. I understand why you have to go through the police instead of Eguchi. You have to finish it, see it all the way through." She began to get up.

Alex pinned her hand on the table to prevent her from leaving. She lowered herself back into her chair. "What aren't you telling me? What's this about being selfish?"

Gaby stared at his hand over hers.

"Don't keep secrets from me, Gaby. That's the worst thing." Alex tried to make eye contact, but she wouldn't look at him. He had to be content with the long line of her neck that led to her upswept hair. A few wispy dark brown hairs had escaped the clip that held the French twist in place and fell about her ear. "It's Marubatsu's silence that tortured me. Like how everything Lester didn't tell you tortured you."

Gaby's voice quavered. "I don't want you to make sacrifices for me."

"It's not fair if you don't give me a choice," Alex countered.

Finally, her head came up. "Eguchi fired me today. His associates won't let him hire Americans."

Alex took that in. "Well. In the long run, is that so bad? Not to be employed by *yakuza*? I know I should feel sorry for you, but I'm kind of relieved. Aren't you, just a little?"

Gaby was silent. After a moment, she said, "The problem is finding another job."

So that was why she felt selfish for wanting him to accept Eguchi's plan. "Eguchi can't promise you a teaching job, can he?"

"No, but with a cleared record, I have a chance of getting one on my own. In another city, of course, but I won't mind moving. I've always liked Osaka. It's a bigger city, but friendlier. They're more used to foreigners there."

"I wish—" Alex stopped and started over. "I'll do anything I can to help you return to the U.S. There are lots of colleges around Seattle. You could stay with me until you get settled— or as long as you wanted. I could get your résumé out to—"

"You're very kind, Alex, but—"

He pitched it to her straight, as if confronting a frightened client with a necessary reality: "How long can you be a stranger in a strange land?"

And Gaby laughed. "My whole life, Alex. My whole life!"

"I don't get it! Why—" He stopped himself, his frustration level too high.

"I had my own moment of truth today," Gaby said. "It wasn't life-or-death-inspired like yours, but when Eguchi fired me, I realized I wanted to be in Japan. Whereas before, I got by telling myself I had no choice. I want to stay, Alex. I'll only leave if it's my last option."

How could she want to stay? She couldn't possibly be happier in Japan than in America. Alex wished he could force Gaby out of Japan for the sake of her best interest. The psychologist in him knew he should respect her decisions for her own life; but the man in him didn't want to lose her. He was biased. He should support her choice, not pressure her to come home with him.

Now that he knew the truth about Cody's death, could he leave matters in Eguchi's hands? Deep down, he suspected he might get nothing by going to the Japanese police. Even if Marubatsu came to trial, a judge could be bribed. With Eguchi's plan, Gaby's reputation would be redeemed and Marubatsu would lose his job. How could he deny her a chance to stop working for *yakuza* and teach again? He had been miserably self-involved since Cody died. He needed to do this for her. "All right," he said. "We'll go with Eguchi's plan."

"Now I feel like I've pressured you."

"Into doing the right thing for myself," Alex countered. "I need to find a better way to rise above it all." The words he used carried the answer.

Gaby picked up on his expression. "Do you have something in mind?"

"Climbing Mount Fuji. It's what Cody was going to do the day he died. I should finish that for him." Alex drained the last swallow of ginger ale. "And to extract as much symbolic meaning out of 'rising above it' as I can."

"If it's symbolism you want, you can't get much more symbolic than Fujiyama." Gaby smiled. She was truly beautiful when she smiled.

"I wish you could come with me."

"Tomorrow? Impossible. But I'll call Junko for you. And you'll have to ask Michael to go along."

Alex made a face. "McKenzie? Why does he have to get involved?"

"As a chaperone. It'll look like you and Junko might be lovers unless a third person is with you. Junko's Japanese friends are shy around foreigners, so it has to be Michael. He's your host this weekend—it would be rude not to invite him."

"Hm. Maybe I'll go to the police, instead."

Gaby widened her eyes.

"Just kidding," Alex said. "All right, I'll ask Michael to join us. Anything else?"

"Borrow a warm jacket. It's freezing at the top. And gloves. You'll want gloves."

"Gloves and a jacket. Anything else?"

"Good luck?"

"I'll need it," Alex said. "Twelve thousand feet is a long way up."

"You'll make it," Gaby said. "One step at a time."

Alex stood beside Gaby on her balcony. The dark air was hot, but not oppressively muggy as before. Alex drew his lungs full and blew them out at the night sky. He could see a few stars, but clouds blocked most of the sky. "Do you see the cowherd and the princess weaver?"

Gaby craned her head for stargazing. "Reply hazy. Ask again later."

Alex gave his neck a rest by looking down at the potted tomato, shadowy and enigmatic in the dark. "So we won't get our *tanabata* wishes?"

"We might get them. It's not all up to the stars, you know." Gaby's face and arms had a bluish cast.

When Gaby caught his eye, something communicated between the two of them that gave him the courage to put his hands on her waist, pull her close, and kiss her mouth. She didn't pull away, so he kissed her again, deeper. Her tongue began to touch his. He eased her back zipper down and slid his hand under her dress, caressing her spine. Her gasp was whisper volume. He kissed the tip of her nose and her forehead before pressing her mouth with another kiss. She flinched and he let go.

"It's not you," she said softly, placing her hand on her abdomen. "It's just too soon."

"It's all right. We can wait." He held her gently, savoring the moment, as hope surged through him, body and soul.

Thirty-seven

In the morning, the washing machine next door convulsed loudly. Gaby pushed aside her dress, dropped in a pile on the tatami floor the night before, and slid open her balcony door. At six in the morning, a few wispy gold and pink clouds rushed across the sky to avoid getting caught in broad daylight, and the air would have been sweet if it hadn't been contaminated by the stink of broiled mackerel rising from Fumiko's apartment below.

Dr. Ono had been right: she felt better, like magic. Her head was cooler and she was hungry. Inexplicably happy. To think that small tumors had been slowing her down for almost a year, and today they were gone. She wasn't used to such a quick fix. She looked down at her tomato plant. Her pink crane had already faded in the sun. Her wish had been for good health: *genki,* two simple *kanji.* Maybe the stars had come through last night, after all. She thought about Alex and a shiver vibrated through her, recalling his kiss.

A car horn blared—not the typical beep of Japanese cars— and Gaby looked down to see an old pink Cadillac swerve around an old Japanese man strolling down the middle of the street. Gaby did a double take. There couldn't be more than one '71 Caddie in Shizuoka, and the only reason for Mr. Eguchi to be in her neighborhood would be to visit her.

Gaby hurried back inside, pulled off her pajamas, and changed into a T-shirt and lightweight jeans. She combed her hair with her fingers and tied it back in a ponytail. She kicked her unmade futon into a corner and closed the paper door on her bedroom.

When the doorbell rang, she paused only long enough to expel a deep breath. Then she opened her front door. *"Buchou-san!"* She tried to act surprised.

"You are up this early?" Mr. Eguchi inquired.

Gaby couldn't help wondering about the logic behind that question. Had he meant to catch her in bed? *"Yes. Would you like to come in?"*

"If you insist." Mr. Eguchi kicked off his shiny leather loafers in her entry and stepped up in yellow socks on her tatami floor. Today, he wore a baggy yellow silk suit over a black T-shirt and goggle-style sunglasses. In her apartment, he seemed shorter, his skin darker, and the gold in his teeth more extensive.

Gaby gestured to her wood table with the two chairs. *"Would you like some coffee?"*

"I don't want to trouble you." Eguchi took a seat and re-garded her scroll painting of the lotus field.

"It's no trouble." Gaby took her bag of coffee beans out of the freezer and started water to boil. *"This is the first time you've been here, isn't it?"*

"Yes. It's very . . . clean." Eguchi glanced around. *"I thought your apartment would be bigger."*

Gaby didn't want to reveal her goal of saving money every way she could, especially in large chunks, like rent. *"Two rooms are enough for me."*

They had never conversed this long in small talk before. Eguchi was by nature *kansai-jin,* open, joking, and yesterday's events had brought them closer. She decided to open the topic of their real agenda. *"About your associates—Ito-san and Murabe-san?"*

"Ah! I was able to postpone the meeting."

"Excellent. I have good news: Thorn agreed to your plan last night. He just needed a little time to perceive its merit."

"That is good. That will help." Eguchi didn't sound as pleased as he should have been. *"You look well,"* he commented. *"Very well."*

"Thank you." Gaby was baffled by his juxtaposition of topics until she remembered he had seen her plastic hospital bracelet. She was touched by his concern, but couldn't believe he would visit unannounced at six in the morning to find out how she was. How was her health relevant to Ito and Murabe?

"Yesterday, Rie got a call from an old woman in the hospital, Watanabe-san. She wants a custom-order funeral, very lavish."

This was Eguchi's way of telling her he knew all about her surgery. Had Mrs. Watanabe gossiped about her American husband, as well? Gaby wasn't sure how much to say. *"I am glad she called."*

"I will see you get the commission, Gebi-san. Even when you have your own troubles, you are a company man. I did not want to fire you."

"I know."

Eguchi waited until she was done grinding coffee beans

until he spoke again. *"We should not have Zone doing favors for us. We are supposed to be helping him, not the other way around. If you are personally obligated to Zone, I must know. I must know exactly how to negotiate with Ito and Murabe."*

So he had figured out Alex had posed as her husband. Gaby picked her kettle off the gas burner when the whistle was airy, before it got shrill, and poured water over the grounds. *"It's different with Americans, buchou-san. There's no obligation for you to worry about."*

Mr. Eguchi watched, saying nothing. Only the sound of coffee dripping into the pot. He cleared his throat. *"So you and Zone-san talked last night?"*

"Yes." Gaby brought him a cup of coffee and poured another for herself.

"Ng." Eguchi took his coffee and blew loudly on it before taking a sip. His eyebrows went up. *"Strong!"*

Gaby set down a quart of milk and a shaker of sugar. *"Oh, I'm sorry. I could add hot water."* She hovered with the kettle.

Eguchi placed his hand on top of the cup. *"No, no, I like American strength."* He poured milk to the brim and took three spoonfuls of sugar. He took a sip of coffee and put his cup down. His gaze drifted to her bedroom door and back again. *"Where is Zone-san, now?"*

It dawned on Gaby that Eguchi thought Alex might have spent the night. She felt guilty, even though it hadn't happened. Yet. *"He's staying with another gaijin."*

"Resutaa-san?" Eguchi's foot began to jiggle.

"No. Michael McKenzie. A teacher at Shizuyama."

"Oh." Eguchi lifted his cup and set it down without drinking the coffee. *"Have you reconsidered returning to America?"*

He was getting to be as bad as Alex. As bad as Dr. Ono and Marubatsu. *"I am thinking more in the direction of Osaka."*

"You are?"

"I am."

Eguchi's face suddenly lit up. *"I could get you a terrific apartment."*

Gaby suppressed a smile. *"Let's wait and see if I find a job first."*

"As you know, I can't help you with that," Eguchi said. *"But I have a friend who owns very nice apartment buildings."*

"Thank you for offering the connection."

"Your apartment could have four or five rooms, with nice windows. You could have a view of the castle. The castle garden is beautiful in autumn. You could watch the maple trees burst into red and yellow from your balcony." He checked his watch and got up. *"I know good restaurants, also. There is a small bistro in Dotombori that floats lanterns on the waterway."*

Gaby followed him to the entry, where he stepped into his loafers, twisting his feet in a kind of disco step to fit them over his heels. *"I'm glad someone is happy that I want to stay in Japan."*

"Ah, Gebi-san." His look was so intense, Gaby half-thought he was about to kiss her. But he pulled his jacket straight and opened the door. *"It is time for me to negotiate."* He had resumed his business voice, straight-faced and self-possessed.

She followed Eguchi out her front door. The sun was warm, the sky pure blue. The back balconies of the apartment building across the street blossomed with bedding and laundry hung to dry. Outside, Eguchi seemed taller and stronger. The sound of washing machines and women beating futons filled the air.

Gaby bowed goodbye. Eguchi winked his special American wink and jogged down the metal staircase to his pink Cadillac parked in the middle of the road.

Fumiko stepped out from her apartment below with a rug beater in hand. In a falsely sweet voice, she called up, *"Ohayo gozaimasu."*

"Ohayo."

"Who was that man?" Fumiko asked.

"My boss."

Fumiko folded her arms, still gripping the wire beater. *"I see. It must be a casual company to dress like that to greet your boss."*

Gaby looked at her T-shirt, jeans, and bare feet. *"It's Sunday, Fumiko-san."*

"And so early in the morning, too," Fumiko added pleasantly. *"After you were up so late last night."*

"Goodbye, Fumiko-san." Gaby saw the Cadillac drive off and went back inside. She wasn't up to jogging, but she felt too good to stay indoors. She put on her running shoes and took her key.

When she went out again, she waved at Fumiko whacking away at her rug and kept going. It was a short walk to where the river was only a trickle, clogged with silt erosion from construction work. She stopped to take her sunglasses off; they distorted the color of the sky, turned the gentle blue an intense, harsh hue.

The rice farmer, standing in his small field, called out to her. *"Nice weather!"*

"It's a beautiful day," Gaby agreed. She slowly walked the uphill stretch that was the beginning of her jogging route. At the crest of the slight slope, she caught her breath.

It had been so long since she'd seen Mount Fuji, Gaby had forgotten how large it was. Her baseball cap visor blocked the top of the mountain from her sight. She took off her cap. Mount Fuji commanded the northern horizon, clear and distinct from its broad base all the way up its parallel sweeping sides to its slightly flattened peak. Its dark blue color had vertical ridges of green at the bottom, where trees grew, rising into mingled shades of purple and brown. A single wispy cloud veiled the off-center notch of the summit. *Feet on the ground, head in the clouds—that is the way to be.*

Alex would be there, at the peak, tomorrow morning, able to see for miles in any direction. She looked around. The road was empty at this hour on Sunday morning. She spoke aloud, *"Ohayo gozaimasu, Fuji-sama."* Convinced no one could see her, she indulged in waving to the mountain. Her arm motion startled a pair of herons from the river. Their wings flapped noisily as they took to the air and then sailed gracefully toward the safety of a bamboo grove.

On her way back, two teenage girls in navy blue school uniforms approached her.

"Hallo. Where are you from?" one girl began.

"Here," Gaby answered pleasantly. "I live here."

This was not an answer the girls expected. As the crosswalk light switched from the solid red man to the blinking white man, Gaby started across. She shouted back over her shoulder, "I'm American." She turned and walked backward to face the embarrassed girls, hands now clamped over their mouths, to add, "I'm a student. I'm learning Japanese. I use chopsticks. And I just love *natto*—yum!"

She reached the other side of the street. Except for the *natto,* it was all true.

Thirty-eight

Alex, Michael, and Junko had shared a taxi from the Fujinomiya train station partway up Mount Fuji, where motor traffic ended in a vast paved oval lined with hundreds of parking spaces. The taxi crept through the curved parking lot behind a white Toyota looking for a gap in the rows of other white cars, like an extra tooth searching for a spot in a smile. About an hour after sunset, the light hadn't quite faded and the cars were dim.

Michael and Junko spoke Japanese in the backseat, continuing what Alex guessed was a flirtatious dialogue that consisted of Michael asking for vocabulary, which Junko politely provided while deflecting the content. Alex sat beside the driver, blasted by air-conditioning at a cryogenic setting, occasionally overhearing English words pronounced Japanese-style: boifurendo, disuko dansu, sutoraaberi dakiri.

After ten minutes of creeping, the Toyota reached the empty spaces at the end of the row and parked. Their taxi zoomed around the end zone and dropped them off in front of a split-level collection of concrete boxes with flat roofs. Alex handed the driver a ten-thousand-yen note. The driver waited. Alex handed him another ten thousand, and the driver unzipped a black pouch and counted off quite a few thousand-yen bills in change.

Alex stepped out into the hot dusk, glad to have a chance to thaw out. Michael took their packs out of the trunk while Junko came up to Alex, unsnapping her wallet.

"I paid the fare," Alex said.

"No, please, we each pay," Junko said.

"Too late."

"I cannot accept." Junko pushed a fistful of yen at him.

Alex, noticing Michael was in no hurry to offer his fair third, said, "Tell you what. You and Michael split the ride back. That's close enough. Okay?"

Junko worked out the math at a point ten degrees off Alex's left shoulder. "Okay," she agreed. "Thank you."

"*Ikimashiyouka?*" Michael asked, dealing out their small nylon backpacks: red for Alex, blue for Junko, and black for himself.

"I want to get souvenir first." Junko gestured to the ugly building.

"And carry them all the way up the mountain?" Alex asked.

"After, I will be tired and not want to buy. And I can get postcard here and mail at the top. You could send to *Sutanton-san* with special . . ." Junko pounded her fist in the air with a stamping motion.

"Postmark," Alex filled in.

"Posto maru," Junko repeated carefully.

"*Boku mo,*" Michael said. "*O-miyage o kaitai.*"

Junko giggled nervously. "Michael-*san* says he wants to buy souvenir also. *Zone-san* also?"

"I'll wait there." Alex pointed to a big blue sign off to the side of the building. He had spent hours on buses, trains, and taxis in the company of Michael and Junko. They had eaten noodle-bowl dinners together at a train station restaurant. Now Alex wanted a few moments by himself before climbing the mountain. There was nothing wrong with Michael and Junko; they were just in their twenties, and he wasn't. He wished Gaby were with him. He missed her already.

Alex stretched his muscles and studied the sign, cut in the shape of a straighter, steeper Mount Fuji. On it, scenic highlights of the mountainside were illustrated in the style of children's books and named in English below the Japanese: Trout Hatchery (two smiling white fish), Shiraito Falls—Otodome Falls (portrayed by four long blue heads of hair tossed over a cliff), The Great Shrine of Sengen (pictured as two cartoon raccoons sitting in a bowl of soup, which made no sense to Alex), Mt. Fuji Woodland Rest Stop (a hiker drawn ball-headed, like a toy peg person, beside six pine trees), and The Ascent of Mt. Fuji (showing the backs of two peg people in big straw hats, one holding a walking stick and wearing a pink backpack, the other sitting on a mound of dirt). A handful of tourist pamphlets were littered beneath the sign, bearing muddy shoe treads or creases from being crammed into a pocket. Alex picked one up. It was a map.

The map was also half in English, half in Japanese. Mount Fuji was divided into ten levels, or stations. The parking lot was at the fifth level; he had already accomplished half the ascent in the taxi! Only foot traffic could continue through the higher stations on the Fujinomiya Trail. The map included stations labeled "Station 9.5" and "New Checkpoint," stations that augmented the original stations, so the 3,776-meter summit was the thirteenth actual station, though it was called the tenth.

Alex was encouraged to read that the estimated time it

took to climb between stations ranged from twenty to fifty minutes. The brochure said the full ascent would take five to seven hours, but noted "time is according to each individual's fitness. Have a safety and consider all your party's strengths and techniques." The section titled "Clothing," however, made Alex wonder what he was in for: "You must wear and prepare for long sleeved shirts, parka or thick sweaters, jackets, long pants and shade caps for guard against the direct rays of the sun. A tough separate-type rain coat is necessary. Umbrellas are of no use." He doubted the nylon shell jacket he'd brought along met the hard-boiled detective criteria of toughness and "separate-type," but at least he hadn't brought a useless umbrella.

Alex looked around in the darkening parking lot. Hikers, mostly student age, chattered in groups as they passed him on their way to the trailhead. Where were Junko and Michael? Had they lost him already? He searched the faces of the people going by more carefully. Alex was half-convinced some quirk of fate like this would stop his adventure just because it felt so weird to begin a long, arduous hike after dark.

A few sparse streetlights had come on, and Alex became aware of the light cast outside through the windows of the fifth station. He wavered between checking for his companions inside the building and staying put by the sign.

Then he felt a nudge at his elbow. He was startled to see Junko. The line of hoops in her ear caught the streetlight in an odd way, and her face seemed warped and ghostly.

"Sorry I am late. The line was long. I bought candy and sandwiches," Junko said. "Here. For provisions."

Alex took a heavy plastic-wrapped disk of peanut brittle and a vending-machine sandwich of indeterminate filling on crustless white bread. "Thanks. What do I owe you?"

"It is present," Junko said. "I insist-o."

"Well, thank you very much. Where's Michael?"

"In the toilet," Junko replied without a trace of embarrassment. "Are you ready?"

"I suppose I should visit Mr. Toilet, too."

"The next station is not far," Junko said. She waved her flashlight up the hill. "You can see."

Alex followed the beam of her flashlight to square-looking lights that could only be windows. He felt a trace of disappointment that the hike would be too easy, a series of short strolls between snack bars and rest rooms.

Michael strode up, backpack strapped over a T-shirt picturing a kangaroo driving a jeep. An orange glow near his hand turned out to be a cigarette. "Is it *gambatte* time?"

Junko pointed to his cigarette. Michael dropped it and rubbed it into the ground under his huge, high-tech running shoe. Junko bent and picked up the butt. "Is not respectful to Fuji-*san,*" she said. "This is the sacred place for we Japanese."

Alex looked down at the litter and butts under the sign. "Sacred" didn't seem to apply to land covered with asphalt, cars, concrete buildings, streetlights, and outdoor vending machines. He could hear the constant buzz of a generator supporting it all. But Junko, carefully escorting Michael's filter to a trash can, had the right idea.

She came back and solemnly placed her hands together. "In honor of Fuji-*san.* In honor of Cody-*san.*" Then she bowed toward the mountain.

Alex bowed, too, and Michael followed his lead.

Suddenly upbeat, Junko cheered, *"Gambarimashiyou!"*

Alex could feel a slight incline under his feet, but the trail was easy, and wide enough for groups of faster hikers to pass them. The trees at this level, evergreens and a deciduous tree Alex couldn't identify, grew short and slanting, as if under constant pressure from the wind. A sweep of his yellow flashlight on the ground revealed only reddish dirt, no plants.

"This is what they call a mountain?" Michael scoffed. "We'll reach the top before midnight."

"It'll take at least five hours," Alex warned him. He stopped on the path a moment to listen. The generator's drone was fading behind them, but except for the voices of other hikers, there was no noise. No animals, no birds. He looked up and saw bright stars, but also dark patches of clouds. He was sweating from the lingering heat of the day, his pants suffocating his legs, and he couldn't imagine needing the wool pullover and fleece gloves Michael had lent him.

They reached the building marked "New Checkpoint 6" in less than the twenty minutes allotted to that portion. This building was smaller than the first, but served soup at a snack bar in addition to a multitude of soft drinks and beer from vending machines. No water was available through the machines, nor was there a drinking fountain. The rest rooms had no sinks, and the toilets were the small, environmental kind that didn't flush. Alex took a swig of water from the liter bottle he'd bought earlier. It was ten o'clock; Gaby would be going to bed about now.

Alex looked up and saw a zigzag line of pinprick lights rising up in shapeless darkness. The beauty of the line of flashlights suddenly struck him. "I get it, Cody," he whispered to himself. The point was to value the experience of the moment, not to worry about reaching the top.

They reached the original sixth station in the prescribed twenty minutes. This was much smaller than New Checkpoint 6 and had no lighting except from its vending machines. After this level, other hikers showed the influence of beer and stumbled into Alex as they passed. One stout man, cheeks flushed, knocked Alex over. He fell on a bed of pumice and granite.

"*Daijobu?* Are you all right?" Junko gave him a hand to help him up.

"I'm fine. Thanks." He rubbed his hip. Noticing Michael farther up the path, out of earshot, he asked, "Are you okay? With Michael? If he's bothering you—"

Junko shook her head slightly. "He is amusement-type boy. I don't mind. I can use to practice English."

Alex found himself relieved. "Let me know if you need him to back off."

Junko bowed and they continued up the path. Alex's fall made him aware there were no longer any trees or, for that matter, dirt. He saw only the bobbing light from his flashlight, his tennis shoes, pumice, granite, and, when he paused to look up, the sky. More clouds crowded out the stars.

The path turned a corner and became a forty-five-degree angle switchback. To the right, up, up, climbing rocks and pseudo-steps, then to the left, up, slide, up, on a slippery gravel grade. Again, to the right. At times, arrows were spray-painted on rocks to mark the path. Some stretches of path had ropes on metal posts, but other sections had nothing to keep someone from sliding off a sheer cliff.

They hadn't even reached the seventh station yet, and he was ready for a rest. Junko had caught up with Michael ahead of him, but they were slowing down. Alex paused to put on his sweatshirt and wool pullover and eat a shard of peanut brittle, reminding himself to be open to the moment. Rocks jutted up to surprise him. Painted on one tall rock were the words "I've been to Rio," but there was no other graffiti.

At the seventh station, a light drizzle came down. It was time for his tough, separate-type nylon jacket. He saw Michael and Junko sitting on an outdoor bench, and huddled next to them. They ate sandwiches and candy. Alex caught himself opening his eyes a few times, perhaps from flash-naps that lasted seconds. Junko yawned twice, and Michael, one gloved hand holding a glove, blew on the fingers of his bare hand between draws on his cigarette. They didn't talk. Keeping awake used enough energy. When Michael put his cigarette butt in the trash can, they moved on.

Alex spotted two more rocks bearing the word "Rio" but no other signs. Only one plant grew, a small bush with glossy leaves and blossoms like white goldenrod. He wondered what color the flowers were in daylight.

This level became even harder. Alex had to hang on to rocks as he climbed around them, testing footholds carefully. He had to keep moving to fight the chill as thick, soft rain pressed down. Dizzy from fatigue and altitude, Alex lost his balance a few times in moments of pure panic. What had he been thinking, doing this hike in the middle of a cold, rainy night?

Cody, he reminded himself. It seemed like days since he'd been at level five, afraid the ascent would prove too easy.

He wanted to be thinking about Cody, but fighting two A.M. collapse syndrome and watching where his feet landed didn't leave room for sustained thought. Maybe that was the point; to fill his mind completely with the coldness of his butt, the soreness of his legs, the wetness of his face, and the damp, sheepy odor of Michael's sweater.

More people passed him. He stepped aside for a few minutes while a Japanese military troop marched up, the leader spiking the air with a repetitive cry of "Each Nissan won!" It took a while until Alex realized he was counting, *ichi, ni, san, yon,* pronouncing *ichi* as one syllable. His ears were hallucinating Japanese into English.

He was ready for Station Eight to be the top. As he searched for Michael and Junko, he noticed the small one-room station was filled with bunk beds. Those who could go no farther could rent futons. He eyed the people sleeping inside with envy. To be dry, maybe even warm, and most of all lying down would be supreme bliss. There were two more shacks, one for outhouses and the other—according to his rain-blurred map— a medical facility. To his surprise, he glimpsed Michael and Junko coming up the path toward the station. He had passed them without knowing it.

As they came closer, Alex saw Michael's arm around Junko's waist. Nothing like hardship to facilitate flirtation, he thought grimly, until he saw Junko was limping. He went downhill and got on the other side of Junko to help her along. "What happened?"

"Some drunken idiot ran into her!" Michael fumed. "She sprained her ankle."

"Are you sure it's a sprain?"

"I'm okay," Junko gasped. They lowered her onto a space on a wooden bench. "It's not so bad as sprain." She flexed her foot and winced.

"There's a medical station here," Alex said. "I'll get help."

He knocked on the door with a red cross painted on it. No answer. Again. Nothing. He went over to the man taking money for futon rental. *"Sumimasen,"* he said urgently, pointing to Junko. *"Sumimasen. Junko-san* . . . hurt. She needs help."

The station master, a thickset man made thicker in a parka suitable for an expedition to the North Pole, spoke a rapid stream of Japanese Alex couldn't understand. Alex physically hauled the man over to Junko on the bench. The man repeated his stream of words at her, and she bowed, saying *"Hai"* and *"Gomen-nasai"* whenever he paused. The man softened some and, after a while, took money from Junko and helped her stand.

"I stay here tonight," Junko told them. "Tomorrow, I think I will be all right. You must go on."

"Absolutely not," Michael said. "I'm staying with you. It's totally mad to continue."

Junko, ignoring Michael, appealed to Alex. "Please go on. For me as well as Cody."

Terrific. Why couldn't he have taken Michael's role, and let young Michael continue to the top for all of them? But the answer was obvious. Michael was here on a lark, to experience Japan and hit on a cute Japanese girl. Junko and Alex were here to honor the one-year anniversary of Cody's death. Cody was Alex's son, not Michael's or Junko's, after all. He was the one who had to reach the top. Somehow. As Cody would have.

While Junko and Michael settled in the communal sleeping shack, Alex leaned against the building and closed his eyes. His body grew numb, almost pleasantly, until Michael roused him to promise to meet up on the way down. Too cold to rest any longer, Alex set out uphill alone.

Around three-thirty, Alex punched through late-night exhaustion into a giddy stagger-onward mode and kept going, through rain and thickening foot traffic. Many climbers carried sticks with bells on the end that rang like chains on a chain gang. The higher he got, the more crowded the path became.

As he ate his last piece of peanut brittle at the ninth station, he observed people stretching and wiping their eyes, as if waking up. Those who had spent the night in rental futons were back on the path to make it to the summit in time for the sunrise.

After "Station 9.5," Alex found himself climbing the mountain *in line*—and when one person stopped, the entire line stopped. Unbelievable. He heard Gaby's voice saying, "This is Japan." Hallucinating again, amid the ringing and thumping of bells and sticks. Soaked through four layers of clothing, he just wanted it to end.

He did his best to concentrate on right foot, left foot, which had become as complicated as a tango step. The man ahead of him hesitated and made bad step choices. Don't fall, Alex willed him. He thought perhaps the stagger was due to beer until he realized the man's glasses were frosted over. Then he saw ice on the path as well, and patches of snow that glowed in the darkness. The air got colder, and the rain came down as ice. This will last forever, Alex thought. Fuji-*san* has no peak. This hike will never end.

He wasn't sure when the hail stopped or when the sky lightened. The change was gradual, from black to gray, from gray to lighter gray. The line stopped frequently now. In the mist, Alex made out a wicket shape that came into view as a *torii* gate, free standing, in the middle of a volcanic wasteland. When it was his turn to trudge through the *torii* gate, he saw the wood cracks were stuffed with coins. There weren't many places left to stick a coin, but Alex found one he could reach, thanks to his American height. His cold, stiff fingers fumbled to get a coin from his pocket: five yen—good enough. He raised his arm and wedged it in. As he passed through the gate, he heard a chorus cry out from above. Again. And a third time. *"Banzai!"* That was it. He looked around and saw everyone facing downhill, some bowing toward cloudy oblivion in the direction of what should be the ocean.

Alex figured it must be sunrise. He hadn't reached the peak in time. He looked at the thick line of bodies on the path.

So many others hadn't reached the top, either. How could they, without going off the path and taking their chances slipping on icy slopes of volcanic scree? He chose to believe it was his good luck to have been under the arch of the *torii* gate at the designated time of sunrise, if not the top, and trudged onward.

Before five A.M., he reached the top and, following the example of the climbers ahead of him, stepped forward to a larger *torii* gate to ring the bell of the shrine at the summit.

It was done in an instant. Immediately, he was pushed aside by the hiker behind him, who eagerly grabbed the bell rope from his hands. Alex turned toward the ocean, shivering, exhausted beyond belief, unable to see a thing. To get out of the way of the bell line, he had to squeeze past a stone lantern as tall as himself and into the courtyard of the shrine.

Here, the line dissipated into a loose crowd. The shrine was a U-shaped, one-story stone building. Large rocks lined up on the metal roof, perhaps to hold it down. There were plenty of signs, but the only one in English read FUJISAN-CHO POST OFFICE above a similar but detached stone structure, with its own line of people extending out its door.

Alex pushed through the crowd to enter the shrine only to find it was but four walls and a roof, packed with human bodies. Despite the herd, it was no warmer inside than out, so Alex went back out.

The sky looked as if it might clear. He could see partial views down the mountainside, including a long line of people yet to arrive. He couldn't descend until the line diminished. He paced and rubbed his hands, wishing he could find a place to lie down. He watched hikers come forward at the top to ring the bell. All were tired, but even the most impassive faces showed at least a flicker of joy when they pulled the rope.

One man stood out as the only one with white hair. Small, wiry, he handed his camera to the man behind him and posed in front of the bell with his arms folded proudly across his chest. After the photo was taken, he bowed, but also shook the man's hand. Alex did a double take. This man looked just like Aoshima.

The brush of white hair, lively eyes, dark skin, and small-proportioned features.

An old man couldn't do this hike, especially not one with a heart transplant. Alex decided he must be hallucinating visually as well as aurally. He desperately needed sleep. He walked behind the shrine where his map indicated a hiking trail around the perimeter of the volcanic crater. Here, there was plenty of room and no crowd, only clusters of hikers squatting on their heels, eating snacks. Alex breathed deeply and headed away from the shrine to have space to himself. Then he saw a smoothly graded road, with tractor tracks.

He was not hallucinating this road. He thought: How did the mail leave the post office? How was the trash removed? How were all the vending machines stocked? For that matter, how had the vending machines been installed in the first place? The sheet-metal roofs? The outhouses? Could it be that "the Ascent of Fuji" was merely an exercise in Japanese torture and discipline, a feat of *nintai*?

His rage at Japan returned. All of his hard climbing had been superfluous ritual if he could have ridden up a back road on a tractor. He felt deceived, cruelly cheated.

Oh, Cody, Alex thought. Help me with this. What did I come here for?

Thirty-nine

"Thorn-*san*?"

Alex heard a familiar man's voice behind him. Another fatigue hallucination.

The man who looked like Aoshima walked around to look at Alex. "Thorn-*san*!" he exulted, grinning broadly.

It was Aoshima.

Aoshima clasped Alex's gloved hand between both of his own and pumped him like an old-fashioned water well. "It is amazing—is that the right word?—yes, it is—amazing. It is amazing to find you here, of all places, today of all days!"

"What . . . how did you get here?" Alex mumbled.

"I climbed! How else?" Aoshima's face was ruddy, but showed no dark lines beneath his eyes. He picked up a polished stout stick he had laid on the ground and cupped his hands over it, leaning his weight against it.

"I didn't see you on my way up." Alex pointed to the graded road. "It looks like you can get here on a tractor."

Aoshima pulled his head back and frowned. "I don't think so. But anyway, I came on foot."

Alex wasn't sure he believed Aoshima. "You must be in great shape. You don't even look tired."

"I took the taxi to level five yesterday morning," Aoshima explained. "I took a nap at level seven, and spent the night at level nine. This morning, I woke at four o'clock to finish the job."

Alex wished he had done it slowly, mostly during daylight. He almost wished he hadn't done it at all. Almost. "Why put yourself through this at your age?"

"I did not want to die before having to climb Fuji-*san*. That is, without having climbed Fuji-*san*. I came today because it is the anniversary of my new heart." Aoshima thumped his chest to illustrate. "I came to celebrate that. This heart got me up the mountain. Are you here for a special reason, Thorn-*san*?"

Alex told him. "Today is the anniversary of my son Cody's death."

He thought Aoshima might stop smiling at that, but the news merely modified the old man's good spirits. "To think we were brought together on the same day! This proves our lives are connected," he stated. He pointed to small stacks of stones placed around the rim of the crater. "It is a matter of destiny, *so desu ne?* What we have in common. We will both build monuments to our children. Together. Me for my Shinsuke and you for your Cody. Side by side."

Alex, paralyzed for an instant, followed Aoshima to a rock pile. Aoshima chose five stones and squatted in the Asian style, flat on his feet with his buttocks almost touching the ground. He turned the rocks this way and that until he found a combination that fit four stones high.

Unable to squat, Alex had to kneel on icy pumice to do the same. He put one of the larger stones, the size of his hand, at the bottom. The second stone settled nicely onto the first but was a bit curved, so that the third rock teetered and the fourth fell off. Knees aching, fingers numb with cold, Alex tried again and again. Finally, he used a different rock at the bottom and the others fit into place. Even after his elbow brushed against it, the stack held. It was solid.

When he stood back to look at the foot-high monument to Cody, he began to weep. He couldn't help it.

"E . . . to," Aoshima murmured in a low voice. "So desu." He moved a few meters away and turned his back to Alex, but didn't leave. He stood as motionless as the two small towers of stones.

At some point, Alex perceived he was weeping into his own shadow, a long, faint shadow that slipped over the crater's edge. The first thought that entered his mind was that you couldn't have a shadow on a cloudy day. Alex turned around, to face the trail along with Aoshima.

Aoshima glanced over and smiled at him in a fatherly way. "Here comes the sun." He lifted his walking stick from his waist, like a giant erection.

Alex looked down a sloping field of pumice studded with gray granite bumps, cut with a zigzag path of people walking back to the first torii where he'd stuck his coin. Below his feet, the mountainside appeared shallow, as if distant hikers struggled over nothing. At the torii, the sweep of the volcanic cone dropped off sharply, and peaks of other mountains in the range spread out in overlapping triangles on either side, their reddish brown pumice gradually blending into distant blues. Straight ahead, at the horizon, the clouds mimicked ocean, a fixed cirrus spray of stationary waves.

Through light cloud cover, Alex saw the circular rim of the sun. It grew bright enough to make his eyes uncomfortable. When it broke free of the clouds, Alex shifted his gaze down to a band of glittering gray that emerged beneath the false sea of faintly pink mist: the Pacific Ocean.

"There," Aoshima said. "That's better now, isn't it?"

"Yes," Alex said. After he said it, it *was* better. A month ago, he could not have imagined anything remotely like this. He hadn't known what would come out of his trip to Japan. He never dreamed he would be standing at the peak of Mount Fuji at daybreak, side by side with an old Japanese man who carried Cody's heart in his chest. A man who had also lost his only son . . . but who had let go of his pain, who had decided to be happy in his son's place, and who had lived well for a long time.

Alex wanted to send Marubatsu to jail, but he reminded himself he hadn't come to Japan seeking justice. He had come to Japan for answers. He had found Junko and Endo. He had found Gaby. And he had found Aoshima. Cody's good heart had powered this old man up to the summit of a twelve-thousand-foot mountain to witness the new day with him. It was, exactly as Aoshima had put it, amazing.

"Better than the temples, *so desu ka*?" Aoshima asked, resting his chin on his cupped hands.

"I'm sure of it," Alex agreed. "Although I didn't see the temples."

Aoshima stood up straight. "What? That is unheard of. You must see them before you go!"

"Not this trip. My time's up."

"You will come again soon?"

"I think so," Alex said. "A good friend of mine is moving to Osaka."

They stood and listened to the bell clang as hiker after

hiker arrived at the gate of the shrine. The sun emerged stronger, fortifying the shadows, burning away the fog. Alex removed his nylon jacket and shook off the water droplets.

"You are going back to America now?" Aoshima inquired.

Alex smiled. "Not going back. Going on." He watched the morning sun clear up more and more of the ocean that spread between the Eastern and Western worlds. He looked to the east, facing home.

Acknowledgments

My heart is full of gratitude for those who provided technical, editorial, and personal assistance:

Gian-Carlo Bava, Barbara Braun, Alison Clement, David Eiseman, John Ginn, Akira Hongo, Shigeko Kumagai, Dorothy Mack, Eric Paul Shaffer, Atsuko Tanaka, Dr. Toshihiro Tanaka, Marian Wood, and above all, my sister, Melissa Carpenter.

SARA BACKER is a poet, essayist, and short fiction writer—and now a novelist of formidable powers, as *American Fuji* amply demonstrates. In the early 1990s, she accepted a position as visiting professor of English at Shizuoka University, unaware that she was not only the first American to hold that position, but also the first woman. The three years she spent in this midsized conservative city halfway between Tokyo and Kyoto suffuse the tone and temper of the novel. Unlike her heroine, however, Backer was not fired but instead was offered a renewed contract for another three-year teaching stint. Much as she'd come to love the people and the country, she opted to return to America, to put what she had learned into fiction. *American Fuji*—an early draft of which was a finalist in the James Jones First Novel Fellowship competition—is the result. Backer is now at work on her second novel.